# The Mysteries of Marigold

# The Mysteries of Marigold

BERNADETTE O'CONNOR

Trade Paperback ISBN: 978-0-6458993-9-9
eBook ISBN: 978-0-6458656-7-7

Print information available on the last page.

The kind press acknowledges Australia's First Nations peoples as the traditional owners and custodians of this country, and we pay our respects to their elders, past and present.

THE
KIND
PRESS

www.thekindpress.com

# CONTENTS

# PROLOGUE

In New York City, Marigold found herself in a world she never imagined. Within hours of arrival, she sat in the darkness, on a stage at a club called St. Christopher's, a harp nestled between her legs, with only one instruction echoing in her mind—'Just do what you do best'. It had been ten years since Marigold played the harp and she'd only ever played it sitting around a fire surrounded by her gypsy family, not in front of strangers in a nightclub on the Lower East Side of New York City.

'Gentlemen …' the dulcet tone swirled like honey around the room commanding silence, such was the power of Madame Rosaline.

'… Tonight, I bring you a rare treat, travelling across the seas from the rugged green hills on the West Coast of Ireland. No! This is no leprechaun, but without doubt, you are in for something magical. Gentlemen, please welcome to St Christopher's, Miss Goldie Mae.'

Indeed, she was out of her depth, yet she wanted it this way. No wilting rose was she and as the light illuminated her on the centre of the stage, she closed her eyes and took herself beyond the darkened room to a memory: sitting in a circle, playing the harp with her two beloved Ma's beside her. Their presence encircled her on the stage and renewed in courage, she plucked the string on the harp and waited while the sound reverberated around the room—touching every corner and the core of every person in the club—such was her power. Silence descended. In the stillness, she commanded their presence and with but another pluck of the string she launched into song, taking all present beyond themselves and the lives they sought to escape. This time, it was not found at the bottom of a bottle of rum. No, it was lying waiting in the realms and the expanse of consciousness beyond all that they knew.

She replaced the harp with a drum and time froze as she sang and danced, weaving herself around the room, caught in her own wonder and drawing all others into it with her.

She finally returned to the stage, bringing her awareness back to the room before pausing with her hand raised, readied to strike the drum and break the trance she had drawn her audience into. Across the room, she sensed movement in the shadows, and was drawn to him, he who was watching in a way the others could not. He was not transfixed by her mystic. He saw her and as their eyes connected, he knew her fully. She gasped in her own remembering, and caught in the magnetism of the moment, their souls rekindled a long lost, yet never forgotten, flame. Flickers of memories held in the pages of time danced between them, a soul tale across many lives of love, loss and learnings. And so it was that once more they found themselves connected in life, the pages blank, readied for their story to continue.

It is time, my sweet Marigold, to write your story once more with Johnny Triboni by your side.

Holding him in her eyes, heart and soul, she tentatively lowered her hand and struck the drum, breaking the trance and the sacred portal of their reconnection. She stood on stage, resplendent in her light, while he rose, adorned by her light, and turned into the darkness.

This was not their first dance. Would it be their last?

# Part
# One

# The Maiden

The ground swelled beneath me as the fire crackled seductively, tantalising my heart. My vision blurred. Reality faded into a nothingness. I grasped at what *was*. The Earth felt off kilter and everything within me was drawn to the fire. *Her* portal demanding, I leaped beyond the edge, dived into *her* emblazoned heart and received the fierce passion she offered. Terrified and trusting, I surrendered to *her* call, relinquishing all remnants of control and releasing all that I was—to *become*.

It was time. I couldn't deny the restlessness that stirred or the longing to dive deep into the fire and move beyond here.

Here, where I was safe and content.

Here, where I was surrounded by love and ease.

Here, where I knew who I was.

Here, I am Marigold.

*I'm Marigold, known for being the golden maiden roaming the mountains, dancing under the moonlight, healing people and animals alike, channelling light and wisdom as I embrace the simplicity and beauty of life with my family, Clara, Caellach and their ever-growing tribe of free-spirited babes.*

Through the dancing flames, Clara witnessed the calling of my soul and her eyes welled at the impending and inevitable change in season. As oft before, I ran into her tender embrace, surrendering to the Mother's arms and her love. I knew it would never be the same beyond here, and I gently grieved the loss of my past.

The little girl who travelled the Burren Hills on the West Coast of Ireland, with her beloved Ma's—Athena and Cynthia. The little girl who chanted to the ancient ones and called home Clara's fractured soul. The little girl who voyaged across the Atlantic to begin a new life in the Catskill Mountains, beyond New York City. The little girl who was trusting, brave and true!

I trusted *her* to come with me for I knew I would need *her* courage, clarity and confidence—together with *her* spirit, spark and spunk—as I ventured into my new life in the city. The sudden intensity of this reality shocked me, too, as I felt ill-equipped to navigate the fullness of New York City. *She* was too much for me, a simple country girl. I faltered, resisting what I knew to be true and desperately clinging to what was safe, what was known, what was easy. *Why would I leave here? How could I possibly leave Clara and Caellach and the kids? Why would I walk away from joy and peace and those who love me into a world where I knew nobody?*

Confusion and tears brought Caellach to my side. Clara gently stroked my hair as she whispered, 'It is time, my darling. This day was always going to come for you. It is love that leads you beyond here. Only fear will hold you here and that will not be good for you or us. A frustrated soul is not always easy to live with.'

She giggled as she ruffled my hair and motioned towards Caellach, her beloved.

'You know what he's like when he doesn't heed the nudge to roam!'

Pretending to ignore Clara's playful jibe, Caellach said, 'Your life here is safe, Marigold, sure … aren't you surrounded by those who love you and the animals, land and mountains? You're awful comfortable here, my girl, but you know as well as I, you can't grow into who you are truly meant to be if you only hang around where it's easy. My best crops grow in soil that nourishes them, but also in an environment that challenges them. They rise from whatever auld Mother Nature sends their way and haven't we seen how they are richer and more bountiful because of the gift of the challenge? Don't they have to figure how to grow into something new!'

'Yeah, but sometimes they get wiped out too, like when the snow hangs around too late in the season and then it takes them so long to recover!' I retorted sulkily.

I knew the truth of his words, but his measured wisdom irritated me. I was reluctant to concede. Threads of my querulous teenage-mind remained active despite now being eighteen years old. Caellach and I had bantered, often playfully, for as long as I could remember. As he declared the ways of the world, I would challenge his wisdom and we would dive into dynamic debates that often lead to one of us storming off aggrieved only to laugh it off later, both wiser for the exploration of the alternate narrative.

'Well then, you just take the time while you're recovering to reflect on what you could have done differently so you don't get wiped out next time. Pretty sure, that's what you'd be saying to me, wise one!' he teased, which annoyed me yet made me laugh because so often we spouted the same guidance having been blessed with Athena and Cynthia, the matriarchs and wise women of our gypsy tribe—our teachers.

'Sure now, Marigold, isn't that what makes "this life thing" all so interesting, trying new things? It would be fierce boring doing the same thing over and over again just to get to the end of your days and think, sure that was a waste. I didn't learn a blessed thing!'

'Maybe I don't want to learn a blessed thing! Maybe I want to waste my life!' I giggled and argued petulantly before inhaling deeply and surrendering to the truth which I had felt niggling for months.

I knew it was time for me to leave the comforts of home and the safety of the love of Clara and Caellach who were oft my parents and big brother and sister and best friends. Caellach had been the ever-present pulse in my life, always telling the story of how he was the first to cuddle me when Cynthia and Athena had taken me back to our camp.

They found me as a newborn, wrapped in a red shawl beside a bed of marigolds in the rugged hills of The Burren. Birthed, I was left in trust I would be found. My Ma's, as well as Clara and Aunt Maeve, ensured I never missed the love of a mother, for they embraced me as their own. They nurtured me—body, mind and soul—teaching me their ways, the way of the *Mother*, the way of the *Soul*, the way of *Love*.

They nurtured my ability to *see* and *know* and *hear* what was not *seen* and *known* and *heard*, through their assurance I never doubted my gifts, who I was, what I did. I lived from my truest expression. Some may have seen me as too confident for a child, precocious even, but my Ma's allowed my free-spiritedness to blossom without limitation.

Clara often shared the story of our meeting. Her journeying into the depths of her soul guided by Aunt Maeve, while I played the harp around the fire for her and all who joined the circle. She says I looked like an angel playing the harp with the golden luminous light of the fire dancing about me. Although, I can't recall this circle as once the music begins to move through me, I enter my own world. As a wild and ponderous little girl, I was magnetised to Clara, loving her infinitely from the beginning. I'd follow her around like a doting little sister does. My nose was well out of place when Caellach captured her heart, but even then, I recognised a love unable to be repudiated and my jealousy abated when they invited me to share their life and loved me as their own.

Our family grew quickly. Sorcha was birthed on the ship as we sailed into the Hudson River with Kevin, Joe, Róisín and Ailish arriving in a timely succession after we settled into life in the mountains. Clara was a natural mother and her heart guided her to nurture each one of us exactly as we needed, not necessarily how we wanted.

Caellach took to the land with gusto, creating a thriving farm that provided an abundance of food to nourish our growing bodies and ample experiences to expand our minds and challenge our souls. Our life was simple. We lived as one, with nature in much the same way as we had in Ireland. We didn't move around every few months, though. A permanent roof over our heads for the past ten years was both a blessing and a challenge for Caellach and I as our gypsy souls craved adventure and exploring beyond home. Ironically, it was this that I was resisting in the calling to leave. This was home. It was easy. I loved my life here. Yet my soul was ready for more and I could not deny the whisper and the fire that burned within. It was time for me to start a new life. It was time for me to move into the unknown.

To let go of Marigold.

To trust in my *becoming*.

*She beckoned from the fire, a mirage of the*
*most magnificent mystery.*

# CHAPTER 2

# The Void

I arrived in the city filled with a terrified excitement which quickly turned to awe and wonder. The hours after arriving at St Christopher's with Aunt Maeve were a whirlwind. I didn't really have time to understand where I was or why I was here. Here, seated alone in the darkness, a wave of terror overcame me and all I wanted to do was run and hide. I felt completely out of my depth. When I heard Madame Rosaline command the attention of the boisterous audience, I was certain I was going to drown. The other girls had roused the audience from their risqué performances, dressed in sequined colourful dresses reminiscent of the roaring twenties. They danced, swayed, shimmied across the stage in a playfully seductive way, teasing and amusing the audience. When they sashayed off the stage, the room was intoxicated by cheers, roars and whistles.

My panic was displaced by a stifled giggle when I heard Madame Rosaline introduce me as some magical being from the ancient lands of Ireland, while assuring her audience I was no leprechaun. Although, I had strangely acquired a new name, Miss Goldie Mae. The pure absurdity of it all was hilarious. I was the antithesis of the other girls in my golden dress, with long blonde hair, no make-up, a harp between my legs. I was also bemused by the idea I may look like a golden angel dropped from the heavens with a harp. Madame Rosaline had insisted I play it. A harp which unbeknownst to everyone, she had tucked away in her private quarters at the rear of the stage. The gold dress had been custom made for me. Aunt Maeve was one of Madame Rosaline's oldest friends, sending through my measurements ahead of time. I knew nothing about what was being planned, but I implicitly trusted that Aunt Maeve, Clara and Caellach would make all the arrangements for my lodgings to ensure an easy transition into city life.

My new home was the boarding house attached to St Christopher's.

One of the conditions for free lodgings was that all the girls must work in the club. I was grateful I had not been coerced into performing with the other girls because there was no way I would be able to kick my legs that high or wiggle my breasts and buttocks as provocatively as they could. I still remained dubious that a skinny little country girl dressed like an angel playing a harp could possibly entertain Madame Rosaline's guests.

'Trust me, child,' I felt her firm hands land on both my shoulders as she purred into the dark. 'I always knew you would come to me and all I ask of you … is you. Be you.'

The light illuminated the centre of the stage. I closed my eyes, took a breath and found the essence of my soul was there waiting for me. *Call them in!* I heard *her* soft voice. Trusting *her* guidance, I beckoned the energy of Athena and Cynthia—my wise loving mothers to join me on the stage. With my next breath, I felt them. They were with me and once again we were sitting in a circle sharing stories, wisdom and love with the rolling green hills that Madame Rosaline had alluded to holding us in their mystical embrace.

My heart burst open as Athena gave me a wink, a nod. I plucked the string of the harp. The note struck every corner of the room and pierced every darkened heart that occupied St Christopher's. My conscious awareness dissolved into a familiar force that was far more than me, expressing itself through me. What transpired on that stage when I surrendered to that force is a mystery—for in my mind's eye, I was a child again in Ireland, playing the harp and dancing around the fire. When my awareness returned, I was no longer on the stage. I was standing barefoot in the middle of the club, surrounded by what looked like middle-aged men transfixed on me. One hand held a drum to my hip, the other lay on the tautness of its skin, the vibration still pulsing through my burning hand. I scanned the silent, dimly lit room and felt the intensity of all eyes, unblinking. I wondered if my performance fell short of the entertainment that Madame Rosaline's guests were accustomed. I soon realised that the soothing vibrations of the harp, coupled with the hypnotic beat of the drum had drawn them into an altered state of consciousness. One I presumed most had not experienced before and it was now my responsibility to bring them back. I returned to the stage and raised my hand high above my head and prepared to strike the drum. Something flickered. I turned instinctively to the left and, despite the darkness, I saw him. Our eyes locked. I sensed his musings as the tiniest smirk danced at the corner of his mouth. Though he was a stranger, he was familiar and my body was awash with the remembering of something old, before this time. It was too much for me to hold and my hand slammed against the drum, shattering the silence, breaking their trance and the magnetism of our connection. He stood and walked into the darkness. Confused, I scanned those sitting closest. They were mesmerised by my light, yet they could not see *me*. He saw *me* but walked away from my light and into the darkness.

*In the darkness, I saw only his light.*

# CHAPTER 3

# Remembrance

---

Bewildered faces searched the room, trying to register what had happened. But as the background music began to play, they quickly forgot anything unusual occurred, cigarettes were lit and conversation resumed. I walked from the stage, grateful I did not have to stand there and attempt to explain the intricacies of them entering a hypnotic state and accessing different realms of consciousness. As the gush of the curtain fell behind me, the darkness stimulated a surge of adrenaline and I ran past the other girls who were staring, equally confused by what had just transpired.

I escaped out the side door into the alleyway, crouched beside a row of bins and breathed deeply, willing myself to come back into form. An electrified energy tore through me, quelling the calm I sought as I trembled with the shock of recalibrating the charge of my energy being with my physical form. *Breathe. Breathe. You're grand, you're coming back, coming back and breathe yourself back in. You're grand.* This was not the first time I had moved beyond my physical body, having danced in the higher realms for as long as I could remember, but never had I been without someone to anchor me as my energy body returned to the physical form. Without the support of someone to stabilise me, another surge of adrenaline stimulated a spiral of panic. I struggled to hold the space.

I didn't see him approach, for my eyes were closed as I was breathing and talking to myself like a madwoman. But I felt him. His presence became overwhelming as he neared. I opened my eyes as he squatted before me and placed his hand on my shoulder. I gasped as our eyes magnetised again. I couldn't catch my breath … as he was the most *man* this *girl* had ever met. Now there was a compelling reason to come back to this realm, into my body.

Visions of shared lives flickered between us. The remembering of our love, ancient, deep and true struck every crevice of my heart. His eyes welled. Through his sadness, a wave of grief swept over us. I grabbed my chest as an aching moan, a painful longing, escaped. I remembered him. I remembered us. And I knew our souls had reconnected in this life, for what reason I did not know, though the surge through my body desired to know.

Taking a sip of golden liquid, his eyes not leaving mine, he offered, 'Drink? It'll take the edge off.'

I swallowed the glass of whiskey down and as it flowed into the pit of my belly, a soothing heat radiated through my limbs, instantly grounding me. Taking one more deep breath, I giggled, 'Holy Mother Mary, what was all that?'

And it was then I truly saw him for the first time. His façade cracked. His face lit up.

'I was not expecting that!' he said, laughing.

'What!' I feigned indignation as I stood before him, dwarfed by his presence. 'You didn't expect *this* to guzzle your whiskey?'

'No, not really,' he grinned from the corner of his mouth, his signature smile, 'Though I did see you throw your shoes aside, dance in your bare feet while banging a drum and weave some sort of magic!'

'Oh my!' I laughed as I looked down at my bare feet. 'Magic … really? You think I'm some sort of leprechaun after all!'

'No, more like a fairy. An impish fairy!' He teased, shattering any remnants of a guard about my gushing heart. He would not look away and I could not look away. As the threads of our past wove us together, the ease of our reunion reflected in our banter.

'An impish fairy! Is that a fact?' Madame Rosaline seemed to appear from nowhere, as we were oblivious to anything beyond one another. Arms folded, eyebrows raised, a formidable force. I would have been terrified had it not been for her bemused expression.

'I came out here to check that you were okay, but clearly you're both fine!'

She looked between us and formalised our introduction.

'Johnny, Goldie Mae … Goldie Mae, Johnny Triboni.'

We smirked at each other, for we already knew each other beyond our names.

I felt somewhat childish when Madame Rosaline raised her eyebrows at me. It was as though her job was to push me into the unknown, while ensuring I didn't get carried away before I understood how to navigate my way.

'Go on back inside now. The girls will take care of you.'

I followed without a further glance in Johnny's direction. Hovering just inside the door I had scurried through mere minutes earlier, I felt changed in a way I could not comprehend. Johnny Triboni had an effect on me, somehow activating long forgotten threads of my soul. Given the agitated conversation I overheard with Madame Rosaline following my exit, he clearly saw it as his duty to protect me.

'What are you doing, Rosaline? You know they won't look after her. They'll destroy her. She's not like them. Can't you see that?'

'Oh Johnny! You've known me for long enough to trust me. Of course, she's nothing like them, but let me tell you that girl can handle them. If anything, they should be worried! Let's not stoop to judging.'

'And sending her out there on the stage with all of *them*,' he spat with disgust. 'Them watching her and wanting her. It's like a lamb to the slaughter.'

'You're letting them get to you, Johnny. You saw what happened out there. They were mesmerised, not by her, but by what she brought to the stage. They don't know who she is. They were captivated by the light, not by her.'

'Do you really think they'll forget? Like hypnosis or something?' he replied, wanting to trust what Madame Rosaline was saying, but reluctant to surrender his fears.

'You were the only one in that room who truly saw her. You were not mesmerised by the light, Johnny. You already know it. If only you would see it in yourself.'

'No, Rosaline, that's what you want to see in me. I know who they are and what they're like. They're dangerous and she's not safe around them. She can't mix with them like the others do. She is not like the others!'

'You think wrapping her in cotton wool is going to help? She came to the city because it was time for her to experience life, to move out of her comfort and I'm not standing in her way. She can look after herself.

She's a lot wiser to the ways of the world than you're giving her credit.'

'Fine, I'll hang around and she can sit with me, so they keep their filthy hands off her.'

I hurried from the door into the darkness of St Christopher's feeling more assured because of Madame Rosaline's belief in me. A familiar surge of power raced from my core and into my heart, bursting it opening and bringing on tears. I could do this. I knew that somehow Johnny Triboni was an important piece of the puzzle.

*The puzzle of my soul.*

# CHAPTER 4

# Initiation

Until now, I'd been sheltered from discrimination, and the condemnation and exclusion my gypsy family had experienced in Ireland, so I didn't understand what it meant to be separate. I had always been warmly held at the centre of my family and in our farming community since arriving in the United States. I was raised with an acute knowing that I was *one* with all—people, animals, nature and Mother Earth herself—even with the realms beyond. I understood that there was no thing separating me and all that existed in both the seen and unseen worlds. I was blessed to only know harmony for most of my eighteen years. This initiation into life in the city had opened up for the first time how it felt to be separate, the outsider.

As I returned to the dressing room after hearing Madame Rosaline and Johnny's tense exchange, I was met by a flurry of over-excited girls teasing and tossing their hair, polishing and perfecting their make-up. I'm sure more sequins and glitter were added to the dresses which accentuated their figures. They were *all* woman, while my undeveloped frame left me feeling very much a girl. I had never doubted my appearance before. I'd never given it much thought, always preferring to muck the cowshed than look in a mirror. Nor had I ever faced criticism or acclaim based on my looks, so I never had reason to consider that how I appeared was not good enough. Surrounded by those girls, the first waves of inadequacy flittered into my sphere.

I refused their insistence on curling my hair, preferring it to hang naturally down my back, likewise their urging to paint my face with makeup. Clarissa, who appeared to be the leader, had earlier asserted that I'd look deathly on stage without makeup, and if I wanted to shine while mixing with Jimmy Triboni's men, I absolutely needed makeup. I had no desire to shine for any man, regardless of who they were. My polite refusal to allow her brush and palate near my face was met with a terse reply, 'Oh, I'm sorry, sweetheart, I didn't realise the hillbilly's had come to town. You might want to scrape the cow shit from your boots before you head on back out there to Jimmy and the boys!'

The vengeance in her words caught me out, but I was far too exhausted to give them much heed. Given she was completing a beauty course, she positioned herself as the expert on shades of eyeshadow, lipstick, false eyelashes and the right brush to use when applying blush. I cared for none of it. The other girls appeared to revere and play along with her game. I did not understand why she was placed on a pedestal by the girls. This social dynamic was a foreign one and it soon became apparent my reluctance to play by the rules was a threat to Clarissa, and so her attacks began.

'So, Irish.'

The girls giggled her on.

'It looks like Madame Bossy Boots has a soft spot for you, giving you a solo and letting you do whatever you want out there. Making a right fool of yourself if you ask me, banging a drum and dancing around like a madwoman in that rag of a dress! You've no idea what real men want. You're hardly a woman … have you seen the size of her tits, girls?'

A gaggle of sycophantic laughter chorused through the room. For the first time, I saw a pack mentality in women. Desperate for acceptance and false power, they didn't know how to accept themselves or claim their authentic power. I wanted neither false power nor their acceptance, which would make my time at St Christopher's challenging.

'Good God, if I lit a match, the place would explode with the fumes from that spray!' Madame Rosaline chastised lightly as the girls' excitement seemed to hit fever pitch. 'Settle down, settle down. You know the rules. You go out there, you have one drink and one drink only. Dance, have some fun, but I don't want to see any nonsense. There's a line. Don't cross it!'

She looked to Clarissa.

'Why do you pick on me all the time?'

'Don't play the victim here. You know exactly what I'm talking about! You all know what I'm talking about, so no playing dumb. Jimmy Triboni and his men are our guests and within the four walls of St Christopher's, you entertain them. But outside of here, you have nothing to do with them. Here they can relax and have a good time. Out there, they are very different men, and you stay away from them. Them's the rules, my girls. You don't like it? Pack your bags but don't come crying to me when your *Romeo* isn't all he makes out to be. It's just a big old game to them, girls. I've made the rules for a reason and Jimmy stands by my rules.'

She paused just long enough for the intent of her message to land with the girls whose giddy enthusiasm appeared to drop a notch or two.

'Right, out you go and have a good time. And remember, Cinderella, upstairs and into bed by midnight.'

I stood still as the girls steamrolled the door eager to make the most of every minute with Jimmy's men.

'Goldie Mae, you stay.'

'I told her she needed to polish herself up, Madame Rosaline,' Clarissa chimed as she swaggered through the door.

'My name is not Goldie Mae!' I projected my irritation with Clarissa onto Madame Rosaline.

'I know very well what your name is, but here it's Goldie Mae. It's time to grow up and leave Marigold on the farm.'

Her intent was clear, but its ruthlessness stung. My vulnerability showed. She softened and took me by the shoulders.

'You're about to walk into a world you don't understand and, unlike your performance earlier, this time you have to have your feet on the ground and your head out of the clouds. You're going to have to be switched on because this time they won't be under your spell!'

She winked, knowingly.

'Watch, learn and discern. It's a game and the men know how to play. But don't worry, they'll be too distracted by the bells and whistles that come with the girls to take too much notice of you. You'll sit with Johnny tonight, nonetheless.'

I nodded compliantly, quietly excited at the chance of seeing Johnny again. Our brief banter had been the highlight of my night.

She continued bringing me up to speed.

'Jimmy Triboni is one of the most powerful men in the city and he's brought his men here for over twenty years. He's dangerous and commands respect, but as long as you know what you're working with, you'll be fine. I know how to play Jimmy at his own game, and he respects me for it, but do not underestimate him. He's unpredictable.'

She spoke with a deadly serious tone and lightness that intrigued me.

'Jimmy Triboni suffers no fool and demands the fullness of my presence and because of that he brings the best out in me. The risk of losing my power to him is real and I'll never allow that.'

I paused, poised to receive the wisdom she was intent on sharing with me.

'When I am with him, I have to be whole. My presence must hold my light and dark and in turn, my heart remains open in the light and dark. It has not been easy to learn, and I don't expect you to completely understand what I am saying. In time, you will because it is your lesson too, and that is why you are here with me. You have chosen this. You were always going to join me here. I was always going to be your guide, at least for this part of the journey.'

At this point, I was completely overwhelmed because Madame Rosaline was so much more than I had perceived. Her relationship with Aunt Maeve now began to make much more sense.

'Cynthia—your Ma—was my friend. She was a good woman. She came to me in a vision many years ago, not long after I heard she had passed. She told me, as clearly as I am speaking to you now, all about you, Marigold. She told me about your light and your gifts and your potency. She said you would come to me. I would teach you how to become whole. How to become a woman. How to reclaim the *Divine Feminine*—she of the light and the dark.'

I stared, awed by her truth and the prophecy of my path.

'Marigold is your light, and you carry *her* with exquisite grace. Goldie Mae is the pathway to your darkness, and *she* will show you how to hold your darkness with as much grace as you do your light. How you meld those threads and how well you hold yourself in the dark will determine who you become on the other side of this bridge. It is always your choice who you become. You always have the power.'

She turned quickly, leaving me surprised by the bluntness of her words. Wise women and men had walked beside me every day of my life, lovingly teaching and guiding me in the ways of the world, yet the gauntlet of truth had never been so intensely thrown before me. Madame Rosaline's passion roused a fire in my soul. I eagerly followed her into the raucous club excited to immerse myself in the dark and begin my lessons.

*My soul's conviction may have been admirable,*
*but my naivety was dangerous.*

# CHAPTER 5

# Soul Contract

Madame Rosaline strode across the club, stopping before a small table adjacent to the main group. With a formality that seemed completely unnecessary yet served a purpose, she proclaimed, 'Johnny, may I introduce Miss Goldie Mae. Goldie Mae, meet Johnny Triboni.'

I extended my hand, which Johnny ignored. Madame Rosaline gently placed her hand on my lower back, guiding me to the seat next to him. Acutely aware of the curious eyes of the larger group watching us, he refused to acknowledge my presence. Drawing heavily on his cigarette, he stared into the darkness of centre stage, knowing the game and determined to give them nothing to work with. The tension encircled me as I sat awkwardly beside him, pondering how this sullen, rude person was the same man who I had bantered with in the alleyway less than an hour before. A formidable intensity enveloped him. He was guarded and wary of his surrounds, as though he was ready to strike at any moment. I was unsettled in his presence. I could feel a fury pulsating through his being that left me wondering what I had done to warrant him treating me with such disdain. I was not accustomed to the sting of rejection, yet it was striking me from every corner of the club. Too exhausted to attempt to understand the absurdity of the entire evening, I surrendered to the experience, silently asking St Christopher, patron saint of the traveller to help this weary wanderer navigate the remainder of the night. A lightness landed and amid the madness, I suddenly found myself again. I reached across the table and took a cigarette from his packet which forced him to look at me and his eyes, oh those eyes, bored into mine. *What are you doing?* I heard him.

'Are you going to light my cigarette, or do I have to get someone else to do it?' I stood up abruptly, refusing to continue to feel powerless waiting for something to happen. 'Fine! I'm going to the bar to get myself a drink and maybe someone there will be polite enough to light my cigarette and maybe even say a word to me!'

Standing with lighter in hand he murmured, 'Just sit down.'

I ignored him and walked to the bar, instinctively knowing he would follow and try to convince me to scurry away before anyone took notice. I couldn't help but smirk when he stood beside me and whispered furiously.

'Will you go on upstairs or come back to the table and stop making a scene.'

'I'm not making a scene, Johnny Triboni. I'm making a statement. I'm not going to sit around like a lost puppy waiting for someone to pat me. So, if you can't even have a conversation with me, I'm more than happy to sit here by myself and have a drink alone. Quite frankly, I prefer my own company more than yours!' I took a large swig of my drink before continuing my rant. 'And if you were hoping I'd scurry upstairs, then you're going to be disappointed, because I didn't pack my bags and leave my perfectly comfortable life to come here and run away as soon as things got tough. If your plan is to avoid attention, I suggest you drop this whole brooding, moody, pissed off look you've got going and just get yourself a drink. Come back to the table and start talking to me like I'm a normal person, which, by the way, I am! The more you ignore me, the more they're going to wonder why you're ignoring me, so technically you're the one drawing attention to us!' I took my drink and turned from the bar.

'Wait!' He gently grabbed my arm. 'What's your real name?'

He lit my cigarette. I inhaled deeply as I sized him up and down. *Did I really want to reveal my true self to him, or do I take Madame Rosaline's advice and leave Marigold on the farm?* I wanted him to know me fully.

'Marigold, my name is Marigold. But I guess here you call me Goldie Mae.' I smiled with sadness because I already felt so different from the girl who had left home that morning. I was losing *her,* but I knew she had to die. It was an inevitable part of the transformative process, yet it was still sad.

Johnny tilted my chin to capture my eye, 'It's okay.'

'It's why I'm here. To grow beyond Marigold.'

His thumb rested on my chin and time paused as I looked into the dark pools of his eyes and reconnected to his soul.

'Don't lose her. I think she's something special.'

My heart ached with the longing of lost love. I remembered his heart and the love I had shared with him for lifetimes. The love I would share with him forever more. Suddenly, a deep cloud of foreboding overcame me and pulled me from his soul, as I sensed ours was not a love for this life. I froze as the desire of possibility that stirred within was just as quickly and brutally ripped from me, as the touch of his fingers on my chin burned with a passion that could never be. I did not understand why, but the wave of grief that tore through his eyes affirmed that he, too, had remembered our love and realised we were destined for something beyond the physical desire we shared in that moment.

He gently drew his thumb from my chin, and I whispered, 'Maybe I came here to find you, so you could help me discover more of me.'

Holding my gaze, he smiled, raised his glass to meet mine. 'May the darkness hold your light and in the golden shadows may you stay true.'

*And it was written.*

# CHAPTER 6

# The Outsider

———

I fell asleep hoping my first night in New York City was an anomaly and believed on waking the following morning that it would take on a different slant. Before the first flickers of light sprung through the curtains, I lay in bed listening to the unfamiliar noises on the streets below. A city that never sleeps, slowly rising to a new day. Like all the rooms in Madame Rosaline's boarding house, my bedroom was simple and practical: a single bed, a rack for hanging clothes and a dressing table upon which sat a basin and jug for water. There was a shared bathroom and separate toilet at the end of the hall, which Madame Rosaline ran strategically via a roster system due to the inevitable conflict it caused amongst seven young women all trying to get out the door at the same time. She had learned from the first girls she had taken into her care, many years before, that the bathroom could be used as a weapon to assert power, especially by young women who had mostly come from lives where they experienced disempowerment on the back of abusive homes, homelessness and prostitution.

I snuck to the bathroom after taking myself to the sanctuary of the higher realms through meditation, intending to complete my cleansing and purification ritual in the shower to provide clarity and confidence upon entering this day. I didn't think I would be inconveniencing anyone by showering early because the roster didn't commence until 6.00 am and Madame Rosaline took the first slot. Unbeknownst to me, the clattering of the aging water pipes acted as an alarm for the girls, as most were not accustomed to waking early. Under Madame Rosaline's rules, the girls were to be dressed and ready for breakfast at 7.30 am and on their way to the respective school, college or university by 8.30 am. Madame Rosaline required all the girls to enrol in further education, determined they use their time under her roof to better themselves so they would be capable of carving their own path and not need to be supported by a man. Through a very firm yet loving hand, she had guided dozens of girls to become empowered, educated and self-sufficient young women. A hidden force in the women's movement.

I proved far from popular for waking the girls early from their slumber, the serene silence in the kitchen as I sipped my tea destroyed by their collective complaints. Madame Rosaline chastised me as we ate breakfast for not abiding with the roster, despite assuring me when we were alone in the kitchen that she would amend the roster and I could take her slot given I was also an early riser. I had been waking before sunlight since the day of my birth, to either met the sun as she rose over the mountains or to milk the cows with Caellach in my later years. There was something about reconnecting with the light as she rose from the darkness, which gifted me calm as I began my day. Perhaps it was the silence and stillness that comforted my soul or the promise of all that may emerge renewed from the darkness of the night.

'Irish here seems to think she can break all the rules,' Clarissa snarled across the table. 'Cavorting with Johnny Triboni, all goo-goo-eyed. You've always told us to stay well away from him, Madame Rosaline, and suddenly she comes along, and you deliver her straight to him!'

I was surprised how aggrieved Clarissa was by what was apparently a gross injustice.

'What I do or don't do is none of your business!' chided Madame Rosaline.

'Maybe you're just jealous, Rissy,' giggled another quiet girl who typically shied away from the drama, but appeared to welcome the rare chance to deride Clarissa.

'We all know you've had your eye on Johnny since the day you got here, but he's never blinked an eye in your direction.'

'Not for want of trying,' said a raven-haired beauty also relishing the opportunity to get her own back.

'But it's true, it isn't fair that she gets to sit with him and perform by herself while we have to do those ridiculous dances!' Another gleefully pounced on the chance to whine about dancing with the other girls, as she had been dancing alone on stages in clubs of a very different kind since she had bloomed into her womanhood at the tender age of twelve. She knew how to draw a roomful of men to the edge of their seats all by herself, and she secretly loved exerting that power over them. Sadly, she also knew the flip side of that coin: being held by a roomful of men, as the woman she called mommy stood nearby, counting her money while they claimed their purchase.

I noticed her catch Madame Rosaline's eye, a silent apology offered, for while her new home had its faults, she was eternally grateful that Madame Rosaline had found her sitting battered and bruised on a platform of Grand Central Station begging for money. Madame Rosaline had lovingly taken her under her wing, surely saving her life. The bond they shared was palpable, bringing a tear to my eye.

'You're all so terribly done by, aren't you?' Madame Rosaline teased. 'Now go on out of here and get yourself an education, so one day you can move out of here and live by your own rules!'

Every girl around that table knew they had been blessed the day Madame Rosaline brought them into her home. And while they would whine given half a chance, they were all equally determined to make the most of this opportunity.

The invitation upon entering St Christopher's was the same for me. I was no different to the girls in this respect. I just didn't think I had wounds to heal or a shadow to rise above, which it appeared they did. Was that innocence, naivety, arrogance or plain ignorance on my part?

Madame Rosaline's fierce tough love as a surrogate mother was the most love any of the girls had ever experienced. Without further complaining, they took to their jobs, cleaning up the kitchen and dining room before scurrying back to their rooms to finish preening. Content with my hair pulled back in a loose braid, a long flowing dress, the rose quartz beads Clara had made me as a farewell gift and the brown leather boots that I wore every day on the farm, I felt no need to return to my room and I bid Madame Rosaline farewell. The excitement of beginning my studies in philosophy and literature at the University of New York surged. I brushed everything else from my mind as I bounded down the stairs to make my way to the subway, eager to explore the opportunities that awaited.

Flying into the alleyway … here Johnny was waiting for me. He took my breath, for I was not expecting to see him. He was leaning against a motorbike, leather jacket slung over his shoulder, cigarette hanging seductively from his lips, and his thick, wavy, black hair combed into a perfect quiff. Reminiscent of James Dean, he oozed sex appeal, yet he had no idea of the impact he had on women.

The world stopped when our eyes met. I saw a glimmer of light dancing through his eyes, and my heart skipped a beat or two as the innocent desire of my maiden stirred. I managed to snap myself back into a normal rhythm, determined not to expose too much. In truth, something inimitable swirled in my heart when Johnny Triboni was by my side. I loved him like no other.

'Jump on.'

He handed me a helmet and stubbed his cigarette with the heel of his boot. I was torn between claiming my independence and mastering the subway or listening to my heart's desire and jumping on the back of the motorbike with my arms around him.

'Thanks for the offer, but I'm going to ride the subway. I have to find my way in this city.'

'You've got plenty of time to find your way. Just let me give you a ride!'

I could tell Johnny was frustrated by my refusal.

'It'll be easier and ... safer.'

'Safer! Excuse me, Johnny Triboni, just so you know, I don't need a ride and I certainly don't need a bodyguard. I'll be taking the subway.'

He called out, asking me to stop as I neared the end of the alley. I was reluctant, yet instinct guided me to hear him out. I turned and folded my arms as he approached, shaking his head in what I sensed was a combination of frustration and concern.

Stopping directly in front of me, he placed his hands on my shoulders and looked me in the eye, but this time there was no spark. Now, he was reminiscent of Caellach: a protective big brother who was carefully steering his obstinate little sister away from danger. Patiently, he explained to me that the city takes a while to understand. He lit another cigarette, looked beyond the alleyway to the bloodline of the city streets already teaming with cars, buses and fast-paced New Yorkers intent on making every minute of the new day count.

'She's a mystery, complex yet profoundly simple. Beautiful on the surface, yet horrifying in the hidden crevices. She is enigmatic in her light and seductive in her darkness. She is everything and some more!' He turned his attention and earnestly declared, 'She will make you or break you, MG.'

I smiled as his passion and his concern touched my heart. 'But that's what I'm here to find out. What will she do to me? Where will she crack me open and force me to grow up and prove I've got what it takes to master city life?'

He laughed. 'New York City is no ordinary city, MG. She is a Queen who will not be mastered. She will give to you if you dance her dance and move with the mystery.'

'Isn't it better to learn her dance through immersing in it, rather than dancing on the edges? To face my fear, rather than give it power?'

'You can do whatever you want, but remember it was you who said that you'd found me to help you find you. So let me!'

'I know. I stand by that, but having you by my side might make it too easy and what if that holds me back?'

'I promise never to hold you back! I'll show you the real New York City and once you figure out how to dance her dance, then she's all yours! I have zero doubt she'll work her magic on you, and you'll douse her with your fairy dust or whatever it is you do.' He popped the helmet on my head.

'You've got me for two hours, Johnny Triboni, and then I've got a date with my philosophy professor.'

'Lucky him, I've no doubt you'll be questioning thousand-year-old philosophical theories within the first ten minutes,' he teased, as he put on his jacket and set his own helmet in place.

'Probably. Isn't that what I'm supposed to do?' I laughed, feigning his reproach.

'Yep, question everything and push them way out of their comfort zone.'

'Do I make you uncomfortable, Johnny Triboni?'

'Completely!' He shook his head. 'From the minute I saw you on that stage you've done nothing but make me uncomfortable.'

I smirked playfully, enjoying the ease of our banter.

'Now jump on or those girls will be down here harassing you again.'

Straddling the bike behind him, I wrapped my arms around his waist and rested my head on his back. All the discomforts and unknowns dissolved, and a familiar warmth came over me. He felt like home and his heartbeat soothed my soul.

He squeezed my thigh as the engine roared to life and shouted. 'Hold on tight, it's going to be some ride!'

*Never a truer word was spoken.* I sensed the danger in holding him too tightly, knowing navigating this path with Johnny was going to be tricky. It was going to be profoundly simple or infinitely complex, and I didn't know which one I sought. But as we raced down the alleyway and dived into the pulse of the city, I trusted it was meant to be and how it played out was beyond me.

*Perhaps it was destiny.*

# CHAPTER 7

# The Authentic Self

Surprisingly, I adapted quickly to life here and found my days took on a defined structure that enabled me to traverse the unknowns with less struggle than I anticipated. Johnny was my constant. He took the edge from my unease. Even though I initially resisted his offer to take me to and from university, I welcomed his presence in the alleyway of a morning and at the front of campus every afternoon. This also made me an easy target for the girls. They took enormous pleasure in brutally mocking my performances over breakfast and questioning my relationship with Johnny. Their ardent curiosity grew from an inability to understand what could not easily be defined and I remained tight-lipped, relishing the mystery and complexity of our soul connection. My silence did little to temper their inquisition. It fuelled the litany of complaints to Madame Rosaline about Johnny and I spending time together outside the club as they were strictly forbidden from mixing with Jimmy's men beyond the confides of St Christopher's. Madame Rosaline refused to be drawn on the subject and would shake her head and reply, 'You don't like my rules, find somewhere else to live.'

After a couple of weeks, all but Clarissa became bored with the topic and quietly accepted that Johnny and I had a *thing* that was inexplicable and through their eyes was insipid. Clarissa couldn't let it go and continued to bait me whenever she had the opportunity, obstinately encouraging the girls to mock me about everything from the books I read, to the clothes I wore, to how I did my hair and my performances. The songs I sang, the music I played, the way I danced were the butt of endless spiteful taunts. I trusted whatever I did on that stage was what I was meant to do. I was always going to seem odd to the girls because I was different. It was blindingly obvious, but I didn't want to belong if it meant sacrificing my true self.

And yet, over those first few weeks, I did betray myself by ignoring the truth of the connection Johnny and I shared. I allowed the innocence of my maiden to overanalyse our relationship in my head. I sought a rational explanation for what I intuitively understood was a soul connection. My confused maiden just couldn't comprehend the intimacy of our relationship, which was charged and palpable but not always in a physical or sexual way. I spoke of Johnny as a friend. Although, it was more than that. I felt a deep love for him. An aching love in the core of my being. I cared deeply for him and wanted to wrap him up and save him from the harsh realities of the world. At the same time, I felt the intensity of his love for me in a similar way. He was nurturing and protective. He knew parts of me that even those closest to me had not discovered and he challenged those aspects. Johnny was a barometer to my truth and would call me out when I showed signs of buying into the stories that my ego wanted to moan about. He forced me to stay true to who he knew me to be. He adamantly denied I was his girlfriend when Jimmy, his father, finally questioned him about the rumours we'd been together outside of the club. He explained that Madame Rosaline had told him to help the new girl settle into the city because she was a 'country girl'. He knew I was so much more than that, yet I did ponder if Madame Rosaline had asked him to befriend me, knowing it was going to be a challenging transition. In truth, it was proving more difficult than I had anticipated to connect with others both at St Christopher's and in my classes.

I perceived that in studying literature and philosophy, I would meet like-minded people who I would readily befriend. I soon realised my view of the world and my interpretation of literature and philosophical ideologies were vastly different to my peers and professors. My questioning of the readily accepted perspective offered by the professors was at first viewed as a novelty, yet it quickly became a source of frustration for my fellow students and those who I had entrusted to mentor me. Following an impassioned discussion with Professor Theodore Johnson, a tweed-jacket-pipe-smoking-academic, it was obvious my questioning was an irritant rather than a stimulus to expand conversations and explore alternate perspectives. In one exchange regarding the character Bertha Mason in Charlotte Bronte's *Jane Eyre*, the esteemed Professor Theodore dictated that she was a secondary character of little importance to the development of Rochester's character. That being locked away in the attic allowed Rochester to grow as a character without the limitation of an insane wife. I opposed his interpretation and proposed that Bertha was an extraordinarily important character who powerfully reflected the patriarchies suppression of the wild woman archetype. She was locked away and labelled insane because she challenged the mould of what society expected her to be. She who said too much. She who felt too much. She who knew too much and saw too much. Bertha was a danger to Rochester's good name and his patriarchal establishment and, like the collective feminine she portrayed, was brutally suppressed to ensure his glorification.

I could not fail to hear the susurrant insults spreading through the lecture hall willing me to shut my mouth and conform.

'Why does she have to question everything?'

'She just argues for the sake of arguing.'

'Angry lesbian.'

'Hippy women's lib bull shit.'

I often left class feeling despondent and wondering whether I should surrender to the collective thinking and go along with the patriarchal narrative, for surely it would make for an easier experience. It was exhausting being the one to offer alternative perspectives, especially when it appeared there was little interest in stretching beyond the comfort of an accepted mindset. And yet, as soon as I jumped on the back of Johnny's motorbike and rested my head on his back, my soul settled. I remembered that my voice did matter and perhaps I was planting seeds that, with time, may open one person or many to see beyond the construct of their programmed thinking. In times of doubt, which tended to pester me in the dark of night, I would reflect on the words Athena had written in the last letter I received before her passing. It wasn't long after I turned thirteen and began my journey into my maiden.

My Precious Marigold,
From the moment you lay in my arms, your soul reflected the wisdom that few are able to bring to this world. The path of the wise woman

is not for the meek. The edge of the circle can be lonely, but it is where your gifts abound. Stray into the middle with caution for the temptation of the ainspiorad—the evil spirits are strong and will seek to syphon the divinity of your soul. When you forget who you are—for you shall—remember to come home.
My heart and soul will remain with you as you journey.
Always, Ma Ma

My saving grace became Central Park, in all her natural beauty. She was a refuge for my soul. The first afternoon Johnny picked me up from class, I convinced him to take the scenic route and ride through the park. This became our path home. I'd quickly kick off my boots and dig my toes into the ground, absorbing the energy and grounding myself. I was relieved to have a little patch of nature to connect with amidst the hustle and bustle. My place to reset my soul and come home. Eventually, Johnny lay on the grass with me, surrendering to the earth. I witnessed him marvel at the majesty of the tree branches above us and the dance of the clouds through the sky.

He knew that just like his morning coffee set him up for the day, Central Park was vital for my survival in the city. I needed this rhythm and stability to keep me grounded, for the temptation to dissociate out of the challenging moments was powerful. It would have been much easier for me to be in higher realms while drifting through my days, completely disconnected from the world around me. Yet, my new life and the pressures it came with were essential for my growth. It was the path I had chosen.

We didn't talk a lot. Not in words, anyway. I never asked him what he did in the darkest hours of the night under the orders of his father. Yet I knew. Some mornings as I bounded excitedly into the alley, a dark intensity would engulf me and though he would avoid catching my eye, I could see the empty dark pools in his eyes that hid the rage, sorrow and resentment. He would thrust the helmet without acknowledging me, before taking a final long draw of his cigarette. His hand shaking as he brought it to his mouth, despite his best efforts to control it. On those mornings, I'd open myself fully to him, knowing he needed to feel me, even though he'd shun me. When I placed my cheek upon his back, I would offer him my heart and all the love it held, intending it to draw the fear from his nervous system, release the tension from his body and dissolve the pain radiating from his heart and soul. His heart would slow. His body would soften, and his chest would heave as the pain would release in his heart-wrenching sobs beneath the helmet.

As we raced through the city streets, violent visions would flood my awareness. Johnny was a voyeur to the intimidation, violence and bloodshed that his brothers and the other men Jimmy employed inflicted on others. They were hungry for power and cold-hearted in their execution of Jimmy's instructions. With every violent blow and splattering of blood, Johnny's body would shudder, and I'd will the transference of the trauma from his body to mine so he may be free from the darkness. Nothing good could come from holding onto such trauma. This was my silent gift to him. The gift he never asked of me.

Aunt Maeve had long before reminded me that as a healer I must be wise in how I support others to heal. She would say: 'Your "wings" are sacred and as you allow the energy of others to move into your being, you must remember to release it from your field, or your "wings" will become dirty, heavy and broken. In turn, the luminance of your light will be dimmed, inhibiting your soul from sharing *her* gifts with the world. Remember, in doing the work for others, you deny them the lessons offered from their wounds. This is not the way of the healer, Marigold. You are wiser than this. A healer is love, and love allows the other to heal. Fear attempts to fix the other. Always walk in love beside the other and show them the way.'

> In meditation, my soul lovingly asked:
> *Are you allowing Johnny to find his own way through his shadow, or are you fixing him? Are you guiding him so he may learn, or are you trying to abate his suffering? Are you holding him in love or fear?*

I convinced myself that my support for Johnny was coming from love, not fear. But in the dark of night, I doubted my motivation as a healer. I wondered if my actions were driven by the depth of my love for his soul, or my fear of losing his soul to the darkness.

I was diligent in releasing Johnny's trauma and cleansing my 'wings' every morning after he dropped me at college. I farewelled him by staring into his eyes and forcing him to connect with me. I would silently assure him *I've got you*, before taking myself to the stillness of the campus chapel. There, I pulled out my healing oils to complete an energetic cleansing ritual Aunt Maeve had taught me not long before I left for the city. Aunt Maeve's intuition was powerful. She could foresee I would need a new tool for holding my centre and maintaining my integrity in the city. Perhaps she had envisioned the journey of my soul through her maiden and into her woman. If she had, I was not privy to her insights. I realised that should I have known what was coming, I would not have been gifted the challenge of the unknown.

*Can one truly be tested when you know what lies ahead?*

# CHAPTER 8

# Fiercely Fearless

I was nearing the end of my first trimester at college when Jimmy Triboni put me on his radar. He had been transfixed during all my performances and hadn't equated me—the ethereal woman moving hypnotically about the stage—as the same *country girl* drinking whiskey beside his sullen youngest son every other night. I was not a threat and thus didn't warrant his attention—until Clarissa stirred trouble.

Clarissa had a way of luring men and manipulating them to her advantage. Frank was Jimmy's oldest son. What Frank had in brute strength, he lacked in brains. He was ignorant to Clarissa's motive in swindling up to him and enticing him into her web. Clarissa had boasted to the girls that she had been seeing Frank outside of St Christopher's. Although wary of Madame Rosaline's wrath, she was determined to worm her way into the Triboni circle. She was never satisfied milling around the edges. Out of all the Triboni sons, Frank was by far the most dangerous, power hungry and entitled. He wasn't clean in his executions and craved short-term surges of power over the long strategic games, which his father played well.

One morning, I gently tried to warn Clarissa to be wary of Frank. She was not open to my guidance.

'Don't think you're the only one who can handle a Triboni man, Irish. I've got Frank wrapped around my little finger! He'd do anything to get into my knickers. You're the one who doesn't know who you're messing with, so you're the one who better watch out, Irish. I'd watch my back if I were you because there's no guarantee lover boy will always be around to protect you.'

Clarissa craved power, too. The malice in her words stirred an unease within. I sensed something more sinister had awoken within her. I trusted my body's wisdom to alert me, yet did not allow fear to dictate my response. I wouldn't let my fear become her weapon.

Later that night, I sat next to Johnny. Clarissa was next to Frank, and Madame Rosaline next to Jimmy, where she kept a close watch on the girls. As usual, Jimmy had no interest in me as I sat next to his petulant son. This night was no different to any other that we had been allowed to stay back to socialise with Jimmy's men, although I could feel Clarissa's malevolence brewing. I noticed her turn to whisper in Frank's ear. He was ignorant to being a pawn in her game. Naively, he played his part, turning to his father. Following a brief exchange, Jimmy looked at me with curiosity—for the first time. Her poison was effective.

Fear and fury flooded Johnny's body as Jimmy approached. I instinctively placed my hand on his beneath the table, trying to steady him. Johnny retracted. But Jimmy Triboni missed nothing, and his eyes flickered at Johnny's reaction to my gesture. I could read his thoughts: *The boy cares for this girl. The boy needs to protect this girl. The boy will do anything to keep her safe. The boy will finally do as I say. The boy will finally show me the respect I deserve.*

'Son, do I get the privilege of an introduction to your little friend here who you've been hiding away, or are you keeping her to yourself?'

Jimmy smirked, knowing Johnny detested identifying as his son. He found it amusing to rile his youngest, yet I saw something more sinister beneath his words. I took heed of Madame Rosaline's warning: 'Jimmy Triboni was not to be underestimated, yet was not to be feared.'

A surge of electricity flew through my body, alerting me to the danger, but I willed it to settle as Johnny had enough adrenaline pulsating through him for both of us. To survive in Jimmy Triboni's world, I couldn't fear him, for then he would have power over me. So, I chose to meet Jimmy Triboni as I had many a wild animal in the mountains—by rising above my fear and facing the threat. I held my centre and forced him to meet me in my power. This was contrary to everything Johnny espoused in dealing with his father and proved to cause a great divide between us. Intuitively, I knew I had not landed in Johnny's life to enable him to stay trapped in his father's world, which he would if he continued to operate from fear. Every time he reacted in fear, he handed his power to this man who relished in dominating and tormenting him with brutal violence, intimidation and manipulation.

To everyone's shock, with the exception of Madame Rosaline who watched on from her table, I rose and offered Jimmy my hand.

'My name is Goldie Mae. I don't hide and I don't belong to anyone.'

Raising an eyebrow, he took my hand.

'Hmm, I see.'

He held my hand longer than necessary, demanding I concede to his power, but I wouldn't flinch. I refused to play his game.

'Perhaps you're not just a simple country girl after all.'

'Looks can be deceiving.' I sipped my whiskey but did not divert my gaze.

I could feel Johnny willing me to sit back down, but I wouldn't. I rose to meet him and all he represented.

I did not fear *him*.

I would not be tamed by *him*.

I would not behave and play by *his* rules.

She, the Divine Feminine had been suppressed by *him* for too long … for far too long.

'Deception. Is that your game?'

'I leave deception to the likes of her.' I motioned my head in Clarissa's direction.

I could feel her watching our exchange, keen to witness the execution of her malicious plan.

'I don't play games. What you see is what you get.'

'Really?' he laughed. 'This feels very much like you've entered the game, Miss Goldie Mae.'

'No, Mr Triboni. I'm not in the game. I prefer to sit and watch.'

'A wise move indeed, Miss Goldie Mae.'

He raised his glass to meet mine and I sensed a glint of respect. As he returned to his table, he nodded discreetly to Madame Rosaline and ignored the fuss Clarissa was making. Madame Rosaline caught my eye. She conveyed respect for the discernment and courage I had in the exchange with Jimmy. In over twenty years, she had never seen anyone meet Jimmy as an equal. Most feared him, cowering in his presence, or they despised him, actively avoiding him. There were those who sought to befriend him and move closer to the centre of power, but Jimmy Triboni did not have friends and he did not let anyone get close. Except Madame Rosaline. Their relationship was a mystery that was unquestioned. She was the only person who knew the man beneath the façade of Jimmy Triboni. She understood his wounds and the behaviours they triggered. She could hold his demons which sought to hurt and disempower others to numb his own pain. She did not condone what he did to others, nor did she condemn him.

'Who am I to judge the journey of another,' she would tell me.

Her level of compassion and unconditional love astounded me. It was evident that Madame Rosaline's soul contract with Jimmy Triboni was complex and challenging and she held it with integrity. Madame Rosaline was there for Jimmy as he recklessly navigated his way through life. She supported the transmutation of his dark to light and held him with something I was only beginning to understand—love expressed through darkness.

*She* was complex and defied the rules.

*She* was misunderstood because of her complexity.

*She* was demonised because she was misunderstood.

*She* was the potency of darkness integrated into the light.

*She* was beyond what we knew woman to be.

*She* was all that woman was being called to *become*, to *remember*, to *reclaim*.

And within, a pulse awakened my remembering of *her* call to reclamation.

I claimed my seat beside Johnny. The force of his emotions struck me. His anger was palpable and threatened to shred the threads that had so gently woven us together. Unable to hold his rage whilst under the watchful eye of his father, Johnny stood abruptly and left the club without a word. My head insisted I race after him. My heart assured me it was safe to let him go, to allow him to move through his fury without me transmuting it for him. He was furious with me for engaging with Jimmy in what he deemed recklessness, but his anger had been seeded long before I appeared in his life. It was this he was being called to reckon with.

I opened the door into the alleyway the following morning, hoping Johnny would be there, yet not expecting him.

'Why did you take him on, MG?'

'I didn't take him on, Johnny. I spoke to him the same as I'm speaking to you now,' I refuted calmly, while willing him to connect with me.

'Exactly, you spoke to him like he was normal, but he's not normal!'

'Beneath the façade, he is Johnny …'

'It's not a façade. It's who he is,' he pulled his hand through his hair frustrated. 'You think you're not in the game, MG, but you are! You're on his radar now and he'll use you to get to me, and trust me, he'll make my life hell.'

He looked at me, shook his head, and his eyes were filled with grief and disdain.

'You've no idea what you've done.'

His condescending tone triggered me, and I met him in my own rage.

'Holy fuck, Johnny, just stop. Stop treating me like I'm a stupid child who doesn't have a clue about life. I get it. He's dangerous and he's not to be messed with. But I didn't mess with him. I just refuse to fear him. I'm not going to shrink myself or hide so he doesn't see me. I'm not afraid to be seen, Johnny, by him or anyone. I held my ground. I held my truth. I held my power and met him with an open heart and mind. Jimmy respected me for it.'

'He doesn't respect anyone. He'll annihilate your heart and fuck with your mind.'

'Maybe he will, but I'm not going to sit in fear like you, giving him an open invitation to destroy me. Your fear completely destroys you, the man I see when I look at you. The one whose smile lights my days, even on the most miserable of days completely dissolves when you're around him. You don't want him to have power over you, but every time you close off your heart in fear of him or what he'll do to me, you give your power to him. He thrives on fear. He can smell it a mile away and when others fear him, he wins every time!'

'Yeah,' his voice was shaking. 'And you know what he does when he smells that fear? He gets off on it. Do you know what he does to people when they cower or try to run away?'

His eyes flickered hysterically.

'Yes, Johnny, I know,' I replied softly, trying to calm the rising panic.

'You don't know. You're not standing there being made to watch it, to hear the screams, to smell the burning flesh … to tidy up his mess.'

Johnny spat with disgust.

I reached out to touch his arm, but he brushed me away and refused to let me in. I needed him to know that I was already in. I had been walking this path with him for months now and I understood more than he knew. I was not blind to the brutal reality of his pain.

I begged him to listen. I wanted him to understand that I take people to a place that is beyond here when I perform. A place where they get to remember who they really are beyond the wounding of their human, where they get to remember the light and maybe that helps them to remember that they carry that light within themselves. Arrogantly, he shook his head when I tried to explain this, and he refused to acknowledge that his father or brothers could possibly be of the light.

I continued, despite his resistance.

'When I take them there, I witness the purging of their pain so they can touch the light. Sometimes it's a big space to hold. That's why I come out here and make sure I come back to me and leave their energy in the heavens to be taken care of by something far more powerful than me. And you are always here to help me come back, Johnny, to help me hold onto my light in this crazy place.'

He softened, his heart opened a little, allowing him to see me as the powerful woman I was becoming.

'I know when you've had a bad night. I feel it as soon as I see you and when I rest my head on your back, I get visions of what you have been through. Like a movie on repeat, I witness the same scenes replaying as they pulsate through your cells, your body's wisdom seeking to expel all that is toxic and all that will suffocate your soul should you hold it,' I continued.

I reached for his hands, but he drew away terrified of poisoning me with this toxicity.

'Please, Johnny, trust me when I tell you I've seen what happens and I know that Jimmy forces you to be there even though you don't want to. I know you refuse to take a gun in your hand and lay a hand on another. I know that you are not responsible for the bloodshed and terror. You are not to blame for their actions, Johnny. It is not yours.'

He crumbled beneath the guilt and shame and cried.

'I am to blame because I don't stop them. My silence makes me complicit. There is blood on my hands. It stains my soul and torments my mind. You see me in the way you want to see me. You want to see me as golden like you. I'm not golden. I'm no better than them and no matter how much I fight it, I'm never going to be free of it. He's in my blood and I'm trapped in his world and once you're in, there is no way out. Can't you see that's why I've tried to protect you? I didn't want you to get drawn into his web, but you went and took his bait and now you're a part of it. Now I don't know what he'll do to you to get to me!'

He slumped to the ground, dropping his head into his hands. I slid beside him and placed my hand on his knee. He pushed it away, but I would not give up on him, even though he wanted me to leave him there in his misery, in his victimhood, in his shadow.

'Johnny, there is always another way and I thought I was showing you that way. The pain can be released. You don't have to stay a victim to your trauma. You can let it go and rise above it and reclaim your light. Then you can see clearer and remember that there is exquisite beauty and light in every moment, even if they are dark and scary. I believed in absorbing your pain and transmuting it as we rode around the city, you would remember your light and that there is another way for you to live.'

In his heart, he wanted to trust me. To open to love and walk with me on the path to freedom, but he stiffened, fear rising ferociously, convincing him that everything I said was rubbish. That it was nothing more than love and light bullshit, a fluffy fantasy fit for a fairy-tale. The only way this Prince Charming could see to protect his princess was to reject me.

'Well, this other way of yours doesn't seem to be working, does it? Because I'm fucked.' He stood up and began walking towards his bike before turning and, with pain in his eyes, he hissed, 'I never asked you to wave your magic wand over me, Miss Goldie Mae.'

The sharp edge of his rejection pierced my heart. I couldn't stop the tears and retaliated bitterly.

'No, you didn't, but you didn't try to stop me, Johnny Triboni!'

I turned quickly and headed for the subway, determined to make my own way as I had always intended. If Johnny Triboni didn't want me and my magic wand, I most certainly didn't want him as my bodyguard.

*All that was, died. All that was to be, birthed.*

# Part Two

# CHAPTER 9

# The Wild Woman

*Buried beneath the calm lies the storm.*
*Shadowed beneath the petal lies the thorn.*
*Veiled beneath the virgin lies the whore.*
*Waiting beneath the light lies the dark.*
*She Comes.*
*Without Invitation. Without Apology. Without Exception.*

I often meandered through the hills to the river with my Ma Ma, Athena. We would sit and she would tell me stories. Other times, we'd surrender to the silence of becoming *one* with the beauty around us. Ma Ma taught me to read the movement of energy in the river, witnessing how it subtly shifted. From a breath of wind on its surface, a stirring in the depths, to the ripples touching the edges, seducing the tree roots or polishing the stones.

Some days, we watched the water trickling. Other days, the water danced joyfully, content in her flow. Many days, the water gushed powerfully, carving her path. Regardless of the day, the water was held by the banks, always. On the day my Mo Mo, Cynthia, died she took me to the river to distance me from our camp. The shock of losing one of our own shattered our usual peaceful community, igniting chaos and hysteria. I was only four years old and didn't fully understand what was happening.

When I was removed from the intensity of other's emotions, I began to shake uncontrollably. Ma Ma sat me in her lap, cradled me in her arms and wrapped me in the warmth of her love. From the time my Ma's had embraced me as a newborn, I had not known fear. My river had peacefully flowed with joy, held securely by the love of our community, especially the constant presence of my beloved Ma Ma and Mo Mo. But with one so violently and suddenly torn from me, the life I had known fell apart and the unpredictability of each moment stirred an unease within me.

Ever the teacher, Ma Ma asked, 'What would happen to all that water if the banks collapsed?'

I stared at the water that gurgled chaotically. Never had it been so fierce and aggressive. Its anger scared me. *What would happen if that raging torrent was not held by the banks?* Visions pierced my third eye demanding I remember, that I remember *her.* Old and wrinkled with long grey hair, she reminded me of Ma Ma, except not serene like she was. *She* was wild. Her hair a mattered mess of twigs and leaves, of grass and feathers. Her eyes darted from one direction to another and she moved frantically from here to there and there to here. She was feverishly hungry for more of something or everything. She could not stop because she was determined to discover it all. *Become* it all. She had to keep moving, wary of those who sought to tame her, contain her bedlam, bringing order to her pandemonium and stifle the wildness that danced ever so dangerously on the edge of sanity. She was too much for this world and had to be stopped.

They had dived towards her, needle readied to jab her with a mild sedative, seeking to tame her, yet before they could claim her, she fractured into a million pieces, her scream piercing the lights of heaven and the pits of hell ensuring she would never be forgotten and forever roam in the light and in the dark.

Lilith, the wild, the misconstrued, the demonised.

Lilith, the fearless, the fierce, the free.

Lilith, the truth, the light, the dark.

I shared with Ma Ma what the river had shown me and how the scream of the wild woman had woken me that morning, before news of Mo Mo's death reached the camp. She kissed my forehead, squeezed me tighter and ever so gently guided me towards the truth of Cynthia's death.

'Marigold, if the banks of the river broke, the water would spill everywhere and no longer go where it should. Some fear it would destroy everything around. For this reason, they believe the banks must be reinforced and secured so the river can be managed or tamed. Those who fear the natural flow of the river, like a hopeless farmer who despairs the loss of crops, will seek to intervene and control the waters. Others, who are able to see from a higher perspective, will understand the river that bursts her banks will create through her destruction. Sometimes riverbanks must be broken for new rivers to form. Sometimes the structure of all that is must crumble for new life to begin. Sometimes that which has been destroyed had to be destroyed so it can start afresh. This is the life-death-life cycle, Marigold. It is the way of all that is. Denial of our natural cycles creates pain and struggle and I assure you, my sweet child, the fields that have been besieged by wild waters will one day become fertile and flourish again, bearing new and magnificent offerings to those who allow the wild waters to weave her magic through their lands.'

'Ma Ma, is this what happened to Mo Mo?'

I was longing for the embrace of my Moon Mother just one more time and yet I trusted she would find me from beyond the veil of death.

'Yes, your Mo Mo lived this life fully. She learnt many lessons and she touched many lives in important ways, including you and me. And while we will miss her terribly, her time in this life has come to an end. She will now be reborn. First in the spirit realm where I hope she rests for her soul will be weary, and when it is time, her soul may be reborn into the earth realm, for this world needs her wisdom, her passion and audacity. I trust in her return and the cycle of all that is. For now, we pray that your Mo Mo transitions held in the arms of the Divine Mother and claims her peace. Amen, Amen, Amen and a little woman.'

'Amen and a wild woman, like my Mo Mo. Not a little woman!'

I passionately reworked Athena's ancient prayer to meet the fire in my belly.

'Yes, your Mo Mo was a wild woman, a rose warrior to the very end,' she laughed.

Slowly, we returned to our people hand-in-hand and allowed our grief to flow like a river with broken banks.

Ma Ma's stories did not always make sense to me when I was young. She was wisely planting seeds, trusting one day when the time was right, those seeds would germinate and blossom to guide me along my path. Some fourteen years after Mo Mo's death, I sat alone on the subway pondering these stories and the wild woman who had unapologetically infiltrated my vision as I had stared into the river. I knew *her*. She lived curled within my womb and when I performed on stage, she stirred. *Her* fierceness and freedom were an antidote to the good girl so revered in most circles. She roused when I rose to face Jimmy Triboni. She was not scared of him. *Her* boldness pushed me to my edge and demanded I now become more … more free, more wild, more passionate, more truthful.

*Her* whispers melded with the millions of untold secrets trapped in the dark tunnels of the subway, the underbelly of the city. A surge gushed, pushing at my edges, threatening to destroy all I knew myself to be. As the darkness invaded the carriage, I doubted whether I could hold my centre and remain anchored in my body. My wild woman arched to meet the potency of the city's darkness. It was seductive in its calling to *her,* and she fought to break free from the confines of my maiden womb and become one with it. Could I hold on to my *self* as *she* ignited in me? I realised that this was the hidden face of the city that Johnny had so ardently sought to shield me from. He saw only my light and doubted my ability to dance in the dark. He had been the banks to my river. Without him holding me, I feared the river gushing through me was going to break these banks and my wild woman would be unleashed on the city.

I had allowed Johnny to be my masculine, to hold my energy, as she flowed through the city. I had betrayed my own masculine and now I did not trust myself to hold the power of my own feminine. Especially the wild woman awakening within. *Her* power and potency scared me and, in my fear, I blocked *her* eruption. I convinced myself to shut *her* down. Tame *her.* Until I was better prepared to manage *her.*

*I will not be managed!*

I heard *her* warning, yet took no heed. I denied the path before me, suppressing the call of my soul and fracturing the sacred thread that anchored me to her. For the first time in my life, I was lost. I began to neglect the rituals that had supported my transition to the city. I did not stop at Central Park on my way home, choosing instead to ride the subway straight to St Christopher's and sit in my room studying. I had no connection with nature, no meditation. I sat at the back of the lecture theatres, silent and shadowed. I refused to allow myself to be seen and heard. Refused to participate in discussions. I went straight to my room after performances. No grounding myself afterwards, or fully coming back into my body. I left my energy fields open to defiling by any stray energy that sought my light—my now dwindling light.

I would not listen to Madame Rosaline, who encouraged me to continue my daily practices to anchor myself and I could only manage half-hearted performances, not able to bring the majesty of my golden light into the darkness of St Christopher's any longer. I refused to go back into the club and socialise with Jimmy's men after performing, especially when Clarissa delighted in telling me that Johnny had asked Sally to sit and have a drink with him. By all accounts they had become an unofficial item, sitting together drinking, laughing and flirting every night. I knew it was part of Johnny's ploy to distract Jimmy's attention from me, but it hurt the tenderness of my maiden heart and I could not bear to witness it.

Sensing my uncharacteristic vulnerability and dwindling charisma and radiance, Clarissa attacked.

'What's the matter Irish? Can't handle a little heartbreak? We all knew lover boy would dump you and move on once your voodoo spells wore off. Upgraded to a real woman, hey Sally?'

The other girls giggled, encouraging her. To my dismay, Madame Rosaline continued to eat her dinner quietly, reserved yet subtly watching and listening, curious to my response. I took Madame Rosaline's silence as a betrayal that condoned their attack and reflected her allegiance to them and not me. I believed she cared for me, but like Johnny, she had abandoned me. Alone and angry, I retaliated.

'He didn't dump me, Clarissa. I was never his to dump.'

I gave Clarissa exactly what she was looking for, a hole in my armour. Madame Rosaline glared at me with a warning to stop. I knew I had handed my power over to Clarissa in that moment, but I refused to take responsibility for my actions and Clarissa dug the knife in deeper, knowing she had the upper hand.

'If lover boy didn't dump you, why are you so miserable all the time? Girls, I think Irish here is missing cock? Is that right, Irish? Are you missing Johnny's cock? Don't worry, I hear Sally here is looking after it for you!'

She fell into fits of laughter and once the girls realised Madame Rosaline was not going to chastise Clarissa, they began laughing hysterically, too. Fuming more at Madame Rosaline's silence than the vileness of Clarissa's words, I threw back my chair, stood and glared across the table to Madame Rosaline, demanding an answer to my question, '*Are you going to let her talk to me like that?*' Her silence infuriated me further. I stormed out, retreating to my bedroom, dived under my bedclothes and into the depths of the victim story I had become enslaved too.

Lost in the torrents of pain, I ignored the calm of my soul voice seeking to bring me back into my heart. I didn't want to be calm. I didn't want peace. I wanted to dissolve into my indignant rage about being misunderstood and betrayed by Johnny and Madame Rosaline. I ignored the knock on my door to tell me it was time to go downstairs and perform. I would not be a puppet on stage for her! I refused to bring through divine light for the men. They didn't deserve it and I wasn't going to share it with them, not tonight, not ever!

'I'm not coming out so you might as well go away,' I yelled at the door, knowing that Madame Rosaline was patiently waiting for me to snap out of my petulance.

'I can't force you to do anything you don't want to do, Goldie Mae,' she replied calmly.

'My name is Marigold. I won't pretend to be Goldie Mae for you anymore. I quit!'

It felt good to tantrum like the child I was desperately clinging to.

'I can see you want to be Marigold. It's so much easier being her. Everyone adores her because she is golden, but clearly life's proving a little tougher as Goldie Mae when you're not everyone's number one. When you're not surrounded in love and when your shadow challenges your light. Welcome to the real world, where your shadow taunts you and you must learn to master both the light and the dark. When it gets tough, you get tougher; you don't just quit.'

'Why are you being so mean? Just leave me alone!' I screamed at the door.

'You know what I see? I see a scared young woman who's fighting the inevitable—you are going to become *her*. You can choose to surrender and allow *her* to move through you, or you can choose to resist. We both know which one is easier. Just depends on how stubborn you're going to be about it and truth be told, I didn't take you as a stubborn one. That's your ego getting in the way. I get it, you're hurting. He hurt you to protect you and you are filled with doubt about whether you can take the next steps without him.'

I heard every word she said and knew them to be true. But I wasn't ready to concede. I wanted to fight. I wanted to feed my victim. I wanted to stay small where I was safe.

'Why don't you just say I've failed this great test, this rite of passage and then I can go back home because at least they love me, and they won't turn their back on me when I don't do it perfectly.'

'Oh please, Goldie Mae, you and I both know you haven't failed anything! This … this breakdown you're having is perfect. It's just the falling over, the dropping into doubt, the succumbing to fear. It's completely normal. It is not a failure to go off your path, to lose yourself and your way. To honour the path of your shadow takes courage and allowing yourself to gently and compassionately accept that this is part of you and your journey will make it easier. Yes, it is uncomfortable, and it will be again, but remember that your struggle and suffering is your doorway to grace. Your shadow is gifting your journey to you, and you must choose how you tend to it. When you stumble, do you get up, dust yourself off and learn from it? Or do you wallow in self-pity, hoping for Prince Charming to come back and rescue you? He's not coming back, Goldie Mae! This part is on you and you alone. You cannot run from it. I see *her* in you. I feel *her* in you and if you don't allow *her*, she will erupt from you, regardless. I know this path and I can tell you it's far more graceful opening to *her* than shoving *her* back into a dark corner, hoping she'll disappear. She doesn't wait for an invitation. She arrives when it is time. And it is time.'

I began to cry because in her words I heard the voice of my mothers, my wise women, Athena, Cynthia, Aunt Maeve and Clara, and I believed I had failed them. I knew better than to behave like this. The shame landed like a boulder in my womb and there was only one way to transmute it. I took to the stage. I opened and allowed the wild waters to break free, releasing the Dark Goddess within me. *She* who wanted to bring to life all the secrets, lies, distortion and deception hidden in the crevices of each and every darkened soul in that club. I rose and came back into the fullness of myself, and as I wildly moved my body about the stage, to the beat of *her* drum, *she* alchemised all remnants of guilt and shame simmering in the shadows for my fall from grace. I did not have to return to my body when my performance ended because *she* was in my body as *she* had always been, waiting for *her* time. *She* claimed *her* time and I was awed by the potency of *her* essence.

*Could my darkness be as divine as my light?*

# CHAPTER 10

# Love Allows, Fear Fixes

As the winter darkness loomed, I surrendered and accepted the perfection of my journey, that it was to be filled with highs and lows, pain and suffering. Grace held me through those tough days when my path was peppered with challenges and I wallowed in my wounds, blaming others for my struggles, aching for Johnny—condemning myself for getting it all wrong. I expected to learn my lessons and complete my transformation quickly, without allowing my shadow to dim my light. Yet my shadow taunted me, and I lost my way over and over again. But I did not give up. Each time, I consciously chose to come back to the present moment. I'd be reminded to be gentle and compassionate with myself, that in allowing the fullness of the experience, I was unlocking a treasure that enabled me to grow and evolve. This was my story, and my soul was the creator, and she was intentionally choosing for it to be more challenging than the past. I was invited to learn about accepting the perfection and beauty of where I was in any moment, regardless of the raw edges.

These days were not easy. I felt dreadfully alone. I missed my family and the comfort of home. Mostly, I missed Johnny. The ease of being by his side, our playful banter, the companionable silence, the way he kissed my forehead when he said goodbye and the erratic beat of his heart that calmed when I held him close. I missed his skin. I missed the smell of his aftershave. I missed the smirk that danced at the corner of his lips filled with love and adoration. I missed the flicker of desire that swirled through the innocence of my maiden when I caught him staring at me, transfixed, a subtle longing for more etched in his eyes. I missed all of him and in the refuge of my dreams I found him. I would hold him tenderly in my arms, stroke the chiselled angles of his face and brush away his worries. With my hand on his heart, I would channel all that I was, all the light that I held and all the love in my heart into his soul and will him back to the light.

I was not afraid of the dark, but I feared losing Johnny to it. I did not believe he could navigate it alone. In my anguish, I was reminded he was not mine to save, and I would return to my heart and attempt to focus on my journey.

Nathanial was always there for me on those tough days, randomly bumping into me on the subway, in the library, at the park or in the alleyway outside St Christopher's, offering me the gift of friendship. His presence was always received with gratitude and awe for the perfection of its seemingly random timing. Nate was likeable, witty, wise, kind and enigmatic. He was Johnny's best friend. His only friend before I arrived, having known each other since childhood. Nate's mother and Madame Rosaline were old friends in the same way she was old friends with Aunt Maeve. Johnny and Nate became closer when Nate moved to the city and worked behind the bar for Madame Rosaline. They didn't associate much at St Christopher's but would hang out when they could and watch ball games or have a beer together. When Johnny was with Nate, he was a different person to the Johnny Triboni the world saw, and it was this normality that Johnny craved. The normality he shared with me, too.

My weary maiden wanted desperately to attach to Nate to fill the void in my heart and ease the burden, but I knew that he was just a friend. A wise friend who never sought to save or fix me. We didn't talk about Johnny much. He met me beyond my heartache and his presence was both his gift and teaching. A reminder of the path of graciousness, where acceptance of the present moment was the only way forward. Nate would say, 'It's a ride, G, one that you signed up for, so go within, go deep and stop trying to control it'.

I loved Nate. We were in many respects cut from the same cloth. He had grown up on a reservation beyond the Catskill mountains and was raised in the ancient traditions of his Indigenous people. His mother and grandmother were widely respected shamanic medicine women who had taught him the ways of old, as I had been taught by my wise mothers. We'd heard the same archetypal stories. Spoke the same language of spirit. We perceived the world through the same lens. We connected on a level that was rare for others our age. Our resonance aligned and yet our souls denied us the path of sacred union. We were confident in the truth of our connection to share this understanding, musing at the wisdom of our souls in always seeking the path of expansion. We acknowledged with thankfulness the significance of what we shared—a friendship seeded in the stars—true soul mates.

News that Johnny had been absent from St Christopher's for a week broke Sally's heart and lifted my spirit. I convinced myself he had finally stood up to Jimmy. At the same time, I was denying the unease in my heart, a deep knowing within my bones that all was not as I longed for it to be.

Nate found me in Central Park on the eve of Thanksgiving meandering through the fallen leaves.

'G, we've got to talk.'

The seriousness of his tone was alarming and ignited a wildness within that had been carefully tempering since *her* rising some weeks before.

'It's Johnny, isn't it? Is he dead?' I witnessed my rising hysteria with curiosity. Like a wild beast, she ravenously tore through my body, freed at last and I was unable to control *her*, a mania edging closer with each breath.

'He's not dead, G, but he's done something stupid and it's better you hear it from me than Clarissa.'

He shook his head, and I could tell even he was dumbfounded.

'Nate! What is it?'

'He's getting married. The engagement notice came out today and it's all over town. Jimmy has arranged it all. It's his lawyer's daughter.'

Nate expressed his concern for me, but our worry was for Johnny and this arrangement which was fraught with danger. Johnny had conceded to his father's demands, and this marriage would tie him to the family business in a way he had never before allowed.

'Even though he despises Jimmy, deep down he's always wanted his love and getting his approval by saying yes to this farce is probably the closest he's going to get. It's a dumb move, but he's desperate and obviously thinks it's the only way he can keep Jimmy happy and you off his radar. I figure in Johnny's head that's a win-win. He protects you and gets Jimmy's approval. But I'm not so sure about his heart.'

'It's got nothing to do with his heart! You told me Johnny's not like his father, that he doesn't play games, but he's exactly like him. It's all a game, a stupid power game. I never wanted anything to do with it and now he's basically selling his soul to the devil to protect me. I don't need him to protect me! For fuck's sake! Nate, this is all my fault. It's all my fault!'

I'm not sure if it was rage or grief or guilt that tore through me, but I screamed into the heavens and fell to the ground distraught. In the distance, I could hear Nate trying desperately to console me.

'G, it's not your fault … he's made his own decision. You're not responsible for that. You're not responsible for him.'

Yet his words were smothered by an eerie voice coming from deep within my shadow whispering, '*You failed him. You lost him to the darkness… again. It's your fault.*' The wild, passionate rage I had tried so hard to suppress broke free and overcame me. *She* raced through my body, bursting through the vulnerability of my edges. *Her* charge was too much for my body to hold. I shut down.

A fever sent me into a delirium within hours of Nate returning me to St Christopher's, and it was Nate who took me to his mother under Madame Rosaline's instructions. Up to this point, she had lovingly allowed me to walk my path, aware of my struggle but trusting in my wisdom to navigate it. Part of me wished she had intervened sooner. Set me straight and forced me to look deeper into the shadows, but I trusted the ways of the *wise woman* and I respected *her* teachings.

*Love allows the becoming. Fear fixes the broken.*

# CHAPTER 11

# Dark Night of The Soul

For three days, I was quite unaware of what was happening. The forced surrender was a welcome retreat from the heaviness of life. I no longer could control the threads of darkness which I had worked so hard to suppress from weaving through the innocence of my maiden. I recall Madame Rosaline sitting beside my bed at St Christopher's and I felt the motherly warmth of her hand in mine. I witnessed Nate carrying me downstairs into the alleyway and laying me across the backseat of a car, and his worry, his smile gentle and his heart tender. Aunt Maeve was with me, compressing a damp cloth on my forehead. She was whispering prayers to the Divine Mother to bless me in my descent into the darkness. There was the drumming, a beat in the background of both my inner and outer worlds that called forth my beloved mothers. I met Ma Ma and Mo Mo in the imaginal realm between the visible and invisible where I so often connected with them. I could not hear them, their loving voices muted, and I was lost, disoriented, confused without their wisdom. I descended with my vision as the fire burned and took me to places I had long chosen to forget.

*There was a farmhouse and a man who lived with me and our babies.*
*The man was Johnny, his soul, not the man I knew in this life.*
*This man was good, and I cherished his light.*
*He was kind and caring and adoring.*
*We loved our babies, but our babies became ill.*

*I was in the market, and I carried a basket.*
*I collected herbs and flowers and stones and bark from a woman.*
*This woman was a friend, she was a wise woman.*
*I emptied the basket onto the table.*

*There were pots and bottles and potions.*
*The babies drank the potions that I made.*
*My babies were again vital and joyful.*
*My heart was full and I was free, having followed my intuition.*

*He didn't like me being free, but he still loved me.*
*He didn't like who I had become, but he still loved me.*
*He didn't like the woman I called friend, but he still loved me.*
*But then he changed, everything changed.*

*He denied me love when I refused to empty the bottles of potion.*
*He locked me in my home when I refused to burn my basket.*
*He beat me when I refused to condemn my friend from the market.*
*He took my babies from me when I refused to repent before his God.*
*And then he handed me over to them, the 'men of God'.*

*I would not renounce my friendship with the wise woman nor denounce her as 'witch'.*

*As I burnt at the stake beside her, he watched with my babies in his arms.*
*Pools of darkness in his eyes were all I could see as I burnt on the inside.*
*I could not feel his heart.*
*I had lost him to the dark.*
*They won his soul, and I failed him.*

*I should have silenced my soul that guided me to choose me over him.*
*I should have played his game to save his soul.*

*It was my fault. I deserved to burn.*
*I willed the fire to take me as I vowed never again to lose him to the dark.*
*Even if it meant sacrificing my own soul.*

I traversed the trauma of this past life in my fevered delirium, adding to my distress and disorientation. I called to Johnny, begging him to return to the light, for his love not to leave me. And in my suffering, I fluctuated between here and there in the void. *Would I stay or would I go?* I was being asked to choose, but I did not know my answer. In my anguish, an energy came to meet me. *She* was mystical. I knew *her* intimately. I recognised *her* as my soul—*she* of wisdom and love. *She* presented with flowing silver hair. *Her* face etched with lines. *Her* eyes crystalline ocean blue. *Her* robes awash with threads of silver, purple and blue. *She* took me to the river I knew as home and then beyond to a ridge high above. On the edge, I showed my fear. *If I leap into the unknown, I may lose Johnny forever. She* held me, acknowledging my fear, and then as one we stared beyond the river to the vastness of the cosmos into which it flowed. I knew my answer.

*I chose me.*

This was my lesson for this life, to choose to honour my path and release the limitation of the belief that I was responsible for any other's soul journey. My soul sought renewal of my commitment to our union, betrothed unto *her* and our chosen plan for this life.

*Will you allow Johnny to walk his path without burdening the responsibility should he become lost in the darkness?*

I will.

*Will you be courageous enough to claim your own darkness and trust yourself with the potency of her power?*

I will.

*Will you allow the Divine Goddess in all her expressions to move through you, reconciling those aspects that have been shunned, shamed and demonised?*

I will.

*Will you rise into the fullness of all you are without depending on another to hold you, remembering you are always held?*

I will.

*Will you trust in the Divine Union of your body and soul with the body and soul of those ready to receive the sacredness of your truth?*

I will.

*Will you allow yourself to be seen, your voice to be heard, your stories to be told and the Divinity within your heart to touch all, without exception or condition?*

I will.

*You know what you are here to do. Allow the blossoming of your fullness, trust in your wisdom to guide you, allow your heart to be full and enjoy every blessing of her fullness.*

*Be not afraid, I am with you always, come follow me.*

I roused, feeling renewed in the early hours of the morning, Thanksgiving having come and gone. My surrounds were foreign and from a mattress on the ground, I scanned the room. Serenity permeated the space, a world away from New York City and her struggles. Sensing my stirring, those surrounding me began to wake. I was greeted by the weary and relieved faces of Aunt Maeve, Madame Rosaline and a third lady I did not know.

'Welcome back, my girl,' whispered Madame Rosaline into the stillness of the space, looking years younger than the woman I knew from St Christopher's.

Aunt Maeve wrapped her arms around my shoulders and rested her lips on my crown, whispering prayers of thanks for my safe return from the underworld. I softened in her embrace and was overcome with relief and gratitude for the wise and loving women who had held me as I transitioned through this, my first dark night of the soul. I was to walk this path many times over throughout my life, each time a little more prepared for the descent, yet always caught off guard and suitably stripped bare. My rawness a portal into the depths that would often call to me, demanding my surrender to the becoming it offered.

'Marigold, this is Sacnite, Nate's mother. We have been blessed to work with her as a gifted medicine woman over these last few days. She is a dear friend and trusted guide for both Rosaline and I.'

Sacnite smiled and nodded, acknowledging me and despite having just met her, I knew her as one does family. *I see you, my sister. It is my honour to fulfill the contract of our souls.* She communicated without vocalising the words and I was humbled by the intensity of our connection. I was awed by her presence which was potent. Her beauty was beguiling, her striking green eyes gentle with a fierce intensity that reflected mine. I knew she held the essence of all I was being called to embody in this life. She mystified me, her presence equal parts assuring and unsettling. A wave of shame flooded my being. I felt but a child who had fumbled their lessons seated before their teacher and yet she did not judge, instead radiating compassion and unconditional love. Her words carved a penetrating presence into the small room, and all became still. Even the flicker of the flame settled, readied to be ignited by her wisdom.

'Welcome back, sister. May you always remember the blessings bestowed upon you in the underworld. We pray to the ancient mothers whose presence is with us now that they continue to walk with you as you reclaim your fullness.'

Her pause filled the room and every thread of my being waited to be rewoven by her wisdom.

'Your soul chose to incarnate with Johnny once more to embody unconditional love. The love that trusts the other to choose their experience. The love that trusts they will find their way. The love that remembers there is no right or wrong.

We pray for him:

May he learn from his choices.

May he grow beyond his story.

May he allow forgiveness.

May he remember love.

And may he find his way home through love and in peace.

So it be. So it be. So it be.'

Across the room, her eyes explored mine in the intimacy of our soul connection.

'You are of the red thread. Born from the bush laden with roses and enmeshed with thick thorny branches, the darkness of its beauty both mesmerising and terrifying. Yours is the blood of the rose, and it was the thorn that carried you into the dark night of your soul. Let it be known now and forever more, you did not need the kiss of a prince to awaken you. You have woken to the call of your soul, dissolving the false gold of your crown with the remembering of your darkness. May you never forget that you are both the heavenly scent of the petals

and the fierce edge of the thorns, the sacred union of light and dark—
you are the *Rose Queen*. May you walk *her* path with courage, wisdom
and love and awaken *her* thread in all those ready to remember the
importance of *her* place in this world.'

Sacnite returned from her tranced state and then walked serenely
from the hut. A wave of grace filled the void her presence left, bringing
tears to my eyes. I had few memories of what transpired during those
days, but I knew I had been blessed by the healing hands of wise
women and I was humbled by the sacredness of the experience.

*She who drinks from the sacred well shall never be thirsty.*

# CHAPTER 12

# Beneath The Veil

Nathaniel drove Madame Rosaline, Aunt Maeve and I back to St Christopher's in silence. The stillness and beauty of contemplation flowed within each of us. I remained fragile in body and mind but renewed in spirit, and I surrendered to the whispers of my soul as we drove through the mountains. *Her* gentle presence reassured me, and I trusted I would not be tempted into my shadow without *her* with me, to guide me through the wilderness and bestow the wisdom that waited within the depths.

My mind desired understanding of all that had happened, but the wisdom of my soul gently assured me: *Mysteries are mysteries until they are not. In surrendering the desire to know, the remembering returns.*

Aunt Maeve reached across the back seat and, squeezing my hand, she smiled, affirming, 'For now, let be what cannot be understood by the limitation of the mind and allow the healing and gifts you received in the underworld to integrate, and trust in the unfolding.'

She winked at me as the wise and loving aunt who had been beside me for so long and who was to stay with me at St Christopher's until the weekend when the other girls returned from their Thanksgiving break.

I whispered to Nathanial as I bade him farewell.

'Thank you for taking me to your mother. She reminds me so much of my Ma Ma. I am so grateful. Please thank her.'

'It was her honour to be one with you, G. You're certainly something! She was humbled in your presence.'

The warmth of his hug was a comfort.

That evening, Madame Rosaline, Aunt Maeve and I sat in front of the fireplace and talked for hours. I listened to them sharing stories and laughing about old times, revealing a different side. I was awed to learn that Madame Rosaline was born and raised on the West Coast of Ireland, not far from where I had spent my first seven years. Her strong New York accent was one she had chosen to adopt when she set foot on American soil over twenty-five years ago.

'I had to leave part of me on that ship because I couldn't bring the pain with me. Creating a new identity was in some ways survival, and in other ways it was part of my healing. The first person I met when I stumbled into this boarding house was Sacnite. I knew it was destined because she became first my friend, then my healer, and has long been a trusted guide. She had moved to the city from the reservation only six months before. Her mother, who was her people's loved medicine woman, told her she needed to explore the ways of the world before she would be called back to take over from her. Sadly, Sacnite only spent fifteen months in the city before her mother suddenly took ill and passed quickly. At only eighteen years, Sacnite stepped into the role her mother had vacated. She has been a healer, teacher, wise counsel and guide for her people since that time. It was not easy for her being called when she was so young and when she had just begun her life in the city, but she never begrudged her calling and is a true reflection of the rapturous grace that comes with acceptance of one's soul path. Nathanial arriving not long after her mother passed also made the transition easier and brought her great joy.'

My curiosity sparked about the path of the wise woman. I asked if Sacnite was pregnant with Nate when her mother died and who was the father? Aunt Maeve laughed at all my questions as we sat by the warmth of the fire with a whiskey opening doors that perhaps would otherwise have remained closed.

'Yes, she was pregnant when her mother died. Nathanial's father was a creative, free-spirited young artist who had a curious mind and unique perspective of the human experience, which intrigued and inspired Sacnite. Their love affair was passionate but sadly short-lived, for he was too young and too attached to his freedom to settle down and become a partner to Sacnite and father to Nathaniel. Her commitment to her soul work saw her sacrifice her one great love, but she always saw Nate as her blessing, and he has brought her much happiness. Like her mother before her, she sent Nathanial to the city a couple of years ago to find his way and explore the world.'

I contemplated my path. Where I had come from on the farm felt much easier than what lay before me. The unknown was daunting, but I vowed to practice surrender and acceptance of the ebb and flow, the rising and falling, the light and dark, all of which I sensed lay before me.

'You know, it doesn't always work out as we might desire, Marigold, but it always takes us where we need to go,' Aunt Maeve reminded me gently.

'So true. It rarely turns out as expected and if it did, it might even be boring!' Madame Rosaline laughed. 'I, for one, never expected I would be pregnant and, on a ship, sailing across the Atlantic at eighteen years of age,' she declared reflectively.

'On discovering my pregnancy, my father sent me to the parish convent where the holier than holy Mother Mary Margaret was charged with hiding my pregnancy and the brutal truth of its origin. I'm not sure how Cynthia heard of my plight, though to this day I remain hopeful my mother confided in her, fuelled by the guilt of failing to protect me from the evil intent of my neighbour. Never will I forget the night Cynthia courageously burst into the convent, telling Mother Mary Margaret that she was taking me with her. A young nun, Sister Catherine was sent upstairs with me to pack a bag and when I came back into the kitchen, I was both shocked, intrigued and secretly delighted to see this fierce woman, who radiated pure light, despite being clocked in a dark robe, with a knife held to the throat of the petrified older nun.'

Madame Rosaline and Aunt Maeve shook their heads and laughed at the memory. This was also the night of their meeting, Aunt Maeve acting as a watch outside the convent rather than wielding miniature swords about the throat of the holier than holies.

'In the most mysterious of ways, Cynthia secured a first-class passage on a ship that was sailing to New York the following day and I boarded that ship excited to begin my new life with my baby. There were three other pregnant girls on that ship who Cynthia had freed from either their families or the nuns before their babies could be cruelly taken from them.'

'What about your baby?' I asked and witnessed her grief and despair as a young woman, stripped raw by the cruelness of life.

'He was born early on the ship, and he lived for two days cradled to my chest. They were the happiest and saddest days of my life and remain with me every breath I take. His wee heart eventually surrendered to the fight and when I refused to let him go, they held me down. The captain and some of the crew and the doctor took him from me and I never saw him again. There were rumours that the deceased, whether they be infants or elderly, were tossed overboard, yet the other girls tried to shield me from the truth. They lovingly looked after me until we arrived at the boarding house Cynthia had arranged for all of us to stay. They all went about their lives, birthing healthy babies and moving beyond St Christopher's, while I stayed. Were it not for Sacnite and her healing gifts, I don't believe I ever would have recovered from the grief of losing my baby boy. That is why I knew I had to take you to her when you became unwell. I knew your fever was steeped in the darkness of loss and Sacnite would support you in finding your way back. I return to her once a year at this time, like a seal returns to the sea to replenish her soul skin when it becomes dehydrated. I work with Sacnite to replenish my soul and renew my soul contracts so I may hold the space I am meant to hold in the city. When you crashed the other day, I recognised that it had all become too much for you. You had lost your seal skin, if you will, and I trusted Sacnite would be able to help you as she has always helped me.'

Once again, I was filled with gratitude for the blessing of strong wise women guiding me through this life.

'We have to talk about Johnny. There is much for you to understand about Johnny and his life before you venture outside this sacred container Maeve is currently holding for us.'

I glanced tentatively at Aunt Maeve who raised her eyebrows and nodded earnestly as an intensity settled upon the room, opening the doorway to remembering.

'When my baby boy died on that ship, my heart closed and even with all the work that Sacnite did with me, I never believed I could love again, not in the way I had loved my son. But I was proven wrong, and I did learn to love again. Johnny Triboni was my teacher.'

She poured us all another glass of whiskey and restoked the fire, preparing to reveal yet more of her heart.

'Dolores O'Connor ran the boarding house. Her husband, John, ran the bar below. They named it St Christopher's, for they had prayed to him for a safe voyage when they set off from Galway many years ago, determined to leave the trauma of their past behind and start a new life in the promised land. The bar was very different to what it is now and sadly, John ended up spending more time drinking from the bar than he did serving from behind it. Dolores made the boarding house safe and welcoming for young women, many of whom were like me, straight off the ship from Ireland. As it happened, Dolores was an old friend of Cynthia's from childhood, and they had managed to remain in contact even when she left for New York. Cynthia arranged for many young women to board ships bound for New York with Dolores O'Connor's address safely tucked in their pocket. Dolores opened her home and her heart to these girls and their babies. While they went off to work to carve out a new life, she would lovingly look after all the little ones. She was a grand surrogate grandmother to many a baby before they went off into the world and, unlike all the other girls who came and went, I stayed and worked in the bar with John and got to know his customers. Most of them were sailors who came in from the ports, but as time went on, a new breed of customers began frequenting the bar, in particular, the Lower East Side Mafia mob. The Irish and Italians are an interesting combination. There's something that bonds them, quite possibly the indoctrination of the Catholic Church and, ironically, their propensity for breaking the rules. Father Michael Casey, the parish priest of St Teresa's, was John's cousin, and he spent almost as much time propping up the bar as he did in the confessional box, hearing the ills of the Mafia men. Some might say *God* brought the Irish and Italians together at St Christopher's though the jury is out as to whether that was a blessing or a curse!'

She laughed, musing on the path her life had taken, deeply embedding her within the New York Mafia.

'Dolores had to get John away from the bar, knowing he was not smart enough to manage the new breed of clientele, and besides, his drinking was running it into the ground. On New Year's Eve 1946, she handed me the keys to St Christopher's, and they sailed home to

Ireland. I've been running things my way since then. John had not kept the accounts in order and financially things were dire. There was no way I could continue to run both the boarding house and the bar, but I couldn't just turn the girls out on the street and renege on my promise to Dolores to always keep the doors open to any girl in need. A young Jimmy Triboni came to me with a business proposition. While I did not know him personally then, I had observed him from afar in the club. He was smart, cunning and suffered no fool. I immediately understood if I was to engage with him, I would have to rise to my fullest so he didn't dominate me in the way he did so many others. He offered to loan me five thousand dollars, which was a lot of money in 1947. But even then, he had access to that sort of money, and I chose not to ask where it came from. In exchange for the loan, which I vowed to repay over the next five years, it was agreed that Jimmy would take a sizeable profit each week, and also confidently bring his men to the club to have a good time without needing to watch their backs. The girls would perform to entertain only. They were firmly off-limits to his men, the exception being the one or two nights each week when Jimmy and his men stayed back after the doors closed and the girls could mingle with them. It was never an issue in all these years because we both set firm boundaries and demanded they be respected. I know he has always respected me for this. I engaged a lawyer to have the contract formalised, and we exchanged paperwork one night in my office over a drink. When I reflect on that night, I see a girl playing grown-ups and while I navigated it quite well, I remained very naïve to the *other* side of life. But that night, who I was died as I crossed into that other realm, and I became a woman. Madame Rosaline was born, and everything changed.'

*Every new beginning comes from the end.*

# CHAPTER 13

# The Sacred Prostitute

Madame Rosaline gazed into the fire. She was lost in timelines past, and I thought she may have revealed as much as she was able to that evening. I looked across to Aunt Maeve who was reclined on her chair with her eyes closed serenely, waiting for the story to continue, obviously already knowing the intricacies involved in the becoming of Madame Rosaline. An unfamiliar vulnerability veiled her, yet she continued.

'He took my hand to cement our deal, but he intentionally held it longer than necessary. Perhaps I shouldn't have looked him in the eye the way I did, perhaps I should have drawn my hand back and looked away … perhaps I should have been the "good girl". But I had vowed when I stepped from that ship that I would never again play to other's rules. I'd never be the "good girl" I was expected to be. The "good girl" didn't fight back when her neighbour raped her. The "good girl" kept her mouth shut when her father sent her away, black and blue from head to toe, to the convent to conceal the shame of the pregnancy. The "good girl" let them come near her baby and only when they took him from her did she fight and find her voice. They said she was hysterical, needed to hush, to settle down, to be respectful, to listen to them, to do what they say, to trust them. Their drugs kept her imprisoned for the remainder of the voyage. They did not realise she had already died when they ripped her baby from her arms. I was the one who walked off that ship, the "good girl" dead, and I declared when I saw *herself*, the Statue of Liberty holding her torch in the air, that I would be free like her. I would never allow a man to dominate me again. When Jimmy Triboni held my hand just that split second longer than appropriate, I knew he was testing me, checking to see if I was intimidated by him and whether I would concede to his domination or meet him in his power. In truth, consciously I had no clue what I was doing, but this force came over me. I was so out of my depth that I simply allowed it, and *she* was courageous and powerful! Unapologetically, I met his eye and his unspoken question with an answer that proved I was not to be messed with. I was a woman who was able to meet his darkness with my own darkness. I was not afraid of him or those parts of me that I had been told to keep hidden. I would not be intimidated by him and play by his rules, walking on eggshells, doing what he told me to, lying on my back with my legs open and my mouth shut, allowing him to take advantage of me. I grabbed his shirt and pulled him to me, kissing him like he had never been kissed before. Then I pushed him onto his back and straddled him, demanding he meet me fully. I stripped him raw, physically and emotionally, releasing years of trauma, and the wounded little boy deep within wept for the first time since his mother died when he was only five years old. In that moment, Jimmy Triboni experienced the exquisite beauty of surrendering to his vulnerability, held in the arms of a woman. This release became his drug because in his surrender, he discovered places within himself he had never been able to access before. In meeting his darkness with my darkness, some sort of alchemical reaction occurs and a lightness, which feels like graciousness engulfs us. It is powerful and transformative for both he and I and, rightly or wrongly, he has been putty in my hands because of it. I am conscious of the power I hold and never have I taken advantage of his vulnerability, never have I dishonoured him or myself, and yet in recent years, I have withheld his drug, refusing to take him to that place, for Johnny.'

In silence, she contemplated the complexities of her relationship with Jimmy, and I began to understand the depth of their soul contract and also her love for Johnny. 'Jimmy is wounded. We all are in various ways, yet Jimmy masks his pain by dominating others. When he feels powerful, the little boy within does not cry as loudly. He hurts others, especially those closest to him, so he doesn't feel his own pain. While I have never spoken to him about what transpires when we are together, I've come to understand that when I take him to other places and allow him to feel something beyond his pain, his wounds begin to heal. But every time he feels insecure or powerless, it is triggered once more and he acts out in the only way he knows how, the way his father showed him. Joe Triboni was a mean and ruthless man and, while Jimmy's actions and the harm they bring to others can never be condoned, I have sought to understand him. In my highest heart, I have found compassion for him. It has been a tough journey with him, for I find myself often feeling disappointed in him, disgusted by his actions and even guilty that in some way I have failed in fixing him because he is still 'bad'. But I know this is all judgement and does not come through a lens of compassion, so I endeavour to see him in the truth of love each day and forgive him, yet not condone the way he continues to express his pain. He does have a heart. I know that, and I do believe—I have to believe—that he will find his way back to living from it rather than allowing his shadowed self to rule his days. He loves me in a way that others will never understand, and he loves Johnny more than any of the others. That is why he challenges him so much. He refuses to give Johnny the love he *needs* from him. He doesn't want to fill this void in him and for Johnny to be powerless in this way. He wants him to know he is enough without his love and thus claim his true power. In this way, Johnny will break the dark ancestral pattern that is woven into their story. Jimmy wants to break it. He hated his father, but he wanted his love and never received it. He has not been able to move beyond that wound and the power of its shadow. He doesn't believe he can change, but he knows Johnny is different and stronger than the rest and can break this curse. It is not an easy path to walk for Johnny, and I have done my best to be there for him as a mother and support him in being free from the Triboni curse. I love Johnny as my own and he is the only reason I have stayed here. Many times over the years, I have questioned my soul path and whether I wanted to continue to play the role I have assumed in Jimmy's life. On a human level, it offers me little. On a soul level, I know I am doing something for the greater good, but it is Johnny who has kept me here. I cannot abandon that boy. I have loved him since the day I laid eyes on him when he was only two years old and Jimmy brought him into the club to get him away from his mother. She rejected him from the day he was born. Jimmy couldn't leave him at home any longer where he would be left crying alone in a cot for hours on end while his mother drank herself into a stupor. I try not to judge others, but I have little respect for this woman who could not find it in her heart to love her baby. Johnny is twelve years younger than his closest sibling and the family regard him as 'the accident'. Except Jimmy, ironically, he was the one who insisted on keeping him. She wanted to abort him, but as Jimmy Triboni's wife and a good Catholic woman, she didn't have a choice. In defiance, she rejected him just as a mother would reject the runt of the litter. In me, he found a loving home. I took him into my arms and held him to my heart, the sweetest little boy you would ever meet. Jimmy would drop him off most mornings and pick him up in the evening after I had fed and bathed him. We never spoke of the arrangement. It just fell into place. I know Jimmy was grateful I had taken care of his problem, and I am eternally grateful for the opportunity to love again. I fought to protect Johnny from the Mafia world and for a long time it worked, enabling Johnny to forge a different path away from the one Jimmy envisaged for him. He would always concede to allowing Johnny freedom, if I withheld my sexual energy. His need to run from his pain through me, so much greater than his need to control Johnny's life. I managed to shelter Johnny from Jimmy's darkest days, which come at the beginning of every year. His mother died suddenly on Thanksgiving when he was five years old. His father remarried on New Year's Eve just over one month later. Every year as the new year dawns, Jimmy spirals, his trauma stirred by the turn of the year and there is little that can be done to stop him from unleashing his suppressed grief and fury. This is why I have to work so hard to be strong over this period. For as long as I can remember, it is why I spend Thanksgiving with Sacnite. She helps me prepare to hold him as best I can during this time. When Johnny was younger, I would convince Jimmy to let him stay with Nathanial and Sacnite during the harshest weeks of the new year. He did not deserve to be exposed to this side of his father, and I did not know what he would do to him. Johnny represents everything that Jimmy wishes he could be. He stands up to his father in a way Jimmy never could. He has forged his own path in a way Jimmy never could, and he has avoided misusing the darkness that resides in him in a way Jimmy never could. Ironically, it is because of all this Jimmy loves that boy, but sadly also detests the mere sight of him. He reminds him of his own weakness, and he cannot bear to face that side of himself, so his self-loathing projects onto Johnny. It seems now, though, with this whole wedding nonsense that Jimmy finally has Johnny where he wants him. I must trust it will play itself out and Johnny's integrity will prevail.'

She shook her head in dismay.

'I convinced Jimmy to let Johnny go to college and then get a job, and I truly believed he was on his path out of the family business. But there was nothing I could do when Jimmy's brother, Albert, who was responsible for keeping the books, died suddenly of a heart attack while in bed with two prostitutes. I kid you not, that's the truth of what happened, but as usual, some fanciful lie was orchestrated and spread throughout the city. Unfortunately, the death of his brother stirred something in Jimmy, and he forced Johnny to quit his job and take over the book-keeping by putting a gun to his head. His own son! For the first time, I felt powerless to help Johnny. Then, within a month, you arrived, and I knew you had come for a reason.'

She turned her focus to me now, and I was overwhelmed by the depth of her despair and her belief in me.

'I knew you would come and live with me when the time was right. Maeve and I have spoken of it for years, but you had to be ready to step beyond the world you knew to become a woman. Sacnite had foreseen many years ago a woman with long golden hair taking Johnny by the hand and showing him the way home … a woman, Goldie Mae, not a girl. That is why we have let you stumble and fall, because Marigold, the girl you were when you arrived here, had to die. Marigold was never going to be able to guide Johnny to his freedom, because it is going to take a lot more than your golden light to draw him back to his heart. You had to go through these last few painful days for the girl within to die and the woman who will be able to hold Johnny to rise from the ashes.'

She came and knelt at my feet, placing her hands on mine.

'I know it is a lot, but I believe in you! The girl you were will always carry the light. The woman you are becoming will also hold *her* darkness and I know when you bring them into union, she will be enough to show Johnny the way, to free him.'

In the background, Aunt Maeve began burning sage and gently

tapping a drum, as she called in The Morrigan, the feared, ferocious and ever-loving Celtic Goddess of the Dark, asking her to protect St Christopher's over the coming months.

I closed my eyes as I felt the air sucked from the room, knowing the essence of The Morrigan was weaving her way into our psyche. Then I heard the whispers of my soul voice and tears welled in my eyes as she unlocked the mystery of my power.

*'Why are you limiting yourself to what can be done in this realm? Your power is beyond this realm, in the unseen. Call him to you in your meditation and dreams and help him to reconnect to his heart and remember all that he has forgotten.'*

I had forgotten. Now I remembered.

If I can see it, feel it and know it, then it *is*, whether visible or invisible. I no longer felt helpless, and the power and relief surged through me in equal measure.

*Amen, Amen, Amen. And a powerful, fierce wild woman.*

# CHAPTER 14

# The Dark Mother

Aunt Maeve went home. The other girls returned to the boarding house. St Christopher's reopened her doors, and I went back to college. Life felt no different to what it had been a week before. Although, everything was different because I was different—stronger, wiser and more open and honest in my heart.

I trusted I could help Johnny remember love despite remaining estranged from him. I was committed to the integration of my healing, honouring the gift that Sacnite, Aunt Maeve and Madame Rosaline had shared with their presence. I spent the early hours of each morning meditating and in prayer and I remained present and mindful in my thoughts and actions as I moved through my days. I spent as much time as I could outdoors close to nature, drank purified water and nourishing food and moved my body through dance in my tiny bedroom, supporting the shifting of those heavy emotions that continued to arise. I would not deny them, nor the truth of my path. I stayed in my body, grounded and aware of my boundaries, even when I was performing, I was diligent in calling in high protection as I connected to higher realms, and was meticulous in bringing myself fully back into my physical form. In truth, I simply returned to honouring my sacredness and listening to the guidance of my soul as I had always done.

In meditation and dreams, I accessed the imaginal realm which bridged the visible and invisible and reconnected with Johnny. No words were spoken, not even thoughts exchanged, just a binding of our hearts forged through presence. Sometimes, we were sitting by a river, wandering in the forest or floating through the stars. Other times, we were lying on the grass in Central Park staring at the clouds or weaving through the city on his motorbike. I trusted implicitly that the reconnection of our souls in the imaginal realm was empowering

Johnny to reconnect to his heart and reclaim his power by remembering unconditional love.

Christmas came and went. I glided through those days with my family on the farm, hiking mountains in the snow with Caellach, cooking traditional Irish soda bread and stew with Clara, making crystal beads with Sorcha and reading books and doing jigsaw puzzles with the younger ones. My heart was full as I returned to St Christopher's on New Year's Eve 1968, wistfully dreaming of all that 1969 would bring to me as I gazed at the stars and the moon from the front seat of Caellach's van as we drove through the mountains. Thoughts of Johnny flooded my mind. I trusted he would find his way back to his truth, yet wondered how he would get there and what we would become: strangers, friends, lovers.

'A little less time in your head, my girl. You're a feeler, not a thinker … stay here,' Caellach gently reminded me, tapping his heart.

As we neared the city, a tension stirred, flooding my body with heat and anchoring me with an inner strength I did not recognise. Feeling the shift in my energy, Caellach reached to squeeze my shoulder.

'We're proud of you. We know it's not been easy, but if anyone can handle this city, it's you. You've got more fire in your belly than anyone I know. Don't be afraid of it, Marigold. It's part of you, but until now you've never really had reason to use it, apart from arguing with me, but that was jest. Down here, there's a lot going on, serious business. Know that your fire can create change if you let it work with you, through you. Do you understand that?' he asked tentatively, an unusual state for one who never doubted the placement of his next step.

'Not really, but sort of,' I suddenly felt very young.

'Let's go in from the cold and have a drink. Matters like this are best discussed over whiskey, that's what Maeve always says.'

We made our way into the bar. I introduced Caellach to Nathanial who was working. To my surprise, they already knew one another. Caellach had held true to his gypsy soul on this side of the Atlantic and every so often he would be called to the wilderness to reinvigorate his soul. Usually, it was only for a few days or a week, although once he spent forty days and forty nights away and Clara and I called him Jesus for months after. He returned from that pilgrimage older and wiser with a hint of sorrow and weariness to his eyes. Whatever he healed within in his ancestral lines and in the soil on which he walked during that pilgrimage remained a mystery. Clara never begrudged him leaving. She knew he needed to roam free in the mountains and to explore and connect with the land and the people of the land. He knew many of the people who lived on the Reservations throughout the northern mountain ranges, was a friend to many, helping anyone in need of a fence built, a calf birthed or a roof repaired. He connected to people, listened to their stories and gave them a shoulder to lean upon while he learnt the ways of their land and the intricacies of their souls. He was at once the wisest teacher and most humble student anyone would ever encounter. I often wondered how I had been blessed to call him my brother, father and friend.

With whiskey in hand, in one of the dark corners of St Christopher's, Caellach guided me to understand who I was, where I had come from and the woman I was being called to become.

'You knew Cynthia as a mother, and she gave so many of us the unyielding, unconditional love of a mother. Yet there was another side to her. One you were shielded from as a child. Because of our own pain, the grief and rage around her death, we have not been ready to talk about it with you, but now it is time.'

I sensed my Mo Mo's presence and my heart expanded like a flower in her fullest bloom to receive her story. Caellach continued.

'Cynthia was full of love and full of fire. She was a rebel—not that she set out to be. She broke rules to create change, not to cause trouble, although she did. "Misbehave but do it with integrity," she would tell me often, for she knew I was like her. The fire I carried within me as a child and young man would often erupt violently and create more harm than good. I have come to understand my life, like Cynthia's, and I believe yours too, is to be a creator of change in a world that is rapidly being driven away from goodness, truth and love. Cynthia's light shone so much brighter because of her darkness, and she used that dark side of herself for good. I have endeavoured to follow her lead. Mind you, I made a right mess of it before I learnt how to hold my fire, when ignited by rage, in a centred way. Cynthia often reminded me, as she tended to my battered and bruised face after yet another fight with someone who wronged me, that all great warriors must learn how to use their sword with integrity. With commitment and diligence, she trusted I would find a way to work with my fire. These days, I mostly work with my light, but sometimes I am called to work with my darkness, and I do not fear it or judge it as bad or wrong. Darkness is misunderstood because its power is too often misused. We must remember that light is only one aspect of the whole and all of creation comes from the darkness of the Divine Mother's womb. Our own light and the light of all becomes more potent when united with the dark. Do you understand?'

I understood. And as my own darkness streamed through my veins, I was overcome with doubt. *Could I hold the dark as Cynthia did and as Caellach does?*

'Sometimes when I go away, it is because I have been called to bring balance to a situation—a conflict, an injustice. On occasions, I have to breathe the fire of the Dragonfae who reside in my ancestral lineage to destroy what is not true, so harmony can be restored. When I feel the fire tear through me, I intend it for the highest good of all that is, and I trust it to create change in ways I do not necessarily even understand and often never see immediately. Cynthia never misused the power of her darkness. Of that I am sure, yet she was vilified by many for her actions and paid the ultimate price.'

Waves of fear gushed through me as a truth long hidden threatened to resurface.

'What happened, Caellach?'

He ignored my question and continued calmly, intent on honouring Cynthia's story.

'As a married Irish Catholic woman, Cynthia had no voice or power. She suffered horrific abuse at the hands of her husband, and even her son, but unlike so many women of her time and even today, she garnered the courage to leave her marriage, her home and her son. She walked out of that house determined that no man would ever silence her, take her power or lay a hand on her again. From that time, it was her mission to help vulnerable women, young and old, to reclaim their voice and their freedom from the hands of the patriarchy. Leaving her son with her husband broke her heart, but if she stayed, she would never be free in spirit. And if she took her son, she trusted her husband would make good on his threat to hunt her down and kill her. He held a rifle to her head, assuring her he wouldn't hesitate in pulling the trigger if she took the child from him. He had laughed and spat in her face when she told him she'd go to the Garda and report him. "Paddy O'Reilly? Sure wasn't he the one after telling me I'd have every legal right to shoot ye if you took my boy." The Garda, the priests, the politicians, they all looked after each other. They still do in every town, county or country. It's the same old story, no matter where you live.'

I felt a rage intensify within him as he ventured into painful waters, and I understood the level of integrity required to hold his darkness in check.

He continued.

'The girls and women who Cynthia sought to help, they were abused and rendered powerless to these men and their systems. Clara, my beautiful, sweet Clara, you know the hell on earth she went through with her brother, that bastard priest, the weak as piss man they sold her off to and Cynthia's own son, Padraig McDermott. A bunch of gobshites, the lot of them. Burn in hell, sure they will, because if I ever got my hands on them, it wouldn't be God given that's for sure and certain, Marigold. I don't trust what I would do to them, should they ever cross my path. That's part of the reason we had to get away. We all needed a fresh start after Cynthia's death and all Clara had been through, but in truth, I couldn't trust myself to be within a thousand miles of them. Rage is fierce. It can overtake you before you know it, take you down paths you never wanted or intended to walk. Sacred rage isn't like that, Marigold. It is measured and clean and doesn't come from wounding. It comes from the heart, and you have to know the difference and keep a check on yourself, always.'

I nodded, understanding both the depth of his struggle and his love for Clara, whom he would do anything for, including surrendering his rage and desire for revenge on those who tried to destroy the beauty of her soul. They had not won, for she was the most beautiful soul I had ever encountered. Perhaps this was what convinced Caellach over and over again to soften the sharp edges of his sword, but never lay it down.

'Cynthia's rage came from her heart and was held so gracefully, but my God that woman was fierce. You never saw it, Marigold. You were too young, and she did most of her work at night. I'd hear them all talking around the fire, and I'd pretend I wasn't listening, but I always was. I'd hear the stories about how in the middle of the night she'd knock on the doors of the houses where husbands bashed their wives, where fathers shamefully hid their pregnant daughters and convents that imprisoned girls and women they labelled as bad, troubled or insane. She'd fearlessly march in and demand to be heard, speaking truth for those who were used to being silenced with a fist or a foot or the threat of a whipping. She'd ask the girls and women if they wanted to be free to start a new life, and when they said "yes", she'd tell them to pack a bag and she would steal them away into the dark of night. According to Maeve, who on occasions accompanied her on these expeditions to act as a watch, Cynthia was terrifying. If the priests, fathers, brothers or nuns acted up, she'd pull a knife hidden beneath the veils of her shawls and this energy would come over her. Cynthia knew it to be The Morrigan, the mythical Dark Mother, with a love so powerful she would strike them all down in the blink of an eye in the name of that love. They would cower in the corner, wet their pants and cry in her presence, pure terror striking their bones. They were powerless against her, because all she needed to do was look through the eyes of The Morrigan into their hearts and they were immediately paralysed. She managed to fly under the radar for many moons, her terrorising escapades not spoken for fear she would return. No one really knows how many women Cynthia helped escape abusive marriages or young women she helped keep their babies. Quite a few like Rosaline quickly boarded ships bound for America, England or even Australia. Others resettled in other parts of the country. She seemed to have friends all over the place and some of what she executed was described as miraculous. Most certainly, there were magic forces working with her.'

A shiver trickled up my spine as I felt the essences of those magic forces weaving their way into my psyche.

*Magic, the making of the impossible possible.*

# CHAPTER 15

# The Rose Warrior

The potency of the Irish whiskey soothed the unease stirring in my soul as Caellach shared my story.

'You were different, Marigold. You were the only one she brought home. You were the daughter she never had, and she loved you like no other. "Left by the fairies," they'd always declared with a warm smile, because you were their magical little fairy. Yet I always thought it was the dragons, not the fairies, that had left you there, hoping the human folk would find you. Now I see it. The fire of the dragon is within you, too. The fairy may have been who you were, but the dragon is who you are becoming. You never questioned your story in all these years, and we have been reluctant to destroy your fairy-tale, but now you are changing, and your fairy-tale must evolve to include the human story. To understand yourself more as you take your next steps, it's important you know the truth of your story.'

I wanted to run, sensing everything I knew myself to be was about to be obliterated, but he placed his hand on my arm, assuring me that all was well, as he always had.

'You were one of the babies Cynthia saved. Your life would have been so very different if she had not intervened. You may not be here at all. Don't look so shocked. While the righteous ones condemn abortion, many babies never had the chance to take a breath after their birth for the shame it would bring to the family. Birthed, burned and buried was the sickening practice that occurred behind many closed doors at that time and probably still does.'

I shook my head mortified that this murderous behaviour went unchecked, probably silently condoned by the godly and legal authorities.

'Your mammy was a young girl, maybe fourteen or fifteen.'

I was confronted by his use of the word 'mammy' because quite naively I had never even considered her, given I was blessed with the love of many mothers.

'Cynthia had a way of telling when young girls were pregnant even though it was often incredibly well hidden. Something to do with a troubled look in their eyes, an ache in their heart and the sense of new life in their energy field. She often sat at the back of churches, her face covered by the mantilla, allowing her to watch the congregation and read the dynamics within families, especially troubled women, young and old. That's where she first saw your mammy and immediately knew she was expecting, even though she had covered it cleverly. The family and priest evidently had no clue, although a cousin who sat two pews behind her watched her nervously. He obviously knew her secret and feared it becoming common knowledge. Cynthia took note and reminded herself to take care of him at a later date, to ensure he never forced himself upon another girl or woman. Rumour has it she did take care of him—with the help of a particular herb dropped carefully into his pint by a complying barmaid who had also experienced his sickening ways. It would be a long time before he was up to using his manhood again!'

I felt nothing but disgust at learning about my biological father. Within every cell of my body lay his energy, the imprint of a rapist. *What did that make me?*

'Cynthia subtly approached the girl outside the church and said, "I see you are carrying a heavy burden. I can help you. Meet me under the bridge at noon." The girl met her later that day. Cynthia explained she could help her find a way to keep her baby and start a new life. The girl was scared, saying she couldn't leave her family because her mammy needed her with the little ones. Cynthia understood her fear. It was not an uncommon response. Cynthia told her she walked along a particular path every morning as the sun rose and if she ever changed her mind, that was where she could find her. Cynthia did not see her again, but only a few weeks later, as she and Athena walked with the rising sun, they saw a bright red shawl lying in a bed of marigolds. Wrapped tightly in that shawl was an infant Athena contested was not more than an hour old, with luminous eyes that stared at her with a knowing that this was exactly as it had been written. In that moment, they answered your call for them to be the mother your mammy could not be. They did not seek out the girl, and no one questioned your arrival into our community, because, from the moment they brought you home to us, you belonged. The four years Cynthia shared with you were without a doubt the happiest of her life, which only added to the tragedy of her passing.'

No one had ever told me how Cynthia passed and for some reason I had never asked. Now the question hung in the silence between us.

'There was a little girl, about four years old, about the same age you were at the time. She lived with her grandmother in the housekeeper's quarters of the local presbytery because her parents had died in a car accident a few months before. Cynthia could tell from the first time she saw her wandering alone by the river that the child was troubled and so she befriended her, as she so often did to the most lonely and vulnerable. It was not long before Cynthia learned that the grandmother was completely enamoured by the old priest, having provided him with more than a clean house and his supper for many decades. Knowing she had found a friend in Cynthia, the little girl shyly shared that her grandmother made her lie with the priest. When he did things to her, the grandmother watched and told her it was "a blessing from God". The girl told her it didn't feel like a blessing, that it hurt, and she didn't like it, but they made her do it nearly every night. Sadly, it was not the first story of its kind Cynthia had heard, yet the beautiful innocence of the child tore her heart open. Having zero faith in the authorities, the godly or legal ones, to do anything to protect the child, she took matters into her own hands. As night fell, she knocked on the door of the presbytery and confronted the grandmother, asking to speak to the child. When the old woman said the child was not there and tried to shut the door in her face, Cynthia stormed up the stairs and found the little girl lying naked on the bed, with the old priest hunched over her. Enraged, she lifted the girl into her arms and held her to her chest before carefully dressing her, while the priest and grandmother stood motionless, terrified by the stranger draped in black shawls. With the girl dressed and tucked under her arm, she turned on them and drew her knife from under the shawl and declared, "May the evil you bestowed on this child be returned to you six-fold." Outside the window, a crow squawked, the sound piercing the air. "May your days be dark, and your nights be cold." The fireplace flickered and roared before spontaneously extinguishing, just as the light above shattered into a million pieces bringing the room to darkness. "And may your heart and soul never know a moment's peace," she whispered into the darkness. She calmly left them in their terror, carrying the child down the stairs and out the door, before racing across the field into the darkness of the night.

There was no warning before the shot struck her mercilessly in the back and brought her to the ground. "Run," she told the child. "Run along the river beyond the bridge. My people will help you." Intuiting trouble, Athena beckoned me to go with her in the direction of the town. She brought her medicine bag, we mounted our horses and we raced along the river guided by the moon. As we neared the bridge, we came across the child cowering, terrified. "She saved me, but they shot her … in the field behind the house," she cried hysterically. I froze in shock, but Athena rose as our Matriarch. "Take her to Maeve. She will tend to her. Then go north. Maeve knows who to contact. Go now, Caellach." I hesitated, wanting desperately to go with her and find those who had shot my beloved grandmother. "Caellach, go, they will be coming for the child," she commanded, as she mounted her horse with the vigour of one many years her junior and took off towards town. I carefully placed the girl on my horse and together we fled to Maeve's some twenty miles away. Athena reached Cynthia who lay in a pool of blood and floated in the place between here and there. With her final breaths, she shared the truth of what had transpired, a story filled with courage and love and the exquisite light of her darkness. Knowing there was nothing she could do to save her, that this life for her dearest friend was coming to an end, she took the sacred oils from her medicine bag and blessing the ground on which Cynthia lay, she called in the ancient mothers and grandmothers to guide her friend home. She anointed her body in a sacred ritual and held her hand as her soul transitioned with unyielding grace. In the stillness of the shadows, Athena felt the fullness of her friend's essence weave its way into the rich dark soil that lay beneath them. The sacredness of the moment was interrupted as the child's grandmother approached with a sack in one hand and a rifle in the other. Athena knew immediately she was the one who had taken Cynthia's life and she now sought to excuse her actions by placing a bag of silver candlesticks and cutlery beside her body. Rising to her fullest, Athena spoke. "This woman is no thief. She fought for those who could not fight for themselves. She was a beloved mother to many, and she was my dearest friend, my sister."

The woman rallied, attempting to defend herself, but Athena silenced her with but one look. "The child will be taken care of, and my people will come to bring the body home before the sun rises." She paused, willing herself to stay in her heart and speak with compassion. "I forgive you, and I pray that as you walk on this land, now soaked in my sister's blood, that you will never forget the errors of your way and, one day, may you find it in your heart to forgive yourself. Be gone, leave me be." I was enraged when Athena shared this story with me many days later when I returned from Mayo. Maeve and I had safely transported the child into the care of a woman who sadly had taken in a number of children from similar circumstances. I was furious that she so readily forgave those who had taken my grandmother's life. I wanted revenge and rallied some of the men to come with me into town, but Athena would not allow it. She held me close over those first few weeks when my pain was unbearable. Oh, Marigold, the rage was fierce, so it was, and it would overcome me and I didn't know what to do with it.

It is this fire that I have had to learn to hold within me and express in ways that honours my integrity. Athena showed me that compassion and forgiveness were the only medicine for my pain and taught me that holding onto hurt, anger and resentment keeps the heart closed and prevents forgiveness and peace from entering. It seeds suffering deep within the psyche. She likened it to drinking from a poisonous cup but expecting the one who wronged us to die. With time, and especially with Clara entering my world, the sharp edges of my heart softened. I discovered forgiveness, and with that I was blessed with peace around the passing of Cynthia. The last letter Athena wrote to me before she passed included a photo of a magnificent rose bush with gnarly thorny branches in the middle of a paddock. She wrote:

As the phoenix rises from the ashes, so too does truth. Our beloved Cynthia, refusing to be forgotten. Her roses were the darkest crimson red you could imagine, almost black to the untrained eye!

We were onto our second whiskey before he finished. Raising his glass to mine, he smiled.

'To Cynthia and Athena, the wisest of women. May they continue to guide us.'

'To our Ma's,' I smiled, meeting his glass.

'I know it's a lot to take in and I'm sure you're wondering why now. I certainly wasn't expecting to share all of that with you when I set off this afternoon. It wasn't until we saw the city lights dancing like stars in the distance that I sensed your fire creating tension within you. I could not deny it was time for you to understand who you are and the fire that is stirring within you. Knowing Cynthia's story, I pray you will understand what is happening when you feel this powerful energy moving through you. Unless you allow it, Marigold, and diligently practice working with it, it will burst from you in distorted ways, dangerous ways.'

I took the stories Caellach had shared to bed with me and tried to sleep, yet was visited by sword-wielding demons, fire-breathing dragons and snowstorms of black roses. While they haunted me, at the centre of every dream stood Cynthia, engulfed by the most magnificent silvery-black angel wings, her heart resplendent as a blossoming red rose. She beckoned me to walk her path with loving assurance that she would show me the way. In return, I implored her.

*Divine Mother, please show me the way so I may*
*show others the way.*

# CHAPTER 16

# As Above, So Below

I chose not to let my thoughts dwell on the stories Caellach had told me about my birth mother and Cynthia's death, trusting they would meld their way into my soul architecture, their teachings guiding me when I needed them. As we moved into the darkness of winter and into the new year, the mood within St Christopher's shifted. I sensed the calling of the warrior within, yet did not know when she would command me to take up my sword.

I wanted to support Madame Rosaline in holding the space, knowing this was the most challenging time for her as Jimmy's wounds unleashed his shadow. She retreated within herself often and was quiet, focusing intently on holding Jimmy level. In her presence, her energy was charged, and her intensity rattled me and propelled the other girls into silence. The mood in the boarding house changed, everyone walking on eggshells. The usual crowd at St Christopher's stayed away, either because it was too cold, or they were wise enough to avoid Jimmy and his men at their most dangerous. It was well known on the Lower East Side that during winter Jimmy Triboni channelled his sinister side, his actions irrationally ruthless and reckless. On those nights Jimmy was about, an ever-present simmering of tension and threats of violence underpinned his every move.

Whilst the crowd was small, Madame Rosaline demanded I perform and bring my fullness to the room. Before I went on stage, I held a clear intention to cleanse what needed to be cleansed from those present and for healing light to infuse the void created. To begin with, I was able to draw Jimmy into that altered state of consciousness, and I trusted he would receive exactly what he needed. However, such was the power of Jimmy's dark threads, his energy began to block my invitation to transcend beyond this reality and I sensed his darkness was actively resisting being drawn to the light.

Witnessing his boredom and mounting agitation from the side of the stage, Madame Rosaline knew I had lost him.

'He's met you. The light you are channelling is no longer enough for his darkness. You have to bring more through, but to do that you have to be more of you. You must tap into your fullness, all that you are,' she later explained.

I knew the 'more' within that she was speaking of. I could feel it stirring, but I didn't know how to bring it through. My fear of failing her when she needed me most overwhelmed me.

'As above, so below. As below, so above.'

She raised an eyebrow, willing me to tap into the remembering of this most fundamental wisdom, but I was blocked. My head rallied against my heart. My fear of not being enough for my wise women, the ones who had walked me to this point, prevented me from hearing my own wisdom.

'You're accustomed to channelling powerful divine light from above. You're a magnificent mystic, but you've become comfortable in that space and the challenge is to go below into the depths where there is equally potent energy. You shy away from going too far into the depths when you are on that stage, but those deeper realms are calling you and their calling is more than a whisper now. I know you feel *her*. I can sense the energy rising through your core as you dance, the drum teasing *her* from where she has been hidden, but it gets to a point, almost like she's about to explode from you, and you shift slightly and push *her* back down and rise to the heavens where it is easier for you,' Madame Rosaline gently reminded me.

The truth of her words was uncomfortable and, despite the urge to resist, I surrendered to her wisdom.

'To go higher, you have to go deeper. It is in the depths your power will be amplified. Your light is not enough to match Jimmy. You need to bring the beauty of your darkness to alchemise his. Trust me, Goldie Mae. The light you draw from the higher realms will become so much more potent when held by the depths of the dark. It is time.'

Later that night, in the confines of my room, Cynthia's presence encircled me, her message lovingly blunt. *She comes whether you are ready or not.* The image of a sword appeared in Cynthia's hand and she fiercely slashed both the ground beneath me and the cords that had shrouded the portal into the depths for *her* becoming one with me. I surrendered as she wove *her* way from the darkness of the womb of the Divine Mother and into my womb where she declared, *I am not learnt. I am known. As you embody me, I become.*

I fell asleep allowing *her*, the fierce, potent thread of my Divine Dark Warrior to weave her magic through my body. In my surrender, I became one with *her*. I became one with the fullness of me and *she* debuted on stage only a few nights later, the call to rise and meet Jimmy Triboni in his darkness appearing sooner than I expected.

*To expect her is naivety. Her mystery is unpredictability.*

# CHAPTER 17

# The In-Between

The following night, I arrived at dinner flustered. I sensed something was wrong as I had not been able to connect to Johnny in the imaginal realm during my morning meditation or throughout the day. Perhaps sensing my vulnerability, Clarissa pounced upon me with the hot news that Johnny had broken up with his fiancé and called off the wedding. With wicked delight, she detailed how Jimmy was so furious that he had beaten Johnny until he lost consciousness and when he finally came to, he disappeared. No one had seen him since, and no one knew if he was dead or alive.

The sordid pleasure she garnered in sharing this gossip sickened me, but it seized Madame Rosaline in another way altogether. She rose silently from her seat, placed her hands on the table to steady herself and glared at Clarissa.

'Tomorrow you will find somewhere else to live. You've had enough warnings, yet you continue to disrespect me and my rules. You don't deserve the privilege of living under this roof. You are a silly little girl playing in a dangerous world and you have no idea what you're messing with. I'm warning you for one last time. Stay away from that family before you end up on the bottom of the Hudson River. Do you understand?'

Her voice was terrifyingly measured, yet when Clarissa smirked at the other girls and failed to answer, something unleashed in Madame Rosaline, and she roared like a fire-breathing dragon.

'DO YOU UNDERSTAND ME?'

Clarissa flew from the room terrified and the other girls followed, for none of them had ever seen this side of Madame Rosaline. Truth be told, it had been over twenty years since she had experienced this ferocity of emotions. She stood at the sink with her back to me and breathed deeply, her tears hidden from view. The anguish of her sobs pierced my heart.

'Rosaline, are you okay?'

'I'm sorry,' she said as she turned to me, her face contorted with grief and rage, her vulnerability palpable. 'I'm sorry, I messed up. I failed Johnny!'

'It's not your fault. It's not,' I gasped to reassure her.

'I should have fought harder. I knew him pushing you away and pretending to have a relationship with that girl was a mistake. I knew he wouldn't be able to keep the façade going, to compromise himself like that just to keep Jimmy happy. I should have set him straight, but he hasn't come near me since they made the announcement. He's avoided me because he knew what I would say, and he didn't want to hear it. Not seeing him for these last two months has broken my heart. I trusted he would come to his senses. Which he has. But at what cost?'

She shook her head in despair as tears rolled down her cheeks, the weight of the last few months finally taking their toll.

'I should have held Jimmy better. He's been worse than ever this year, and he's also avoiding me now. I think he's finally realised that I'm the drug that keeps his demons at bay, and he doesn't want to keep them under control. He wants to unleash them. But doing that to Johnny is too much. He's crossed a line and ...'

In her pause, she rose, and her energy shifted, carrying a charge that scared me. I did not know what she was going to do. She turned to me, fire in her eyes.

'I'll take care of Jimmy. You must find Johnny. Call to him.'

Madame Rosaline closed the doors to St Christopher's, ducking into the night, enigmatic as ever, to 'take care' of Jimmy.

I retreated to my room, sinking into a deep meditation. Still no Johnny. He wouldn't come to me. I willed myself to sleep imploring, *Johnny, come to me. Please, Johnny, come to me.* I found myself in a dream, but there was still no Johnny, only an abyss, before a bridge formed on the horizon. I moved towards the bridge. The city that lay on the other side was both familiar and not so. It was the city I knew held Johnny captive and I was desperate to reach him, but as I neared the edge of the bridge, it all began to dissolve. I reached through the realms, desperate to connect to the city that harboured

Johnny, keeping him from me. I could not hold on and I plunged into the space between the here and there. It was here in the void I found Johnny, plummeting past me further into the abyss. Despite my scrambling and screaming, I could not reach him. I feared I had lost him forever and woke calling his name. My heart was pounding, the sheets dripping with sweat and in a tranced state, I dressed against the cold and ran into the dark. Like a wolf mother, I moved with the grace of primal instinct, knowing exactly where I had to go. *Johnny, wait for me. Please, Johnny, wait for me.*

The bridge lay before me. It did not disappear as I approached. My years of hiking through snow-laced mountains served me well as I raced across Brooklyn Bridge towards a bench at its centre. *Come sit with me.* I could well have been hallucinating, but was assured of my sanity when I saw Johnny sitting on the bench, waiting.

Waiting for me.

'Johnny!' I called as I moved ever closer. The world slowed as he turned towards me, before throwing his head into his hands and weeping. I pulled him to my chest and held him through his agony, vowing to hold him for eternity. When his sobbing finally subsided, he held my face in his hands and stared into my eyes, searching for answers.

'How did you know I was here?' he stammered.

I silenced him by gently placing my finger on his lip which was swollen and split, dried blood encasing the wound. He had bruises blackening both eyes which were bloodshot and tormented. His jaw was inflamed and tinged a dark blue. He winced with each breath, the expansion of his chest aggravating fractured ribs. He stared blankly at the railing of the bridge, and I suddenly understood the unimaginable and squeezed his hand tighter, unable to find words to meet his admission.

'I couldn't do it, MG. I stood there and looked down into the darkness and I've never wanted anything more. It's the only way I could be free from him, from all of this. But then something held me back. My body just wouldn't move and you were my only thought.'

He shook his head, the magic of divine love a mystery to him while the reality of what could have been tore through me. I grabbed his face in my hands and kissed every part of it. I sobbed as I held his head to my heart relieved that my love had been enough to keep him here. He was safe in my arms and for hours we sat on that bench in the freezing night air, unable to let the other go, held in a mysterious vortex where we were blessed with temporary immunity to the external world.

'I'm sorry for hurting you. I was cruel and I knew it, but I didn't know how else to protect you. If this is what he can do to his own son, think about what he would do to you to get to me. I'd take a thousand of his beatings over letting him lay a hand on you. Nothing else matters to me but you.'

He paused, caught by the truth of his own words, while the pain in his eyes pierced mine.

'I naively thought that going along with his plan of setting me up with Isabella would distract him from you and also get him off my case. In some ways it worked, because he backed off and gave me space if I said I was with her. I was able to avoid him and get out of his dirty work because he really wanted to keep her old man happy. Apparently, I was Lenard Rosenthal's solution for keeping his daughter on the straight and narrow. She'd become quite the handful for them, pushing boundaries that threatened to destroy their Upper East Side image. We came to understand we are both trapped by our families' expectations and her life was as complicated as mine. Being together loosened the reins for both of us, meaning we had more freedom and for a while it worked. The lie worked, but I was miserable and so was she. It wasn't real. We were never actually together, not in that way as a couple. She's actually been in a relationship with her best friend for over two years. Knowing their families would never approve of their relationship, they've kept it hidden. But they've had their suspicions and that's why her father approached Jimmy and arranged the whole marriage thing. We couldn't keep living a lie, so we figured it would make it easier for her to reveal her true relationship with her girlfriend if I broke up with her. Her father was furious. He'd thought "a few fucks from a real man" would put an end to her relationship. I kid you not, that's what he said about his own daughter! But according to Jimmy, I wasn't man enough to "fuck the lesbian out of her" and her father, whose been Jimmy's lawyer for the last twenty years, dumped him as a client and now a whole heap of legal stuff has been thrown in the air, especially the attempted murder charge against Frank. It was a given that Frank would be acquitted of the charge by claiming self-defence, even though the guy he beat within an inch of his life was attacked from behind and didn't have a weapon. Without Rosenthal's sway with the judge, Frank might end up behind bars for a long time, especially if Jimmy can't get a new lawyer on the books or find some more cops to pay off or take care of the witness so he can't testify. In Jimmy's eyes, it was all my fault. As he beat me, he told me I was nothing but an embarrassment and not worthy of the Triboni name. Not that I care because I don't want to be associated with that name. I hate it and I hate him. I said as much as he held a knife to my throat and told me if Frank ended up in jail, my life wouldn't be worth living.'

He continued to stare at the railing and into the darkness beyond it.

'My life isn't worth living anyway, MG, because I can't escape him. I hate myself for going along with the plan to appease him. I hate myself for not having the balls to leave. I hate that people fear me because I'm his son and they automatically think that I'm like him. Because I'm not. I'm nothing like him and I never will be.'

He stormed to the edge of the bridge and held onto the railing, banging his hands hard against it. It took all that I was to resist the terror that screamed inside my head, telling me to jump up and save him. Instead, I allowed him to face his self-hatred and rage, trusting he would turn around and come back to me, resisting the urge to jump. Fortunately, he walked from the railing and stood in front of me, calmer than he had been all night.

'MG, most of all I hate myself for pushing you out of my life. I love Rosaline and Nate. They know I'm not like him and they care about me. But you saw who I really am before you even knew me. For some reason, I know you love me despite who I am.'

'How can I not love you, Johnny Triboni?' I smiled as my heart filled to bursting. 'There is so much light in your eyes. It was all I could see the first time I saw you. And I knew then, like I know now, that there is so much more to you beyond the tough exterior that the world perceives. You're nothing like Jimmy because you feel it all, Johnny, and that is why it hurts so much. If you were like him, it wouldn't hurt because his heart is cold and dark.'

'I'm sorry for being so cruel. I could feel you hurting so much. I hated myself for it, but then somehow when I thought of you, I would only feel love. It was the thing that kept me going these last couple of months, but I've missed you.'

'I've missed you too, Johnny Triboni.' I smiled.

My heart filled with relief.

'Do you think we can figure out a way to see each other without stirring Jimmy's suspicions?'

What was next was unclear. There was much to navigate, but staying apart wasn't an option anymore. The connection we shared was without definition, but we chose not to seek to understand it and simply enjoy whatever time we got to spend together. To the outside world, the Johnny and Goldie Mae thing was done, having proven to be but a ripple amounting to nothing. Yet when it comes to ripples, there is always something bigger being created, even if it cannot be seen.

*Wise are those who remember the untapped*
*power that lies in the unseen.*

# CHAPTER 18

# Whispers of Warrior

Johnny dropped me back to St Christopher's only after assuring me he would stay at Nate's apartment for a few days. I couldn't sleep. I was physically and emotionally exhausted. Everything from my crown to my soles vibrated, demanding I remain present in my physical form rather than dissociating into the dreamworld where I sought refuge. I rose before my alarm sounded and, while reluctant to begin the day, I welcomed the opportunity to dive into my morning routine. The structure felt like the perfect antidote to the chaos circulating through my body and mind.

Fresh from the shower with a towel wrapped around me, I was caught off guard as Clarissa barged into the bathroom, ambushing me in a corner. I was unusually rattled by her presence, and she obviously meant to catch me by surprise to maximise the impact of her attack. Refusing to be drawn into her game, I told her I'd finished with the bathroom, but my gentleness irritated her. She unleashed a righteous tirade.

'Don't play all innocent with me. I heard you come sneaking up the stairs at 3.00 am. She'd let you get away with anything! One set of rules for the golden child and another for the rest of us.'

I'd heard it all before and didn't reply, so she zoned in on Johnny.

'Did you find him all black and blue? Did you kiss him better? Did you mend his broken little heart? Did you fuck him? Could you handle a Triboni like I can?'

In her hysteria, she edged closer to me, dishonouring my sacred space and triggering a wound so old and so deep that it ignited a fire.

'ENOUGH!'

The eerie fierceness was reminiscent of what I had witnessed in Madame Rosaline the previous night.

'Get out of my space … now!'

My eyes glazed as a remembering flickered through my consciousness, the violent dishonouring of my sacredness by a group of men, the impingement upon my space and my terror rendering me immobilised, unable to defend my honour.

*Never again,* my soul silently commanded, as a peaceful presence enveloped me and a dark, potent force radiated through my body and exploded from my heart, physically pushing Clarissa against the bathroom door. I moved forward, reclaimed my sacred space and paused, trembling with the knowing that in the blink of an eye I could annihilate the wounded little girl cowering before me. But I would not misuse this power, so I allowed only love and compassion to touch her as a voice that was not mine, yet familiar, spoke through me.

'Pack your bags and leave St Christopher's before the other girls wake. You have insulted the goodness of Madame Rosaline, and only you are responsible for the path you now choose. May your journey be blessed.'

She scurried from the bathroom, and I sat on the edge of the bath shaking as the ferocity of the energy pulsating through me began to settle. I prayed silently to the Divine Mother.

*Holy Mother, Mother of all that is,*
*Pray for me now.*
*Hold me with Love and in Grace as I surrender to you.*
*Reveal in me all that is hidden, so I may remember the truth of who I am.*
*Infuse me with the courage to live my truth, to nourish all that is with Love.*
*And with your graceful, merciful and loving hand guide me.*
*Divine Mother, please show me the way so I may show others the way.*

I embraced the Divine Mother's presence and renewed my faith in the power of *her* love, in all its expressions, to be a transformative gift to Johnny and Madame Rosaline, Clarissa and Jimmy and all others. I floated through my day with *her* presence humming within, carrying an intensity and lightness that seemed to perfectly balance each other.

I was concerned when Johnny failed to meet me behind the campus carpark as agreed on parting in the early hours of the morning, but I was immediately assured by my heart's knowing that he was safe and had finally surrendered to sleep. I, too, longed for sleep and the comfort and security of my own bed, yet I knew I had to find energy for the performance that night as the doors were reopening. I trusted Madame Rosaline had taken care of Jimmy, yet I felt a calling to rise from deep within my womb.

A light circled St Christopher's that evening. The recent unnerving energy miraculously disappeared, and I allowed myself to be fuelled by the buoyancy. Even the girls who had been reluctant to perform over the last few weeks excitedly prepared their hair and makeup when they heard the club was almost full again.

I observed their merriment with interest and wondered how much of the change related to the overall mood within the club and how much was due to the absence of Clarissa's toxic energy. Without her, they were friendly and welcoming. There were no snide comments. I was relaxed and enjoyed their playful tizz.

Olivia, a talented artist, asked me gently if she could do my makeup and for some reason, I trusted her to support me in my transformation. I gazed astounded by the exquisite beauty and mystic reflected in the mirror as she captured my hidden essence, which was ready to take centre stage. My eyes were darkened around the edges, the upper lid layered with a light moss green and sprinkled with gold, the under edge and inside corner touched ever so delicately with a soft rose red, the effect transforming my eyes to a silver-grey colour that commanded attention. My cheekbones were accentuated with a sharp edge and etched in shimmering silver and my lips blossomed with renewed definition and fullness and were coated a dark silver grey that glistened and paralleled my eyes in colour and commanding presence. I was moved to tears when Gwendolyn, one of the quieter girls, sat beside me and took me by the hand.

'You look beautiful, Goldie Mae. You always do, but tonight is different. I'm wondering if you would like to wear something I've just finished making. I've been working on this piece for the last couple of weeks. It's different to anything I've ever made before and when

I've been working on it, you are always on my mind. I finished it this afternoon sitting in front of the fire. It was just so peaceful upstairs this afternoon that I just kept tinkering away and it's done and I'm wondering if you'd wear it tonight, Goldie Mae?'

'Really? Are you sure, Gwenny?'

'Of course!' she beamed excitedly and stood to dress my forehead with her masterpiece.

'I could only ever see you wearing it. No one else could hold *her* chemistry,' she mused mysteriously, entranced by the beauty of her creation.

It truly was exquisite. An intricate web of tiny crystals that sparkled like diamonds and teardrop pearls woven into a delicate crown that danced across my forehead and intertwined its way into the golden folds of my hair.

'You look like a Queen, Goldie Mae,' she whispered as she finished securing it in place and stared into my eyes in the mirror.

Stunned by the truth revealed in the image before my eyes, I pondered how Olivia and Gwendolyn had managed to capture my essence, for I believed she was deeply hidden within me. In that moment, I realised she had been quietly expressing herself through me for some time. She was the girl I knew myself to be, enriched with an edge that instantly transformed her into the fullness of my maiden and I silently celebrated, knowing I was more powerful in finally allowing myself to see what had been hidden.

I stood at the edge of the stage, my crown adorning my head while my feet remained bare. I giggled as the girls exited the stage filled with frivolity from their spirited performance. Madame Rosaline caught me before I took to the stage and looked at me stunned.

'Have I done something wrong?'

'No, not at all. You look simply magnificent. There is indeed a transformative hand at play this evening. But now is not the time for us to count our blessings and drop our guard. Once you begin to weave your new brand of magic, be assured there will be resistance, but trust in your power. Surrender and allow *her* to move through you.'

She shook her head, overwhelmed by the magical force weaving its way through her club. I walked onto the stage for the first time without an introduction and the unapologetically fierce fullness of my maiden unveiled herself. *Her* new distinctive energy wove its way into my dance and my drumming took on a deeper resonance that seemed to throb rather than hum. I didn't really understand what transpired once I entered that space. It often remains a mystery. I could feel a different intensity move through me and a raspy fierceness to my voice when I sang. As I moved around the room, a sensation similar to what I experienced in the bathroom that morning began to vibrate beneath my feet and coil its way into my pelvis, through my womb and rise through my spine before exploding from my heart. I closed my eyes as the intensity of the vibration once again shocked me and threatened to obliterate my physical form, but in my mind's eye a guiding hand I knew to be Cynthia's gently offered me a sword sheathed by threads of roses. Taking it in my hands, a surge of electricity raced through my body and anchored me into the depths, fuelling my power and allowing me to raise the sword above my head before striking it fiercely into the ground before me. My eyes opened and magnetised to Jimmy. He was transfixed.

*I See You.*

A voice within me spoke to him and while it was carried on the vibration of unconditional love, there was an unmistakable and formidable warning in *her* intent. While I held him motionless, *her* radiance, *my* radiance, filled the room, striking all those around me. I was accustomed to channelling divine light from higher realms that flowed about the room gently enchanting the audience, however, this frequency was razor sharp and with consummate intent, it penetrated the heart. This energy had not come from the higher realm. It had risen from the depths of my womb, from my darkness, and it was unapologetic in its transformative powers.

Paralysed by the prodigious potency of my fullness, I witnessed it touching every hidden corner within the room and within the souls of those before me. I was awed by the alchemical beauty unfolding, layers of rancid darkness obliterated, revealing a raw purity, the magnificence of each and every soul blinding. Overwhelmed by the vulnerability of being stripped bare, a collective unease stirred throughout the club and threatened to erupt, and I doubted my capacity to hold the space.

*Have I gone too far?* I tried to return the sword bestowed upon me, but she would not take it back, trusting me to honour *her* sacredness and to use *her* infinite power with integrity.

Humbled, I claimed the sword and received the blessing offered to me, and holding the space, I allowed the transformation to be complete. I struck the drum held in the visible realm and broke the trance. I quickly exited the room as they returned to normal consciousnesses, profoundly different in ways they would never find words for, having experienced the divine potency of my Dark Goddess. I did not feel called to race outside into the chilly night air to bring myself back into my body, for I was more embodied and grounded than I had ever been.

This work was different, and *her* transformative powers remained a mystery to me. Yet in trust, *her* energy was activated whenever I took to the stage after that night. I would not consciously invoke *her*. She preferred to awaken with me and demanded I surrender and allow *her* to wind through my body, like a tightly bound cobra before slithering *her* potency throughout the room and striking unsuspecting targets. *She* knew who she was after. The darker the core, the greater *her* challenge, and she would persist at alchemising the outer layers night after night. I never doubted the power of *her* fierce, loving touch in creating change.

Jimmy changed. I don't know exactly what happened, but I'm sure Madame Rosaline had more to do with it than me. I sensed a collective sigh of relief when his ruthless and reckless ferocity tempered.

A renewed calm flowed throughout St Christopher's and fell across the city like a blanket of pure white snow. Madame Rosaline was not resting on her laurels, for she knew Jimmy Triboni, the sharp edges of his wounds and the complex intricacies of his soul better than anyone. As a falcon perched high on the mountain top, she maintained a vigilant watch, awaiting his next move.

'Do not be fooled. This is more a pause than an ending,' she prophesied when I commented on the easing of tension.

*Beware of the eye of the storm.*

# CHAPTER 19

# Gypsy Soul

Spring danced on the horizon and the promise of new beginnings beckoned. I was excited about what the turn of season would bring. It was always such a vibrant time living on the land, life literally birthing and blossoming before your eyes. I longed for the reinvigoration it offered, ready to leave the darkness of winter. However, a feeling that all was not as it seemed lingered, and I could sense the calm surface of the new season was hiding some turbulence—waiting to erupt.

'I've heard you all going on and on about this party up in the mountains, so I'm closing the club for the weekend and away you go, the lot of you,' Madame Rosaline declared over a mid-week dinner. 'Let your hair down, be wild and free, but make sure you watch out for each other and, as always, honour yourself.'

The girls were ecstatic. It was a rarity for most of them to leave the city. They busily began organising lifts and borrowing tents and sleeping bags. We would be camping on the farm of one of Nate's best friends. Their excitement was intoxicating, though my unease prevailed. I expressed my concerns to Madame Rosaline, but she would not indulge my fears, ever measured and peaceful in her navigation of dangerous waters.

Neither Johnny nor I had mentioned we were meeting up most afternoons, but she knew.

'Listen carefully, my girl, something is brewing. I can feel it in my waters as you do, yet it is not a time for fear. Wisdom tells me it is better we are all out of town this weekend. From what I've heard, things aren't looking good for Frank. The name of the judge who is to preside over the case was leaked and he has some personal vendetta against Jimmy, which does not surprise me. The district attorney has a strong witness, and he's confident there is enough evidence to finally prosecute a Triboni. Strangely, there are no hands willing to be greased by Jimmy's dirty money to sway the case in the other direction. It's never happened like this before. Money has always talked and assured him of his power in this town. But he's losing his grip on that power. His tower is crumbling, and he knows it. I don't know what he will stoop to in order to reclaim that power. I've been strongly guided to close the club and spend the weekend with Sacnite while you girls go to this party with Nate. We can come back afterwards and review where to next. Let's take one very conscious step at a time. And look, let's be honest, there are worse places to take a break than the Catskill Mountains.'

Nate's flatmate, Jez, was a born creative, making magic happen with mini-music festivals played on his family's land. Nate assured me it was simply Jez's band and two others coming together to entertain a diverse group of friends, including other musicians, the St Christopher's crowd and a group of young Irish immigrants, one of whom was in Jez's band and another dating Gwendoline.

The night before I was to leave for the mountains, I had gone to bed mildly excited about the weekend and the opportunity to do something different, conceding that perhaps Madame Rosaline was right. A change of stimulus would be good for me. But I woke during the night agitated, my heart racing, my hands sweating and my head throbbing. I couldn't quite process what was happening as the space around me stilled. Then there was nothing. Not even my breath. Not even my pulse. Just a deep vastness and through it came the whispered wisdom:

*Do not run from what you fear.*
*I will hold you as your heart expands.*
*All that is not of love shall be divinized.*
*Nothing but love shall remain.*
*Nothing but love. Nothing but love. Nothing but love.*

My racing heart led me to believe it was a warning, and my aching head impeded my ability to discern between the voice of love and the voice of fear. I became increasingly agitated and confused as the adrenaline surged my body, blocking my intuition to guide me to the truth. I found Madame Rosaline in the kitchen, staring at the flickering flames of the fire with a freshly brewed pot of tea before her. She rubbed myrrh, frankincense and lavender oil on my head as I shared the message I had received. The message was crystal clear despite my mental fogginess. She suggested it was a reminder to face my fear of connecting with others.

'Perhaps you're being pushed out of your comfort zone because you've been hiding behind your magical mystic for too long. The fear of being seen in your human expression, beyond the veil of your gifts, completely terrifies you.'

I wanted to object, but the truth in her words struck my heart and I began to cry. I was scared.

'What if nobody likes me, Madame Rosaline? What if this...' I gestured to my body. 'What if I don't belong? What if I'm not good enough for them? What if I make a fool of myself? When I think about that, I want to run and hide. I'm happy by myself. Why do I need to connect to others, anyway?'

'This is fear, not love, speaking. You are being invited to live love, which will require you to open your heart and overcome your fear.'

I didn't let people get close. I trusted few to truly see all of me because somewhere deep within I feared rejection. Positioning myself on the outside had allowed me to avoid being where I could be rejected. Despite the discomfort of this truth, I trusted this experience had landed to challenge me to step from my shadow, the part of me that blocked me from connecting with others and exploring who I was when I was truly seen.

'You may be surprised by the gifts waiting for you on the other side of this weekend. The most powerful ones are the most unexpected!'

She placed her hands on my cheeks and looked me in the eye with deep concern.

'You are young. Your spirit is free. Let *her* dance and be filled with joy this weekend. Do not become trapped in this mess. It will ruin you. I know Johnny told you and you didn't believe him, but please believe me ... once you are in their world, it is very hard to escape it.'

I threw my arms around her in gratitude for her love and guidance and bid her goodnight.

Caellach and I wound our way out of the city in the campervan.

He had laughed when I asked if I could borrow the campervan earlier in the week, saying, 'Once a gypsy, always a gypsy my girl. It's in our blood.'

I felt the excitement rising as the city faded into the distance and Caellach began singing Irish folk songs that spoke of love, land, loss and hope. They touched the webbing of my soul and stirred a longing for home. A desire for the simplicity of my old life and Marigold—the girl I once was. I was eighteen, yet I felt an intense weariness, my time in the city having stretched me, even though it hadn't even been a year. It felt like many lifetimes had been lived in a short period and I welcomed this time away.

I joined Caellach in song and let my soul soar as I remembered sitting around the fire with my Ma's. Athena on one side, Cynthia on the other, holding my hands, telling me the stories of the songs and calling in the ancient ones, the ancestral mothers and fathers to sit with us. In connecting with their presence, we trusted them to support us on our journey, to guide and protect us. I silently invoked my Ma's and felt the beauty of their presence in the van with Caellach and I. To them I whispered, 'Please, my beloved mothers, protect me and guide me with grace on my path of truth. Help me keep my heart open as I face my fear and be nothing but love.'

As Caellach finally surrendered the driver's seat as we hit the mountains, he mused, 'Nothing but love… Wise words. Harder in practice, but it's all I know you as, Marigold, pure love.'

With renewed confidence, I successfully made my way through the mountains and back to the farm, where Caellach handed over the keys, convinced I was more than capable of driving the van through the winding road to Jez's property some twenty miles away. I relished the chance to play with the kids and have a cup of tea in the sunshine with Clara, her willing me to fill her in on all the news.

*Where to start?* I pondered and decided it was best to dance around the details, sharing bits and pieces about classes and the girls and St Christopher's. I refrained from mentioning Johnny. It was far too complex and confusing to try to explain over just the one cup of tea and I was eager to hit the road and embrace my fears.

My gypsy soul exploded with rapture as I made my way through the mountains, soaking up the beauty and simplicity of the experience. I understood this was what Madame Rosaline meant when she said there were unexpected gifts waiting for me on this adventure. The pure bliss that enveloped my being as I drove that campervan was quite simply, perfection. I could have happily kept driving and adventuring into the unknown. The temptation to run away by myself was palpable, but I followed the calling of my soul and arrived at Jez's beautiful property, trusting in the growth this path offered me. Who I was to be when I again drove this road I did not know, yet I trusted who my soul sought for me to become.

*And so it was.*

# CHAPTER 20

# Forget Me Not

The river called me. The mountains called me. The trees called me. Solitude called, too. I parked the van by the river on the perimeter of the property, shadowed by the mountains, surrounded by the trees and away from the main house and out-sheds where everyone else had set up their campsites. I longed to sit by the river with a book, sipping hot tea or go for a hike in the mountains. But before I could shy away in solitude, Olivia, Sally and Gwendoline raced down the drive and across the paddock to greet me.

Their enthusiasm hijacked my plans, and I wandered up the hill arm in arm with them, enjoying the frivolity as they gushed about how gorgeous some of the guys were. Though not the Irish lads who lived with Gwenny's boyfriend Patrick, nor the couple of fellas who worked behind the bar at St Christopher's with Nate. According to the girls, the dreamy ones were the musicians, with their long hair, paisley shirts, flares and circle rimmed glasses. I was intrigued by their fascination with them, for they were a world away from the crowd who frequented St Christopher's and were quite the novelty for the girls who had never really moved in alternate circles.

It was ironic that this group should have been 'my people', given I had lived as part of the alternative circles my whole life. However, I immediately felt I was not quite vibrant enough for their edgy spiritual vibe. *Nothing but love …* my heart whispered when I found myself in judgment of them. I circled with them for a while, open to connecting before finding myself drawn to the Irish lads who were happily drinking whiskey and beer, no time or inclination for the marijuana and psychedelics that were being passed around. They much preferred to have a drink and the craic than passionately discuss altered realms of consciousness while declaring their love for everyone and everything. The lads drank like there was no tomorrow but balanced it with stories from home, reminiscing about their mammy's home cooked dinner, the smell of peat burning in the range, the pub on a Sunday afternoon after clearing their sins at early Mass. Most had grown up on farms and after finishing the basics of school they were forced to leave their home and homeland, for there were no jobs about for their kind. At fifteen, they'd packed a suitcase, bid farewell to their family, surely breaking their mother's heart, and took on the Atlantic to see what the United States of America, the land of promise and plenty, had to offer them. They were happy enough where they'd landed, with plenty of construction work in New York City to keep them busy and a strong Irish community to appease some of the homesickness. Well experienced in holding my own with Caellach, I relished the banter and played along when the lads gave me an awful hard time about my name.

'So where are your people from, Miss Goldie Mae?' Paddy asked, intrigued. 'You've quite the mix of accent there. You're certainly no Dub like Michael here, thanks be to God.'

Their booming laughter filled the camp as they mocked Michael, the only Dubliner and therefore 'city boy' amongst them. I vaguely told them my people were from the West Coast.

'It's a big coast, that West Coast, Goldie Mae! Where exactly?'

When I told them I'd moved around a lot, they laughed more than ever.

'You're not a knacker are you, Goldie Mae? Ah, surely not!'

'I'm not a knacker!' I protested jovially, 'You can call me….'

I paused playfully, and they shook their heads.

'Knacker!' they chorused.

'I'm not a knacker! You can call me a wanderer, a gypsy soul!' I giggled.

'Feck off, gypsy soul, me arse! You're a knacker through and through, Goldie Mae!'

They all laughed, and I loved once again being part of the craic. It felt like home and I hadn't realised how much I missed being around my people. Caellach and Clara were sharp witted and light-hearted, our conversations often dynamic, impassioned and filled with laughter, but since moving to the city, I had become quite serious. I was naturally cheeky, flirtatious even, but I had lost that edge, my wit and imp tempered. In sitting about the fire with the lads with a whiskey in hand, I reclaimed that part of me I had unknowingly lost, and was more at ease than I had been in an age.

As dusk fell, Paddy pulled out a fiddle, Michael, a tin whistle and Rory, a bodhrán, and before anyone knew what was happening, they took over the stage and regaled in their merriment. After a solid hour of playing and singing, which brought all of us to our feet, Rory asked if I sang. I was secretly chuffed he asked.

'So, my little knacker from somewhere on the West Coast, do you know Galway Bay?' he winked at me, knowing too well the sweet place that Galway Bay held in the heart of every Irish emigrant to have sailed from the West Coast.

I took the bodhrán from him and began the gentle drumming of the taunt goat skin. Closing my eyes, I took myself back onto the ship as it sailed from Galway Bay some ten years before. I'd left behind my homeland, my roots and my loved ones. All I had ever known was behind me on the shores of Galway Bay.

And I sang, the words flowing in waves of grief.

*If you ever go across the sea to Ireland,*
*Then maybe at the closing of your day,*
*You will sit and watch the moonrise over Claddagh,*
*And watch the barefoot gossoons at their play.*

*Just to hear again the ripple of the trout stream,*
*The women in the meadows making hay,*
*And to sit beside a turf fire in the cabin,*
*And see the sun go down on Galway Bay.*

*For the breezes blowing o'er the seas from Ireland,*
*Are perfumed by the heather as they blow,*
*And the women in the uplands diggin' prates,*
*Speak a language that the strangers do not know.*

*For the strangers came and tried to teach us their way,*
*They scorned us just for being what we are,*
*But they might as well go chasing after moonbeams,*
*Or light a penny candle from a star.*

*And if there's going to be a life hereafter,*
*And faith I'm sure there's going to be,*
*I will ask my God to let me make my heaven,*
*In that dear land across the Irish sea.*

The vibration of the drum caressed the core of my aching heart. Slowly opening my eyes, I was met by stunned silence and the tear-stained faces of the lads. *Bless their hearts.* Rory drew me close to his chest.

'Thanks a million, Goldie Mae. You're a gift from heaven, sure ye are.'

'My name's Marigold, not Goldie Mae,' I whispered.

Claiming the name my Ma's had given me was suddenly of profound importance.

Standing back, he held my shoulders and stared into my face, nodding.

'Jesus, Mary and Joseph, Marigold … Mary the Golden One. I should have feckin' known. You are from heaven!'

He shook his head, bemused.

'Will you sing again for us now, Golden One?' he asked gently.

'Yeah, Irish, sing again and make us all cry for our mommies.'

I turned around, stunned to see Clarissa standing behind me. However, I did not recognise the girl who had left St Christopher's only a few weeks before. That girl was gone and before me stood a bitter, hard woman whose face I was certain held the remnants of bruises.

'Clarissa,' I stammered. *How dare she! How dare she come here and pierce my joy!*

She'd tagged along with a couple of the girlfriends of the boys who worked behind the bar, apparently keeping in contact with them after leaving St Christopher's.

'Doesn't take you long, does it? Always knew you were sly! Ditched the Italian for a leprechaun. How's it feel to fuck a leprechaun? Why don't you sing about that, Irish?'

'Mind yourself!' Rory warned, startled by the vicious attack.

'Oh please, she doesn't need your protection. She's not as innocent as she makes out. She's been fucking the prince of the Mafia for the last year, swooning around Central Park thinking no one's watching.'

'Why don't you just feck off? You're not welcome here!' Rory motioned for her to leave, but I knew she was just warming up. This attack had been brewing for months and she was not about to walk away.

'Oh, you're so chivalrous, Farmer Joe! I'm not going anywhere. I wouldn't want to miss a minute of the action here. Please do sing again, Irish! Entertain us all with your little lullabies, transfixing us with your witch spells.'

The girls she had come with surrounded her and laughed, egging her on.

'And when I get home, I'll tell my Frank you were fucking a leprechaun and he'll make sure Johnny finds out. Maybe that'll break the spell you have over him!'

Clarissa glared at me, and I had never witnessed such hatred.

*Nothing but love.*

I refused to be drawn into her wicked web, but it took everything in me not to react and scream that Johnny would never listen to a word she said because he's not stupid enough to believe the filth that comes from her vile mouth. Yet, I didn't say a word. My silence was more powerful than any words would ever be. I drew Rory away by the elbow, sensing he was close to erupting. Having seen a wild Irishman or two in my days, I knew better than to let this exchange continue.

'Watch her!' she screamed as I walked away, her hysteria rising. 'Under the sweet and innocent act, she's dangerous. She causes trouble wherever she goes. You know your precious Johnny copped it again last night because of you, Irish … You hear that? Blood dripping from his cracked skull because of you!'

She shrieked with an insanity that stirred the increasingly familiar sacred rage resting in my womb, waiting patiently for the moment to rise, to create order from chaos and yield *her* divine fire to protect the sacredness of my soul.

*Nothing but love.*

Love is an expression beyond the scope of limited eyes. Those who only want to see love as light will condemn *her* dark expression as bad or wrong or evil, for they fear *her* power. Those who do not know the fullness of love will never see the potency of love expressed through divine rage. Rage that swiftly silenced the fearful little voice in my head that begged me to *settle down* and be a *good girl.* My soul refused to be diminished, to be silenced, to play by the rules. Nothing could stop *her* as she rose through my core, curled *her* way up my spine, dived through my heart and pierced my physical form. Striking the ground in front of Clarissa, *she* ignited the grass  creating a ring of fire that sprang to life surrounding her, paralysing her in terror. With loving ferocity, the blessing of the Divine Dark Mother penetrated Clarissa's heart. *May these sacred flames cleanse the shadows that stain your soul and may you find your way home to love.*

Nobody dared move, held in both shock and awe by the power of *her* passion, *her* fire, *her* magic and mystery. My own legs began to give way such was *her* force and Rory gently held me by the elbow as the flames faded from the conscious eye, but their mark forever imprinted on the subconscious of all who bore witness to *her* formidable power. Trembling as the energy continued to rapidly recoil into my form, I asked Rory to take me to my van. He put his arm protectively around my shoulder and that one simple gesture reminded me so much of Caellach that I burst into tears, my vulnerability escaping from knowing I was safely held. The tension gently dissipated as we wandered down the hill and I marvelled at the night sky, the stars glistening more brightly than I had seen them in an age.

'You're like them, Marigold. Like the stars, you shine in the dark like nothing I've ever seen before. You're a grand girl, so you are, and don't be listening to the shite that one carried on with, you hear?'

I was touched by his affection.

'Thank you.  She's always been horrid to me, but there's definitely an unpredictability to her malevolency now.'

'Ah well, I think you put the fear of God into her with that fire dancing at her feet. Jesus, the look on her face! I don't know how you did it, but would you believe me when I tell ye, I saw me Granny, God bless her soul, do the very same thing once to the parish priest. A complete gobshite, so he was. He's after refusing to baptise me little brother because he was born with the Downs Syndrome, you know. Dear God, the rage coming from me Granny as she marched to the door of that church. If you weren't after seeing it with your own eyes, you'd never believe it, but I did, and dear God, I'll never forget. As sure as I saw it there tonight, a ring of fire right around him and the whole fecking church, so it was. She terrified the bejesus out of me, me auld Granny, but she had a heart of gold and wouldn't harm a fly, but don't cross that line. She reminds me of you, so she does! I miss her. Good auld stick she was … now off you go into ye fancy van before I get all sentimental on ye.'

'Goodnight, Rory, and thank you, well, you know, for being there for me.'

'No bother on ye, Marigold. It was good auld craic there this afternoon, with the singing and dancing. T'was grand sure it was until herself stepped in. Anyway now, mind yourself, Marigold. I'll see you in the morning. God bless.'

As he went up the hill into the darkness of the night, I stared at the stars and the glorious moon. How I loved to ponder the mysteries of the world, to commune with the spirit world, seeking to understand everything from what happened to Johnny, whether he was okay, whether I should stay here or go and find him, to the viciousness of Clarissa's attack and why the good guys, like Rory and Johnny, could never see me as more than a little sister to hang out with and protect. I contemplated the idea of Rory seeing me as something more and what it would have looked and felt like if he had stayed with me in the van. I enjoyed the rush of energy that accompanied those thoughts as they flooded my body, but I was immediately struck by guilt, these thoughts a betrayal of Johnny. I did not understand my guilt because I knew in his eyes I could never be more, yet I wondered about his heart. *Was I more in his heart? Could I be more if his heart allowed it?*

I could no longer deny my desire to be *his more* and as I drifted to sleep, I prayed to the Divine Mother to keep him safe, to hold him in her loving arms and like warm honey, a sweet remembering flowed through every cell of my being.

*Now and always, Johnny Triboni, you are my cushla*
*machree—the vein of my heart, my beloved.*

# CHAPTER 21

# Heaven on Earth

---

Crisp mountain air filled my lungs as I hiked the mountain with the rising sun. I breathed deeply, mist billowing from my mouth from the union of warm breath and chilled mountain air. I marvelled at the creative power of opposites as the light of the sun merged with the dark of the soil to germinate the seed, in time creating the flowers and the trees. I soaked in the magical simplicity and mysterious complexity of nature in her finest as Mother Moon set and Father Sun rose, majestically illuminating the forest, which gently stirred with the waking birds and animals. I bathed in the changing colour of the sky, savouring the touch of the wind's kiss on my cheeks and listening intensely to the stillness, the doorway to the Divine Mother's wisdom. I stopped on the ridge of the mountain and sank further into her magnificence, surrendering to the silence and comfort of once again being held in her arms.

*Show me, teach me, hold me,* I implored her in my vulnerability. My heart was expansive yet still raw and tender from being broken open, time and time again. Humbled by the rising of love that embraced me, I placed my hand on my heart and surrendered to her wise counsel.

*Let love lead you.*
*Let love plant the seed.*
*Let love filter through the layers of all that is.*

*Let love rouse your soul.*
*Let love crack open the seeds of change.*
*Let love sprout the beginning of the new.*

*Let love reignite the Divine.*
*In you. In him.*
*In all that is.*
*My gift to you.*

*Nothing but Love. Nothing but Love. Nothing but Love.*

I remained in that space for a long time, allowing the transmission of her words to seep into my heart. Slowly and steadily, I made my way down the mountain, filled with gratitude and relishing the calm, centred and reassured presence within myself. In rapturous oneness—with the mountain, the sky, the birds, the animals, the trees and the flowers—I wound my way back to the river, her icy waters beckoning me to become one with her. I stripped bare and dived into her pristine freezing waters, arousing and invigorating every cell, muscle, organ and bone in my body, ensuring there was nowhere else I could be but present with that moment. With my heart wide open, I trusted I was held no matter where my path took me. Returning to my van, I rekindled the fire, ate a late breakfast and drank tea before wandering up the hill, my heart filled to bursting, my soul blissfully at peace, the greatest gift to an ever-expanding soul.

The music vibrated, stirring the wild and free crowd who danced and sang, wonderfully claiming their joy. I ran into Rory as I neared the main house.

'Well, if it isn't herself? We were about to send out a search party, sure we were!'

He pulled me into his chest and held me tight, awash with relief despite his jest.

'Now you'll have drink with me won't ye, Golden One?'

I laughed and he chastised me when I asked for a water.

'Sure, you're going awful soft on me now. Your man over there, Johnny, he's only after drinking just the water himself.'

My eyes must have lit up because he laughed.

'Well now, if I hadn't seen it with me own eyes, there can't be any denying the spark in ye eyes, Golden One. Your man, Johnny, he's up there by the fire. We've been having a bit of the craic with him, stirring him about his leather jacket and movie star looks. He can take it well enough, sure he can. Mind, the girls are going *gaga* over him, but you wouldn't be after seeing him raise an eye to one of 'em. Keeps looking over his shoulder, so he does. Anyone would be thinking he was waiting for someone in particular!'

He smirked and raised his eyebrows at me.

'Go on with you now. You look like you're about to jump out of your skin, sure you do.'

I gave him a playful thump on the arm and a quick kiss on the cheek.

'Mind yourself now, Golden One,' he called sincerely, as I darted away towards the large circle of people around the fire.

But I was only looking for one and he wasn't hard to spot, his broad shoulders and leather jacket a dead giveaway. I crept up behind him and placed my hands over his eyes, a charge racing through my body. He placed his hands over the top of mine and held them for a few seconds before drawing them down to his lips where he gently kissed them, treasuring the moment of our reconnection. He rose and drew me into his arms. In that moment, nothing else mattered and nobody else existed. Relieved to have him safely in my arms, I rested my head against his chest and melded into him, never wanting to be separated again. I imagine we stood like that for an age, my deep surrender as he gently kissed the top of my head. I cherished every beat of his heart. Eventually, we sat by the fire in an intimate bubble. In hushed tones, he opened, finally letting me into his world, trusting me to support him and love him beyond the darkness of his family.

'He's losing power and he's desperately trying to hold on. It looks like Frank will be found guilty. The DA's got a solid case and the only way Frank will get off is if they take out the witness. Frank's more than willing to do it, but Jimmy insists I do it, because it's my fault we lost Rosenthal and the case has gone to shit. He said it was about time I proved myself a man, and when I refused, saying I was done, out, that I wanted nothing more to do with him or the family, he became enraged. I've never seen anything like it. His eyes became blank, a void of nothing, and I saw him reach for a baseball bat. That was the last thing I remember before I was pulling myself up the wall splattered with blood, my blood. I was conscious enough to know what I was doing, and that I had to get out of there. If he struck me a second time, I'm sure I wouldn't be here now. I expected to be struck again as I climbed the stairs out of his stinking dungeon office, and I vowed I would never return, and I won't, MG. I'm never going back. I'm finally free!'

He laughed as I had never seen him before and I grabbed his face and stroked the cut on his temple, terrified of what could have been. The possibility that I may never have held him again brought me to tears, tears of pure relief and gratitude, that he was here, beside me.

'How did you get here?' I asked, trying to piece together the timeline.

'I made it to Nate's and he took me straight out to his mom's. Rosaline arrived there yesterday and between the two of them, they stitched me back together, my head and my heart. I went there, doubting myself, still believing that once you're born into a family like that you can never be free from them, but Sacnite and Rosaline did some of their healing magic and showed me I could be free. A weight lifted from my shoulders and my heart. I saw a different path, away from Jimmy and the whole Triboni family. The only person I saw on that path was you, MG.'

I marvelled at the man before me. Finally free from the tension that had suffocated his light, the dark moodiness he projected was replaced with the luminance I had always seen, and he did not shy from it. Quite the contrary, he embraced his newfound buoyancy and the freedom to express himself without reservation, taking hold of my hand.

'I know what I want,' he said, gently brushing a stray hair from my face and tucking it behind my ear, never taking his eyes from mine.

'I want to be free from them forever. I don't want them in my life, MG. I want you.'

His words were filled with raw truth and possibility, and for the first time since the night we met, I recognised the fullness of desire in his eyes. I may have died a thousand deaths in that moment. I wished it to last forever in the deepest crevice of my sacred heart. The screams of my fear to run, to protect my heart from further hurt, to save my soul from the agony of abandonment, were silenced by the vastness of the portal that bound us. Nothing could draw me from love.

*Nothing But Love.*

I placed my hands on the log we shared, anchoring myself to the present, to the love that danced magically in the space between us. Not having a clue what I was to do next, I took a deep breath and surrendered to my soul, trusting in her to guide me as she always had to the path of my highest truth. Into his eyes I sank, finding his soul, where the gravity of his passion welled.

*It's always been you*, he whispered across the realms.

I took his hand and walked to the middle of the group dancing to the music. My body moved, drawing him to me, intent on expressing to him the fullness of my yes. Never would I have imagined that Johnny Triboni would be so free to meet me fully. His body bound to mine and moved with reckless abandonment as our joy filled to overflowing. We laughed and sang and flowed as one in the sacredness of our portal, where only he and I existed—embraced in love.

I did not know who was surrounding us, watching with curiosity.

I did not know what music was playing or how we danced.

I did not know how long we stayed in that space together.

I did not know when it started to rain.

I did not know when everyone else left us alone on the dancefloor.

All I knew was Johnny and our love.

As our souls wove into one, we became still, holding each other as the surge of energy from above and below pulsated through us. I shivered as it burst through my crown and yoni at once, stealing my breath and threatening to overwhelm me, but he did not falter in steadying me, taking one hand in his and gently grabbing the base of my skull to tilt my head, compelling me to meet the passion in his eyes.

*Stay with me. Stay open*, he demanded, and though terrified in my vulnerability, I trusted him to hold me as I surrendered even further into the depth of his soul. Never had I been taken to this place before, not with another. This was so different to the places my soul danced when *she* rose into the realms or dived into the depths. This was more, so much more, the more my soul had longed for.

Held in the rawness of my woman by the potency of his man, we became one—a sacred union of our souls—and in this remembrance, tears were drawn from my eyes for the sheer beauty of it. Threads of our energy entwined until there was no separation between what was his and what was mine. Together, rising and falling, holding and releasing, in an intimate dance to the edge and beyond, we flew above it all as one, suspended in the divinity of grace, the most amazing grace, which I had long desired, yet never known. I wanted nothing more than to keep it alive for eternity. As the rain streamed from the heavens upon us, blessing our union, we were alone on the dancefloor, as one, dancing to the beat of our sacred drum.

*Johnny Triboni, then, now, forever, I dance*
*with you in the rain.*

# CHAPTER 22

# Fall from Grace

The crow cawed, callously clawing me from nirvana.

Momentarily bewildered, I gasped as a surge of lightning raced through me, forcing my awareness to the physical world. I trembled … my arms wound around Johnny's neck. His hands shaking as they cupped my face, our breath shared as his lips quivered ever so lightly upon mine. Time froze and immobilised in the intimacy of our embrace, there was nothing but the warmth of his breath meeting mine and the burgeoning possibility that danced on our lips in anticipation.

The crow cawed, zealously commanding attention.

My everything begged me to stay with him, my soul whispered her sweet longing to kiss his tingling lips and meld with his physical body which ached for me.

*Do you remember this? Do you remember us?* his soul murmured.

I remembered lifetimes dancing in his arms. They cascaded through my mind's eye and with him, I remembered home. *Take me home, Johnny*, my soul filled with longing, begged.

The crow cawed, violently piercing my everything.

The malicious sniggers surrounding us forced me to pull away from Johnny and obliterated the divine thread that bound us, a jagged edge bastardizing the exquisite beauty of our connection. The sword of shame, humiliation and foolishness penetrated the purity and brilliance of my soul as a group of girls giggled and sneered, mocking the sacred intimacy Johnny and I shared. The fullness, the truth and beauty of all that I was had been exposed, and their scornful, shaming stares struck the rawness of my soul and activated my deepest fears. Clarissa was front and centre, leading the ridicule and belittling our union, dirtying it with her vicious, vile tongue and tarnishing its purity. She relished the opportunity to attack me, publicly shaming and disgracing me for my sensuality and sexuality, for the expression of my wild and free maiden on the verge of claiming her woman.

She had waited for this day, her snarky comments and vicious attacks had never rattled me when I had danced and moved in my sensuality in my performances at St Christopher's because I knew that energy, having claimed it long before I danced on that stage. But I had never danced with another with *her* and, while the sensual weaving of myself into union with Johnny was innate, it was new and exposed me to enormous vulnerability. Clarissa jumped at the chance to debaucher the virginity of my maiden.

She took what was divine and tarnished it.

She took what was pure and dirtied it.

She took what was ours and made it theirs to desecrate and dishonour.

Her smirk took my sensual maiden and turned her into a silly little girl who was playing a game she was ill-equipped to take part in. I was out of my depth and made a fool of myself, so before I could grab hold of the doubt and shame that tore through me, I ran from them.

I ran from the woman I was becoming.

I ran from the path of my soul.

I ran from Johnny and our union.

I ran from love and into the eager arms of fear.

Johnny reached for me when my eyes turned from his to theirs, his hand gently resting on my jaw, willing me to return to him. But I took her bait over his love. He grabbed for my hand as I released from his embrace. But I would not allow him to hold me. He called for me to stop when I closed my heart and ran from him. But I would not listen to his pleas above the little voice in my head that cruelly told me I was foolish and had imagined it all. That what I thought we shared was no more than a fantasy stemming from childish desires. That I'd let it get out of control and humiliated myself in front of all those people. Worst was the thought that Johnny was laughing at me, too, that he thought me a silly little girl with a crush. It was more than I could bear, the possibility of ridicule in his eyes, and I ran despite his calls for me to stop.

I fled to the mountains, and I climbed far from them and their vicious taunts. I climbed until there was nothing but me and Mother

Nature and she willingly absorbed the tears of shame and grief that bled from me. They did not subside, an endless torrent gushing from me, drowning the cries of my soul to go back to him, to believe in the power of love we shared, the union we had created. But I did not want to think of it, so great was the pain of humiliation. Instead, I turned from it and sank into the self-pitying wounding of my maiden, she who remembered victimization and was not ready to let it go. Can one step define a lifetime?

*Oh Johnny, my beloved Johnny!*
*I'm sorry for abandoning you.*
*I'm sorry for not trusting you to hold me.*
*I'm sorry for leaving you to believe you were not good enough.*
*Oh Johnny, I'm sorry for failing you.*

I wasn't to know Clarissa would strike as soon as my back was turned. She took advantage of his vulnerability to fill her desperate need for power. I was careless leaving him there, knowing how much she sought to bring me down. I didn't realise how dangerous she had become since leaving St Christopher's. I wasn't to know Clarissa had taken to psychedelics, predominately LSD, and accessed a path to other realms. She claimed to have discovered her spiritual gifts and felt it her duty to share these gifts with others, whether they sought her insights or not. Nor was I to know that Clarissa had begun messing about with energy, connecting to spirits and reading cards, without any understanding of boundaries, protection or the ability to discern what energies she was connecting with. She was driven by malice and the desire for power. She had no interest in understanding how to work with energy with any degree of integrity. One of the most important lessons my mothers ever taught me was respecting the power of energy and the sacredness of other people's energy. They guided me to always use my energetic gifts with integrity because without integrity our spiritual gifts are not gifts, they are dangerous.

While I wasn't to know what Clarissa was up to when I ran to the mountains, she knew exactly what she was doing when she launched her attack on Johnny, exploiting his confusion and the tenderness of his heart. Of course he was confused by being abandoned without explanation, despite moments before being bound as one in love. My reaction confused me, but I ran from her vicious claws and left him to walk straight into her trap. She manipulated his head and heart, turning him from love to fear, from light to dark, from good to bad.

Nate found me hiding on the mountain ridge as the sun began to set, a murder of crows circling me insistently with their loud, rambunctious squawk. For a couple of hours, I'd arrogantly refused to heed their warning and return to the campsite. Instead, I waited like a sulking teenager for someone to find me. I hoped it would be Johnny, searching me out and listening to me rationalise why I had left him and how horrendous Clarissa had always been to me. But Johnny did not come. Nate appeared, sweating and distressed, having spent hours looking for me. Never had I seen him rattled and it alarmed me. He was always the calm presence amidst the storm, the level head in the drama, wisely guiding others through 'life's little hick ups', as he called them.

'Something's not right, G. I can feel it in my gut. I don't like it. Something's happened to Johnny … I don't know what. He was a mess when you left. Clarissa took him aside and then he just left. He took my car and he's gone.'

As the crow's caw stopped, an eerie silence pierced my heart and opened my vision. I could see through realms. I saw Johnny distraught as I ran from him. He ran to catch me, but when I did not stop, he went to my van and sat by the river to wait for me. Then I saw Clarissa come and sit with him, placing her hand on his thigh, tilting her head in faux concern. I became so enraged that the vision began to blur. I couldn't see what happened next and I turned to Nate distraught.

'What did she say to him, Nate? What has she done?' I cried.

'The last I saw was you and Johnny dancing in the rain and I thought, finally … and then I went and helped get tarps to cover the equipment. By the time I came back, everyone had dispersed, but I had this odd feeling, so I went looking for you and Johnny. Before I got to your van, Johnny raced past me in my car and didn't stop when I flagged him down. I figured something must have happened between you two and he had gone looking for you, so I wasn't too concerned. Then Clarissa came up the hill towards me, smirking like it was all a big joke to her and I knew she'd stirred up trouble. But when I asked her, she looked at me blankly and in a stupid voice said something like, "I am not Clarissa. My name is Luna Star. I come from the seventh dimension and the earthling named Clarissa offers herself as a channel for my guidance." She said she'd used cards and the cards had spoken to him, to show him the way. And then she said, "He goes now to free his soul from his father in the only way his father knows, through blood." She thought it was hilarious and walked off laughing. I don't know if she was high or seriously deranged, but either way she's dangerous, and she's somehow tapped into Johnny and sent him to the city to do God only knows what.'

I was livid with her, and with Johnny for listening to that rubbish, but mostly with myself for letting Clarissa get to me. My anger blurred with shame and guilt and layered upon my humiliation and self-pity. I purged relentlessly as we raced down the mountain, but when we neared the bottom, Nate turned to me, took me by the shoulders and shook me.

'Enough of this bullshit, G. Just grow up, for fuck's sake! You really want her to win? Because that's exactly what's happening here. Her pathetic little performance is working a number on you, and the longer you stay caught up in it, the worse it is for Johnny!'

I paused, poised to argue, the rawness of my heart seeking comfort in righteousness, but he softened before I could say anything.

'I'm sorry, G. I hear you and I get it … I really do. We need to be there for him, no matter what she's done, no matter what he's done. We have to be there for him in the way that you and I know. Let it be love that shows him the way through whatever she's walked him into.'

I knew his words as true and I breathed deeply, releasing all that didn't serve me, all that was not of love from my body, mind and spirit as we made our way back to my van. Whatever happened next, I vowed to be guided by my heart, not from the rawness of my wound. An eeriness permeated the property. Torrential rain had settled in and many of the campers had chosen to leave while the remainder hung close to the shelter. The revelry of the previous night and earlier in the day had dissipated, and a heaviness hung in the air. Nate decided to borrow a car and head into the city in search of Johnny, while I agreed to wait at my van in case he returned.

'He will come back to you. Call him back to you and hold him with you, no matter what. Follow your heart, G. I promise I will be back by sunrise and if he is not back and I have not found him, we will navigate it from there, okay?'

I nodded, trusting in him and his wisdom. In Nate's absence, I drew myself into a meditative state and asked to be shown a higher perspective, to see beyond my pain to truth. I saw Clarissa as a small child, reaching for the love of her mother but being cast aside, unseen, unheard, unloved and I understood in witnessing the intimacy of my connection with Johnny, her own desperate desire to be loved had driven her to destroy ours. I trusted Johnny and I were stronger than her malevolence and I prayed I had not lost him by running from him. In surrendering to a flood of compassion for Clarissa, my heart expanded, and I was able to access the imaginal realm, the place where Johnny had met me so often before. I called to him and though he did not come to me, I believed he could feel my presence, the pulse of my heart through the realms, willing him to return to me. I stayed in that space for hours, present with nothing but my heart and his, aware only of our love, and I called him home, to me and our love.

*From the shadows he walked into my arms, shrouded by*
*a veil of darkness, his soul siphoned of light.*

# CHAPTER 23

# Purification

His eyes were ghostly, his face pale and splattered with blood which caked into the creases that formed about his eyes and in the furrow of his brow. This was not the face of the man I had held in my arms that day. The man I had danced with in the rain had died. The man before me was broken. The essence of his being had been destroyed, the light of his soul eradicated.

Gently, I took his hand, for I did not want him to run from me.

Carefully, I walked him to the river, for I did not want him to fall.

Tenderly, I undressed him, for I loved him beyond the layers of his story.

Lovingly, I guided him into the waters, for I trusted her to cleanse him.

Gracefully, I washed him, my hands reaching into the depths of his soul, touching all that was traumatised and bruised, alchemising it to love and creating space for his light to return.

Instinctively, I traced my fingers around his lips and demanded his eyes. I knew in our union he would remember his truth, the goodness and divinity that resided within, masked by the darkness he believed himself to be.

Tentatively, I drew his lips to mine, for I did not know the way, but as he felt the quiver of my lips on his, the veil lifted, and he rose to meet me. The man I knew and loved returned. He kissed me gently as the waters gushed around our legs and I gasped as my body responded to his with a longing to be one with him.

Gently, he took my hand, for he did not want me to run from him.

Carefully, he walked me from the river, for he did not want me to fall.

Tenderly, he undressed me, for he loved me beyond the layers of my story.

Lovingly, he guided me onto the softness of the blanket by the fire, for he trusted her to warm me.

Gracefully, he stroked the tenderness of my body, his hands reaching into the depths of my soul, touching all that was shamed and scared, alchemising it to love and creating space for my light to return.

Instinctively, he traced his fingers around my lips, and they spoke a thousand words, across time and space, that landed in my heart and tore me open so that nothing lay between us.

Tentatively, he drew my lips to his and I surrendered all I was to him and trusted him to show me the way, to guide my maiden into woman.

And then, we were one, connected in a love that extended beyond the physical experience of our bodies entwined. Nothing existed but the sensation of his body bound to mine and the threads of our souls weaving an exquisite tapestry of pleasure, bliss and rapture, a surrendering to an endless expansion into everything. He was me and I was him. Our souls as one flew through higher dimensions in pure ecstasy.

Across the realms, the crow cawed and once again tore through us and the intimacy of our union. He pulled away from me.

'I'm sorry, MG, I should not have touched you. I should never have taken your purity, your goodness. I'm so sorry.'

I held him, shaken and confused.

'You didn't take anything from me, Johnny. I gave myself to you as you gave yourself to me. That was the purity, the only truth, Johnny. Didn't you feel it, too?' I asked, distraught.

The fear that what we had shared was not real to him fuelled the instinct to pull away and close my heart to him again. But I could not do that to him. I could not do that to me. Not again. I would not abandon my heart. I would not abandon him. I sobbed as his eyes faded beneath the veil of darkness.

'Johnny, come back, please!' I begged as I clawed at the rawness of his chest. 'I'm here, Johnny. I promise I won't leave you. I love you, Johnny, please come back to me.'

I pulled at his face, desperately forcing him to look at me, but his eyes were devoid of the love and passion that had ignited them only minutes before.

My soul whispered, her presence an antidote to the waves of fear terrorising me.

*Stay with him.*
*Hold him as he descends.*
*Hold him as he rises.*
*Be the love that tends his soul.*

'She told me you ran away because I was not good enough for you, that I would never be good enough for you until I freed myself from my family. I was confused, because I knew I was enough for you. You showed me when we were dancing that I was everything to you. I felt it and I knew it was true. But then you ran away, and when I called you and you didn't stop, I thought I must have imagined being so close to you as we danced, that I must have done something wrong. I thought I'd upset you or hurt you or worse still, dishonoured you, the beautiful you. I would never do that, MG.'

I tasted the saltiness of his torment.

'I could never do that to you. You are my everything,' he murmured, begging my soul to believe him.

I passionately kissed him, hungrily absorbing his pain, drawing it into my being, alchemising it, desperate to assure him that I believed him and in our love.

Determined to reveal his truth, in the hope of my understanding, he gently drew himself from my lips and explained.

'When he hit me across the head with the baseball bat the other night, I knew that was it. I was finally done with him and all of it. And in being free from them, I realised that I could be with you, that you were the one I was meant to share my life with. I came here with Nate because I wanted to see you, be with you and when you came up behind me and put your hands over my eyes, I was sure that you felt it, too. And then we danced, and it was crazy, magical and I'd never felt that before. I didn't know I could feel like that in this life. I don't have words for it, but you showed me what was possible, and that was all I wanted, to share that with you forever. But when she said you had run because I wasn't good enough for you, I doubted it all because I've never seen myself as good enough for you. Because you are pure, and I am tainted. I've feared from the first moment I laid eyes on you that night at St Christopher's that I would ruin you. It was the weirdest thing. I knew you even though I had never met you and I loved you then and I love you now. And I have stayed away from you, in this way, because I feared all the bad that I carry within me would defile your goodness. I made myself ignore this insane desire I had to hold you and kiss you and make love to you just like this and so I forced myself to see you as a little sister, to protect and tease. I could still love you, but it was safer that way. But I couldn't ignore it once we danced because you showed me you knew it, too, that you loved me and wanted to love me like this, to be with me. You showed me all that I am and all that I can be.'

He turned away, ashamed and unable to face me, until I drew his face back to mine and demanded his presence.

'Johnny, I see only you, the essence within. *He* is who I know, *he* is who I love.'

'How could you possibly love me when you know what I have done?'

'Because I love you, Johnny, all of you, without condition.'

My lips brushed his gently, my fingers stroked the beauty of his face. There was nothing but love.

'Oh Johnny, you've taken me to the edge of all I knew love could be and forced me beyond it, breaking my heart over and over again, demanding I become more. More love, more true, more divine, all because of you.'

He softened, his lips meeting mine, receiving my love, craving my love.

'She followed me down here to the river and told me she understood because you had never thought she was good enough, either, and that I was unworthy of you because of my family. I was so confused and stupidly believed her. Then she pulled out these tarot cards, telling me there was a message wanting to come through for me. She pulled three cards and told me one was about family, another death and the third spoke of freedom and the light. She asked me who was the light and I told her it was you. She said that my freedom lay with you, but it had to come from cutting off my family and death. I honestly didn't understand what she meant. The only thing I really heard clearly was my freedom lay with you and she must have picked up on this. She just went on about the only way you would ever see me as good enough for you would be if I was free from my father. And the only way I would ever be free was to get his approval and prove I was a man. She asked me what he wanted me to do to prove I was a man to him and when I said "murder", she nodded her head and said something like "Of course, that's why the death card is there … I think you know what you have to do, Johnny, if you want her back." And I didn't even question it. It was like something took over me, possessed me, and I took Nate's car and …'

I was so enraged with her for her malevolence, him for his stupidity and myself for leaving him as easy prey for her malicious game. He met my fury with his own.

'You were the one who ran away from me and messed with my head. You danced with me like a lover and took me some place where everything was perfect and I thought it was real. But then you left me and I thought I must have imagined it all, must have pretended it was real because I wanted it to be real. I was so confused, MG. I didn't know what to do or think, and I just had to be done with it. I can't keep living like this and I believed once it was done, you and I might be more than just a fantasy, that maybe you would finally see me as worthy of your love.'

'You were always worthy of my love. You've always had my love, Johnny. I'm so sorry I confused you and hurt you so much. But why didn't you just stop? Surely you realised between here and the city that there was another way, that it didn't have to be like this?' I sobbed.

'Because she came with me,' he declared bluntly.

'She didn't!' I cried. 'She didn't go with you, Johnny. She was here the whole time. She spoke to Nate and told him what had happened.'

He stared at me aghast and shook his head.

'No, MG, she was there with me. I could hear her the whole time telling me that I knew what I had to do, that there was only one way. That you would never love me if I didn't finish it once and for all. She just kept saying it over and over and over.'

'Johnny, she wasn't there!' I cried in frustration and fear.

'But she was, MG. She was in my head the whole time, even when I went to Frank and told him I'd do it, that I'd kill the witness for him. She was telling me to do it, that it was the only way. She kept whispering to me, *do it, do it.* And Frank was only too willing. He drove to the guy's house, telling me he had it all planned. But instead of him pulling the trigger, I would do it. I didn't want to, MG, but I truly believed it was the only way I would be free, and then you would love me as I love you. I stood there as Frank pulled this guy out of bed and threatened him to stay silent and mocked him when he wet himself. I just stood there, watching it all like it was a movie, not really aware that I was part of it. And then I heard him say, "Shoot the fucker!" and I heard her say, "Do it, Johnny, shoot him, shoot him. Jimmy will be proud of you." And something about that, about *him* being proud of me, snapped me out of it. I didn't want him to be proud of me, because if he was, then it meant I was like him, and there is something I want even more than you, MG, and that is to be nothing like him.'

He paused, took a deep breath and looked at me, determined to own his truth.

'I turned the gun from that poor guy and looked across the room at Frank. He reminded me so much of Jimmy. I hated him, and the hatred in me compelled me to shoot. And I did. I shot Frank and blood went everywhere, all over me, all over the room. He fell to the ground, and I ran. I don't know if I killed him or not, MG. I think I killed him. I think he's dead and I did it.'

*Nothing But Love.*

I drew his distraught face to mine and whispered gently to the depths of his soul.

'It's okay, my love. It's okay, Johnny. It's okay… '

I held him and stroked him as his body trembled in shock, soothing him, wiping away his tears. In truth, I didn't know what to do next because I was so far out of my depth. All I could hear above the erratic throbbing of his heart was the calming wisdom of my soul. *Trust in your love. It is enough.* But my gentle loving caress was not enough. His body trembles turned to spasms and his sobs to howls which pierced the silence of the night and activated something deep within me.

*Was it love or fear that awakened her?*
*I did not know. I have never known.*

I surrendered to *her* as she wound her way from the darkest corners of my womb through my core and to my heart. *She* obliterated the fear encircling it and her fullness erupted, pulling his eyes to mine, commanding he stay in my presence as I straddled him, my nakedness ripe. I braced myself, gripping the broad musculature of his bare shoulders and my lips enveloped his. My passion demanded he meet me, and I drew his trauma into the fierceness of my desire and my longing for him. I moaned in exquisite ecstasy as his agony penetrated me, tearing through the core of my woman. I ached for more from him, demanded more from him and I took more from him, drawing more of his pain, more of his sorrow, his anguish, his shame, hatred and guilt. I opened to receive more of his everything and arched my body, rhythmically spasming, as I unapologetically released to the darkness of the night sky stars, the heavens and the cosmos. Over and over again, all that I drew from him, pleasure and pain erupted from my woman. I would not stop. I could not stop. Like a wild beast hungrily devouring, I took from him until there was nothing more to release, until he was cleansed of the darkness that shrouded his light.

*Was it love or fear that drove her?*
*I did not know. I have never known.*

'MG, come back. MG, please don't leave me,' he pleaded as his lips caressed my face, his heart and eyes searching to find me.

But I did not understand, because I had not left him. I was her and she was me, yet I had become engulfed by her potency and Johnny had lost me. I held his face in my hands, took a deep breath and assured him.

'I'm here, Johnny, I'm here. I am *her* and *she* is me. I never left you. I will never leave you again.'

He pulled me to his chest, clinging to me, sobbing, but this time his grief came from love, pure love, and I welcomed the gentleness. He brought his lips to mine, ever so lightly, inviting me to become one with him again. Taking me by the hand, he guided me into the van and lay me down on the bed. Slowly, tenderly, he made love to me. His fingers danced across the breadth of my body, his lips tantalised every inch of my skin and stimulated every aspect of my being. The shadows encumbering my essence magically melted, and the potency of love within me exploded, becoming one with the love of all that is. Together, we explored the realms of here and there, entwined through all time and space, neither here nor there, our story forever mapped in the celestial masterpiece.

Sheathed in love, I surrendered to sleep with the gentle touch of his fingers dancing across the naked crest of my spine, the reverent trace of his lips down my back, seven sacred kisses forever embedded in my soul.

*I remember nothing else. Nothing else existed but our love.*

# CHAPTER 24

# Into My Arms

Was it the cawing of the crow that woke me?

Was it the gurgling of the river, her edge rising with the awakening sun?

Was it the distant crunching of gravel beneath car tyres?

Was it the howling of the wind that shook the van?

Was it the icy coldness that raced through my veins and sent a shiver through my spine?

I woke unsure if I was here or there.

I woke aware of everything and nothing.

I woke knowing what I did not want to know.

I reached for him, but he was not there. The weight of his jacket anchoring me to the mattress.

The crow's caw demanded I move.

The river's gurgle demanded I move.

The gravel's crunch demanded I move.

The wind's howl demanded I move.

The icy coldness paralysed my body and demanded I stay.

I would not move. I could not move. But nothing could immobilise the guttural howl that tore through me, piercing the dawn and compelling me to rise.

Outside the van, the sudden stillness suffocated me. I could not breathe as I scanned the scene. The remnants of a fire, a stool, a bottle of whiskey beside the stool, a half empty glass on top of the stool, my journal beneath the glass on the stool. A gust of leaves blew across the grass, disrupting the sickeningly suffocating stillness, callously reminding me that it was not a static scene. I gasped as my breath returned with ferocity and jolted my head up, forcing my eyes to see beyond the foreground to what I did not want to see. What I would never unsee.

There was a tree, above a rock, beside the river.

Nailed to the tree, above the rock, beside the river, was a piece of paper.

SHE KEEPS THE JACKET!

Hanging from the tree, above the rock, beside the river, was Johnny. His body swung in the breeze. His body swung in the breeze. His body swung in the breeze.

Johnny swung in the breeze from a tree, above a rock, beside a river, obliterating my heart and violating my soul. He bore life and his life had held me just before. Before, I slept, and now he was without life and the rope around his neck held him and nothing held me as I stumbled to the ground.

*I should have held him.*
*I should have never let him go.*
*I must hold him.*
*I must never let him go.*

I ran to him and then Nate was running to him, too. And then there were screams, primal, tortured screams, but I do not know where they came from. And then Nate cut the rope, but I do not know how he cut the rope. And then the body went thump. Nate could not hold him, and Johnny's body went thump on the rock beneath the tree, beside the river.

*I should have held him.*
*I should have never let him go.*
*I must hold him.*
*I must never let him go.*

I drew him into my arms. He was cold and blue and hard. I touched his face. It was hard and cold and blue. I kissed his lips. They were blue and cold and hard. I drew him into my arms and there was chaos and screaming and crying and arguing, but I would not let them take him from me. I drew him into my arms, desperate to meld into one again so we may never be separate. I would not let them take him from me.

They did not know, all those making noise in trying to take him from me. They did not know that we were one, that we could not be separate. Johnny knew and I knew that we were one, but not them. They could never know, never understand how we had been one. But if he was gone, then only I knew. I was the only one who held our secret. Only I knew the bond we shared, the ecstasy we created, the magic we made. Only I knew the potency of our love.

*What if it wasn't real? What if it never happened? What if it was a dream? How could he do this after that? Maybe this is all a dream and he's not cold and hard and blue in my arms.*

I squeezed him hard. I punched him hard. I thumped him hard to see if it was real. It was real, but was our love real?

*How could he be hard and blue and cold in my arms if he loved me? How could he leave me if he loved me? How could he leave me if my love was enough? He would not be blue and cold and hard in my arms if my love was enough.*

Even though I did not want to believe it, I could not deny he was gone and that my love had failed him. Johnny Triboni, the pulse of my heart, the love of my life, the mate of my soul, was dead in my arms, no breath, no heartbeat, no essence pulsating through his body.

*From my arms, they took him. From my soul, they took me.*

Part
Three

# CHAPTER 25

# More Than Words

Thunderous clouds veiled the sun as the paramedics finally prized him from my arms. Nate wrapped his arms around me, gently, ever so gently, guiding me into the van, away from the prying eyes of vultures mesmerized by the horrific scene. I sat on the bed. The bed that held the memory of our love, the intimacy of our love. Nate wrapped a blanket around me before seeing the jacket, Johnny's leather jacket, lying atop the tangled sheets. Reverently, he draped it over my shoulders. I shuddered as his smell, the tobacco mixed with aftershave and hair cream, activated the memory of who he was before he was a dead body in my arms. Frozen, I stared into the void, seeking only for the nothingness to absorb me, to free me from the present. Yet I did not want the past where I had failed so completely, nor the future where I had to live with myself and without him. I wanted nothing but him and the nothingness beckoned me, implored me to get lost in it and, perhaps, I would find him there, lost in the nothingness, too.

Nate placed a glass of whiskey in my hand and sat beside me. Words were inept, for so much had to be said, but pointless because they would make no difference. The silence was an empty portal of agony and despair that engulfed us and hungrily devoured Nate's sobs. From the depths of his soul, he wept for his best friend and all that was lost. His anguish crushed my already shattered heart, but I could not give him anything because there was nothing in me to give. All had been taken. The time would come when we would have to talk, to seek to understand the incomprehensible, but for now, we sat as shadows of who we were mere hours before, in the silence of shock.

Caellach came. I don't know how he knew to come, but he was there, and he took me home into the loving embrace of Clara. She held me in the arms of the mother as I broke and cried and rocked and howled until I slept in pure exhaustion. Caellach drove Nate home to the reservation and stood with his arm around him as he broke the news to Madame Rosaline and his mom, in turn, breaking their hearts. Nate was a pillar of strength. He held them, as he had me, accessing the power of the most Divine Masculine. I remain awed by the man he rose into that day, despite his own heartache. Madame Rosaline asked Caellach to bring her to me and they arrived late in the night. In her arms, torrential waves of grief and guilt poured from me and she held me, despite the enormity of her own pain, without the need for words, the story told through my anguish.

I woke on the lounge, the house in darkness, and crept outside and into the van. I wanted to lie where we had lain. I wanted to feel him as I had felt him. I wanted to be there with him not here by myself. I was alone for the first time since I had awoken alone in this bed almost twenty-four hours before, and my pain was raw. Razors sliced the tenderness of my heart and I cried, drawing the sheets around me, inhaling his scent, longing for him to be in my arms. Tears gently dampened the sheets, but they were different tears now, from a place so deep it could only be accessed when I was alone.

Beneath the shock, confusion, anger and shame was a well of grief unlike any I had experienced before, for I knew grief, having lost Cynthia and Athena. I mourned them, yet their physical absence from my life was tempered by our spiritual connection. This was different. The human loss was crippling. The girl who loved the boy, the girl who gave herself to the boy, the girl who knew that the boy she treasured chose death over her was sad, ever so sad. The pain was brutally deep and raw. I turned to my journal, grasping for a way to articulate my sorrow, but as I drew it from my satchel, I remembered seeing it that morning, before I had seen Johnny hanging from that tree. It was lying on the stool by the fire with the whiskey glass on top of it. Even though it carried the most private musings of my soul, I had not given it another thought. Nate must have put it in my bag at some point, or had I? I shook as I attempted to piece together the missing pieces of a puzzle and suddenly everything became clear. I frantically tore through the pages, searching for the message I knew waited for me.

# CHAPTER 26

# The Underworld

Some*thing* propelled me through the mountains, and I reached the main road as the sun rose.

Some*one* guided me into the city, and I reached St Christopher's as the streetlights dimmed.

Some*where* from the darkness, a voice beckoned me, and I reached into the depths of the subway tunnels, descending into the underbelly.

Some*how,* I knew he was there. I reached for him, welcoming the invisible hand that drew me ever deeper into the pits of hell on the promise of reunion.

A voice claimed my all, body, mind and soul.

*He is here. Come, find what you have lost.*

I rode the subway, staring into the emptiness of the silent carriages, searching for his face. But all I saw were blank faces, the soulless eyes of those who were trapped beneath the façade of who they needed to be to get through just one more day in the game they called life.

My desperate longing to find him opened me to everyone and everything. I witnessed the torment of souls, the festering of wounds and the entities that attached to their energy fields, torturing their desire for peace and happiness. I could not turn away as the shadows that stained their souls sought to meld with the magnetism of my light. They revealed their stories and the threads of despair, horror, trauma, wrath, agony and vengefulness danced before my eyes. Their inner demons, desperate to be seen and freed, were held hostage, suppressed by the distractions of life, work, alcohol, drugs, sex and whatever it took to avoid facing the pain of the past. They begged me to take them, to absorb them into my fields, my light a welcome refuge from the darkness of the souls they inhabited. But I held my boundary, despite the collective dagger striking my edges. *It's not yours,* the invisible voice whispered, and I scanned the carriage, searching for the owner of the voice. Then I saw it, at the other end of the carriage, a shadowed apparition. Its eyes were black pools that fixated on me. A potent eerie presence commanded my focus, demanding I be drawn into its vortex to come face to face with it. I could not resist its pull and, on entering its sphere, a ghostly voice encircled me.

*You don't deserve light. You are bad. Your love is poison. Your love killed Johnny.*

A second haunting voice joined the chant.

*You don't deserve light. You are bad. Your love is poison. Your love killed Johnny.*

A choir of voices spun through my head, swirling manically.

*You don't deserve light. You are bad. Your love is poison. Your love killed Johnny.*
*You don't deserve light. You are bad. Your love is poison. Your love killed Johnny.*
*You don't deserve light. You are bad. Your love is poison. Your love killed Johnny.*

The echoes systematically penetrated my body and mind. I was powerless to the viciousness of its attack, its potency destroying my armour and forcing me to claim its shadowed presence. I did not want to see it, hear it, know it or own it. But I had no choice and all I could hear was its truth. I shuddered as it infiltrated the purity of my light. Its eyes did not leave mine. It was without emotion. There was a job to be done and it was unapologetic in its delivery. I hated it for forcing itself upon me, but I loved it for the pain it caused me. My love killed Johnny. My love was poison. I am bad. I do not deserve the light. I believed it and wanted to feel the pain of the trauma I had caused Johnny. I wanted to be punished. *Who was I to think I could heal Johnny? Who was I to think my love was of light? Who was I to think I could save*

*Johnny's soul from the pits of hell? Who was I to think I could play God?*

I had misused my power and I deserved to be punished.

'Punish me!' I screamed into the vortex … 'Punish me for killing Johnny!'

But it did not flinch. It did not waver in its hold on me, forcing me to own the deluge of sludge that had settled upon my soul. And then it drew a knife. I willed it to pierce my heart, to end the pain it inflicted upon me, but it did not touch me. Instead, it sliced the energy that held us as one and the vortex was obliterated, releasing me from its shadowy hold. A waterfall of light flooded me as I curled into a ball on the seat at the rear of the carriage and I surrendered to sleep or death. I did not know, nor did I care.

I woke with a start, terror tearing through me as I battled confusion. I knew not where I was nor how I had got there. I only knew the devastating ache of loss and the brutal remembering that Johnny was gone and I had to find him. If I found him, it would not be true. He would still be alive and my love would not have killed him. I raced from the carriage as it pulled into the next station and determinedly roamed from platform to platform, train to train, station to station, moving ever deeper into the depths of the city's underbelly in search of Johnny, for I knew he waited for me somewhere. But was it too late? Had I lost him in this vile pool of darkness forever?

In my devastation, I begged for him to find me. Instead, the shadowed phantom descended onto the platform before me, its eyes once again transfixing me and luring me into its vortex, which was oddly warm and safe. Held by the darkness, it forced me to remember that which I did not want to remember, and fragmented images penetrated my mind's eye. A woman, face down in a river, hands tied behind her back. A little girl roaming alone in the snow. A monstrous man lying on top of a young woman. Three dead women hanging from a tree side by side on a mountain. Short, sharp snippets of memories, foreign to my conscious mind, yet familiar to my soul, tearing me open and exposing me to the darkest trauma of my past. I was brutally forced to see those memories I had turned away from in this life. Those I had hidden in the vault of my soul. But now, I was in the darkness of that vault. I could not run and hide any longer. The blue grey face of Mo Mo, lying dead in a field. Crows surrounding her, squawking hysterically. Were they mourning the loss of one of their own, the divine dark warrior? Or were they preparing to devour her, to gorge her soulless eyes, pick at her marbling flesh? They terrified me, the caw hauntingly familiar. Friend or foe, I did not know then or now. I wanted to reach for her, save her from them, but I couldn't get to her and no matter how hard I tried, I remained trapped in the vortex, a prisoner to my past, its intensity amplifying the more I sought to escape. It did not falter, eyes demanding my presence stay with the excruciating agony of witnessing my beloved Mo Mo dead and to feel it in its fullness. Futilely, I screamed in frustration because I wanted to save her from the crows, from those who threatened to violate her sacredness and feed off her fading light. Yet I was paralysed, rendered helpless by a sickening truth held in the core of my heart. *My Mo Mo was dead because my love was not enough to save her.* I descended into despair as a torrent of horrendous thoughts battered my stricken heart and tore shreds from my soul.

*She had rescued me, but I could not rescue her.*
*Her loved saved me, but my love was not enough to save her.*
*It's my fault.*

It tore through my core. I screamed in terror. I begged to be released from its vicious claws, to be freed from the vortex. I could not take any more. I felt the coldness of death dancing at my edges, but still it would not release me. Wave after wave of energy shook my body, and when I knew I could take no more, a sacred sword sliced open another portal. I saw Johnny hanging from the tree, his body swaying in the breeze, the contortion of his hands, the fixation of his jaw … The dark empty pools of his eyes transfixed me, and a primal howl released from my hell into the ethers.

*I could not rescue him.*
*I loved him, but my love was not enough to save him.*
*It's my fault.*

Cynthia and Johnny had left me because my love was not enough to keep them here with me. They had died because of me and the light I had always believed shone so brightly for others faded. It was my fault. I descended further into the darkness, into the hell I deserved for failing those I loved. I hungrily drank in the shame and guilt, but the energy within the vortex suddenly shifted, refusing to allow me to wallow in self-pity.

Across the void, an intensity commanded my focus, a dark mysterious energy swirled as a mist, until it took form as an exquisite Dark Goddess, whom I remembered, where from I was not sure. She offered me a rose, luring me towards her. As I moved closer, inching in trust, *her* form altered, and *his* eyes bore into mine with renewed intensity and demanded I remember him. He did not move yet the luminance radiating from him was overwhelming, somehow more potent because of the darkness he held and love, like I had not experienced before, wove its way towards me. It teased open my heart, its purity dancing delicately across my soul, willing me to release all that was false, all that was from fear, all that was of ego and shrouded my soul. I could not resist as he penetrated my being and silently beckoned me to breathe ever deeper in union with *him*, graciously releasing all I was not, over and over, until I became so light, there was no room for darkened thoughts. An explosion of love moved through every cell of my body, bringing light to the darkness, calm to the chaos, peace to the anguish.

*His* energy was nothing I had experienced before. A potent expression of love borne of the heights of light and the depths of dark. As it enveloped me, I knew only peace and a beam of light radiated from him, striking my third eye and opening my vision, allowing me to see an exquisite vastness, the limitlessness of both Cynthia and Johnny's souls that extended so far beyond their human form and the human experience I shared with each of them. I witnessed their life, a pulsating energetic masterpiece, and was humbled by the beauty of the golden luminous threads that wove through the later stages of this life experience for both of them. I understood that my soul had created a thread in their exquisite tapestry, filled with so many threads, so many stories, so many soul contracts. And I *knew* I was not responsible for their deaths, for they were so much more than the relationship that they shared with me. I wept with the knowledge that my love had been enough. I had not failed them. In truth, my love had been a gift to them. It was my love that had allowed them to walk the path their soul called them to, even if that path had caused me heartbreak. Grace moved through me, allowing me to receive the gift of my heartbreak, remembering that at the core of every wound resides the light of truth that liberates the soul over and over and over again.

I stared across the vortex to the energy that held me through it all. I did not understand *him. Was it he or she? Was it angel or devil? Was it light or dark? Was it mine or outside me? Was it real or imagined*? It was beyond definition. It was the Divine and I fell to my knees in reverence of its most exquisite beauty that shone, alchemising my darkness to light. *He* reached out and I rose to take his hand, becoming one with him and infinitely trusting in him. *Go home,* was all I heard before falling. In allowing him to hold me, I surrendered and fell deeper and deeper into nothingness. There was no thing but me and the huge expanse of nothingness. As I dropped ever further into it, I became it and it spread through me, dissolving my body from form and I was but a mist, a stream of light energy floating through the darkness. For there was no light, only darkness, but I was not afraid because I knew I was safe in the embrace of love that held me, yet allowed me the freedom to expand into the nothingness. The purity of love wove through me, and I became the everything. I touched the sides of all that was and a surge tore through me, seeking to explode through the darkness which suddenly felt like it was restricting me. I had outgrown the vastness of the nothingness, and I remembered there was more beyond the darkness and a longing stirred in me, a longing that was so familiar. I felt pain move through my ever-expanding form. Waves of pain moved through me as the desire for more drove me to push and then surrender before pushing again. As the waves of longing intensified, I roared, stretching and bursting through the darkness of nothingness into the light of the new world.

I shielded my eyes from the blinding light and attempted to regather the tethers of my soul that felt extraordinarily vulnerable and raw, threads of my soul reluctant to be here. Or was it that they did not want to bear witness to what the light was about to illuminate in the darkness? I felt *his* presence again calling to me, and in trust I moved to the edge of the platform, near to where he stood on the subway tracks. Illuminated in light, he mysteriously transformed into a woman who was gentle and loving. I knew her as Mother Mary, the safe harbour for the troubled soul. She held a baby wrapped in a red shawl. I paused and her eyes penetrated mine, commanding I go to *her*, to remember her.

I knew her, the infant she held in his arms. Some place within me had never forgotten the moment I emerged from the darkness of the womb into the light of my life. Now I was being called to see her fully, her innocence, her beauty, her trauma and pain. I could not move, paralysed by the terror of reliving her trauma and feeling her pain. I did not need to see it in her eyes to feel it bursting from her tiny broken heart, because I knew within the deepest recesses of my own heart, determinedly hiding it so no one would ever know, that Marigold— the golden one—was in truth, brutally wounded and broken at her core.

*Take her away! Take her away!* I implored her, the terror rising with increasing ferocity. But she knelt on one knee and carefully placed her, the newborn baby wrapped in the red shawl, onto the tracks and turning to me she whispered, 'Claim her!' Then she turned and walked away before dissolving into the invisible realms. I couldn't believe she left her for she had held her in love, and she believed she was safe. I couldn't believe she left me, for she had held me in love, and I believed I was safe.

Now she was alone. There was no love, and she was not safe.

Now I was alone. There was no love, and I was not safe.

I screeched into the ethers. *Please don't leave me. Please don't leave me. Please don't leave me.* I fell to my knees, my legs spread apart as I rocked back and forth, moaning in excruciating pain, my mouth frothing as I tore at the roots of my hair in madness. *Come back. Come back. Please come back for me!* I knew nobody was coming for me and nobody was coming for *her*. I begged Cynthia and Athena to come, to go to her, to save her, to pick her up and make her feel safe, make her feel that she was enough, make her feel that she was loved, make her feel that she was the most magical, mystical fairy baby ever born.

But they didn't come, not this time.

There was only her and me and no one else to save us.

A spark ignited at the base of my spine and surged like a raging serpent through my body. It propelled me to dive from the platform onto the tracks and scoop her into my arms. I cradled her to my chest, connecting her to my heart, assuring her that she was loved, that she was safe, that she was enough. I stroked the milky softness of her cheek and she gazed lovingly into my eyes, and I knew her, and she knew me. I was her and she was me. I promised her I would never abandon her or hide her away in the brokenness of my heart. As I held her to my heart and she held me in her eyes, the broken pieces of my heart melded together, a golden scar intricately woven into my core. Immersed in love, I did not notice the vibration of the tracks, nor the wind gushing through the tunnel signalling the approaching train, nor the screams of the people waiting on the platform. But through the ethers, I heard Johnny call to me, *MG, MG*, and I snapped from my tranced state. My eyes tore about, wildly trying to make sense of the scene and his voice, which again beckoned me. *MG, I'm here. I'm here, look up.* I saw him there, standing on the stairs, the light from the outside world illuminating him. His own light blazed with such radiance that I began to sob. He had made it. He had made it through to the other side. From the darkness of his hell, he had found his way back to the light.

I glanced at the babe in my arms, but she was gone and all that remained was the red shawl in which she had been so lovingly wrapped. My eyes darted about, desperate to find her. I promised I would not leave her. I drew the shawl to my face and inhaled hungrily. Her smell, the beat of her heart, the softness of her skin and the sweet whistle of her breath imprinted on my soul and I heard her whisper, *I am within you. I always have been. I always will be.* I quickly drew myself onto the platform, just as the train raced into the station, knowing she was with me, always. Ignoring the hysteria I had ignited about me, I flew to the stairs where Johnny reached out his hand, silently inviting me to follow him to the light.

*I surrendered and he took me home.*

# CHAPTER 27

# Divine Darkness

Asleep at the side entrance to St Christopher's, Caellach found me as the sun rose. It was four days after I left in search of Johnny, still wearing his leather jacket and covered by a red shawl. Cradled in Caellach's arms, he soothed my confusion with gentle reassurance that, 'I was grand, all would be grand.'

I was not aware of anything that had transpired during my absence, and he did not ask me for details. He took me inside where Madame Rosaline, Aunt Maeve and Sacnite were overcome with relief to see me. They were not surprised by my return. In their wisdom, they trusted in my journey and in my return home when it was time. I murmured to Madame Rosaline through the fogginess of my mind, 'I found him, and he showed me the way out. I went into the dark and he showed me the way back.'

In the moment, I did not understand my words, nor the potency of the story contained within them. To most, they would be but the mutterings of madness. Perhaps they were, for there is a fine line between sanity and insanity, especially for those who move between realms. Yet those surrounding me did not doubt the truth in my words, understanding the enormity of the transformative journey I had undertaken. They tended to me with great care, offering me sips of water, wrapping me in warm blankets and holding me just tightly enough to assure me I was held without suffocating me. Sacnite prepared a warm drink with the herbs, remedies and potions she had brought with her. With each sip of the magical brew, I was ever so gently brought out of my confusion, my nervous system resetting from the shock and my energy fields returning from the underworld. I blinked my eyes, slowly readjusting my perspective and connection to the earthly realm, before once again closing them to connect with my breath, choosing to become fully embodied once more. As the last threads of my being returned to my body, I burst into tears as the intensity of my experience struck my human consciousness and flashes of what had transpired poured into my mind. Caellach and Aunt Maeve attempted to piece together the missing days and nights, a blurred timeless void, splattered with images of Cynthia dead in the field, Johnny hanging from the tree and my infant self abandoned on the rail tracks. I stared into space and, too fragile to hold it alone, words purged from me as a jumbled mess, a release that freed me.

'I had to find him … Johnny. I had to find Johnny. I knew he would be in the dark, so I had to go into the dark to find him and something took me deep down into the subway, way down into the yukkiest, the murkiest parts. I knew he would be there, and he was. Not to start with, I had to search for him, so I did. I didn't stop until I found him, and I did, in the end. But he was no longer in the dark then. He was on the stairs, making his way back up onto the street, up into the light. He called out to me when I was on the track. I was stuck there, holding her, the baby, the tiny newborn baby, the one who had been left there, all by herself. I couldn't leave her there all alone, so I jumped onto the tracks to save her, and I held her so close to me, so she knew that she was loved, that she was worth keeping, that she hadn't done anything wrong to be left there all alone. I told her that she was perfect, that she was more than enough, that she was loved, and her tiny little heart raced at a terrifying pace, but once she looked into my eyes and felt my love, it settled and came into one with mine. And we were like that, just staring into each other's eyes, until I felt a train coming towards us on the track, but I could not leave her. I would not leave her again. I promised I would never abandon her, just like I'd promised Johnny that I would always be there for him. And I would have stayed on that track with her in my arms, but I heard a voice calling to me, calling *MG* and only Johnny called me that. I followed the voice and saw him standing on the stairs, saturated in light and he told me to follow him, and the baby was gone, but she told me she was within me so I could never lose her. You know, I can still feel her within me now. For as long as I can remember, something has been missing inside me, inside my heart. I never really knew what it was, just this little hole, but I think

I ignored it because I have always had so much love around me that I had no right to feel empty inside.'

The faces of those surrounding me were strewn with tears. Not tears of pity or sorrow, no, they were tears of love, for these people, my people, understood me and the depth of healing that had occurred within me.

'It's strange, but then I guess it's not, because I know spirit works in mysterious ways, but I went into the darkness to find Johnny, and somehow, I found the real Marigold. I didn't find her in the light. She was there, in the darkness, waiting for me to have the courage to find her.'

I breathed deeply and released my need to understand any more at this stage, trusting insights and awareness would come around what had transpired in the tunnels of the subway in the weeks, months and years ahead.

Madame Rosaline looked heavy with sorrow, for not only had she held vigil for the last few days awaiting my return, but she was also deeply grieving for Johnny and my heart ached for the loss of the man she saw as a son.

'I'm sorry for the stress I caused by leaving. I know it's made it harder for you, but I promised I would be there for him, wherever he went. I know he made it back out of the darkness and to the light and he was so beautiful, flooded in golden light as he stood on the stairs. It was him, Johnny Triboni, the most blinding light in the darkness, the light that saved my soul from becoming stuck in my own hell.'

Madame Rosaline sobbed, finally able to allow the brokenness of her heart to weep.

'Thank you for holding him, for being there for him, for loving him. I believe you, I really do, because I could not feel him these last few days and then this morning, before the sun had risen, as I stoked the fire, I felt him standing behind me and I heard a whisper, *Mother*. I convinced myself my mind was playing tricks, wishful thinking induced by exhaustion, but now I know it was him for sure and I know he loved me as a mother. That was all I ever wanted to be to him … so he knew the love of mother. Thank you, my sweet girl, for your courage in going to the places that none of us ever want to go and very few are able. Queen of the Light meets Queen of the Dark!'

I smiled, but I was not sure about my becoming Queen of the Dark. She scared me.

The intensity of the mood shifted. A human normality returned when I declared I was ravenous. As Sacnite and Rosaline rose to the kitchen to prepare breakfast, Caellach and Aunt Maeve helped me up the stairs. I allowed Aunt Maeve to undress me in the bathroom and tenderly wash me with a soap Sacnite had blended in preparation for my return, and the deep energetic cleanse that would be required. Shocked by the endless waterfall of filthy water that poured down the drain, I tensed as I thought of what had penetrated and attached to me during my time in the underworld. Aunt Maeve sensed my tension and intuiting my thoughts, as she so often had before, she appeased my worries.

'All will be well, my precious. Sacnite and I will take care of everything and only the gifts you received in the darkness shall remain with you.'

I could have fallen asleep under the cleansing waters while her fingers ever so lovingly dissolved the tension in my body, mind and soul, allowing the integration of these gifts. Though, it would take years, decades, perhaps even lifetimes, for the integration to be complete.

Wrapped in a robe, with my hair carefully braided, I sat before the fireplace and hungrily devoured a bowl of porridge, two slices of soda bread with lashings of butter and another cup of Sacnite's magical brew. A companionable silence flooded the room as we ate, the physical and emotional demand of the last few days finally landing. I looked about the room into the weary faces of those surrounding me and felt pure love and admiration for each of them. Caellach who had been by my side since the beginning and loved me as big brother and father, the Divine Masculine presence in my life. Aunt Maeve who had become the wise matriarch of our little tribe, always offering a gentle yet firm guiding hand. Madame Rosaline who had become threads of mother, mentor and friend to me since arriving in the city and offered me an anchor through unsteady waters. And finally, Sacnite who brought a calming presence and divine commitment to her service as a healer, medicine woman and shaman. She was deeply connected to the earth and the skies. She was the embodiment of the mystic and reminded me so much of Athena that my love and respect for her extended beyond our few meetings. I thought then of Clara, my surrogate mother, my sister and friend, who had stayed with the children, ever the safe harbour, assuring them that everything would be okay for she had a deep faith in the Divine. She had prayed daily in her own sacred way that I would be found, and Caellach had assured me that he had made the phone call to let her know I had made it home.

They did not make a fuss of me, despite understanding the enormity of my journey through the underworld and my vulnerability as I re-entered this world. In their wisdom, they knew that those who descend into hell and come through it are stronger and wiser because of it.

I stared into the fireplace, the flames sparking provocatively, willing me to see the truth of the dark energy who had held me in the vortex, forcing me to see all I did not want to see, forcing me to remember that which I did not want to remember, forcing me to feel that which I did not want to feel.

*Was it the Devil?* It was dark, but it did not radiate fear. Quite the contrary, it made me feel safe, loved and courageous enough to lean into the terror that sought to cripple me, had crippled me for so long.

*Was it the Dark God?* The goodness held in darkness, which I had begun to dance with in my feminine but never encountered in my masculine?

*Was the Devil the Dark God?* He who had been misunderstood, condemned, demonised and thus feared?

I did not know the answer and I did not know if I was to trust this energy, regardless of name, but it intrigued me and lingered within me, compelling me to explore it more. Somewhat confused by the heat rising through my body, I looked around to Madame Rosaline. We exchanged a look which made me realise that she knew this energy, the fierce, forceful love of the Dark God, that demanded I open to it, surrender to it, receive it and the gifts it sought to bestow upon me. To begin, I did not want to take what was offered, for it terrified me, but the more I resisted the more it forced me, without saying or doing anything. It was nothing but love that penetrated my energy field and drew me further into the darkness of my own soul, which surprisingly was safe, comforting and nurturing, so I knew it to be love, a deep and dark divine love. A love I had not known. Something within me stirred, a deep desire to experience it again and to know it fully. The confusion overwhelmed me. I silently sought answers from the wisdom of Madame Rosaline, she who understood better than most, the energy of the divine darkness.

> *Can you love the darkness and honour the sacredness of*
> *your light at the same time?*

# CHAPTER 28

# Blood Sister

---

I fell asleep in the healing hands of Sacnite and Aunt Maeve and woke some hours later, bewildered by the midday light that streamed in. Madame Rosaline was seated beside my bed, eyes closed in deep prayer. My stirrings roused her, and her eyes bore into mine, their agony cracking my heart and compelling me to reach out and grab her, begging her to tell me what was wrong.

'Nothing is wrong, and everything is wrong,' she replied forlornly. 'Such is the complexity of life. I know he is gone but he is not gone. Gone from here, yet still here, but somehow that doesn't stop the pain in my aching heart.'

She allowed the tears to roll down her cheeks and shook her head in disbelief.

'I can't believe I lost him, too. He was the son who filled the void of the one I had lost and now he, too, is gone and I'm angry and confused and sad. I'm just so sad!'

Together we sobbed, allowing the deep grief to pour through us without resistance, shame or fear. Like a river, it flowed, allowing a lightness and beautiful, reassuring presence to settle between us.

'The funeral is this afternoon,' she declared matter-of-factly. 'I don't know if I can face them, those people who are calling themselves his family. They were not his family. I don't want to witness the game playing, the big Mafia funeral, the fake tears, the wheeling and dealing. It won't be about Johnny. It'll be all about them. Goldie, you've got to know they're pointing fingers, looking for blame outside of themselves. They're blaming Nate, saying he took him to the festival and gave him drugs. And they're blaming you, saying you put some sort of curse on him. They are blaming you both, because they cannot see how he could have possibly taken his own life. They just cannot see it.'

The sting of blame struck me. Yet did not surprise me. Instinctively,

I knew Clarissa would be conspiring against me.

'Did Nate tell you what happened?' I asked sombrely.

'No, Nate has not spoken. He's been searching for you day and night and will not speak to his mother. Sacnite is worried about him and has gone looking for him to tell him you are home and to prepare him for the funeral. He deserves to be there as his best friend, the only real friend he had before you came along.'

She smiled wearily and I knew I had to tell her exactly what had happened that day and night, all the pieces of the puzzle that led to Johnny hanging from that tree. I had to tell her, so she could stand in that church before all those people, knowing the truth of what had transpired. I had to tell her, so I could stand beside her in that church, knowing someone else knew the whole truth.

'I have to tell you everything, Rosaline,' I began with a serious tone.

Without reservation, I told her everything that had transpired. From Johnny and I dancing in the rain and coming into sacred union in the higher realms, to Clarissa laughing and humiliating me, causing me to run away and leave Johnny in her malevolent hands. I shared how she cast some sort of spell over him, pulling cards and telling him to go to the city because death was the only way to get Jimmy's approval. Tentatively, I told her how Johnny succumbed to Jimmy's demand, telling him he'd murder for him. Yet in the moment, he couldn't shoot the witness and turned the gun on Frank, coming back to me splattered in blood. I stumbled when I came to the next part, for it was personal and yet I felt a need to share with Madame Rosaline.

'I took him into the river and washed away the blood. I cleansed him and then we made love, and it was so beautiful and holy,' I sobbed, despite attempting to maintain my composure. 'But then, well, something came over me and I brought him inside of me again and I drew from him all that was not pure, all that was not of light. I could not stop, and I knew I would not stop until he released into me all that was not divine,'

I paused. Madame Rosaline waited, honouring the sacredness of my story.

'It is so hard to put into words and it sounds wrong in some way, but I took from him all of it, all his pain, his shadow and anything that was evil that had touched his soul. I held him within me, drawing it from him, absorbing it into me, before I released, and I witnessed it being taken back to the light. It was so powerful. Johnny brought me out of it, though I would have kept going, for as long as I needed to, however long it took to free his soul. But he took me by the shoulders and looked me in the eye and I saw only light again. I saw Johnny and I knew his soul was free.'

I looked at her, the shame desperate to wash over me, but her eyes were nothing but pure love and adoration.

'Oh, my girl, my darling girl, I did not know. I did not realise you had shared your sacredness with him.'

'Rosaline, I'm so confused. I don't know if what I did was right or wrong. I followed my heart and allowed that energy to work through me, but I don't know if Johnny wanted it or if I took from him without his permission. But my body knew what to do and he didn't stop me until the end, until all of it was gone, the vile darkness. But then he took his life. Is that my punishment for doing the wrong thing? For taking his power? For misusing my own? Athena always told me if we misuse our power, then it will come back on us three-fold. Johnny killing himself must be punishment. But he made love to me again, after that time, and it did not feel like I had done anything wrong. It was perfect. He made me believe it was perfect, that what we shared was holy, but then he hung himself. I don't understand, Rosaline. Was it punishment?'

'You are exhausted, my girl, and you need to nap again before the funeral. But I will quickly tell you a story that I hope helps you understand the gift you gave to Johnny, and in turn, the gift he activated in you.'

She took a long sip of her tea before explaining.

'Once, long ago, in the ancient times when the feminine was revered for all her powers, including her sexual energy, the Priestesses of the Sacred Temples, the holy women, embodied love. They were a vessel for love, and they expressed it through their sexual energy, allowing it to flow through them and into every crevice of the earth, offering healing and transformation. Woman and men, traumatised soldiers from war or those suffering mysterious ailments would be sent to the holy women for healing. Through intimate union, physical, mental, emotional, spiritual and psychic wounds would be healed through the power of their sexual energy. Just as you did with Johnny, these powerful holy women would draw the pain and trauma from the wounds, cleansing their soul and literally transforming them back to their wholeness, their divinity. These women were revered for their power and valued for the sacred healing gift they offered. Yet, with the rise of the patriarch, *her* power was deemed a threat, and she was demonised and shamed. She was called whore, prostitute, sinner. Yet those of us who reclaim this power will not be shamed. We receive with honour the name of Sacred Prostitute. It is only those who do not understand and fear *her* power that continue to shame her and try to suppress her power. But in you, as in me, she has returned, and her power is a transformative force in this world.'

She smiled with pure adoration in her eyes.

'The path of the sexual healer is not for the faint-hearted, for the outcome of our work may not always be as our egoistic mind would like it to be. But as a channel for divine energy, it is never about our desire, and we must always remember to surrender and allow the divine to work through us and guide the other on their path. I know that you fear what you did for Johnny was not enough, because he took his life. But without you, he would have left with that trauma weighing on his soul. Because you purified his soul, Johnny became whole and reclaimed the light of his soul, allowing him to rise from the darkness of the underworld. And for that, Goldie, I thank you.'

We sank into silence and allowed it to say all that words could not. Finally, I understood Madame Rosaline, the complexity of her relationship with Jimmy and the path of her soul. In turn, I began to understand my own path—my dharma. No longer was I to be she who walked the golden path, shining my light. No, my soul was calling me into my Dark Goddess, she who is courageous enough to walk the path of darkness, to *become* the darkness and transmute all that is not divine within it, so the light may shine ever brighter through it.

Madame Rosaline broke the silence with a weary, melancholic voice.

'I always believed I would be able to bring Jimmy through from his shadows into the light, and when I did, Johnny's life would be different, and he would finally be free. But that never happened. Jimmy's shadows are as active as ever, but at least Johnny is now free and, because of that, so am I. My soul contract with Jimmy Triboni is complete, even if he has not found his way home and remembered who he is. It is no longer mine and I am so very grateful for your part in bringing this to completion for me. So many have judged me over the years for my relationship with Jimmy because they could not understand it, but I know the truth of what it was and was not and this afternoon when I stand in that church, I will hold my head high knowing I, too, am free. I will not hide in shame as they expect. I was a mother to that boy. I will stand in that church to honour both him and me.'

'And I will stand beside you with my head held high, despite what they are saying about me. I now know the truth of my relationship with Johnny. I will not hide in shame as they expect me to. I was his beloved, and I will stand in that church to honour both of us.'

*That's my girls, love whispered through the realms.*

# CHAPTER 29

# The Sacred Circus

Madame Rosaline took my hand, Nate took the other, as we walked up the stairs to the cathedral. In return, I was supporting them with the energy that pulsated through me, declaring I was powerful beyond measure and commanding I claim my sovereignty. On my entrance, glowering eyes of the mourners and spectators turned towards me, yet the only eyes that touched me were those of Johnny when he appeared at the end of the aisle, waiting for me, as a groom would a bride.

*No hiding in the shadows for you!* I could hear him.

I straightened my shoulders, and lovingly swathed Johnny's leather jacket over my long black dress, tilting my chin to command the full presence of my luminance. Johnny held out his hand and beckoned me. *Come, my beauty.* I walked down the aisle, drawn to him, and led those who loved him towards their rightful place in the front pew. Madame Rosaline and Nate followed closely behind me, their support ever present. Aunt Maeve, Sacnite, Clara and Caellach in turn followed them. Many would have expected us to hide in the back, if we dared come at all. I would not be hidden or relegated to the back so those who sought false narratives did not have to confront the truth. They were not strong enough to face the truth that lay beneath the mask of their pitiful charade.

I smiled as I drew closer to him, for his spirit was exquisitely pure and, in that moment, he was as real to me as he had ever been in life. *Nice jacket,* he winked as he escorted me into the front pew on the left side of the aisle. *I saved this for you because you are My Girl, my everything. Please never forget where you belong nor lose the courage to claim your place.* Then he disappeared into the ethers as the chords of the organ began to play the first of many melancholic tunes that took the heaviness of the cathedral to another level. I tuned out into my own bliss as the archbishop, bishops and a gaggle of priests from throughout the city recited prayers and diffused incense over Johnny's coffin. There was not an essence of the Johnny I knew and loved reflected in the service.

A man they referred to as The Most Reverend Anthony Agostini took to the pulpit. Between long dramatic pauses, he spoke about how tragic it was for such a great man as Jimmy Triboni, a highly respected man and a pillar of the community, to suffer such a heartbreaking loss as the unexpected passing of his beloved youngest son from an undiagnosed heart condition causing a fatal heart attack. I was shocked at how the lies tumbled from his mouth and were received without a blink of an eye by those present. It was the story that had to be told, suicide being a mortal sin in the eyes of the Catholic Church and shameful to the Triboni name. The true story, that Johnny Triboni hung himself from a tree had spread far and wide around the city, yet everyone knew to play their part, keep their mouth shut, sweep the uncomfortable truth under the rug and silently accept the story that had been concocted to protect Jimmy's honour and the Triboni name.

If I was angered by their denial of the truth, I could not feel it in that moment, for the complete absurdity of the façade being enacted became almost comical when an uncle who had flown in from Italy for the occasion presented the eulogy, despite never meeting Johnny. He told stories of how much the family loved Johnny, how he was the centre of their world and how his mother saw him as a gift from God, given he was so much younger than his siblings, and had doted on him from the day he was born. I felt Madame Rosaline stiffen at the vulgarity of this lie, for Madame Rosaline had been the one constant in Johnny's life and it was she who adored, nurtured, encouraged, celebrated and protected him. The falsehood being so publicly proclaimed was painful to witness, but she bore it with extraordinary grace and integrity, not flinching other than to squeeze my hand, assuring me she was okay. Their lies only sought to drag her from love into resentment and rage. She would not go there. She would not give them that satisfaction. Madame Rosaline was too powerful to play their game.

I was fascinated how stories could be fabricated to suit a particular narrative and how others, who knew them not to be true, could so readily accept the lies and play along with the game, the rules of which were dictated by those in positions of power. I had never lived in this way. I lived by the rules of the heart: truth, goodness and integrity, and I pondered the collective psyche of humanity. *What makes us tick? What makes us behave in the way we behave? What makes us hand our power over so easily to those in positions of power?*

As I looked along the pew at those whom I shared my life with, I felt the pain that each of them carried for having navigated their human life. Both Aunt Maeve and Clara stared at the altar. They were not affected by the fairy-tale stories being told, but were reliving their own stories and the trauma they had suffered at the hands of the church. The sounds, smell, rituals and righteous energy coming from those adorning the altar had triggered deep, painful wounds within both of them and, as they sat there, they were invited to once again explore their wounds, for in honouring them and the lessons learnt from them, they would grow stronger. It is through our wounds that divine light enters our body. Our wounds are a blessing, a doorway to more love. I hoped I would be as courageous as Aunt Maeve and Clara to become *more* because of my wound, especially the loss of Johnny. And as they expanded from their wounds, my heart burst with love and tears trickled down my face. They were not tears for Johnny, they were tears of gratitude for those who stood beside me.

I would remember this experience, not for the farcical way they dishonoured Johnny, but for the way love cursed through my whole body and assured me that no matter what path I walked, the doorway to love, to this magnificent bubble of grace and peace and clarity was always present and available to me. I smiled remembering this divine truth, and Johnny's mother must have caught my smile, my bliss triggering her because she began to scream hysterically, propelling herself onto the coffin.

'My baby, my baby boy,' she howled wildly, determined to claim her part in the performance, to take centre stage and not merely be tucked into a pew to demurely pat her eyes.

'You!' she screeched, turning dramatically towards me and waved an accusatory finger at me.

'You brazen whore! How dare you show your face here! How dare you sit there smiling, knowing what you did! Knowing it was you...'

she paused for dramatic effect, '… who killed my son!'

She roared loud enough that even the people who had assembled outside the cathedral to catch a glimpse of the *show* could hear, and I guess they were getting their money's worth, for it was turning out to be quite the Shakespearean performance.

She sashayed towards me and, taking a deep breath, she continued her onslaught.

'My baby is dead because of you. You came to this city looking for trouble and you brought nothing but trouble. You think I don't know what you did to my boy, *my* Johnny? She showed me the cards and they showed the whole thing.'

She pointed towards Clarissa who was dressed decorously in black, and whose eyes glistened with malevolence, clearly thrilled with my public shaming and blindly ignorant of the potential consequences, ethically, morally and spiritually, of her overt misuse of the tarot.

'You listen to me, missy. We own this city, you understand. We own this city and if we don't want you here, you'll go. With God as my witness, you will go one way or another!'

I did not flinch despite her threat. Feeding from the strength of my steely resolve, those by my side did not react, either. All seven of us sat motionless, staring straight ahead, unwilling to give them what they sought, more drama. I'm not sure if it was our tenacity, integrity or our unity that infuriated her, but her hysteria escalated.

'Witch! Witch! You cast a spell on him and put him under your control. He was never the same after you came here, my sweet baby boy. You turned him against us, you sorceress, you filthy slut, seducing my baby, taking away his innocence. They told me, they all told me what you would do when you danced at that club. Club, meh, brothel is what it is!'

Turning to Madame Rosaline, she lost sight of any dramatic script she may have prepared, becoming completely hysterical.

'St Christopher's, a holy name for a heathen house and you enticed my husband there every night, you vile woman. Every night!'

Her voice pierced the corners of the vast cathedral and a deadly silence followed as the crowd anticipated more insights into the dark secrets of Jimmy Triboni's marriage.

Sadly, no one attempted to stop her spiral into mania. In some ways, it offered them the entertainment they had hoped to witness, but I have never understood why her husband, sons, daughter or the presiding clergymen did not intervene and offer her any support. Despite being the target of her attack, I was overcome with compassion for her and wondered what her story was behind the façade of the Mafia wife. In turn, I considered what lay ahead for Clarissa who was carving her path into the Triboni family as the next Mafia wife. Did she have any clue what that life really involved beyond the mask of power and riches?

In the pause, Madame Rosaline's eyes bore into hers and she whispered calmly as a mother would to a child.

'Stop. It is not the time, not now. We are here for Johnny.'

Her words seemed to break the momentum of her mania and she stared blankly into Madame Rosaline's eyes before a single tear rolled down her cheek. I felt her heart break open, and the love she held for the baby she never wanted poured through her. She was overcome by pure, raw grief. I was not sure whether she was grieving the death of her son, or for having denied herself the gift of loving him. She turned her eyes to mine, lost and forlorn, and reached out a hand, tentatively stroking the leather of the jacket adorning my shoulders.

'My baby,' she murmured in an agonising whisper.

It was in that moment, Johnny appeared again. Placing his arms around his mother's shoulders, he whispered, *'You are forgiven.'*

She flicked her head about, confused, clearly feeling or hearing something. She looked again to me, and I silently assured her with a smile and slight nod that what she had experienced was real. At that moment, Nate rose and walked around the pew, placing his arm around her shoulder, as Johnny had done, and gently escorted her back to her seat.

*'Thanks Nate,'* I heard Johnny whisper.

Nate smiled at me as he returned to his seat, and I understood he too *knew* the wonder of Johnny's spirit.

As they carried his coffin from the altar, *'Amazing Grace'* echoing through the church, I wept as the girl who loved the boy, the girl who would never wrap her arms around him on the back of his motorbike, the girl who would never lie in Central Park staring at the trees with him, the girl who would never tease him until he cracked a smile, the young woman who would never make love to him again and the young woman who would never have a future with the man she loved. An indescribable ache brought me to my knees. I could not bring myself to stand as the sadness, the grief, the disbelief tumbled from me in the most sacred pain. Within it, I heard Johnny whisper.

*'Never forget us. Never forget you. If you get lost, come find me and we can dance in the rain.'*

Encouraging the others to follow the procession, Nate stayed with me. Placing his hand in mine, he held me. Together, the tears silently streamed down our cheeks, a shared love of a man so few bothered to understand. We knew and loved the real Johnny Triboni, the man who was so much more than just the son of Jimmy Triboni. We sat, hand in hand, heart to heart, for a long time as the raw waves of human emotions washed over us, as one in our sorrow, our love and our thoughts.

*Could I have done more? Did I do enough? I wish I could have saved him.*

A transmission from the wisest threads of my soul silenced his doubts.

*He didn't want to be saved. He wanted to be loved and you loved him. Love is always enough.*

I turned his head to mine and took his eyes in mine, determined he may never forget the truth.

'Nate, I know that Johnny found his way home. I was with him there. His soul is at peace, he is finally free.'

And together we took a breath and let him go, releasing our attachment to Johnny's spirit, freeing him from this realm while knowing he exists beyond here, while I was assured our souls would meet on the rainbow bridge, the imaginal space between here and there.

We walked silently hand in hand from the cathedral to St Christopher's. I contemplated the other bridge I was precariously traversing, the one from maiden to woman. So much had transpired in the last few days, weeks and months, and I was not confident that I was getting it right. I doubted my next steps. A gentle assured voice of wisdom spoke from my heart.

*There is no right way. There is only the next step.*

# CHAPTER 30

# Holy Rage

After the funeral, we came together as a family at St Christopher's to share a meal and celebrate the life of Johnny. Nate stuck close to me, holding my hand as we sat at the table, anchoring one another as the desire to move beyond the human suffering called to us both. Here, the reality of grief weighed heavily and the lightness in the great expanse of consciousness felt so much easier than remaining in the present. I focused on those seated with me, treasuring the connection and securing it as a sacred imprint on the vast timeline of my soul. They were family, bound by heart rather than blood. I knew them in a way I did not know others. My essence resonated with each of them individually, and I loved them in a way that was hard to comprehend— as a soul family. I relished the beauty of reunion as we shared food and wine, and exchanged stories, wisdom and laughter.

Our sacred space was brutally obliterated by a ferocious banging on the door below, rattling St Christopher's and all who gathered within the sanctuary of her walls. The shattering of glass tore us from our seats. I grasped at the table in shock, the ferocity of the attack penetrating the vulnerability of my psyche. Nate grabbed my shoulder to steady me and motioned to his mother to come to me.

'Mom, she needs a hand.'

With another assuring squeeze of my shoulder, he quickly turned to follow Caellach and Madame Rosaline downstairs to address the chaos that had interrupted our gathering. Sacnite came to my side, anchoring me back into the present before calling back all parts of my being that may have fractured with the shock. She smiled that gentle, knowing smile of the wise woman.

'We are always here for you, Marigold. If you get lost, come home. If you forget, *we* will call you home.'

Jimmy Triboni was drunk. Madame Rosaline, Caellach and Nate

escorted him away from the private quarters where Clara, Aunt Maeve, Sacnite and I remained, but his rage tore through the floor and walls, piercing every corner of the building. Abandoning Johnny's wake, he was violently seeking solace from Madame Rosaline. He knew she was the only one who could hold him in his darkness and dissolve his pain.

'Fuck me, woman, just fuck me!' he bellowed vilely. 'For twenty years, you gave it to me whenever I wanted. Now you won't. Why won't you fuck me now, woman?'

Drawn to bear witness, I watched with awe from behind the stage curtain as Madame Rosaline stood above him, filled with composure, unapologetic in her power and refusing to react to the onslaught of his demands. Caellach and Nate stood behind Rosaline, alert and ready to intervene should she allow them, *only* if she allowed them.

'Please make it go away, Rosie,' he begged, his rage tempered by desperation. 'I can't stop seeing the boy … hanging with a rope around his neck.'

He faltered, staring pitifully at Madame Rosaline.

'Take it away, take it all away, woman … Why are you punishing me?'

Madame Rosaline gracefully maintained her silence, refusing to save him from his inevitable descent into the darkest of personal hell. She knew she had moved beyond the contract she had for so long shared with his soul. Her presence, so still and silent, appeared callous to the human eye, but in the eye of the heart, she was nothing but love. Even I, some ten feet away, could feel it radiating from her. She appeared to grow in stature, expanding with the compassion and mercy flooding her being. And yet her silence reignited Jimmy's rage, for he was helpless without her, needing her to dissolve the ugly truth that gnarled brutally at the edges of his soul. He needed her to free him from the guilt and shame that overwhelmed him more than the pain of his mother leaving him ever had. Madame Rosaline knew she must allow him to suffer, for in suffering there is always the invitation to grace should he choose to seek that within his own heart. Madame Rosaline's silence riled him. So many paths lay before each of us, so many possibilities that would be determined by what happened next. He inhaled deeply and like an iceberg breaking from land, the silence fractured, and potential timelines shattered as he began his final assault. He made his choice.

'It's your fault the boy's dead. You and that little whore. You might as well have put the rope around his neck, the two of you. Your little apprentice! Did you teach her how to spread her legs? Did she fuck him like you fuck me? Did she fuck with his head like you fuck with mine? You better watch your back, woman. You and the little whore better watch your back, because when I give the word, with God as my witness, you'll be done. Both of you.'

No longer could I hide in the darkness. No longer would I hide my darkness.

The veil of the curtain flew across the stage. I emerged in the fullness of my power and walked slowly towards him. Madame Rosaline held her space standing fiercely, her arms by her side, palms facing towards Caellach and Nate, who were readied. She knew as I walked towards Jimmy that I had been called to rise to meet his darkness and she would not stand in my way. This was part of my initiation and she would honour my journey.

He took a slurp of his drink and spilled it over himself, before stumbling to the ground as he lurched in my direction. Clumsily pulling himself onto a chair, he stared at me with a hatred deeply seeded within. Its toxicity was so poisonous he could no longer contain it and he venomously projected it onto me. He smashed the glass and held it like a knife ready to pierce my heart, but I was not afraid of him.

The fire rose from the sacredness of my woman, precisely the place which he sought to denigrate with the vileness of his words. It raced through me and into my womb, igniting a sacred rage. The fury of the Divine Dark Goddesses, whom I had come to honour, Morrigan, Lilith, Hecate, Medusa, Isis, Eros, all exploded within me, refusing to be vilified and denigrated any longer. Standing above him, centred in the fullness of my power, the eye of my soul bore into the eye of his and as pure holy rage soared from my womb and burst through my heart, *she* demanded truth.

'Enough of your lies, Jimmy Triboni. Now you will hear the truth. Johnny loved me and he hated you. Johnny didn't kill himself because of me. He killed himself because of you. He put a rope around his neck because he hated you. He threw that rope over a branch because he hated you. He swung from the tree until the life was sucked from him because he hated you. He may have proved he was a man in your eyes by firing that gun, but he would rather be dead than live knowing he was like you. He didn't want your approval; he wanted your love, but you could never give that to him. He would rather be dead than live another day waiting for your love. He would rather be dead than risk becoming a man like you. Johnny killed himself to be free from you. This is the truth, Jimmy Triboni, and may it burn through you, haunting your every moment until the day you die. Let there be no rest for your soul until you repent, Jimmy Triboni.'

I walked up the stairs to my bedroom and lay on my bed, shaking from the intensity of the energy that moved through me. I breathed deeply, moving with this insatiable energy, refusing to suppress it, allowing it to move through my body. Each breath seemed to fuel the fire. I was overcome by waves of rage that held no regard for my physical body and tore at my edges, commanding release. My eyes closed and, in the darkness, Johnny was hanging from the tree, swinging with the breeze. Suddenly, the fury erupted on another level and my body began convulsing. This energy was too much for me to hold and too much for me to resist. I surrendered all of me to all of *her*. I tremored and quaked as she expelled the fullness of her rage, thousands of years of burning holy fury tearing through me. I recall no more. What happened after I lost consciousness remains a mystery.

I was woken by screams as Clara raced into my room and dragged me from my bed, down the stairs and into the alleyway. Smoke was billowing through the windows which cracked violently as the fire cackled and tore ferociously through the building, destroying all that was St Christopher's and all who remained within her guarded walls. Sirens and flashing lights pierced the night sky, drawing my attention away from the building and to Clara, Caellach, Aunt Maeve, Madame Rosaline, Sacnite and Nate standing beside me. Not a word was said between us as we watched the exquisite beauty and tragedy of the end.

The charred remains of Jimmy Triboni were found slumped in a chair in the confines of Madame Rosaline's office. I do not know why he was alone in there. I do not know how or where the fire started. I never ask Madame Rosaline. NYPD, who were tasked with investigating the fire and the circumstances of his death, did not ask her either. And so, it seemed, Jimmy Triboni would take the truth of Johnny's death along with his own, to the grave. Few in the reclaimed glory of New York City mourned his passing.

*The pages of a book turn in a mysterious way. New chapters begin where another ends.*

# Part Four

# CHAPTER 31

# Let Her Be

---

My Dearest Goldie Mae,

It is 3.00 am and Nate will be arriving in only a few hours to take me to his mother. You are in the room beside me, and I do not know if you are asleep or tossing and turning as I have been. You will not speak to me and while I understand your desire to withdraw, my heart aches for you and I wish you would come with me, or at least stay with Nate. Alas, you are a stubborn one—us Irish woman so often are! There is so much I wish to share with you before I leave. But, as your door remains closed to me, I write this letter to you in the hope you will read it before you leave. While it pains me, I will let you be and trust the path you choose to walk. I, too, trust that my words, wisdom and love will be received when you are ready.

You rose to the challenge and committed to your path. You got back up when you fell and learnt from your experiences. You believed in yourself, and you showed up confident in your truth. I am proud of you.

Yet I understand that you believe you failed and, in some way, got it wrong. There is no right or wrong way. There is only her way and how you meet her.

You are learning and you learn through experience. Often it is in the mess that we become masterful. Please know that you did not fail. You met her in the fullness of the teacher, and she is a tough teacher. But you are wise and courageous and tough enough to meet her challenge. She has chosen you as she once chose me.

I allowed her, the Divine Dark Goddess, to work through me. She is pure, unconditional love expressed through the darkness of the feminine. A beauty so intriguing and exquisite that people are drawn to her not knowing why, often leaving shell-shocked from the encounter. She will bring divine disruption to your life and activate a profound and highly uncomfortable growth. She does not hold back. She will not apologise for destroying the egoistic thoughts and patterns that rule your life. She acts only from the deepest love. What you call harm, she calls liberation, freeing you from the constraints of the path you are walking, the prison of your egoistic ways. She is the force that creates the change for you to go beyond where you are at. Though you may curse her, ultimately you will celebrate her presence in your life. She will realign your soul to a path of truth, to a path of love, and she will not apologise, for you unknowingly sought her and she came to your call. Let her be.

She birthed as a creation of the holy rage that tore through me the night they took my baby from me, and I have never fully understood her. Her seed had been planted long before, germinating patiently, waiting for the time to come forth into the world. She came from the fire that had been brewing within for lifetimes and her destructive loving sword severed me from who I was and all I knew my life to be, signalling my journey into the dark. She is a mystery that cannot be understood until she is experienced fully, and even then, she will remain a mystery.

May your journey through her, with her and in her be blessed.
Always, Rosaline

*Birthed unapologetically from the fire,*
*Seed cracking, refusing to be contained.*
*Timelines created from destruction,*
*From the fire, she rose.*
*The wild,*
*The passionate,*
*The fierce,*
*The dark truth.*
*Birthing the new, from beneath the veils, she who was hidden.*
　—Róisín Dubh, *the Dark Rose.*

*Would I be enough to honour her sacredness*
*now I had been chosen?*

# CHAPTER 32

# The Soulless Vessel

I did not ask to be chosen. I did not want to be chosen. I wanted to be nothing. *She* was nothing. The ghostly young woman reflected back at me through the plane window, eyes devoid of light and the spark that once defined her as the 'golden one'. Marigold was gone, obliterated in the ashes of St Christopher's. Her golden locks were brutally chopped to sever any connection to the past and a black pixie crop now framed my gaunt and pale face. Thousands of miles distanced me from all those I loved and those who loved me. I was not worthy of their love for I was bad. I was evil. I was a whore. I was dangerous. *Bad. Evil. Whore. Dangerous.*

The vicious final words of Jimmy Triboni had catalysed a toxic concoction of thoughts in my mind that offered no respite and subjected my mind to a constant and merciless barrage of abuse. I was too weary to fight and hold strong in my truth. My heart closed and, in the emptiness of my vessel, my soul fractured, splintering beyond my human form, taking with it the beauty and purity of all I had known myself to be. My soul, the essence of my being, became lost, and I had no desire to reclaim her. I surrendered to the chaotic void that engulfed me, allowing it to take me down whichever path it chose, for I was but a soulless vessel devoid of dreams, passion and the spark to create the life I had once desired. I did not care for the life that lay before me, so it did not matter where I went as I spiralled into recklessness.

I could have drunk champagne, danced in diamonds and bedded princes in ancient castles, or woken up beside toothless strangers in squatters' quarters in London's East End, surrounded by hypodermic needles with my underwear missing. I did not care.

My fall from grace was brutal.

I arrived in Los Angeles on a Sunday afternoon and within a few hours I found myself drinking whiskey in a hotel bar in the middle of

West Hollywood. I was far from the glamour associated with Hollywood in my black leather pants and boots, Johnny's jacket encasing my gauntness. I was too dark and moody for any of it. As I tinkled the ice in my drink, I was overcome with a sense of freedom unlike anything I had felt before. It was not an expansive freedom, like when I danced in the higher realms, connected to the all of everything. This was a distorted freedom that came from being completely untethered from the all of everything, including my soul. I had failed the light and tainted my divinity when I abused the power of my darkness. I was free from the onslaught of shame and guilt at my failing, the betrayal of my soul, my truth, my divinity, because I no longer cared. I had one small bag that contained a change of clothes, my journal and a substantial wad of cash. Nate had insisted I take it even though I was reluctant. I cruelly refused his invitation to stay with him in the city or to go to the reservation with his mother and Madame Rosaline. I had to leave. I had to be alone. It was safer that way, for everyone.

I threw down the remainder of my drink, desperate to drown memories of the past, yet they continued to surface in blurred snippets, determined to be remembered. I ordered another whiskey. And then a double. I sought to erase anything that was attached to then, them— *her.* After the fire, Clara and Caellach pleaded with me to go home with them, to return to the love and safety of my family. I did not deserve love or safety as I had sparked the fire that killed Jimmy Triboni. I was a murderer. It was better that they continue to live with the memory of the Marigold they knew, the surrogate daughter and sister, who was good, loving, kind, light and wise, rather than a murderous monster.

Madame Rosaline seemed to understand my need for space and assured Clara and Caellach that she would look after me. She acknowledged the energy that continued to vibrate viciously through me and invited me to walk with her, to breathe with her, to dance with her, to move my body and work with the energy rather than allowing it to overpower me. This time, I stubbornly ignored her guidance and wisdom, burying the letter she gave me as she bade me farewell at the bottom of my bag. I no longer wanted to learn how to work with the dark threads within me, for I had proven they were too powerful for me to hold with integrity. I could not be trusted to carry their potency as Madame Rosaline had. I would never be as wise, graceful and filled with integrity as the women who had guided me my whole life.

The damage was done. There was no way back. I surrendered to my despondency, choosing to reject Madame Rosaline's guidance and the whispers of my Ma's. I suppressed the calls of the Dark Goddess who had awakened from the archives of my womb. With all the free will I could muster, I forced her back into the deep, dark dungeon where the patriarchy had kept her imprisoned for thousands of years. It was safer to be free from her, free from her seductive call to dance, free from the whispers of my heart to allow her, free from the murmurs of my soul who had become her before I severed my connection.

I drew heavily on my cigarette and determinedly rewrote my story. I was no longer the golden one. In the space of ten days, I had driven the love of my life to hang himself, had a psychotic episode while lost in the subway, been seduced by the devil, burnt down my home in rage—murdering the head of the Mafia in the process—and brutally pushed away everyone and anyone who had ever loved and cared for me. *I am nothing.*

I grabbed another note from the wad of Johnny's money, the dirty money he had siphoned from under his father's nose and intentionally withdrawn from the secret deposit box the week before his death. He asked Nate to hide it for him, making him promise that should anything happen to him, half was to be given to me and the other half Nate should keep for himself. Johnny must have known something big was going to happen that weekend and he did not want all that money, over fifty thousand dollars, to rot in a secret deposit box when it could be used to set us up for life. I did not want his money, nor did I want to set up my life. I had turned my back on the only life I knew, and I was determined to use the filthy Mafia money to putrefy the remnants of my life.

I'd never been drunk, yet a couple of hours later, after quite a few more whiskeys, I surely was and, overcome with a longing to sleep, I booked myself a room at reception. In my drunken state, I flirted with the two young men manning the desk, but I certainly didn't invite them to my room. I ignored the knock on the door. When the door flew open and a shadowed form entered, my instinct to scream and defend myself abandoned me. I recoiled under the cover, hiding, terrified for my life. I did not see his face. I closed my eyes as he pulled back the covers and placed his hand across my mouth, but I recognised his voice from the reception desk.

'You know you want it. Girls like you always do.'

And then he stroked my face and every cell in my body sensed the primal presumptuous desire pulsating from him and I froze. *She* died and I felt nothing.

Nothing, when he forcefully stuck his tongue in my mouth and down my throat.

Nothing, when he viciously grabbed and squeezed my breasts.

Nothing, when he tore my underwear away and thrust himself into me.

Nothing, when he released inside me.

Nothing, when he kissed me, telling me we'd do it again.

Nothing, when he left the room, and his friend came in.

Nothing, when he licked hungrily the wetness left between my legs by his teammate.

Nothing, when he then turned me over and forced himself inside me.

Nothing, when he tore my flesh as he grunted and groaned.

Nothing, when he squirted on my back and rubbed it all over my body.

Nothing, when he rolled me over and rubbed it in my face.

Nothing, when he licked my face like a dog.

Nothing, when he slapped me and called me a filthy slut.

Nothing, when he told me he'd be back for more.

Nothing, when he left.

Nothing, when no one else came.

Nothing, when I showered my battered body.

Nothing, when I curled into bed.

Nothing, as I fell to sleep with the words of Jimmy Triboni in my head.

*You're a filthy whore.*
*A filthy whore who deserved it.*

# CHAPTER 33

# The Seductress

If I was to be a whore, I'd be a high-class whore, not merely a piece of meat for bell boys. And so, the following morning I booked a suite for a month in the Chateau Marmont. No questions were asked when I paid the full amount in cash. I quickly learnt that no questions were ever asked if you had enough money to keep people quiet. I polished my style: slick black pixie hair, bright red lips, a tailored black dress that sat an inch too short above my knee and stiletto heels. Johnny's jacket and dark, oversized sunglasses finished my look and became my signature.

I was an enigma. Nobody knew if I was a movie-star, nightclub singer or the high-class whore I was channelling. I bedded many men. So many men. Men of all ages and status. I never took their money. It was nothing more than a game, a power game that I was intent on winning every time, and I felt nothing. No guilt, regret, shame, remorse, nothing! Some I lured to my suite, wetting their desire, waiting until they were hard and readied, only to refuse them entry. Some upped their game to little effect, some moaned, releasing their desire like pubescent boys. Some complained of blue balls and called me frigid, a tease. I cared not for their sorrows or name calling and stood by the open door of my suite, signalling their exit, ready to scream rape down the corridor should they refuse to leave. They never came back looking for more. They knew not to mess with me. I was fiercely determined to punish any man who sexually desired me, all the while seducing them so they would desire me. Fools! They blindly walked into my trap every time. I was the one who dominated. Never again would a man dominate me.

Within weeks, my own desire for sexual power escalated. Bored by the ease of my conquests, I upped my game. Alone in my corner seat in the cocktail bar of the hotel, I tinkled the ice in my drink and, behind the dark lens of my sunglasses, I watched and waited. A man I had never seen before, dressed in a suit with an air of self-importance, confidently took a seat at the bar and curtly ordered a drink from the barmaid, leering lustfully at her as she walked away. While I remained determinedly disconnected from my once strong intuitive senses, my primal instincts were suddenly activated, and I recognised *him*. More accurately, every cell in my body remembered the energy thread of *his* frequency. You see, the rapist carries a distinct archetypal energy pattern and once you know it, especially once you have experienced it, your body never forgets it. The bellboys were in their infancy when playing with this thread, and I'm certain I was their first foray, but this man with his arrogant assuredness was different. My body's heightened response left me in no doubt he had lured hundreds of women into his sordid web. This time, I was intent on overriding the primal fear response which screamed at me to flee.

*No! Not this time!*

This time, I would not flee, nor would I freeze. Never again would I freeze and allow them to take my power. An electric charge raced through my body, a fire stirring in my womb as I made a silent vow.

This time, it's *my* web.

This time, I will lure *him* in.

This time, I will dominate *him*.

This time, he will know how it feels to be used like a piece of meat and tossed aside.

As the distorted, dark energy vehemently roared through my body, I caught his eye. With the slightest tilt of my chin, I motioned for him to come. And he did. It was not hard!

It was not hard to entice him to his room.

It was not hard to seduce him.

It was not hard to strip him bare.

It was not hard to make him hard.

It was not hard to tweak a point on his neck.

It was not hard to witness the terror in his eyes as paralysis struck.

It was not hard to shove a sheet in his mouth to silence him.

It was not hard to mount his hardened cock and drain it for *my* pleasure.

It was not hard to hear him sob as I casually smoked a cigarette.

It was not hard to wipe his flaccid cock dry and brand it with my cigarette.

It was not hard to smell the burning of flesh.

It was not hard to warn him to never again disempower a woman.

It was not hard to walk out of his room to the sound of his muffled screams.

It was not hard to sleep that night.

In fact, it was the best sleep I had had in weeks. Vengeance may not be sweet, but it did bring a strangely distorted sense of peace.

He could not look at me the following morning when I casually walked into the restaurant for breakfast. I was not surprised to see him sitting there. I knew the paralysis was temporary, Caellach having shown me what to do years ago in case I ever crossed paths with a wild animal in my meanderings through the woods. I knew he would pretend it never happened, business as usual and all that, but as I sat silently watching him from across the restaurant, my eyes still veiled by the sunglasses, I enthusiastically observed his vulnerability and shame.

Assured in my power, I went immediately to reception and extended my stay by another month, realising it would not be hard to attract more of his kind to be tamed, shamed, denied and deprived, all the while feeding my power and siphoning theirs, so they might know exactly how it feels to be on the receiving end.

And so it was that for a time, Chateau Marmont became my web, where my abusive, distorted feminine convinced herself she was bringing balance to the abusive, distorted masculine who dishonoured the sacredness of the feminine. Every other night, I would strike. It was never hard to execute my signature act, from paralysis to branding to walking away and feeling nothing. No remorse, no regret, no recollection. The power of *nothing*, a welcomed gift from the bellboys to my damaged dark feminine. I fulfilled my role in her plan to exact vengeance. I was all too willing to do whatever she asked of me.

Did I do it for the sacred feminine?

*Absolutely not.*

Did I do it for the wounded feminine?

*Every fucking time!*
Did I bring balance and create change?
*Absolutely not.*
Did I create more wounding and division?
*Every fucking time!*
Did I act from a divine place?
*Absolutely not.*
Did I know that my behaviour was distorted?
 *Every fucking time!*
Did I care?
*Absolutely not.*

I dived into the world of distorted darkness, believing I belonged. I had no desire to ascend from the darkness, to reclaim my light. I was intent on a rapid and catastrophic descent.

I do not know if it was chance or divine intervention when I was offered a job with a new rock music magazine called Cornerstone. The founder, who I did not know by name but had seen many times having meetings in the cocktail bar over the past few weeks, took a seat at my table.

'I've been watching you and you've been watching me. You read people. I like that. Can you write?'

'Yeah, I can write,' I replied, my curiosity sparked for the first time in months.

'Are you done with this place? Time to move on?'

I loved how matter of fact he was and respected that in all the times I had seen him, he had never come onto me, unlike most of the men who frequented the bar. In realising that he didn't desire me as others did, he felt safe and so I entertained his offering.

'What exactly are you suggesting?' I queried, inhaling on my cigarette.

'On the road, all over the country, overseas if you want. Following the bands, getting the behind-the-scenes story. You know, get to know them, the real people behind the façade, and then tell their stories from a fresh perspective, through the eyes of a young woman. I want you to write for my magazine, Cornerstone.'

'Sure, why not,' I mused, for I had no attachment to where I was, nor a plan for where I was going.

He shook his head and smiled.

'You're just what I've been waiting for. What's your name?'

I had not spoken my name, only scribbled it on hotel registration forms.

'Róisín Dubh.'

'Right … the dark rose! I'll run you through things the first week, but then you're on your own. You're going to have to look after yourself, Dark Rose, you understand?'

His energy nudged at the corners of my cold-closed heart, yet he didn't break through my protective guard.

'I'm more than capable of looking after myself.'

'Fair call. It's why I've offered you the job. I know you can hold your own, I've been watching you for weeks. I know what you get up to.'

Was he chastising or commending me? Either way, I didn't care for his judgement.

'You want me to do the job, I'll do it my way. You get your stories, but you keep out of my business.'

'Exactly as I intended. I'll see you down here for breakfast tomorrow morning. We hit the road at 9.00 am and your first story is due in forty-eight hours.'

I took a breath as he walked away. A door had opened, and I'd said yes. There was no going back now. I had nothing to lose and nothing to gain.

*Que sera, sera, whatever will be, will be—a Doris Day musical, it was not to be!*

# CHAPTER 34

# Dark Mirror

I leapt into my new gig with reckless abandon. There was endless travelling on planes, buses and RVs, wild partying, sleep deprivation, deadlines and meaningless sexual encounters with more men than I cared to remember. Truth be told, I didn't remember what happened most nights as I ended up so drunk I would fall into bed with anyone. I numbed with marijuana, while alcohol to excess unleashed my wild side, enabling me to keep up with the hard-core partying with the bands I was following. I'm not sure who introduced me to cocaine, but I was wickedly grateful when I discovered its magical power to kick my brain into action. I could write for hours and submit my articles, notoriously meeting the endless deadlines at the last minute.

After about six months on the road, I toyed with the idea of quitting. I felt like the job was holding me back. I wanted more partying and less responsibility. I certainly didn't need the pay as I still had plenty of Johnny's filthy money stashed away should I need it to fuel my decadent destruction.

In many respects, I was a free spirit, free to move from city to city, club to club, band to band, man to man. Yet I was also devoid of spirit. I was completely detached from everyone and everything, though men were strangely enthralled by my enigmatic and apathetic attitude. I was an anomaly because in the music industry it was all about who you were connected to, with success reliant on knowing and being adored by all the right people. In contrast to many playing in that world, there was nothing to know and nothing to connect to in me, yet still they were drawn to me. I was a mystery they sought to explore, to unravel and understand, a challenge to conquer. I didn't care for their intrigue, and offered no challenge, mindlessly saying yes to their eager invitations to explore me. But, one after the other, they were left bitterly disappointed when I gave them nothing to appease their curiosity. In the nothingness, I had no fear. There was no fight, no flee, no freeze. I really didn't care what they thought or said about me, because when all was said and done, they didn't care either. A meaningless fuck was still a fuck. My complete surrender meant I said yes to invitations to jump on private jets to party with the rich and famous in Hollywood, Monaco, Paris, London. I danced in the halls of palaces throughout Europe before falling into bed with a prince or two. And yet it didn't matter whether they were royalty, movie stars, rock gods, record company or film studio executives. To me, they were all the same and I gave them the same. Nothing! My heart never flickered in their presence, no matter the adoration, gifts or lines of cocaine bestowed on me, and with every empty encounter, my soul drifted further still from this life.

I dreamt of my death often and understood the self-destructive path I was rebelliously choosing was a dangerous one. I was tempting fate and devoid of fear. Should death take me from this life, it would be a welcomed relief, the descent into darkness complete. Then I could dance with my own fucking devil in the afterlife, punished for *all* of it, all that I had done wrong in this life.

Despite months of debauchery, surrounded by every drug imaginable, I had never been offered psychedelics. If I had been offered, I would have accepted. But on some level, my debased subconscious blocked it, ensuring I avoided access to higher realms where I could dance in the heavens and expand my consciousness. I had done that my whole life. It was my most natural way of being—my *home*. But I didn't want to go *home* because I knew my ever patient, understanding, forgiving and unconditionally loving soul would be waiting for me there. In my shame, I simply couldn't face reconnecting with *her* essence. I had betrayed her light and her divinity—my light and my divinity.

After almost a year of recklessness, my body began to break down, begging me to stop, to nurture and nourish it. I arrogantly refused to listen, ignoring the crippling fatigue, paralysing headaches, constant dizziness, recurrent sinus infections and aggressive bouts of vomiting and diarrhea. Incapacitated often, I would be confined to bed, but being stuck in a hotel room stirred my anxiety. My demons began circling, infiltrating my every thought, penetrating my dreams and terrorising the nothingness I gripped onto desperately. Somehow, garnering just enough strength, I'd get out of bed and get dressed before launching myself back into the void of darkness that had become my life. It was safe in there and with seemingly endless lines of cocaine, I energised myself just enough to stay there. Nobody blinked an eye because if you wanted to stay in the scene, you had to be in the game.

I missed deadline after deadline, and when complete exhaustion overcame me and I was close to comatose for three days, I convinced myself that my work was killing me. I quit. My editor suggested I take a few weeks off to rest and recover, even go to rehab, but I had no intention of stopping to recover, let alone go to rehab. I wanted to party harder, to push the boundaries ever further, without any accountability.

In quitting my job, I had no reason to be of sound mind, to keep myself going, to push myself to show up in life. I did not simply quit my job, I quit life and beckoned death. Like a demonic thread, heroin began circling around me. I had never used it, despite its ever-increasing presence around me. And much like psychedelics, on some level, I was blocking it from entering my realm. Without psychedelics, I unconsciously avoided a return to the light. Without heroin, I unconsciously avoided death. Somewhere, the suppressed wisdom of my being knew that injecting heroin into my body was certain death. Its poisonous venom would mark the full stop to this timeline. For a long time, I avoided it, until I was done, and it hungrily came to my call.

*He* came with the heroin.

*He* who was without a name.

*He* held his own in the darkness.

*He* magnetised me into his vortex.

*He* held me in his darkness and the world around me ceased to exist.

*He* commanded I see truth and remember who I was as the needle filled with the poison.


Before it was able to pierce my vein, I collapsed, began to have seizures and lost consciousness. What transpired between that moment and waking up alone in the bed of my hotel room, I can't remember. The confusion and exhaustion that had tormented me for months was gone, replaced by a clear head and an abundance of energy. I took my time to rise, then showered, deeply cleansing my body, mind and spirit before leaving the hotel to walk through the city streets. I had never bothered to leave the hotel or the clubs in Chicago to explore the city and connect with normal people. I was so immersed in and captivated by the music scene I had separated myself from the normal world without even realising it. I found a seat by the window of a café and sipped a cup of tea. I watched with intrigue as the world passed by. Businesspeople made their way to work. Mothers walked children to school. Couples strolled hand in hand. I eavesdropped on conversations around me and relished the normality of their lives. A longing for something unknown stirred within, making me uncomfortable. Turning my focus to the muted sounds of the outside world, I saw *him*, the enigmatic voyeur who had captivated me the night before, standing directly across the street. His presence stimulated visions of the club, the needle and the madness in the eyes of the lowlife who had prepared to inject me, intent on sharing its wickedness with me before dragging me into his dungeon and reaping his reward.

Devoid of discernment and without a care for my life yesterday, I couldn't see it, but now I could see the truth of the path I had chosen before *his* presence had captured me. I remembered his eyes and how they had held mine. They anchored and held me in a space that offered me protection from what I have no doubt would have been the end point of my life. Now he was there, standing across the street, waiting for the green light. His jeans clung tightly to his thighs and butt and his leather jacket and boots commanded a 'don't fuck with me' vibe. I was more centred, clear and calm than I had been all year. I could feel his presence despite the distance between us.

He entered the café and sat at the back. I wondered if he would recognise me. I was attracted to him. I felt him in a way I did not fully understand and it excited me. He removed his sunglasses, his eyes a turquoise green that appeared otherworldly and were contrary to his tanned skin and short jet-black hair. He didn't look at me, although I sensed he was as aware of my presence as I was his.

I was struck by the importance of consciously choosing my next step, something I had neglected for a long time. I knew I had to choose between following the inkling in my waters to approach him or run. Gripped by an overwhelming urge to vomit, I raced to the bathroom, reaching the toilet just in time. Collapsing onto the floor of the toilet cubicle, I wept with exhaustion and relief knowing that something had significantly shifted within me following last night. I could not help but wonder if he had something to do with it.

After a time, I composed myself before returning to my table to discover a perfectly penned note.

*'Gentle steps sound the loudest. There is always a way home.'*

I turned to look for him, knowing he was the messenger, but he was not there and there was no sign anybody had even been seated at the table. My intrigue was overrun by irritation. I ran from the café straight back to the bar and ordered a whiskey, straight. I did not want to take gentle steps. I did not want to be told what to do. I had taken gentle steps my whole life and look at the mess I had created. I wanted to destroy everything on my path! I sculled my drink and ordered another, righteous indignation fuelling my rage.

*Don't tell me to walk gently! Don't tell me to be quiet! Don't tell me to settle down! I don't want to go home and be the good girl! Fuck her and fuck you, whoever you are!*

As I downed drink after drink, visions of the past hit me like the waves I had witnessed as a child as I crossed the Atlantic, wild and brutal. Bellboys smugly trading places, Johnny's distraught eyes framed by splattered blood, picking wild flowers with Athena, the musty smell of healing vaginal wounds, bloody powdered noses in toilet cubicles, crows screeching from trees, Cynthia's coffin being lowered into the rich dark soil, Jimmy Triboni leering at me with disdain, Johnny's swollen face with the rope around his neck, fire encircling Clarissa's feet, fire bursting from the windows of St Christopher's, fire pouring from my darkened heart and hungrily devouring the soft flesh of Jimmy Triboni's slumped drunken body. I ran from him, from my pain, from my shame, from my darkness and straight into the lecherous arms of a masterfully manipulative and cold-hearted lover.

*The punishment I deserved.*

# CHAPTER 35

# Devilish Destruction

Samuel Snyder didn't hand pick me. I hand picked him. Even if he tried, he could not have selected a better woman to hang off his arm in public and devotedly dote on him in private. Devoid of identity, esteem or confidence, I was putty in his narcissistic hands. A misogynistic maestro, he manipulated me to fuel his repulsive hunger for power and control and relished the chance to intentionally and cruelly destroy another.

He was the lead singer of a band that was fresh on the scene. They were creating an impressive name for themselves. Strutting into the bar, he scanned the room, and I seductively drew him to me. It was not hard to seduce him. He was good looking and oozed confidence. I was clear on my intent and took him to my room and fucked him. He took me to his room and fucked me, to show me who was the boss, because he needed to be in charge. My connections in the industry were an added benefit in his desperate hunger for fame. It could be argued I was a handy rung on his ladder to the top. I was also without a job, and he gave me reason to stay in the music scene. I wasn't ready to leave. It suited my self-destructive path far too well. A match made in heaven!

The following day, after snorting lines and fucking all night, he took me shopping, adorning me in designer clothes, bags, shoes, all the things I was meant to desire as a woman. He brought a hairdresser and make-up artist to the hotel room to show me how to create a 'rock-star-chic' image. I had no interest in any of it, however, if he was choosing me as 'his girl', then he sought to model me into his image of the perfect rock star girlfriend. I knew what he was doing. I went along with it.

Most nights, I was so wasted, drunk and high that by the time he came off stage, I had little recollection of what happened. It was a heady mix of sex, drugs and rock 'n roll, without the responsibility and accountability of having a job and deadlines to meet.

I threw myself fully into free-fall, leaping off the edge of the cliff into the darkness of the unknown. I gave Samuel Snyder my power. I made it so easy for him to manipulate and dominate me that he became bored within a few months and his adoration suddenly turned to rejection and degradation. He took from me what he desired in the bedroom or in his dressing room after leaving the stage. He would walk in, high on adrenalin and whatever else he had pumped into his system before going on stage, scull a quarter-bottle of scotch, then grab me and bend me over whatever table, chair or cupboard was in the room. Once he was finished with me, he'd kiss me hard, telling me that he loved me and that I was his girl, before leaving me to go party with the rest of the band and the inevitable groupies that flocked to them.

Over time, he stopped saying he loved me, then stopped calling me his girl, then he wouldn't kiss me. Instead, he'd grab me by the arm and turn me around after he finished fucking me and look at me with disdain, almost repulsion. One night, he finished performing and barged into the dressing room. He was agitated. He tore my clothes from me, forced himself inside me and then grabbed my face, peering into my eyes. I saw nothing but hatred and loathing. He stared at me like that as he continued to fuck me and when he finished, he spat in my face and called me 'a disgusting fucking slut.' I didn't object. When he told me to get out, I didn't move because I was naked, so he punched me in the face. It didn't hurt. Not the first punch, nor the second or even the one that drew blood from my nose. I felt nothing and as he pushed me out the door, I stumbled past three young groupies who, in their eagerness to enter his realm, did not blink an eye at my bloodied, battered face, nor my naked body.

I slumped against the wall, unable to grab a gown or towel to cover myself and closed my eyes. I willed death. I was done. An overwhelmingly peaceful silence filled the space. I allowed it to embrace the brokenness of my body and the rawness of my heart, revealing truth. Once, I knew only love for myself, adoring and honouring the sacredness of my being. Now, I lay naked, bruised and bleeding, my sacredness decimated. Grief poured from me.

In the depths of my surrender, I became aware of a presence

nearby, yet felt no fear. Through my blurred vision, I saw a shadow coming towards me. Its form was illuminated by the stage lights in the background. I did not resist, and it moved ever closer. It was both familiar and foreign, and only when it was close enough for me to see clearly, did it pause. It was *him*, he of no name who mysteriously appears and disappears. He did not step closer. He did not speak. He did not reach out to help me stand. He simply stood there and held me in this space where nothing moved, and yet everything was revealed by the light that streamed from his darkened form. I could not recoil as the truth penetrated my heart. In my mind's eye, I witnessed the abuse I had experienced over the preceding weeks, which I had allowed in my alcohol and drug dissociated form. I wept as I looked upon the dishonouring of my sacredness and as I remembered the beauty of who I once was. The depth of my self-betrayal tore open the tenderness of my heart. Unexpectedly, I felt it beat once more. A slow, measured pulse drew me within and in that quiet place, I clearly heard the wisdom. *Darkness frames the dawn. Rise with the dawn and come home.*

He turned away, his dark form fading into the light from which he had come. In turn, the light in the corridor disappeared and in the purity of the darkness, I knew only peace. Within the peace, a flicker of light broke through and a single tear rolled down my check. I remembered that I was the light that flickered. No matter how far I had strayed, no matter how many times I had turned my back on my truth, my light, the essence of the girl I was, could never be destroyed. Relieved, the light claimed me and I remember nothing more.

I woke some time the following day, alone in a new hotel room where I felt like I had slept for a million years. The crisp clean sheets cradled my body which felt strangely regenerated despite its battering the night before. Similarly, my mind was clear. With the toxicity siphoned, I recalled that the last time I had woken with clarity of mind was following my last intimate encounter with *him*, he of no name. I did not know who had brought me to this room, how my suitcase had ended up tucked beside my bed, or who had delivered a basket of fresh fruit, water, lemon and ginger tea, a jar of comfrey ointment and a vial of the sweetest smelling rose oil I had ever encountered. I sensed he had something to do with it.

I drew the rose oil to my nose and as I gently inhaled the memorable scent, I smiled, imagining my beloved Athena, ever the medicine woman and loving mother, sneaking into my room in the middle of the night, quietly delivering me all I might need to begin my healing. My heart expanded as I allowed myself to feel my Ma Ma, for it had been so long since I had even let myself think of her. She, like all who loved me, had been pushed into the furthest corners of my mind and the deepest, most hidden crevices of my hardened, cold heart. And yet here she was, bursting through every layer of my protection, to fill my heart once again with the richness of her love. I indulged in her loving presence as I soaked in the bath and courageously reflected on the night before. I touched my face, aware that the bruising which should be blackening had already begun to fade. The cut to my lip and the tear of my anal tissue from the brutality of his penetration were miraculously almost healed.

Buoyed by the mystery of my healing, I bravely opened to my emotions. I wrapped a robe about my tender body, tied a towel around my hair and methodically rubbed the ointment and oil into my skin. As I sipped the lemon and ginger tea, tears of shame and regret trickled down my cheeks and I did nothing to stop them. For many hours, they flowed as a healing river and when they were done, I simply felt sad. Sad for what my life had become. Sad for all I had thrown away. Sad for all I had pushed away. Sad for having abandoned the one who loved me more than any other ever could, my soul. I had lost my way and maybe, just maybe, it was time to heed the wisdom of those who loved me and go home. I sobbed and snoozed throughout the afternoon, deeply content in the silence and sanctuary of the cocoon in which I had so carefully been delivered. I woke in the early evening to discover a note under my door along with a bunch of roses.

My Dearest, Rosie,

I am in town tonight. Meet me for dinner?

A car will be downstairs at 8.00 pm.

Yours, Luca.

*An invitation. A crossroads. A choice.*

# CHAPTER 36

# The Invitation

Luca Johns, Cornerstone's founder, publisher and editor, who offered me the job at Chateau Marmont the year before, had become as close to a friend as I had during that time. He was a savvy businessman, clever publisher and brutal editor, with high standards for all his writers, yet he had a soft spot for me and always made time to meet up with me should our schedules align. I was reluctant to leave the hotel room, relishing its sanctuary, but strangely, I welcomed the idea of his company, conversation and connection.

I did my best to cover any bruising with make-up, but toned down my usual rock-chic look. In truth, I didn't want to be her anymore. I just didn't know a way out. Once again, Luca Johns came into my life at exactly the right time. I was relieved he had chosen a restaurant away from the hotel, and not frequented by those in the music scene, for I was certain word had spread about what had transpired the night before and I couldn't bear to see anyone I might know.

I entered the restaurant and Luca waved me in his direction. As I approached his table, I noted he was seated with another person and my body charged with knowing. His back was to me, yet I knew it was him, he of no name, and I froze. As before, he terrified and excited me all at once. I was not used to feeling so intensely, having worked so hard to numb my feelings for so long. Luca rose to greet me and drew me into a hug before gently touching my jaw.

'He will pay for this.'

Tears welled, his care stirring the raw edges of my heart, and I took a seat, not looking to my side, yet remaining acutely aware of the presence beside me.

'Rosie,' Luca continued. 'This is Gabriel Rodriguez. He's an independent talent scout for the record companies. I asked him to join us for dinner.'

Awkwardly, I acknowledged him, but then directed my focus solely on Luca and we made small talk. He seemed to have a clear idea about how I had been filling my time since I had quit working for him, and he was intent on getting me out of that scene.

'This whole festival thing is taking off after Woodstock and they're attracting a lot of new bands. Gabriel here is about to head on the road, travelling about and seeking out new talent to sign. I'd like to cover some of these breakthrough artists before they make it mainstream. Cornerstone has to show it has its finger on the pulse—no—it has to *be* the pulse. I'm proposing a three-month contract, a profile a week, a full article each month. All expenses paid and you'll travel with Gabriel. He has the contacts, and he knows where to go. I think it will be good for you, Rosie, to get away from all this.'

Gabriel excused himself at this point, as the conversation was heading in a more personal direction, even though I knew he had seen me at my lowest. I doubted Luca had any idea how far I had fallen, and I bristled at the thought. He stared at me with concern.

'Rosie, I know they've hurt you. Perhaps I should have protected you more, but I figured when I threw you into the lion's den that you were the lion. You still are, but the lion who can't discern will get eaten up and spat out. Putting no end of shit into your body to hide the pain just fucks with your head, kid, and you know it. I know it. Stops you from seeing clearly. It becomes one mass distortion, and it's sucked you in. Now, you can stay in there, but you won't last much longer, or you can get clean, get your head straight and get back on track. That's what this is, Rosie, a chance to find you again.'

'What's with him?' I asked, referring to Gabriel.

'He's one of the good ones, Rosie. There's not many of them, but I trust him, and I trust him with you. Like I said, it's different to the hard-core rock scene. The festivals are fresh and new, and Gabriel's already got his head around it, so I trust him to show you the way. All you have to do is follow his lead. He's the path out of this mess, Rosie. What do you think?'

I shrugged my shoulders like a petulant teenager. I was being offered a lifeline but refused to acknowledge it.

'He leaves here on Thursday. Have a think about it overnight and call the office tomorrow. I've got to go. I'm watching that fuckwit you got yourself messed up with perform. Might be the beginning of the end for him if I've got anything to do with it. Stay clear of him, okay?'

I nodded, and a tear rolled down my cheek as he rose to leave. I quickly wiped it away as Gabriel returned to the table and Luca shook his hand, bidding him farewell. I refused to acknowledge him as he sat across the table from me.

'I'm staying at the same hotel as you, so I can meet you in the foyer Thursday morning, 7.00 am,' Gabriel declared briskly.

They were the first words he had spoken directly to me, and they triggered a rage I could not suppress.

'Who the fuck are you and why do you keep interfering in my life?'

He ignored me and curtly replied, 'He's asked me to take you with me, because you're his best writer and I'm doing him a favour.'

'Just leave me alone. I don't need you hanging around!'

'You think I'm actually choosing this? You think I like watching you degrade yourself and destroy your life? You're beyond a train wreck, because you don't stop once you've crashed. You don't learn any lesson, you just keep going back for more. And you know what? I'm done. Come with me on Thursday or not. I really don't care.'

He left the restaurant and my moment of triumph at successfully antagonizing and pushing him away dissolved as the echo of his words flooded through my head and pierced the tentative buoyancy of my heart. *I really don't care.* His presence was confronting yet comforting, holding me in a way that assured me I was safe. I believed that on some level he cared. I didn't know I was longing for another to care for me, to watch out for me, until once again it was taken from me. An agonising arc of abandonment tore through me, reawakening the seemingly never-ending wounds of rejection pitted across the tapestry of my soul and the ever-vicious, destructive voice screeched in my head. *What's the point? Why would anyone care for me? I'm not worth loving. I'm vile, disgusting, repulsive. I'm a disappointment to everyone. They would all be so ashamed if they knew what I had become. I'm a failure and no matter how much I try, I'll never be enough. So, why bother. What's the point? There is no point.*

I left the restaurant, flagged a cab and directed it to the darkest club in the city, the one widely known to be a favourite of drug dealers, pimps and criminals. I approached a dealer I had seen in the hotel lobby a few days earlier. He told me to meet him in a dark room out the back in an hour, when his 'peak hour' had ended, and he would 'sort me out'.

'No point having the goods if you don't have the equipment to deliver it with, sweetheart,' he crooned with an evil smile.

I sensed his enthusiasm for injecting young women with heroin ran into more sinister waters than merely an added extra from a kind-hearted dealer. But I did not care. My intent was clear. As the dark liquid hit my heart, it would stop it and put a stop to the endless nightmare, the train wreck as Gabriel had so accurately described my life. I would return to the afterlife knowing there would be much for my soul to review, to reflect upon and heal. I was too far gone. There had been too much damage done for me to make amends while I still lived and breathed in this realm. I convinced myself that my soul would take the hit and sort it out beyond the veil. If Johnny Triboni could do it, so could I!

There would be no note, no explanation, no farewell, no apology.

*Ar dheis Dé go raibh a hanam. May she rest in peace.*

# CHAPTER 37

# Mahala, Come Home

I rolled up my sleeve. He tied the band around my arm and tapped at my vein. I closed my eyes and sank into my heart. There was a peace, a stillness as I took a breath, willing it to be my last.

'Fuck off, mate, this is a private party!'

The darkened dingy room became flooded with light. Gabriel stood in the doorway, golden rays streaming from him. As he drew me in, everything froze, and nothing existed but truth. I saw the needle angled, ready against my flesh, and as he drew my eyes to his, I heard. *The baby.*

*The baby!*

A sharp, excruciating pain raced through my abdomen. I retracted my arm to brace myself. My sudden movement pierced the vortex and the light immediately receded from the room. The dealer howled.

'What the fuck are you doing, bitch? Do you want it or not?'

I stumbled from the room, barely able to walk. Gabriel was nowhere to be seen and I wondered whether he had been there at all. I dragged myself into the restroom and as I collapsed onto the filthy floor, a gush erupted from my vagina and I screamed in agony. There was no one there, no one to help me. I was alone, but I understood on some level that I had wanted it this way. I had to do *this* myself. I dragged myself onto the toilet and endless bright red blood covered the bowl. No amount of wiping or patting could suppress it.

I recovered myself enough to walk from the club, wave down a cab and ask it to take me to the nearest hospital which was two blocks away. Our Lady of the Blessed Virgin Hospital, was where, according to their mission statement, no person would be turned away or without care— unless of course you presented as a young, intoxicated and dishevelled woman, who was alone and experiencing profuse vaginal bleeding and excruciating abdominal pain.

The taxi driver kindly walked me to the entrance. However, from the moment I entered that hospital I did not receive another hint of mercy, compassion, kindness or care. Without examination by a doctor, the nurses put me in a room and left me for hours on my own, crying and screaming as the waves of horrific pain tore through my body. They had ignored me when I told them I was bleeding heavily and I heard unmerciful murmurs of 'miscarriage', 'unmarried', 'heathen', 'serves her right' and 'God's will'.

At some point, I realised that I was birthing, but alone and terrified, I could not centre myself enough to listen and follow the lead of my body. Without a steady, kind and reassuring hand to show me the way, I screamed in agony and fought every contraction, resisting the innate pulse of my body to bring the baby into the world.

After many hours of this torture, a stone-faced older woman came stomping into the room. As soon as the door was closed, she flew across the room, launching herself in my face and gripped it violently.

'You need to stop this nonsense now, do you hear me? Women do this every day without all this fuss.'

Her eyes were inflamed with rage, but she pulled herself off me and, straightening her uniform, she smirked.

'Your type are all the same. You get what you deserve. For my Lord Jesus Christ always ensures the work of the devil is punished.'

The nucleus of my cells burst open and purged a primordial rage that would not stop, could not stop—I refused to be silenced again in shame.

'ARGH … ARGH … ARGH … ARGH … ARGH … ARGH.'

The rhythmical beat drew me into an eerie, deep calm, quelling the pain and shock, and activating the power of all that I was as a woman. With each cycle, I drew ever closer to my sovereignty and in the fullness of *her* power, I birthed my baby into my own hands and drew him to my chest. He was tiny with an almighty cry, a sound etched in my heart for eternity. Yet before I could look into his eyes, stroke his cheek or kiss his lips, she tore him viciously from my arms. Then there was silence, a strange silence, a false silence, a heart wrenching silence. Abruptly, the silence was broken by chaos as the room became awash with frantic people screaming as my blood flooded the purity of their sheets. I resisted the pull into the void and fought desperately to stay with my body because I would not leave my baby. I would not abandon him. I knew the absence of mother. My heart held that aching wound and I refused to inflict that trauma on my baby. I called on my soul to save me and as I willed myself to live, she whispered, *Mahala, come home, all is forgiven.*

*Beneath the veils of darkness, she had waited patiently,*
*trusting I would find my way home.*

# CHAPTER 38

# The Triple Goddess

For over a year, I had unconsciously moved through life, existing rather than living. I had never lived that way, and it was only in birthing my baby that I was awakened. In returning to my awareness, I found myself alone in a different room with stark white sheets holding me in place. Gradually I remembered the hospital, the old nurse and then, my baby. I leapt out of bed and ran into the hallway, the surge of blood gushing down my legs failing to stop me. A younger nurse quickly escorted me back to bed, telling me I needed my rest, but I insisted through sobs that I didn't need rest, I needed my baby. She ignored me, anxiously looking to the door as she tucked me back into bed, straightening the sheets nervously.

'Bring me my baby,' I began steadily, and still she ignored me.

'Bring me my baby!'

I gripped at her arm, dug my fingers desperately into her flesh.

She pulled her arm away, nervously whispering, 'Please be quiet. Don't make a fuss. You don't want her coming back in here.'

The fear in her eyes startled me. I realised she was terrified of the older nurse who had taken my baby from me.

'Bring me my baby, now!' I hollered louder.

'Bring me my baby, NOW!' I screeched as something primal stirred within and drew the older nurse back into the room, furious and eager to tame me.

She slapped my face and demanded I stop making a scene. But I would not stop the primitive wail of the wounded mother until my baby was in my arms. She slapped me harder, pulled clumps from my hair, pinned me onto the bed, threw cold water over me, but still I would not concede to her demands to subdue me. The more she tried, the more I allowed my agonising rage to pour from me, terrorising those surrounding me. It was only when she placed her hand over my mouth to silence me that I stopped, frozen in shock and horror, as truth flooded my awareness.

I *knew*!

I *knew* she had placed her hand over my baby's mouth to silence him, to punish me. The world stilled and time froze, because anything could have happened at that moment. Potential timelines darted across the cosmos, for *this* had not been written and as my muscles contracted, I readied to tear her head off. In the void of the complete unknown, Gabriel suddenly appeared at the door. He walked towards me, and they cowered in his presence. Gently taking my face in his hands, my eyes in his, his presence bore into mine and a force I had never encountered before penetrated both my heart and soul. It was beyond this world, the earthly realm, and came from somewhere in the darkness of the cosmos.

He *was* the darkness of the cosmos. He was not of form. He was pure energy, divine dark energy, and he demanded that I merge with him. I could not resist and as my energy melded with his, this incredible force moved through my being, a fierce, solid charge that enveloped me from the depths to the heights. Telepathically, he instructed me to let go of it all, the all of everything, the all of nothing, and drop. My soul surrendered to his lead and dropped, beyond the earthly realm, beyond any realm, beyond the divinity of source itself, to a concentrated energy containing the all that is.

*Consciousness.*

'*Go to her,*' his voice commanded through the cosmos.

In consciousness, I found her, the purest expression of my soul, she who had been calling to me, willing me to remember, though I had not been ready to hear, until now.

She stood on the edge of the cliff, staring beyond the vastness of the sea. I recognised the cliffs as my home in The Burren, the rugged green hills overhanging the mighty Atlantic. She was mystical and captivating, a silhouette that danced between the flickering light and dark. As her hair blew wildly with the wind, I was reminded of the mythical Banshee, she of the hills, caves and mountains. She who roamed freely, howling and shrieking, heralding death, calling in the darkness and holding the souls who transitioned through the veil and those who remained, guiding them into the dark cave of grief, anguish and loss. She was at once both terrifying and the most exquisitely gentle being you could ever encounter. Athena had introduced me to her essence as a child, guiding me to trust in her and her call to the darkness, explaining, '*She is elusive and only comes in the very dark of the night. In darkness, you will grow. When you hear her call, go to her.*'

I moved ever closer, floating through time and space to reunite with her, noting the thick, velvet black cloak adorning her shoulders. She was regal and held a staff by her side, reflecting her sovereignty. Like the shepherd, she called her people home to be held in the safe haven of her dark cloaks. As the wind blew, she turned to meet me and I remembered she was ancient, from before this time, from before all time. Her weathered face, etched with lines, held the wisdom of all time. Her eyes were limitless pools of unconditional love and her staff now morphed into a sword and I knew, with honour and integrity, she would unapologetically use her sword with the will of the Divine to intervene in the restoration of Divine Law. She was the ancient one who was at once the wise crone, the warrior mother and the wild maiden. I knew her as my beloved Athena, who was wise, my fierce protector Cynthia, who was warrior, and my free-spirited Marigold, who was wild. Humbled by the power and potency of her presence, she took my hand and welcomed me home. In complete trust, I surrendered to her and, embraced by the darkness of her cloak, I became one with her and was blessed with remembering that she was within me. I was her and had always been the *Wise Wild Warrior, the core of my soul.*

*She* who had called me from afar.

*She* who I had forgotten.

*She* who I had ignored.

*She* who I had run from for fear of her power.

*She* who demanded I now claim *her*, anchored within me.

*I am fierce and wild and unapologetic in my power.*

*I am the creator of chaos and the fuel for fire.*

*I make others uncomfortable because I illuminate truth.*

*I will raise my sword without apology in the name of Divine Law.*

*I am the safe haven for the divine darkness that magnifies the light.*

*I have waited on the edge of this cliff calling your name for lifetimes, knowing you would come from the depths of your darkness and remember me—remember you.*

In that instant, I was pulled back through the portal and into the hospital room where there remained nothing but his eyes holding me transfixed, safe and assured in the fullness of my presence. I knew nothing but love. I loved him fully, without expectation or apology, and in the divine darkness of his soul, my soul found her home and in Gabriel, I found my home.

'Get off her, you vile creature!'

Our union was smashed by the abhorrent screeching of the older nurse.

'Who are you? You have no right to be in here. She's to be left alone,' she spat.

'No, you have no right to be in here.'

She dropped back towards the door as he turned towards her.

'And *she* has a name.'

'I know her name,' she snapped furiously.

'Róisín Dubh,' she spat again, rolling her eyes at the name I had given when admitted, the name I had been running with since abandoning who I really was.

'This is not Róisín Dubh. This woman is Marigold Ciara Grian,' he professed forthrightly.

I was humbled that he knew my name, that he *knew* me fully. He took a step towards her.

'You judged and treated this woman without compassion or care because she had no band on her finger. In the shock of the baby coming early, she left her ring on the dresser. Shame on you,' he declared without the hint of reservation.

He held her shocked gaze for a moment before she ran from the room, terrified by his power. He turned and walked towards my bed. Taking a plain silver band from his pocket, he placed it ever so gently, ever so lovingly, ever so solemnly, on my finger.

*And so it remains.*

# CHAPTER 39

# Sacred Sorrow

'Get me my baby now!' I demanded of the young nurse who was trying to hold back her tears.

'Your baby did cry. He was very small, but he was alive. I will make this right. Never shall it happen again. I promise you this.'

She left the room, returning with my baby who she carefully handed to Gabriel. We did not see her again. I knew she would never be the same for witnessing all that transpired that day. In being present to both the distortion and divinity of darkness, she would become a powerful creator of change within that hospital, the church and the medical profession. *Blessings upon her.*

Gabriel gently yet firmly closed the door, claiming a sacred space for me to be with my baby boy. Tears rolled down my cheeks as I reached for him. Gabriel placed him in my arms. He was tiny but he was ever so perfect with sweet cherub lips and long dark lashes against the translucency of his skin.

He was cold, ever so cold. I drew him closer, placing him on my chest, willing my beating heart to warm him and there I stayed, gently kissing his tuft of soft black hair, inhaling the purity of his essence for an eternity. Gabriel sat beside me on the bed, a protective arm about me, not saying a word. His presence held me and somehow assured me that my own heart would continue to beat despite the lancet that had torn through it. It was an unimaginable pain, but I treasured the hours I spent holding my perfect baby boy. I feared he would be harmed in some way because he had come so early and had been created from my destructive darkness, but he was not. He was perfect, ten fingers, ten toes, long lean arms and legs. I rested my hand upon his ribs and felt for the beat of his heart again. I knew I had felt his pulse, his beat, his essence when I had first held him in my arms, before she cut him from me, ripped him from my arms and took his life.

I willed myself to again feel his pulse, to remember his life force, to know his soul.

A small smile crept across my face when the memory of his heartbeat reconnected with my own. I knew forever my precious baby boy would remain in my heart, healing my heart. My love for him guiding me forward, always towards love. *Nothing but love.*

I napped and wept, wept and napped. Gabriel spoke, ever so gently, after a few hours.

'Shall we go?'

'Where?'

I did not know what step to take, but I would follow him. I would follow his lead on the path of love.

'There is a church across the street. An old friend of mine, Michel, is the priest. He is a good man.'

I nodded.

'Will he bless him and treat him with the dignity he deserves?'

I had heard horror stories of what they did with babies like mine in hospitals like this. There was no honouring the sanctity of life when they threw them in incinerators, discarding them as no more than trash. Not my baby. He would be honoured.

He captured my eyes as he stood and assured me.

'Michel will help us make arrangements.'

He left the room for but a minute, returning with fresh blankets to wrap around my baby boy. He helped me stand and dress, my clothes having been unceremoniously thrown into a brown bag when they were stripped from me on my arrival. I carefully slipped into Johnny's jacket. It was comforting in its familiarity, yet strangely heavy. Gabriel put on my boots as I would not let go of my baby, then laid out the fresh blankets on the bed.

I unwrapped my precious boy and laid him on the new blankets. I kissed every finger and every toe. I trailed my fingers along the perfect ridge of his spine and laid my head upon his chest. My tears flooded his heart, and I enveloped him in those blankets, sealing in my love for an eternity.

I vowed I would walk from that hospital, past every one of those doctors and nurses with my head held high, cradling my baby just as any new mother was entitled. Nobody dared to stop us, for I imagine we were a formidable sight walking through the corridors, our dark presence intimidating. I was called to stop as we passed the nurses' tearoom. The old nurse was sitting in there, surrounded by peers, and I took her eyes in mine and whispered with clear intent.

'Should you ever take the life of another baby, I will come in the middle of the night with my sword and slice the throat of your precious grand babies, Samuel, Thomas and Christopher, who sleep under your roof every Saturday night.'

I trusted from the look of shock and terror upon her face that my sudden intuitive insight into her family was accurate and, with the further intervention of Father Michel in the confessional box, she would never take the life of another baby.

My whole body shuddered as we walked through the doors of the hospital into the crisp evening air. I wasn't sure how many hours, or even days, had passed since I had entered, yet I felt like a foreigner in a strange land walking back out those doors. The traumatised young woman who had entered had, through the fires of hell, been transformed into a woman, a wild, wise warrior, and strangely, I was overcome with the deepest gratitude.

Father Michel was, as Gabriel had assured me, a good man. He was more than good, he was a true man of Christ; gentle, compassionate, courageous and decisive. He did not blink an eye as Gabriel explained briefly what had occurred and that I would like for the baby to be cremated and his ashes returned as soon as possible. He simply nodded.

'I will make the arrangements, though it may take a day or two. I recommend staying in the hotel down the street. It is clean and run by wonderfully kind people. They will nourish you both and allow you rest, for you need it.'

He turned towards me, resting his hand upon my knee, and I was overcome by the remembering of a father's love. Even though he wasn't all that old, his presence was so soothing to my soul that a tear ran down my cheek as I allowed myself, for the first time in a very long time, to feel the absence of Caellach and his calm assuring presence in my life. Oh, how I missed him. I longed for the comfort of his embrace, and to renew my trust that everything would be alright, to help me reconnect to my faith in the Divine. Sensing my loss, Gabriel placed his arm softly about my shoulders and I surrendered. I stopped fighting love. I stopped resisting life and I softened into his embrace and into this, my new life, and whatever it held for me.

'What name have you given your son, Marigold?' Michel asked quietly.

I did not know the answer, for I had not considered naming him. He did not need a name to be forever in my heart. I stared at the baby in my arms and realised that naming him would claim him as real, affirming he had existed, not just in my heart but in my arms.

'Xavier,' I whispered, 'Xavier … my saviour.'

'Javier, a powerful name for a strong soul.'

He paused and closed his eyes, dropping into stillness and deep prayer. Almost immediately, I was overcome with peace as radiant love flowed through him, blessing my sweet Xavier's soul.

'Rest now in peace, Javier, with blessings upon your mighty soul. And blessings upon you, Marigold. May your journey home be gentle.'

He allowed me time to prepare for the separation from my baby, though nothing could truly prepare me for that moment and it remains the most heartbreaking moment of my life. I held my baby to my chest for the last time and inhaled his essence. I then took Johnny's jacket off and wrapped it around Xavier and kissed his sweet little lips before passing him over to Michel.

'Please make sure the jacket stays with him, holding him as he … as he goes.'

I kissed his forehead and stroked his cheek, awed by his perfection.

He was divine.

He was my divine gift.

He was my divine saviour.

Never a day passed where, in my remembering of him, I was not blessed with a flicker of pure unconditional love within my heart.

*My Xavier, the light in the darkness that guided me home.*

# CHAPTER 40

# Teacher Awakens

I rested and slept fitfully for the next two days before Michel came to the hotel with a small box containing Xavier's ashes. We took a cab straight to the airport and boarded the first flight to New York, intent on finalising Xavier's earthly story. It was strange to be back in the city I had once called home. I had avoided all shows that required me to return there over the previous year, but I knew I must now return to write the final chapter of my time there.

I did not contact anybody I knew. Gabriel had made enquiries over the past few days to ascertain where Johnny had been buried, and we went straight to the cemetery. In one hand, I held a small box containing the physical remains of my son. My other hand was held gently and reassuringly by Gabriel.

He helped me to my knees. I placed my hands upon the earth, eager to feel Johnny again. Intentionally, I had denied him for all these months, blocking him from connecting to any part of me, particularly my heart. I had pushed him away, refusing to meet him on the rainbow bridge, denying him even my dreams. I was afraid to feel him and his love in case it touched my heart and awakened my soul. Yet it was not he who had done that but my baby boy, who would now rest with him. In my rawness, my heart and soul torn open, and I felt his soul call to me through the earth that held his body. From the realms, the tears of his spirit fell upon me.

*Oh, Johnny.*
*Oh, Johnny Triboni, how I love thee.*
*How I always loved thee.*
*How I will always love thee.*

I sprinkled my Xavier's ashes upon the grave, my endless tears dampening the soil as I entrusted him to Johnny.

'Please take care of my baby, Johnny. Hold him as I will, love him as I will and let him never forget me, as I will never forget him or you.'

I collapsed onto the earth which now held the bodies of my loves, their time here on earth so fragile and heartbreakingly fleeting, yet their impact on my soul monumental. Because of them, I garnered the strength to go on.

'From now on, I promise I will take care of myself and be true to me. I'm sorry, my darling Xavier, that you did get the chance to know me, who I really am, that I couldn't be your mammy.'

Inhaling the air, I was gifted the memory of his pure sweet scent and, rising to my feet, I anchored into the earth. I was here, in this moment, in this life, and I remembered that only I had the power to choose what I did with this moment and my life. I vowed to Johnny and my Xavier as I stood before them, that I would always seek to choose the highest timeline, the path of love. Of course, it would not always be easy, and I understood at times I would make it incredibly hard for myself, harder than it needed to be, by allowing fear and doubt to rule my head and hijack my heart. But now, I would return to the *way of the soul*, the way my wise women had taught me. I would seek counsel from within, listening to the wisdom of my soul, regardless of what my head or the pain within my heart said.

Gabriel stood beside me, present, solid, silent, accepting and trusting.

'Thank you for finding me and holding me through the darkest of my days,' I whispered. 'If the invitation still stands, could I come with you on the road? I'm not ready to return to my family just yet. It's been … It's been a lot and I need time before I see them again.'

He smiled and the darkness of his eyes filled with light.

'Of course. We'll fly back to Chicago tomorrow to pick up the RV.'

As more tears soaked the sacred earth, I farewelled my boys, my loves.

Gabriel held my hand as we left the cemetery and slowly walked towards our hotel.

'I don't know how I ended up being there with you during all those horrible experiences. I've been as confused as you. All I knew was something powerful drew me to you. But I've been contemplating it over the last couple of days and I'm starting to understand why. You see …,' he paused for a moment before continuing a little awkwardly. 'When I left the monastery, yes, I was studying to become a priest. That is how I know Michel. My family were enraged and ashamed of me because for a Catholic family, it was the greatest honour for a son to be a priest. In their eyes, I had dishonoured them. Except for my grandmother. She was a deeply spiritual woman and different to the rest of my family. We had this unique bond and when my family turned their back on me, she invited me to stay with her. After I had wallowed for a week—because they were indeed dark days for me— she demanded I get out of bed one evening and sit with her. She scared me sometimes because she was so blunt. She suffered no fool and refused to enable me to spiral any longer. She told me it was time I moved on with my life. She knew I was destined for bigger things, well beyond what the church offered me. She shared that before she left her village in the mountains when she was a young woman, long before she married my grandfather, the Shaman had taken her aside and stated that one day her grandson would be a teacher, but not in the traditional ways.

She had never forgotten, despite never mentioning a word to another person, and when I entered the monastery, she was devastated, believing I had lost my way, that the church was an ending, not a beginning for me. She took my eye and declared, "You have been called beyond there and now your true journey to become the teacher begins.

It hurts my heart to say this, but you must leave Peru to discover you." I guess it was the permission to leave I had been unknowingly waiting for, and in many ways, my family were glad to see the back of me, my presence a reminder of the shame I had brought on the Rodriguez name. Only my grandmother came to the airport with me. As we bid farewell, she handed me a card which I have read a million times over the last seven years, both comforted and confused by it.'

He pulled the worn card from his wallet and shared her gnosis.

'My Gabriel, to become the teacher, one must walk the path. This path will not be easy for you, but you will always find your way back through your heart. Do not forget your heart beneath that hardened shield you too often raise against the world. The student arrives when the teacher is ready. She will be golden but lost in the dark. Honour her path, show her the way and in turn she will teach you more than you could ever know alone.'

Again, he paused, clearly overwhelmed to finally share this truth with me.

'I saw you long before you saw me. You just kept popping up in bars and hotels across the country and I *knew* you were the one my grandmother had foreseen. Even in the darkness you were immersing yourself in, I could only see your light. It was impossibly hard to witness what you were doing to yourself, and I didn't know how I was meant to help you. I prayed on it, and I randomly found myself in those horrible moments with you. Something would happen to you when we connected, so I just followed my heart. And now we are here. I've spent days contemplating what it is all about, and I believe my grandmother's prophecy is true. I held you through your darkest days and now, if you allow me, I will walk beside you as you learn to hold yourself in the darkness. We cannot deny it. It is within you, within me, within all of us, and we must learn to trust it. It can be a beautiful creative force, or it can be dangerously destructive. Both are important because both are teachers.'

He hesitated before turning and walking away. I waited in silence, trusting in his return. And he did, his eyes dark and sorrowful, brimming with truth.

'I feared for a long time that my grandmother would be ashamed of me because I messed up. But now I understand that she knew I would stumble, fall and hit rock bottom, and learn some really harsh, yet important lessons. You see, I had always been the good boy, always seeking to make my father proud. That was the only reason I entered the monastery. I left Peru in emotional turmoil and with no idea what to do with my life. I arrived in LA and found myself in the music industry and my first few years were really messy. I was totally seduced by the whole scene and my dark side ran wild. I dishonoured myself, misused my power and forgot who I was. When one of my friends died in my arms from an overdose, I finally had enough and went to rehab, and got off alcohol and the drugs. I move around a lot, and I am in the scene but also out of the scene. It has allowed me to practice living with integrity in a very dark industry. Most people want me to go back to being who I was before rehab, you know. I was more fun, less intense, easier to relate too, easier to manipulate! But I never will. I know who I am now, and yeah, I might be way too intense, abrupt and aloof for most of them, but I don't care what they think of me. They're not important. My heart is what's important to me and it guides me. It takes me into dark places, but I try to bring goodness into that world and maybe I make a difference, maybe I guide some down a wiser path.'

He dropped into silence, appearing to process all that he had disclosed in opening his heart to me. I was both humbled and honoured in his trust. In turn, I trusted him to guide me on the next part of my journey.

'There's a festival in Wisconsin up near the border this weekend,' he continued, returning to his abrupt style and resetting boundaries, his own and those that we would operate within. 'I had to figure this all out myself, be my own teacher, so maybe this is meant to be easier for you. But it won't be easy, and I won't be easy on you. There are rules if you want to walk this path with me: no alcohol, no drugs and no sex. They are the seductive dark threads, not necessarily bad, but they can lead you off the path way too easily if you can't yet hold yourself.'

I nodded in understanding and acceptance. I longed for the new way and his hard line would support me in staying true to it.

'First, I'm your teacher and I won't always be gentle and sweet. It's not who I am. Learn or don't learn, it's up to you. I figure we'll both know when it's done. Second, I'm a friend. I won't rescue or babysit you or enable victim behaviour, but I will be here for you to lean on if you need. Beyond that …,' he paused and stared curiously at me for some time. 'I guess that remains a mystery that is best left in the unknown.'

He was direct and clear with his boundaries. I knew where I stood, what we were and what we were not. I smiled as I heard the whisper of my soul, *We're in!*

'We're in,' I nodded, offering him my hand.

He took it.

'May God help us both!' he murmured with the hint of a smile.

*And so, our journey began.*

# Part Five

# CHAPTER 41

# Beyond The Storm

My body, mind and spirit needed time and space to heal. There was no rush and Gabriel allowed me to move at my pace with no expectation of what I was meant to be doing. I heard the festival music and the crowds, but I wanted no part of it. It was but a distant noise of the external world and I was deeply immersed in my internal world. Nor did I have the energy, as my body was physically rebuilding from the torrent of abuse I had subjected it to for well over a year. Gabriel ensured I ate nourishing food, drank mountains of water and herbal teas and that the RV was dark and warm so I could sleep as much as I needed, day or night. I asked him to walk with me, sometimes early in the morning or late in the night when he returned to the RV, as I longed to once again be held by Mother Nature. We didn't really talk on those walks. I relished the silence and solitude. I was alone for long periods of time, Gabriel allowing me to do what I needed. He was always busy with work commitments, and yet we were acutely aware of each other's presence.

After a few months, when I became stronger in my body, my emotions rose forcefully to the surface and I could do nothing to suppress them. Grief, sorrow and agony expelled in torrents of tears and muffled howls into my pillow day after day, night after night. I allowed them to flow. However, I knew more was required to allow the rage, anger, guilt, shame and regret to move through my body and be transmuted.

One morning before the sun rose, after yet another restless night where my unease turned to panic, I ran into the forest that bordered the festival. I kept running until I fell to the ground in exhaustion. It was only when I found myself straddled across the dampness of the mossy rocks that I surrendered and, held by the great Mother herself, I purged. I knew if I did not dispel it fully, it would come back to haunt me as trauma always does. The guilt and shame were by far the hardest to release. My head told me every story about how I did not deserve peace and freedom, how I had betrayed my soul, my family, my wise women and how they would be ashamed if they knew the truth of who I had become. Flashes of dark memories infiltrated my mind. No matter how much I cried or thrashed or moved my body, I could not escape the sickening shame and galvanizing guilt that sought to trap me in the past, blocking my way to claiming my new life. I called on my soul, my guides, the Divine, beseeching them to release me from this pain, but *she* would not raise her sword to free me while I remained in fear.

*What are you afraid of?*

I could not answer the query of my soul because the noise in my head hijacked my truth. No matter what I did, I could not free myself from the charge of these emotions. I was stuck in the turmoil of my past. That night, as I sat alone on my bed, filled with anxiety, despondency and irritation at my inability to transcend and transmute my emotions, Gabriel entered holding a drum, an Irish drum, the bodhrán.

'This may help,' he said, placing it beside me on the bed.

I wanted to fight him and his intuitive knowing, but I paused and began to sob instead, hoping he would hold me and make it all go away. But he promised me he would not make it easy for me and he refused to enable my victim. He turned to leave and go back to the festival, but as he walked through the door, he turned with a final glance.

'Damn it, Marigold. You know what to do, you've done it your whole life!'

Driven by a renewed force, I drew the drum to my nose, inhaling the familiar scent of goat skin. I rose, heading outside to the small fire Gabriel had built. Closing my eyes, I inhaled deeply. On exhaling, I rested my hand upon the taunt skin, as familiar to me as my own skin and I wept. I was immediately taken home to my gypsy family, anchored by Athena and Cynthia. With the bodhrán resting tentatively upon my thigh, I began to drum. As my hand connected with the skin, threads of my being connected to my wild, wise warrior, and she asked me again.

*What are you afraid of?*

This time, as I drummed, the answer was clear. *I'm terrified that I got it wrong. That all the things I did to harm myself and others have tarnished my soul forever. I'm scared that no matter what I do, the damage is done and there is no way back. I'll never make it home.*

BOOM. BOOM. BOOM.

I thumped the drum, rage pouring through me, and I guided it inwards, towards that part of myself that insisted on condemning and punishing me. I rose and began to move my body wildly as I sought to release not the guilt, not the shame, not the regret, for they would go when this vile voice within me had been transmuted. It fought desperately for supremacy, seeking to silence the roar of my wild, wise warrior who would no longer allow the judgement of who I was, *all the parts of me.* Her wisdom spoke directly to my heart and rose above the critical chaos of my mind.

*Judgement of who you have been is holding you hostage to the patriarch.*
*You are worthy in all your expressions.*
*You are enough in all your expressions.*
*You are loved in all your expressions.*
*Your light and your dark in its divinity, dormancy and distortion.*
*The Divine does not judge.*
*The Divine loves the all of you.*

I danced and drummed as I received her truth, weaving it into my cells, my layers, my soul tapestry while I simultaneously disabled the critical vile voice within my head. I stayed grounded in my body as I danced and drummed, feeling the flow of energy moving through and around me. The battle raged between what sought to hold me back and what sought to move me beyond the stories of my past.

I gradually slowed down my movements, dropping into a gentle hum. Resting my hand on the skin of the drum, I witnessed and experienced the energy settling within and around me, claiming it all, for it was pure peace and contentment.

Oh, how my soul relished the beauty of that moment! And I held onto it, despite the shock of opening my eyes to see a crowd encircling me. I had not been aware of their presence whilst I was in my embodied trance state, but as I glanced about the group, it was evident they had never witnessed such primal healing. No words could explain, nor did I feel an obligation to rationalise what they had observed. They had been called to witness the inner workings of my sacred space, and I would not be shamed for the fullness of my woman, her wildness, her rawness, her ugliness, her darkness, her light, her rage, her agony, her too muchness. I turned my back to them and returned to my bed where I slept peacefully for the first time in months.

*An arrow in the script of the patriarch.*

# CHAPTER 42

# Inner Peace

I woke renewed, proud of myself for facing my demons and reclaiming my power from them. I enthusiastically shared my experience with Gabriel though he did not seem overly impressed. The more I divulged about my healing, the more irritated he appeared to become, which began to annoy me. *Couldn't he give me something?*

'Can you stop now, please? I'm pleased the bodhrán helped you moved things within you, but don't think that it's done.'

'What do you mean? Can't you just say well done?'

'No, I can't. I won't let you succumb to comforting illusions. You agreed to let me guide you and I told you it wouldn't be easy, nor would I be soft on you.'

I'd been working so hard over the past few months to overcome addiction, heal my body and tackle so many wounded parts of myself. I believed I had finally made a significant breakthrough. I wanted and needed his validation.

'You know better than that. You don't just learn the lesson, reclaim lost parts or awaken new parts of yourself and then think the job's done. I won't let you walk that path and bypass the real work. It starts now. It's hard to integrate these changes and hold on to them when you are challenged, when you are threatened, when it doesn't feel safe. Of course it's going to feel safe to be a warrior when you're hanging out alone in the RV or wandering through the woods by yourself. But can you hold her out there in the world? Every evolution will be challenged. Many stumble at the first hurdle because their ego tells them it's done, but it's not. The energy may have shifted, but the body, where the memories are retained, will reveal where there is still work to be done. To move from one who has learnt a lesson to one who has mastered the lesson requires a complete rewiring of the body's nervous system and reweaving of the soul.'

I understood everything he said. I'd been raised by the wisest of teachers, who taught me the way of the soul, but it was different actually living it. It was hard.

'All I wanted was for you to say well done, not to criticise me.'

'I'm not criticising you. That's merely your perception. And look what happens when you feel you are being rejected. You contract because it doesn't feel safe anymore. You become defensive or you dissociate so you don't have to deal with it. That's your way of staying safe and if you can't overcome that, you are never going to be able to bring the all of you out into the world. Because the truth is, it isn't always safe out there. You are going to be judged, rejected and condemned, and you are going to be scared. But you've got to get to the point of trusting yourself, especially those powerful dark threads that hold you, support you and protect you. They can't if you run from them every time something makes you uncomfortable.'

'Just leave me alone! You're the one that's making me feel unsafe. You and your preaching.'

He smirked and raised his eyebrows, totally calling me on my victim behaviour which only infuriated me more. However, in my petulant silence that followed, I quite humbly could see how my fear-based reactive patterns continued to disempower me.

'Okay, okay, I get it. So what do I do now?'

'Do you trust me?' he asked more gently, sensing he had brought me to the other side.

I nodded, and he told me to put my shoes on and get some water and food together because we were going into the mountains.

I relished each breath and felt a renewed connection with the beauty of nature as we briskly hiked into the mountains. She spoke to me, the air and water, the rocks and moss, the trees and bushes, a choir of Mother Nature's making, singing only of love in a perfect harmony. I kept my focus here because, in truth, I was nervous about where he was taking me. I knew it was going to be beyond my comfort. After some time, Gabriel diverged off the trail and I followed him deep into the forest, where the canopy of tree branches blocked even the sky and we found ourselves in the shadows. And yet Gabriel was not fazed, confidently taking one step after another.

'Feel for me. Trust me,' was all he said until he abruptly stopped.

His hand reached for me and guided me onto what I assumed was a large fallen log. We sat in silence as his hand held onto mine. It was incredibly peaceful, but in the passage of time as the silence and darkness intensified, I became uncomfortable. It was a relief when Gabriel's voice broke the silence, his first question gentle.

'Why don't you feel safe in your body?'

I didn't know what to say and he continued more bluntly.

'Why can't you trust your body?'

I pulled my hand from his, not comfortable with the intensity of his energy, nor his questions.

'Why can't you accept her, even now, after she showed you her beauty and her power?'

I wished he would stop. I did not want to face this, face myself.

'You remembered her in the hospital. You allowed her to cleanse your soul, and you allowed her to heal you last night. But as soon as it gets uncomfortable, you dissociate, leave your body and lose your power. Why?'

I was determined not to react and run, though fear demanded I escape. I exhaled.

'Because it's safer *there* than it is *here*. And when I go there, I can find someone to comfort me, to make me feel better. My Ma's or Johnny or a guide or an angel, or I just drop into the light and then I feel safe.'

'But when you're there, you're not here, and you become powerless here in your body. It's like you unplug yourself, weaken your boundaries and protection and then you're susceptible to anyone or anything.'

Everything Gabriel was saying made sense.

'It's what I've always done. Like a default switch,' I whispered.

'Of course it's a default. It's a deeply unconscious behaviour you've adopted to keep yourself safe, but it doesn't. It's holding you back and you're not going to get any further until you master this. Your body is essential to your soul's journey. The mastery is in finding there while staying here.'

The clouds billowed overhead, engulfing us in shadowy darkness that stirred at the edges of my comfort. In desperation, I sought to understand this pattern. Gabriel guided me.

'Remember, it is a feeling, not a thought. Get out of your head and into your body. Where do you feel unsafe in your body?'

I was immediately drawn to my heart and, resting my hand upon it, it flittered erratically, like a bird caught in a trap. With one breath to centre myself, I asked the wisdom in my heart to show me what I could not see. Instantly, a vision engulfed my awareness and I understood.

'Gabriel, I have to go back.'

'Back where?'

'Back to where it began. Back to when I first escaped my body when I was alone and scared and there was nothing. Back to when all I had been promised in coming into this life had not eventuated. You see, when I was born, the young woman who birthed me left me amongst the stones on the mountains. I have done so much work around this before. I have been there before and held the infant that I was and told her she was loved and that she was enough. But I see now there is more that I must do. Then, I would have been terrified, abandoned and rejected. To protect myself, I must have dissociated from my wee little body and gone beyond this world to where my soul knew it to be safe. I don't think it was ever really an issue when I was a child, before I moved to New York, because I always had people around me who loved me and made me feel safe. I didn't really know fear until I moved to the city and then Johnny sought to protect me, even though I adamantly refused the need for a bodyguard. I realise now that he was the anchor keeping me in my body, assuring me I was safe, and then he left me.'

I became overwhelmed by the memories as I continued on.

'I know it is up to me. I have to learn how to anchor myself to stay in my body even when I feel unsafe. I can see how it has diminished my power, but more importantly my presence. It takes me away from life and all that it offers me, even those parts that are terrifying or triggering. I understand how important they are, because they are the lesson, and how powerful it is for me to stay within my body and experience them fully.'

'So, what are you going to do?' Gabriel asked, firmly planting responsibility for this journey in my hands.

'I'm going back to her to transmute the pattern, my response to fear.

I'm going to stay up here tonight with her, in the dark, alone, and we are going to do it together, just me and my infant self. I'll be okay. You go back and do whatever it is you do all night and I'll come back down in the morning.'

'Okay. I trust you can do this.'

And he left. Alone and awash with courage, I closed my eyes, placed my hand on my heart and inhaled deeply. As I exhaled, my awareness took me to the place of my birth where my mother was holding me, staring lovingly into my eyes. I was safe, one with her, not knowing nor expecting separation. I absorbed the love bestowed upon me by my mother, reinforcing my deep inner knowing that I was loved. I was enough. I could see it in her eyes. It was undeniable. I knew what I needed to do to transmute the trauma of separation, the wound of abandonment and the fear of rejection. Through the realms and into *her* ear, I lovingly whispered. *You are not alone. I am here with you. You are not alone. I am here with you. You are not alone. I am here with you.*

My mother stroked my cheek and kissed my forehead, in much the same way I had with my own baby boy. Now I had experienced the loss of a child, her despair in leaving me was palpable and tore open my heart, exposing its rawness. From this place, I witnessed two angels appear on a golden ray. As my mother placed me on the ground, one angel wrapped its wings around her, comforting her torment, while the other wrapped its exquisite wings around my infant self, cocooning me in golden light, assuring me I was safely held in love and that my soul would always be safe in my physical body.

I joyfully witnessed my infant self breathe with relief and surrender into her little body, trusting it fully to protect her. I stayed with her in my mind's eye until Cynthia and Athena came upon her and scooped her lovingly into their arms. Knowing she was safe, and the next chapters of her life would be written in nothing but love, I prepared to leave the timeline and return to the present. But before I left, I was called to acknowledge the safe space within my own body, deep within my heart, where I held the healing of this memory and my precious infant self-cocooned in love.

Through the night, I was tempted by my fear, particularly as the darkness engulfed me, but I remained in my body, anchoring myself with a mantra. *I am safe in my body.*

Despite the occasional surge of adrenaline, I never once sought to escape the sanctity of my body and I experienced both relief and pride as dawn broke, knowing I had been tested and passed. I would be challenged beyond the mountain, in the real world, but I was confident in my power.

I wandered back down the trail, contemplating the path before me, when I became aware of a presence in the distance. It was golden, like the angels who had embraced me in my vision, and as I moved closer, I received a transmission of pure love, which illuminated the divinity of *she* who lay within me and also, *he* who was before me.

Gabriel did not see me as I approached the tree he was resting against. He looked exhausted after what must have been a restless night waiting for me. He had not returned to the festival, instead allowing me the space I required while remaining at the end of the trail in case I called to him.

I was humbled by the depths of his love for me as my guardian angel, my guide, my teacher and I pondered whether, in his human form, he could love me as man to woman. I sensed it was beyond the contract of our souls, but in remembering the vastness of my soul and honouring the calling of my heart, the seed was planted.

*All is possible when no thing is impossible.*

# CHAPTER 43

# Radical Acceptance

We bathed in a crystal clear stream at the bottom of the mountain, her crisp cleansing waters soothing to my soul. I was not ashamed of my body, nor intimidated by Gabriel's strong, lean body. Silence, our preferred language when he was not downloading wisdom, held us in a sacred space, allowing me once again to claim a deep inner peace and reconnect to the sense of oneness I had been so familiar with before the storm of my life. And despite Gabriel's presence, maybe because of his presence, I was able to surrender to the solitude enveloping me as I floated in the stream, allowing the morning sun to kiss my tender skin and heal my bruised soul.

We slept that day after nourishing our bodies, for neither of us had slept the night before. Without invitation, he came and lay with me, placing his arm around my waist. Held in his embrace, I fell asleep, allowing all that had transpired the previous night to be woven into the tapestry of my soul. When I opened my eyes a few hours later, he was gone, yet I could still feel his presence beside me. He had a charge that was extraordinarily hard to define. I believe everyone felt his intensity when they were with him, whether they wanted to or not. Often, he spoke, yet not through words and his message was always clear and often bluntly revealed truth, for he was not about playing games.

The space beside me almost pulsated with the imprint of his presence and I longed for him, in what capacity I was not sure. Before I could resist, the memory of waking without Johnny beside me struck every part of my being and I began to shake. I did not want to remember him not being beside me, him being in my bed, him being within me. These memories had been purposefully blocked from my mind; they were laced with a passion I had not felt with another. Nothing I had experienced since came close to the sensuality and sexuality I shared with Johnny. The more I fought these thoughts and memories that flashed through my mind, the more my body ached with desire, pulsations moving through my yoni and into my womb. I gripped the sheets beside me to steady myself as the waves of longing demanded to be met. This only made it worse as Gabriel's energy was etched in the sheets. I remained present with my body as his energy moved within me and as my desire rose, I surrendered, unable to contain the fullness of my sexual energy. As a surge of yearning tore through my being, I released with an exquisitely agonising gasp. I breathed deeply, inhaling and exhaling, staying within my body, refusing to run from the fear of my own sensuality, trusting I was safe in my sexuality. Startled by the opening of the door, I quickly pulled the covers over myself, attempting to hide what I knew Gabriel would see, would feel, would *know*, and I was ashamed.

And there it was! Shame, still lingering in the shadows.

'Get dressed.' Gabriel said in a candid tone, once again leading me to believe I had done something to upset him.

I dressed quickly, my black uniform of the past having been replaced with the simplicity of jeans, t-shirt and sandals. My hair had begun to grow longer and had returned to its original golden colour. Without doubt, on every level, I was an evolving landscape, aspects of me eroding while new parts awakened, the dormant threads of who I once was slowly being reclaimed.

I met him outside. With no explanation, he grabbed my hand and guided me across the paddocks towards the festival, through the crowd and towards the main stage. We had attended over twenty festivals, yet never had I watched any of the artists perform, nor had I mixed with the crowd, preferring my own space to heal in solitude. Now, I was surrounded by people. I felt overwhelmed, for I had not connected with anyone except Gabriel for months. He did not stop to tend to my discomfort, so I focused on my body and breathed through it. I trusted him, yet still I was nervous when he began flashing his VIP card and weaving us backstage. Once we were positioned on the edge of the stage, he turned to me and stared me in the eye.

'Be *her.*'

'What?' I queried, blind to his intent.

'The best way to overcome your fear of something is to face it, and the best way to overcome a fear of yourself is to become *her*. Just let her be.'

'You are not serious!' I retorted, realising why we were at the side of the stage.

'I watched you the other night when you played the drum. You drew a crowd without even knowing it. *She* ... you lured them in and seduced them, connecting with them and touching places within them that they had never felt before, activating them, awakening them. You were fucking healing them before my eyes. You have absolutely no idea of your power and you keep hiding it beneath the sheets!'

'You were watching?' I felt a wave of shame with the knowing that such a raw aspect of myself had been exposed to him.

'I'm the teacher. I'm always watching!' he declared bluntly before allowing the hint of a smirk to dance on the edge of his lips, momentarily breaking the intensity, before continuing. 'You were filled with shame when I walked in on you just before, but you've nothing to be ashamed of. It is *your* power. But I get it. I know shame because I've carried it within me as well and it's toxic. It will destroy you, your magic, your mystery and your majesty.'

Not since he had challenged the old nurse in the hospital had I heard him speak with such passion and he turned away in his vulnerability, attempting to anchor himself.

'Marigold, you get to choose right now whether you keep feeding that shame and giving power to all those stories you hold within yourself, or whether you leave the stories behind and rise up to meet that divine part of yourself that is so fucking sensual and sexual and wild and exotic. You claim *her* or she will end up rotting inside of you, and that is a fucking waste to all those people out there who are waiting to be touched by *her*.'

It was too much, it really was. The last thing I thought I was capable of was performing on stage in front of all those people and allowing my wild Dark Goddess to come out and play. In truth, I was scared to let her out of the cage in case she ran wild and caused utter destruction again. I desperately fought him.

'I did claim *her*, and she might have been sensual and sexual and wild, but she was dangerous, not divine. So far from divine—you saw how that ended! You were there to see the disaster my life became when I allowed her to run wild and do as she please.'

He took me behind the stage and stood directly before me, so I had nowhere to run.

'Marigold, just stop the bullshit. Is she really dangerous or is that the story you are telling yourself to stay safe?'

'I don't know… Maybe? But she doesn't keep me safe. She almost ruined my life!'

'But that wasn't *her*. That was you distorting her and misusing her power to destroy yourself, to punish yourself. That is very different. You know *her* in her truth, and once, you did hold her with integrity. Once, you completely accepted and allowed *her* to move through your body. But then, Marigold, you blamed *her* for the rope going around his neck. But it wasn't *her* fault. It wasn't YOUR fault, Marigold. You know this already, but you are still using it to keep her hidden.'

He knew what he was not meant to know about the hidden crevices of my heart. And he had determinedly, yet compassionately, struck the lingering remnants of this wound.

Tears rolled down my face, the memory torturous.

'I know it wasn't my fault. I know it wasn't *her* fault. But after that, with all those men, she was … bad, to put it mildly. She hurt them and me.'

'No, she wasn't bad. You weren't bad. You misused your power because you were stuck in your wounded maiden, trying to figure out how to become a woman while actively punishing yourself at the same time.'

'Can we just go home and talk about it there?' I begged, becoming increasingly anxious with the emotions arising within me and the flux of people coming and going from the stage.

'Stop and take a breath. This is uncomfortable for both of us, but it's the next step. Please trust me.'

He softened and we sat on the grass behind the stage, which was quieter and more private, for Gabriel to continue his teachings.

'You already know so much of what I share with you. But in the here and now, you need to hear it again, to receive it in a new way. You keep judging yourself for getting it wrong, for misusing your sexual energy. But an energy that is dormant for so long, that then awakens, like a wild animal released from a cage, will express itself in ways that are not wise. But that is simply because it does not yet know the wisest way to express itself. It is only through the wounds and pain of the distortion that the wild animal learns how to hold its power and to use it in ways that serves all that is. Some, the ones not quite ready, not quite courageous enough, will run back into the cage, believing it is easier and safer there. That may be best for a time, if that time is used to contemplate the path forward and garner the courage to come out once again. But it is the one who stays within the cage, fearful of who they are being called to become, who will abort their true nature for the safety of what is known. They will die, their soul will fade and all that will remain will be an empty vessel living a meaningless, but seemingly safe, existence. While the wise ones, those who have the courage to move beyond what is known, they practice holding the energy of their fullest expression and discern when and how to use it, not from their head, but from their heart. They understand that they will make mistakes and they are okay with that, because their journey to mastery is not dictated by perfection. In fact, it is guided by imperfection. When you move beyond judgement into acceptance of all you have been, all you are and all you will become, then you return to the centre of your heart and claim the throne of your soul. And from there, you can allow *her* in all her expressions: the messy, the beautiful, the vile, the graceful, the death, the rebirth, the student, the master.'

*When we judge the student, we can never become the master.*

'Can you be compassionate with yourself? Back then, you were still learning how to hold the fullness of your dark threads, your sexual, sensual, wild, exotic energy! She is powerful and potent, and I imagine it is not easy to hold *her* energy with integrity. Sure, you messed up, but did you learn? Did you learn from the mess? Are you wiser, softer, stronger … truer … because of all of it?'

'I have learnt now. My baby boy forced me to learn. To reflect on what I did, why I did it, and I have tried to forgive myself, tried to forgive them.'

'Can you accept her, the girl you were, with forgiveness and compassion? Can you love her and allow her, the woman waiting to be reclaimed to be part of your life, in a divine way? Because she is something special, and her spirit, her spark, her passion, her power is needed to help others to see beyond the here and now, to consciousness. That's what you do, Marigold. You take people beyond the limitations of *here*. You show them *there* and who they can be.'

I pondered his invitation. I realised that once I had believed that to be loved, to be enough, I had to get it right all the time, to be divine, and only express myself from my heart and soul. But I was learning, or rather being shown, that I was worthy of being loved, whether I was *this* or *that*, divine or distorted, 'good girl' or 'bad girl', acting from love, or from ego and wound. It didn't matter. All was worthy of being loved, and that was my challenge, to accept all of me, because the Divine loves all of me, in my light, my dark and in the shadow where the invitation to growth lies. And in Gabriel's eyes, I knew he did, too.

Our trance was broken by the stage manager bellowing over the railing at the rear of the stage.

'It's time, mate. If you want her to go on, she's got to go on now!'

I sensed he was doing Gabriel a huge favour and, though he may have begrudged it, few denied him what he asked.

'Okay, you're right. It is time. Time I claimed *her*, regardless of whether I get it right or wrong. I have to let her be.'

He handed me the bodhrán.

'There is no right or wrong. There is only *her*. Only you, Marigold. You are worthy of love, any which way.'

He kissed my forehead and held me by the shoulders. In his anchor, I felt my wild, wise warrior stir within my womb, and I knew I was ready to allow my desire to be wild and free and unapologetically sexual and sensual once again. I was ready to claim *her* and share *her*, claim me, and share the potency of my gift with those who were ready and able to receive me.

*And once again, I rose to meet my soul's calling.*

# CHAPTER 44

# Heart Wisdom

I strode onto the stage and, with an exhalation, I released memories of taking the stage for the first time at St Christopher's. I honoured who I once was, loving her for all she had been and all she had taught me. Then, I chose me. I hit the drum with my hand and stared into the audience stilled in anticipation for my birth. As she entered the world, my body moved innately, twisting, turning, thrusting, and my voice sounded in chants, moans, howls and screams. I stayed within my body, feeling every movement, present to every sound released, aware of each shift in the flow of my energy, the unfurling of layer upon layer upon layer, the shedding, the rawness of birthing the new.

I did not shy from the eyes of those before me. I held them, seeing them and knowing them in the fullness of *their* truth, inviting them to reveal all that was hidden in *their* shadows. All that was not for this world to know, all that was too much, too shameful, too dangerous, too offensive, too provocative, too intense, too taboo, too extreme.

All they believed was not allowed in the light.

All they had been programmed to judge as wrong.

All they had refused to accept within themselves.

All they denied and fought desperately to suppress, creating struggle and pain, disharmony and disease.

And into the light, their shadows rose, tentative at first, fearing judgement and condemnation. But, as I held the darkness and honoured the shadow, individual and collective, it danced without apology, freeing itself from the darkened corners of the soul and claiming its divinity. A light blossomed, swirling through the crowd, inspiring me to anchor even further into my depths, determined to draw more of the shadows from within the beings before me.

Standing motionless, I became aware of a staff in my hand, anchoring my warrior, holding me within my body as I expanded into battle, knowing it would be used in love to dissolve the distortion of darkness. And like the shepherd, I would show others the way through the void of darkness, befriending it, trusting it and working with it to activate the light. I rose ever taller, expanding in every way as the devilish darkness boiled to the surface of the crowd. The misuse, corruption, betrayal, manipulation, vengeance, greed, hatred and evil taunted at the edges of the collective. Those who did not know this energy danced untouched by its eruption. Those who had indeed tampered with the undivine expressions of the dark were drawn into my sphere.

I rose.

Like a giant Goddess, I expanded my presence, more able than ever to hold the darkness across all its expressions. With a strike of my drum, I became aware of my wings unfolding. Gold-laced and as dark as the midnight sky, they drew forward those who were ready to receive my presence. With each waver, they came closer, laying down their shame for dishonouring the power of the darkness, their guilt for dishonouring the sacredness of others and their regret for dishonouring their truest expression of self. So many came forth under my spell to dissolve the stain upon their soul and reclaim the sacred beauty of their dark threads. I watched and witnessed the purging, from quiet sobs to hysterical screeching, from a moan to a howl, from gentle swaying to feisty thrashing of bodies, and from within the crowd *they* appeared—the bellboys. Those who raped me. They walked side by side towards me before humbly stopping and dropping to their knees, stripped of shame and guilt. They were filled with despair, desperately begging for forgiveness. I was unsure whether they were real or apparitions, fragments of my past drawn to the present and into my presence. Regardless, I held them in the fullness of my darkness, my heart expanding ever more, knowing nothing but love. Though filled with compassion, I would not offer them forgiveness, though I had forgiven them within my own heart.

*Forgiveness will only be received by hearts that have forgiven themselves.*

I implored them, and all those who stood alongside them, to open their hearts and to see themselves with compassion and forgiveness, through the eyes of the Divine who does not condemn the path we walk nor the mistakes we make. In opening to forgiveness, we are invited to live in truth, to walk both in darkness and light, guided by the divinity of the heart. As they forgave themselves, their own divinity kissed the edges of their darkness and a great light reflected from their beings. As a witness from the stage, I was awed by the beautiful kaleidoscope of their energy field.

Inspired by the transformation, my wings stretched further still, weaving through the realms, drawing an energy who had long lingered in the shadows to stand before me. The stage, the crowd, the bellboys, all became a blur, except for him and as he stepped forward, he demanded I see him fully. I paused, confused, and suddenly I knew him intimately, for I had come from him, and I carried parts of him within me. He showed me then, in my silent recognition, how he pinned the young woman against the wall of the pub, pulling up her skirt and forcing himself into her. She did not cry out, she did not flinch and her eyes, capturing mine, were nothing but shock and terror. My own body began to buckle, the strength of my dark-winged warrior failing to hold her and the truth of her trauma.

*The crippling truth of the trauma of my creation.*

As a witness to this truth, I doubted myself.

'You can and you must, Marigold. Believe in *her*.'

Gabriel's voice travelled through the realms, carrying the wisdom of my own soul, acting as a ballast to steady my ship. Through him, I believed in the power of my darkness, the wild, wise warrior, to face the horror of this shared truth. I arched my back, releasing a primordial roar and, drawing into my fullest expression, I courageously entered the portal opened to me by the man I knew to be my biological father. This young man had raped the young woman who, in turn, had birthed me, ashamed, alone and terrified in the darkness of The Burren. It was in my creation that her nightmare had begun, and I held her in my wings, assuring her that from the darkness, a light would be born.

*I was that light, the light born from her darkness.*

He drew my mind's eye back to him to reveal his triumph at stripping her sacredness, pilfering her power and claiming his lust-filled desire. I prickled at his smugness, dangerously close to armouring my heart, drawing my sword, ready to destroy him. I knew I could, for he was not a man who could meet me in battle. He was weak and yet, I understood that I was a reflection of him, the cells throughout my body, holding his story as my own. As I sought to vilify him, so I sought to demonise those aspects of myself. Visions of those men whom I had lured into my web and, in abhorrent vengeance, dishonoured, came towards the stage, and I realised I was no better than the man who had raped my mother, forcing my creation.

*How could I have done to others what he did to her?*
*How did I allow myself to become him?*
*How can I possibly forgive him?*
*How can I possibly forgive myself?*
*Oh, how could I ever forgive myself?*

I sobbed, broken and, as I fell to the ground, I begged those I had dishonoured to forgive me.

'I'm sorry, please forgive me. I'm so sorry, please forgive me.'

Then I surrendered to the darkness, trusting she would take me where I needed to go. And she did. The exquisite beauty of my darkened wings wrapped around me, and I was held, cocooned within my own being. My heart thumped, assuring me of her presence, and in the void between each beat she whispered.

*Love her (dom dom).*
*Accept her (dom dom).*
*Forgive her (dom dom).*
*All of her (dom dom).*
*Even the most ungraceful (dom dom).*
*Especially the most ungraceful strokes upon the masterpiece of our being (dom dom).*

From the ground to the beat of my drum, I drew my head, stared into the portal, and, from the forgiveness of my soul, my heart poured onto him and her, nothing but love.

*May my love dissolve your terror, my mother.*
*May my love shatter your shame, my father.*
*May my love offer you forgiveness, to thy self and the other.*
*May my love be a blessing of gratitude for the gift of my life.*

I rose and, with one final strike of my drum, I claimed the all of me whence I came, all I had become and all I was to become. The portal closed. The trance broke and, in my return to reality, I turned to the side of the stage and reached for Gabriel, *Please hold me*, amidst the cheers, chants and celebration of the crowd.

*And he did.*

# Part Six

# CHAPTER 45

# Inner World, Outer Reality

Gabriel carried me from the back of the stage to the RV, lovingly placed me into bed and kissed my forehead.

'That was big. Sleep now.'

And I did, gratefully surrendering my everything and allowing my energetic exhaustion to take me deep into an integrative realm, where there was nothing, no dreams, no awareness, just complete stillness in the depths. I woke, feeling as if I had slept for lifetimes, yet discovered it was only mid-morning. An excited calmness stirred within my body as I reflected on the depths of my journey the previous night. While I knew I must be gentle with myself during the integrative phase, I was excited to immerse the new version of me into the world. Knowing I had Gabriel by my side filled me with an added surge of enthusiasm for my path ahead. He would not allow me to graduate until I had mastered his teachings, which first must be tested. But in truth, I didn't want to be tested anymore. I just wanted to move on with my life.

I floated into a fantasy of what could be. He intrigued me, and I could no longer deny I desired more. I was also confused and infuriated. At times, he appeared to see me as more than his student or friend, and other times there was nothing, he was only my teacher. I believe he intended it to be this way because my desire to know him was a distraction from knowing myself, and he would not allow me to digress. Perhaps, if I mastered the seemingly never-ending soul lessons, then I may be able to graduate from student and he retire from teacher and then… well, that was where my mind wandered into fantasy. My illusions were quickly dispelled when I got out of bed and discovered a note on the bench.

'Marigold,

I've been called to New York City. You know what to do to integrate last night.

I'll be back in a few days. Not sure where we are going next.

Gabriel.'


I mulled over his note as I ate, while the familiar sting of an old wound stirred in my heart. I allowed it to surface, first anger because he had left me, next my fear of failing without him by my side, and finally the ache of abandonment which led me to questioning my enoughness. I let it all rise and I did not judge my emotions, nor myself, for experiencing it all over again, even though I had tended to this wound so many times. I needed to move my body, to release the charge of these emotions threatening to hijack me and sabotage all the work I had done to claim my empowered self.

I ran, not away from the emotions, but into them, allowing them to move through my body. When I reached the mountains, I climbed higher and higher until I began to feel lighter. Then I danced, moving my body to the internal beat of my drum, until I knew I'd moved beyond the grip of my emotions. And then I laughed, with joyous relief, because I had overcome a test, gifted to me in the midst of my transformation when it would have been so easy to slip back into my old pain patterns. But I didn't. I rose. I stood on the mountain top with my feet solidly rooted in the earth, filled with power within my core and the hugest blossoming of love from my heart, fuelled by a download of magnificent energy through my crown. I allowed myself to celebrate me in all my magnificence and relished the surges of energy pulsating through me and from me.

*Take it where it is needed,* I told the wind, trusting myself in a way I never had before as a channel for the Divine. I now trusted in the fullness of my being to hold the all of me with integrity, the light and the dark. In turn, I accepted I was worthy to be a channel for the Divine, regardless of whether I stumbled and fell on my path, whether I was light or dark, good or bad, graceful or ungracious. And the joy, pure bliss I experienced in claiming this birthright was inexplicable, a treasured memory held within my heart and nurtured by my soul.

I journalled and rested before heading across the paddock to the festival. I had not ventured into the crowd itself, having detoured to the back of the stage the previous day when I had Gabriel by my side. But I felt called, a deep desire to be amongst people, not on the stage performing for them, but rather with them. I wove my way into the middle of the crowd, witnessing the blending of light and dark and speckles of all the other colours, the mix of all that is. I danced as me—Marigold, not Goldie Mae, not Róisín Dubh—with the knowing I was at times a little or a lot of them all, wherever the rhythm of life was. I trusted. I danced. Whomever my soul called me to be, I could become in any moment if I choose to follow her lead. For I always had the choice and I laughed aloud with the freedom of being me in all my expressions and in remembering I always had the power to choose me.

*I choose me. The all of me.*
*I accept me. The all of me.*
*I love me. The all of me.*

Hours passed as I danced in ecstasy with my soul, joyous in my becoming. In my bliss, I witnessed the merging of the inner light, the pure essence of each soul within the crowd. A blanket of exquisite colour moved as one to the beat of the universal heart, and I saw with my own eyes the expanse of consciousness within the collective field. That vision inspired me to forge ahead on my journey, for I understood that as my consciousness expanded, so, too, did the collective consciousness. And since that moment, I have never stopped believing that it is possible for humanity to move to higher frequencies, to an elevated expression of *being* on this planet. I trust humanity to evolve to a place where the unique manifestation of each soul merges into the most exquisite, unified field, the creation of sacred union upon the earth.

I mused as I lay in bed that night, that after all I had been through, all the work I had done, all the wise women and men who had guided me, that it was a few thousand strangers in a paddock in the middle of nowhere who showed me the way beyond my own journey to the *journey of all.*

The following night, after spending much of the day deep in nature, grounding my energy and feeling the movement of these profound shifts through my body, I chose to go to the afterparty, where the musicians, performers, crew and other VIPs like Gabriel hung out away from the festival goers. Gabriel had never invited me to go with him and I had no desire to mix with these people, but something called me that night and I followed. As soon as I approached, utilising my connection to Gabriel to get through security, I sensed the energy amongst this group was vastly different to that of the larger crowd. Where the festival goers were free and easy, intent only on having a great time, this group held an intense edge. On the surface, they were drinking, laughing, singing, dancing, but beneath the surface there was disturbing murky energy, manipulative, calculating, lustful and greedy. I became aware of eyes leering in my direction. I stood at the edge of the crowd, and I understood they were seeking to invoke fear so they may intimidate and dominate and in turn take my power. But I was not fearful. I was consciously aware of my own power, not just in my head. I could feel it within my body as I anchored the strength of my wild, wise warrior and held their gaze, meeting them in their darkness and unapologetically assuring them that they had no power over me. Without a word spoken, for none were needed, they turned away, returning to those eager to play their game. The game I would never again partake in.

I witnessed, without judgement, the intricate dance of their ways and pondered how Gabriel navigated this crowd. This was where he spent his nights, in the midst of this murky energy. He appeared to have mastered *detached connection*, to be connected to another or a group while remaining completely sovereign. And once again, his mastery intrigued me, because I was only able to hold my space there by placing a protective shield around me, remaining completely detached and discerning whom, if anyone, I connected with. I viewed it as an invitation to connect, but one I chose not to accept from a place of love for myself. I contemplated, as I observed the dynamics of the party, how so often throughout my life I chose to sit on the edge of the circle, avoiding connection because I didn't feel safe to connect and that my protection came from a place of fear, not as an act of self-love. One depleted me and rendered me powerless, the other, the one I now chose, was extraordinarily empowering. From this renewed position of power, I intended my energy, the vastness of my being, to share the love I felt pulsating within me to all those around me. Within a moment, beneath the dark façade that had dominated my earlier perspective, I witnessed a shift, a swirl of energy that appeared to activate the light within each person in the tent. The soul essence miraculously flickered, like streetlights at dusk, and I was blessed with the remembering that each one of them was more than the role they were playing in that moment, in that scene, in this life. Awed, I observed their lights, again a myriad of colours, bind together in an exquisite tapestry, affirming what I had learnt from my own dance with the darkness. Despite what was happening on the surface, the light within each soul never wavered. It was always there, ever patiently waiting for the moment of remembrance and the chance to burst through the heart and illuminate the path for their beloved.

I understood these people, trapped in the game, lost in their life, having forgotten the truth. I was there only six months before and my heart overflowed with compassion and mercy for every one of them. I did not know their story and how they ended up in the midst of darkness, but who was I to judge? I accepted them without condition, for I saw beneath the layers of their façade and there was nothing but love and light within their darkness. In that moment, I gained a clear insight into the power of my presence as a creator of change. If I could hold others with radical acceptance in unconditional love, without fear and without trying to fix them, then perhaps, if they were ready, or rather when they were ready, they would simply receive my love as an invitation to begin their journey home.

*Home to their truth—the universal truth of unconditional love.*

# CHAPTER 46

# The Priestess

The festival ended and the exodus began. The paddocks returned to normal, though the lands were never the same because the soil was fundamentally changed from the experience. And so it was with all who attended the festivals. Many left with a deep sense of gratitude for all they had experienced, grief for the ending of the experience and trepidation about re-entering the 'real world' as the person they had become because of the experience.

Over the previous months, I had moved on from festival to festival untouched by the experiences, having been deeply immersed in my own world. This time, it was different. I had not only performed, but more importantly, I had courageously woven myself amongst both the festival goers and the performers and I was different because of these experiences. Yet I was not wary of returning to the real world. I was eager and excited to live beyond my own cave and share the woman that I had become with the world.

Gabriel returned and appeared untouched by the shift in energy with the ending of the festival or from within me. His capacity to remain this way in the world astounded me. Remaining focused on the task at hand as each experience ended, he looked to the next almost like he'd ticked a box. Or was that the mastery of letting go? I wondered if Gabriel regarded me as a broken little bird to mend and if, when the job was done, he would move on and simply let me go. I did not know where we would go next, but I carried a lightness in my heart and my soul voice was ever present, meeting my contemplation with gentle wisdom.

*You know the truth.*

I did. There was more to our connection, but Gabriel refused to allow me to see beyond the here and the now. Unlike Johnny, whose essence I remembered as soon as we connected because we had danced on timelines together for millennia, Gabriel was impossible to read and his soul was unfamiliar. I did not recognise him as an old soul companion and believed this incarnation was a first encounter for our souls. The concept both excited and terrified me, for never had I known one who was so divinely dark, mysterious and enigmatic as him.

Quiet and moody, he entered the RV, and I sensed his troubles. In his body, I felt agitation. In his heart, I sensed confusion. But his soul was nothing but love, the purity of one who is a channel for the Divine. I understood I was not the cause of his demeanour, yet his presence unsettled me, so powerful was his touch upon my fields. He offered no explanation as to where he had been.

'I'm going to LA. It will be a long trip. I can drop you at the airport if you want to go home to your family, or you can come with me,' he bluntly stated.

I sat within my heart before I answered.

'Gabriel, I'm not ready to leave you. This journey is not complete.'

I witnessed relief, though he did not acknowledge it, not then, because he was not able to receive me fully. My gypsy soul loved a road trip, and I did not allow Gabriel's brooding to dampen my mood. My perception of the world around me was once again fundamentally different because of the new heightened, yet grounded, level of consciousness I had accessed. I relished the ease and inner contentment afforded me by this transformation. In truth, I had become bored focusing only on my healing, evolution and becoming. I was ready to just be, to take this version of myself, with all I had learnt and become along the way, into life. I longed for the simplicity of cooking a meal, listening to music, dancing in a bar or around a fire, writing, painting, playing, reading, connecting, chatting, laughing and singing for no reason other than pleasure. I pondered, for I did love the art of contemplation, particularly on a long road trip, if simply living a life of pleasure was actually the key to continuing to grow. Sure, I understood that we grow from our struggles, that in the depths of the rich dark soil we are nourished and evolve, but what if the enjoyment of life was my spiritual practice? Could pleasure and play be stimulus for my soul growth?

*The flower blossoming from the rich dark soil also needs the kiss of sunlight to thrive.*

As we made our way across the country in silence, I consciously chose to blossom in the sun. My time in winter had been tough, but I had honoured it, and as I emerged from that season, I was different—stronger and wiser, lighter and darker, and both grounded in my body while deeply connected to my soul. It had been some season, one I remain forever grateful for, but it was time to move beyond that story and claim my new life.

*And so it began.*

After eight hours of solid driving, Gabriel finally pulled into a rest station. On exiting the vehicle, he murmured something about going for a walk to stretch his legs.

'No, no, you're not! You are going to get changed and we are going to that bar across the way, and we are going to have fun.'

'I don't do fun.'

'I know and it's boring, so I'm hijacking the classroom and tonight I'm going to teach you how to have fun.'

'Fuck, Marigold, I'm wrecked. I just want to go for a walk, eat and then sleep.'

'Excuses!' I refused to concede. 'You've been in your head all day and it isn't helping you to move this.'

I waved my hand dramatically in front of him.

'This stuck-ness, whatever it is. You need to move your body and get out of your head. No excuses. You're following my lead tonight, Mr Rodriguez!'

He shook his head and headed back into the RV to get changed, his defiance dissolving under my authority.

We ate dinner in silence. I did not mind because I was in the real world. I relished the music playing from the jukebox and the banter of normal people who surrounded us. Normal, such an uncelebrated way of being, for I truly believe normal can be extraordinary. I certainly felt it in these people, in some small town in Mississippi, who just got on with life, enjoying the simple pleasures of a meal, chatting, dancing, singing, laughing. In the simplicity of their joy, I witnessed a blanket of light, flickers of stardust, in all colours of the spectrum streaming from these extraordinarily normal people. *What a delight!*

'What are you smiling at?' he broke his silence to enquire.

I laughed.

'Nothing in particular, but a bit of everything as well. Just life, Gabriel. I figure it's worth a smile.'

He shook his head, bemused, but I could tell my lightness had drawn him from the depths of his despair. Sensing I had a window to work with, I reached for his hand.

'Gabriel, may I have this dance?' I asked with mock sincerity and implored with faux dramatics.

With but a little tug of his hand, he rose to meet me. He stood beside the dancefloor watching as my body moved with the music and I sang along to the songs playing from the jukebox. I laughed in exhilaration, thrilled to be simple, light and free just like the girl I had once been, she who I loved so dearly. Gabriel did not move to the music nor sing along to the songs. He was so uncomfortable about allowing himself to let go and have fun, to be wild and free. I adored his vulnerability, for he never showed this side, and it spurred me on. In my giddy, flirty, playful state, I took his hands in mine and began to dance with him, sidling up beside him.

'Surrender to the music, Gabriel. Allow *her* to move you. Stop resisting *her!*' I teased.

He rolled his eyes and smirked at my mockery, silently knowing he was in a losing battle. I took him by the hips, drawing him to my body and slithered before him, seductively enticing him to release control and meet me in play. And then he drew his arms around my waist, relaxed his body into mine and together we moved as one, slowly at first and then increasingly wild as the intensity of the music increased.

There was nothing sexual in our connection. It was all play, dancing without any reason except to experience joy, and I saw the bliss in his eyes as he spun me about and I threw my hands into the air, drunk on delight. We danced and laughed and sang our way through the night, oblivious to everything and everyone around us, focused solely on the moment and one another. We only left the dancefloor when the lights turned on.

'Time to take your party for two elsewhere,' the barman called.

We weren't ready for the night to end so we walked hand in hand through the quiet suburban streets, under the light of the moon.

In the lightness bestowed upon him through pleasure and play, Gabriel opened up, chatting with me in a way he never had before. He shared stories from his childhood, his life in Peru, his family and the burden of responsibility placed upon him by his parents. He talked about his time in the monastery and his reasons for leaving, as well as purging stories of his decadent early days in the record industry when he first moved to LA. I allowed him to flow from one story to the next, without judgement or expectation, and held him in my heart. I witnessed as he detangled himself from the chains that had bound him and limited the beauty of his expression. Free from the constraints he placed upon himself as my teacher, he met me as a man, in his truth, filled with wounds, shadows, shame, guilt, sorrow and memories of happiness, joy and love.

'I've been terrified of losing you if you ever found out about my past. That's why I went to New York. To put an end to stuff that has been haunting me for too long, to write the final chapter, if you will. I have to be honest because I haven't made things easy for you, nor should they be easy for me. When I first moved to LA, I was offered a job by this guy, Wolfgang, who was really well known and connected in the music industry. I thought I'd made a big breakthrough when he offered me a job doing essentially what I'm doing now, scouting for new talent. But he preferred young women, very young. In LA, there are always plenty of them wanting to be the next big star, on stage or in the movies. And many of them are genuinely really talented, so it wasn't hard for me to select the gifted ones and send them his way. I honestly didn't know what I was doing in sending them to him. But then again, maybe on some level I did, and that is what I have always struggled with. You see, after working for him for about two years, he invited me to a party at his mansion in LA. I spent a lot of time on the road, so I had never been around for his infamous parties. So, I went along, and I was shocked, naively many would think, to see about a dozen of the girls I had sent his way, floating about the mansion. They were clearly drug-fucked and obviously only there as entertainment for his guests, most of whom were middle-aged men with high-profile roles in Hollywood's film or music industry. I didn't want to see it, didn't want to acknowledge what was going on, so I drank whatever I could get my hands on and dropped an obscene amount of acid. Anything to escape the truth. But when he brought this girl over to me, she must have only been about seventeen. I couldn't ignore the reality. "Gabriel, my good man, you remember Mary-Jo?" I remembered her. She had an extraordinary voice, from a small town in Montana, with stars in her innocent eyes and a huge dream in her heart. "You gifted her to me and what a blessing she has been. Now it's your turn, Gabriel. Enjoy!" He patted me on the back and walked away laughing. I stood staring at this girl whose eyes were lifeless, her heart empty, and her dreams obliterated by that man, but only because I had sent her to him. I left and never turned back. I couldn't face it. I couldn't face her. I couldn't face myself. I couldn't face the truth.

I quit working for him but descended into a pretty dark place for about two years because I was filled with self-loathing. I guess I figured if I fucked myself up enough, I might forget my part in the whole thing. But when my friend died in my arms from an overdose, I turned a corner and I've been clean ever since. And I suppose since then, I've been trying to learn the lessons that you've had to learn, and how to still be in that dark world but make it better in some way. I've been trying so hard to get it right, and then when you came along, I knew you were the one my grandmother spoke of in her letter. I figured my whole journey could amount to something positive if I could help you rise from your darkness, show you the way back. I believed you were my redemption because I had turned my back on all those girls I sent to him and his evil friends. Now I could make it right and guide you from the darkness and back to your truth. And you've done it. Despite everything you've gone through, the most horrific experiences, you've mastered the mystery of your darkness and claimed its power. You've managed to weave it with your light, creating *you* … this divine masterpiece.'

His honesty and vulnerability overwhelmed me, but I let go of my thoughts, focused on my heart and allowed my soul to lead. She rose to meet him, radiating pure love, providing the safe haven for him to continue to reveal his truth and purge his pain.

'I guess I realised after you performed on stage the other night that you no longer needed me as your teacher, because you are fucking amazing! But still, I didn't feel I had done enough to make amends for what I did to those girls. I felt so responsible for ruining their lives, their dreams and for just abandoning them. I had to take action in an attempt to clear my conscious. You slept so peacefully after you had performed and tended to your demons. I knew I wanted that same peace within me, and I felt called to New York. It was what I should have done years ago, but I always resisted. This time, I did not hesitate. I filed an official report with the FBI regarding Wolfgang and the child-sex trafficking ring he was part of, as well as providing the names of the others I knew were involved. I told the investigators all I knew, my part in it and what I had seen, but also what I knew within my heart. That those girls I sent to him were not the only ones. There were hundreds more, some older, but many younger again. I'd heard the rumours over the years but was so ashamed of my involvement that I ignored it. I am, like so many others, complicit in allowing what is a well-orchestrated operation to continue. The FBI are investigating. In fact, they assured me they had been actively investigating for a number of years and my information would move the case forward. Whether it does or not is outside of my control. And should I be held accountable once their investigation is complete, then I will accept their punishment, for I take full responsibility for my actions, conscious or unconscious. I've faced my shame and guilt and I've opened myself to forgiveness, forgiving myself, so that I may be worthy of love.' He paused momentarily. 'I pray that I can move beyond here and perhaps let love in.'

He lowered his eyes in the rawness of his truth, yet his vulnerability made my heart burst with love and the all of me longed to hold him in my arms. But this was his experience, and I would not interfere. No words to reassure, no touch to comfort. Instead, I held the space with nothing but love flowing through me, allowing him to continue. Taking a deep breath, his eyes welled as he spoke.

'Even though I've done so much to move beyond this point, I sat beside you all day today and was overwhelmed by your goodness, your joy, your beauty, your lightness, your everything. To be completely honest, I still feared that all I had done was not enough, that I was not worthy to sit beside you, to walk beside you, to be more than a teacher to you. But tonight, when you held me, dancing and laughing at me and with me, that fear completely disappeared. And now I feel free. Finally, there is this deep peace within myself because tonight you helped me remember that I am worthy of love. I see it in your eyes and feel it when you hold my hand, and that's enough. Truly, that is enough, because regardless of what happens next, you gifted me this. You brought me back to love, Marigold. That is a blessing, and I could never ask you for more.'

*Never shall the raw radiance of his heart be erased from my soul.*

I stroked the side of his face, his light more potent than ever against the backdrop of his darkness.

'What if you didn't have to ask me for more?'

My lips softly brushed over his and I gasped, overwhelmed by the magnitude of my longing for more.

'What if my heart desired to offer you all of me?'

His hands cupped my face. His eyes pierced my soul. His heart searched mine and found only truth, for there was nothing but love. I was nothing but love.

'You are everything, Marigold.'

I surrendered into his arms, his mouth passionately meeting mine and I began to weep, sweet tears of sorrow and joy. He kissed every tear drop, honouring the vastness of my heart before drawing me to his chest. We rested in the most exquisite harmony for an age. As we melded into the other, timelines across the cosmos shifted, ancestral lines were healed and the angels sang as our souls rewrote the contract for our lives.

A sacred union destined yet not given. Through our struggles and pain, our lessons and learnings here on earth and in the humbleness of our human form, it was written.

*Forever scripted in the Divine Tapestry.*

# CHAPTER 47

# The Queen

Gabriel and I were unknowingly writing our own tale, one penned in the beautiful complexity of truth—reflecting the light and dark, radiance and shadow, heart and wounds, human and soul. A simple tale it was not, the intricacy of our souls and the preparation for union was to take commitment, time and patience.

Gabriel met my passion when we returned to the RV. Laying on the bed, I began to undress him, my body and soul longing to be one with him. Gently, he drew my hand away.

'It is not time.'

I trusted his knowing yet was dying with unfulfilled desire.

'Ah!' I flopped on the bed beside him playfully as he leant over my face and kissed me gently, smirking at my dramatics.

'I want this as much as you. You've no idea.'

'Ah, I'm pretty sure I do!'

'I want to love you in the way you deserve to be loved. I have more work to do to fully know I am worthy of your love. Because if I don't believe it within every part of my being, then I will not be able to give the all of me to you. And you deserve nothing less.'

'Thank you for honouring me and my sacredness.'

He kissed me again, more passionately, his eyes welling as he looked upon me.

'You are beyond sacred. How anyone could ever have harmed you, I cannot comprehend.'

'You have to stop kissing my like that or I am going to die lying right here beside you!'

I laughed and playfully straddled him. Sitting above him, adoring his dark beauty, I remembered his golden presence as he held me in the depths of my darkness, and I knew I would never love another, nor another ever love me, in the way that we loved.

'I know this sounds strange,' he began somewhat awkwardly.

'Oh, you know I love strange, the stranger the better!' I giggled.

'The other day, when I was in New York, after I had been to the FBI, I went walking in Central Park. I needed to move my body and just breathe. Anyway, I got a coffee and sat on a bench and this old guy wandered along and sat beside me. He looked dishevelled and dirty, and I presumed he was homeless, so I offered to buy him something to eat and a coffee. As he sipped his coffee, he stared into the park and mused. "You know, I've walked here every afternoon for the last month and you're the first person who has shown me kindness. So many people walk by not taking notice, caught in their own world. Or they don't think I'm worthy of their attention, their generosity or least of all their company. You know when you sit with another whom you judge as unworthy, your own worth is eroded. When you sit with another whom you see as worthy, despite their appearance or what they may have done in the past, you reinforce your own worth." I was intrigued by his wisdom which so many had forsaken because of their prejudice, and I had this feeling there was no other place I was meant to be in that moment. So, I let go of all thoughts about Wolfgang, the FBI and even you. I gave him my presence completely, trusting in the moment, and I waited, sipping my coffee, for him to speak. He said, "You are an anomaly, son. You sit beside me, honouring my worth, but you do not see yourself as worthy. This is something you must tend to, for those who sit beside you can never claim their fullness without you meeting them where they are at. You know, in ancient times, the Queen would be initiated before claiming her throne, but he who was chosen to initiate her would spend months preparing for this most important role. You see, if he did not see himself as worthy, then he would not be able to honour her fullness and she would never truly be aligned to her power. The initiation was the most sacred of rituals, the two becoming one in the bed chamber! My son, you must claim your worth before you initiate your Queen, or she will never believe she is worthy of her power. May you be blessed." He rose and, without another word or a backward glance, disappeared into the abyss of the park. I'm actually not sure if he was real or not. I figure I'm not meant to know, as long as I received his message, which I did. So, while every inch of my being wants to make love to you right now, I won't, because it's not time. I must do more to know I am worthy to love you the way you deserve to be loved, to honour you the way you deserve to be honoured, to initiate you into your Queen.'

*There were no words.*

My love for him was ever patient, and I understood the depths we must descend to move beyond our shadow and rise into the heights and reclaim our fullness. I assured Gabriel I would be there for him, like he had for me, as he danced with his own devil and transitioned through the underworld to confront the darkness of his soul.

The following day, we drove for a number of hours before we left the highway and ventured from the known roads onto those that were unsurfaced, raw, winding and bumpy, yet we trusted the path. The further we went into the woods, the less we spoke and the more I felt Gabriel separate himself from me. The boundary he had placed between he and I, as student and teacher, felt like it was returning one brick at a time, and each brick felt like a stab in my heart. I longed to reach out and touch him. I longed to caress his face and swim in the pools of his eyes. I longed to feel him deep within me, to move as one in perfect harmony. I longed to fall asleep on his chest in union with his beating heart. I longed for *all* of him, but I had to allow him to walk through his shadow, to die this death of his old self and awaken to the man who he was being called to become. I trusted *he* would return to me.

The initiatory journey is a painful, overwhelming and, at times, terrifying one. I knew this was not the first time he had embarked on a deep spiritual transition. He knew what lay ahead in the darkness of the woods, yet the vision of *our* divine plan, no matter how vague it remained, compelled him to walk where most men were not able. I knew he was capable of this journey, courageous to stand before his demons and beyond worthy of the reward that would be bestowed on him on the other side. I had to trust he believed as deeply in his soul as I did, for without trust, the shamanic death that lay before him would be far more traumatic than it needed to be.

Surrendering to the higher forces that had guided him to this point, and allowing them to hold him through the fears and doubts that hindered him, would see him wildly break through this cycle and be birthed again to embark upon another life within this life. A life I knew was to be shared with me, more expansive and more powerful than either of us could comprehend in the simplicity of our minds. We understood that the sacredness of our union was fundamental to our soul missions.

He built a fire beside the RV on the edge of a dark, foreboding forest in the middle of who knows where. He sat for some time with his head in his hands, melancholic yet accepting of the journey that lay before him. He looked across the fire and, finding my eyes and my heart, he spoke a million truths.

'You have shown me who I can be, and the potentiality of what we can be. Because of you, I will walk into those woods and face my greatest fears. I do not fear my darkness, I fear the light within it. I always have. But it is time for me to claim it, and while I have walked this path before and faced many of my demons, I trust I am being called to stand before them once again. I understand others have remained locked away, hidden in the deepest vaults of my soul, but they are ready to be seen, to be understood, to be honoured as truth and, should I have it in me, to integrate them as part of my divinity, no longer banishing them to the dungeon in shame.'

He dropped his head, the shame, guilt, humiliation and regret seeping from him. I realised there was much darkness within him that he had hidden from me and himself, but I trusted he was ready and able to alchemise it into pure, potent light.

'Marigold, I am so grateful that you came into my life, because you have forced me to address stuff that I haven't wanted to acknowledge within myself and the collective masculine. You believed I was your teacher and you the student, but can you see that you are the one who has taught me? Being in your presence, I've realised that my masculine, and the distorted masculine that the collective has become, simply is not worthy of the sacredness of the Divine Feminine because we have dishonoured her for so long. It is time I faced all of this from this life, past lives and all that I am being invited to heal for my ancestors and the collective. It is huge, I know that, and I only hope I have it in me to do what I am being called to do.'

'Gabriel, you have this in you. You are more courageous and powerful than any other I have known. I will be here. I will wait for you. I've waited lifetimes for you, for this, for us.'

Tears rolled down my cheeks as the truth of my soul overwhelmed me. I held his face in my hands, closed my eyes and drank in his essence.

*May you have strength beyond strength,*
*my warrior, my beloved.*

# CHAPTER 48

# Divine Union

---

I sat before the fire Gabriel had crafted for me and stumbled through my own pain, completely unprepared for the depths of my own healing his journey offered to me.

I grieved.

I grieved him leaving me.

I grieved his impending death.

I grieved never having been seen and loved so fully.

I grieved the lifetimes of being dishonoured as a woman.

I grieved the forgetting of my own sacredness which allowed me to be dishonoured.

I grieved each and every wound that stirred in my heart.

I grieved those who had abandoned me and, in turn, those I had abandoned.

I grieved for all the times I abandoned my Divine Self, giving my power to fear.

As I headed to bed, I looked into the vast darkness of the woods and, with all that I had, I sent Gabriel my love. I vowed to the moon and stars above, to the trees that surrounded me and to the earth beneath my feet that I would never abandon my Divine Self. She held the key to the well of love within me and I always wanted to know love on this magnitude.

In the middle of the night, a storm broke. Rain lashed the windows, wind rocked the vehicle, thunder pierced the silence and lightning illuminated the darkness. I moved between being gripped by fear for Gabriel, who was alone with the elements, and complete calm, trusting in the magic of the moment. The intermittent waves of terror derailed my attempt to sleep and so, I began to pray, the words flowing from me like a long-lost river.

*Hail Mary, full of Grace,*
*The Lord is with thee.*
*Blessed art thou amongst women and blessed is the fruit of thy*
*womb, Jesus.*
*Holy Mary, Mother of All, pray for us now and at the hour of our*
*death.*
*Amen.*

Over and over, I recited the prayer and was gifted with the presence of Mother Mary, who I envisaged walking into the woods and taking Gabriel into her arms like an infant. I sought to understand more, to see and know more, but I was directed back to my heart where my power lay, to be the holder of space, the safe haven as the storm wildly awakened what remained hidden. I remained in my heart, allowing the prayer to flow from my mouth like warm honey, comforting me. Finally, I drifted to sleep.

I am not sure if what happened next was a dream or occurred as I travelled the astral realms. Either way, it was a magical and mystical experience. I found myself in Ireland, as often I did in my dreams, always around The Burren and by the sea where often I would be met by Athena or Cynthia. But not this time. This time, a woman wrapped in a thick woollen jacket with a scarf around her head tentatively approached me. She had a fierce determination in her eyes, driving her to overcome any obstacle, even if it meant traversing realms.

*'My child, I heard your prayer. Take my rosary beads, pray with them every day and may you never forget the love of the mother.'*

She was so real, her words so clear, her love so engulfing that I awoke snug beneath my blanket, with only silence outside, the storm having passed. My stomach cramped aggressively, breaking my tranquillity. I reached for my womb, confused because I was not due to menstruate, though I could feel the dampness of the sheets beneath. Perplexed, I raised my hand from the sheet. I was bleeding and also mystified to see rosary beads wrapped around my hand. They were made of the same glistening garnet stones as the beads given to me in the dream. I shuddered, the shiver running through my body, and I understood that someway, somehow a miracle had occurred while I slept. My energy fields were electrified as I pondered the mystery. Even though I had experienced magic my whole life, from the magic of a sunrise to the act of kindness from a stranger and the alchemical healing in the fields of The Burren, it was the *magical mysteries*, the miracles, that completely awed me. Overwhelmed with gratitude, I drew the beads to my heart and offered thanks to the Holy Mother for blessing me. I asked that she support Gabriel as he journeyed, knowing the power of her presence on his path. Closing my eyes, I became aware of warmth rising from the ground, through my feet and channelling through my body. At the same time, an influx of energy flooded my crown, meeting in my heart and expanding beyond me, creating a portal, which I entered. In the distance, I saw the woman who had given me the beads. She acknowledged me and motioned to dive deeper into my heart. I followed her guidance and was shown her face, the face I had first known, and then lost.

Across the realms, I called to her, *Mammy*! But she did not hear for she was completely taken with the babe in her arms, and I remembered the love in her eyes as she whispered blessings upon my soul. She drew her rosary beads from around her neck, the ones that now lay in my hands, and she whispered the Hail Mary before praying.

*Holy Mother, I pray to you,*
*Hold my baby with your love, oh blessed of all mothers, so she may never know the absence of my love.*
*I beseech ye to pray for me, now and at the hour of my death, for never shall I forgive myself for what I am about to do.*
*Please send the gypsy woman to find her, please may she find her.*
*Amen.*

She sobbed and tears streamed onto my infant head as she held me to her breast. I felt her heart beating and within it her love. Kissing the top of my crown, she secured the red shawl and placed me on the earth before turning to walk across the fields towards her home as the first hints of sunlight kissed the horizon. Again, I called across the realms, *Mammy*, and she paused, quickly scanning the surrounds for the voice carried by the wind and I knew she had heard me.

*Mahala, come home, Mother, all is forgiven.*

I cried tears of joy as I returned to the earth plane, for as Gabriel had journeyed to reclaim his Divine Masculine so he may honour me, I had been taken on a journey of my own to reclaim my Divine Mother, in preparation for my initiation into my Queen, the Divine Feminine.

It was a little too much for my mind to comprehend that the beads now lying in my hands were the ones my mother had held as she swaddled me in the red shawl. Yet to honour the miracle and the mother I never knew, I vowed from that day forth I would pray with them, trusting that my prayers would keep our souls connected until one day, through another miracle, I may be blessed to be reunited with her in the flesh.

I welcomed the chance to return my blood to the earth, binding me to Mother Earth, and washed the stained sheet in the river before bathing in her cleansing waters. I relished the solitude and ever-present hum of the natural world that embraced me as I deeply integrated my healing. I journalled of my experience so I might never forget its power. I prayed, sang, danced, ate and slept, not knowing when Gabriel would return from the forest. I understood he must complete this journey alone, though I longed to connect with him. I slept restlessly that second night, disturbed by dreams that doubted Gabriel's return and stirred my abandonment wound. *Why can't I be free from this pain?* I asked despairingly of my soul. She answered. *It returns so you do not become complacent. It invites you to remember the power of love and to always choose love over fear.*

As the sun began to set the following day, Gabriel emerged from the edge of the forest, unkempt, raw and weary. His immersion into the depths had obviously been gruelling. Over the previous days, I had envisaged this moment and had seen myself running to him, throwing my arms about his neck and holding him close, but I was unable to move from my seat beside the fire, overcome by shyness. This exquisitely tender man was a stranger, *though I knew him fully.* He sat beside me in silence, taking my hand as he stared into the fire and, for an eternity, we stayed, content in the presence of the moment, tentative to move beyond it.

'I'm sorry for all I have done. Please forgive me.'

As the woman who loved him, there was nothing to forgive and I wanted to assure him of this, yet instinctively, I understood he spoke not for himself and not to me. This was bigger than us.

He spoke as the masculine to the feminine, asking to be forgiven.

His eyes revealed the horrific oppression, abuse and torture of the Divine Feminine over thousands of years at the hands of the masculine. He had borne witness to it all and now sought forgiveness for the collective masculine. I reminded him that only those who forgive themselves are able to receive the energy of forgiveness offered by another.

'I forgive myself for dishonouring the sacredness of the Divine Feminine,' he declared as he wept. 'And I forgive myself for dishonouring the sacredness of the Divine Masculine.'

We received the forgiveness offered by the other on behalf of the collective. Through the living expression of our sacred union, we did our part to heal the wound of separation between the Feminine and Masculine, to bring unity where for too long there has been division.

We bathed in the waters of renewal and in infinite trust, I surrendered to him as the Divine Masculine. He knelt before me, honouring me as his Queen, and reverently drank of my sacred blood, which I offered to him from the sanctity of my divine chalice. Illuminated by the fullness of the moon, held by the strength of the earth and warmed by the glow of the fire, in the purest expression of our human and cosmic self, our hearts and souls wove as one, creating a *Divine Sacred Union.*

We transcended all time and space and passed through the veil into the dark void of the unknown. We floated and danced blissfully as one in the infinite love of the cosmic womb, and she carried us to a piercing golden light, where we remembered our oneness with all and knew infinitely the ultimate truth—the unity and sacredness of all that is, the wholeness of *all.* In the sacredness of our union, we were a pulse that harmonised with the all of everything. We relished the honour of sharing the power of our union, its potency rippling through all realms and across all time, an awakening of *our* destiny.

*It was written.*
*In the stars, in the sands of time, in the books of old and those yet to be
written.*
*It was, is and will always be.*
*The sacred mysteries hidden in the vaults of time, the sacrament of
becoming One.*
*No thing, no one, no force can unwrite what has been written.*
*No matter how hard they try, the truth will always return.*
*The Mystery of All That Is.*

Part
Seven

# CHAPTER 49

# Nothing But Love

A new story cannot be written until the final chapter is complete, so, before we embarked on the unknown journey of our souls' mission, beyond our destiny point, both Gabriel and I needed to tie off loose ends. We took our time travelling across the country, finding enjoyment in every moment of our sacred union. Upon finally reaching Los Angeles, Gabriel sold the RV, finalised all outstanding contracts in the music industry and closed his business. We took a couple of weeks to pack up his apartment and wrap up his life on the West Coast, whilst also savouring that time as a normal young couple, relishing our freshly ignited love. We went on dates, strolled hand in hand through the markets, snuggled in the cinema, kissed under streetlights as well as spending endless hours in bed, exploring each other's bodies and indulging in the ecstasy of our sexual connection. There was a beautiful humanness to be discovered in our union, the power of pleasure and play once more fuelling our expansion.

At times, there was nothing more to our love making than pure physical pleasure. Other times, we traversed realms and landed on timelines, where I somehow found myself merging into the darkness of other souls' traumas before alchemising it to light. When this first happened, it was incredibly confusing and confronting for me, yet Gabriel managed, as always, to normalise the extraordinary, encouraging me to trust in my healing gifts that had flourished from the sacredness of our union. I came to understand that because I infinitely trusted Gabriel, I would surrender my whole being as we made love. With no resistance, I unknowingly offered myself to the Divine as a pure channel for her energy to work through me for the good of all. The charge of our sexual union took us into altered states of consciousness, where we would be taken to those souls who needed healing, especially those who needed to be brought from the darkness back to the light. My body connected with their energy patterns and often the trauma I witnessed would express through my physical form, while Gabriel held the space for me, never doubting nor interfering, allowing my body and soul to do what I was called to do while he anchored and protected the sacredness of my being.

I could not have accessed this gift without Gabriel and, as we surrendered with trust and curiosity, we were more frequently taken to these realms during our sexual union. We cheekily referred to it as our *sexual trip*. Who needed LSD or plant medicine when we had each other! We were the medicine. It was our *thing* and we held it sacred, never sharing stories of these experiences with others, for at that time, we believed few would truly understand. These experiences helped us understand our divine plan and also expedited the necessity to heal our relationships with our families.

We had both estranged ourselves for a number of years. Gabriel had left the monastery and Peru seven years prior. I had not connected with my family for almost two years since running from New York. I would not allow myself to wallow in guilt and shame for the hurt my absence caused those I loved most. I understood that we often turn our back on those we love most to heal our wounds, to discover forgotten parts of ourselves and to honour the journey of the soul. I had aggressively pulled away from my family, but I was proud of the person I had become because of the experiences I'd had, freed from the safety of my family.

If I had returned to the farm or stayed with Madame Rosaline or Nate in the city after Johnny passed and St Christopher's burnt down, then I would never have had the experiences I did, as traumatic as they were. And in turn, never would I have descended to the depths that I did, to discover and learn to love the exquisite darkness within myself that magnified my light. And never would I have found the love of Gabriel—my divine counterpart. I knew I would return to my family so much more than I would ever have been should I have stayed with them, safe and comfortable. I truly believed I was returning as the phoenix who rose from the ashes, courageous, powerful and wise.

Some, through their journey of becoming, come to understand they must sever all connections to their families for their souls to continue to evolve. Fortunately for both Gabriel and I, the foundation offered by our families would be paramount to our soul growth, individually and in union.

Reluctant to be separated, we chose to travel together, first to Peru, where Gabriel tearfully reconciled with his mother and father and reunited with his extended family. His beloved Grandmother took my face in her hands and greeted me.

'Golden One, it was you. Thank you for finding him. Blessings be upon you and my Gabriel, always.'

Two weeks later, we flew to New York and, travelling north to the mountains, I could not contain the plethora of emotions that exploded from me as we navigated those winding roads. My return to the city had triggered renewed grief for Johnny and my baby boy. Though much had happened since holding them both in my arms, they were never far from my thoughts and always in my heart. The ache deepened as we neared the farm, and I grieved the loss of not returning to my family holding my precious baby boy in my arms.

*Oh, how they would have adored him!*

A sorrowful well opened and it was impossible to contain the suppressed grief of the separation from my family. They were my everything, Caellach the constant in my life from the day I was born and Clara ever present from the time I was seven. I had abandoned them, yet had not allowed myself to feel the loss, knowing it would have drawn me back to them before it was time. It was a season, the winter I had to have to become *me*, and the warmth of their love would have denied me the need to activate my own fire, to warm and nourish myself and love myself without condition.

Unprepared for my return, Caellach dropped the wheelbarrow he was pushing down the drive and ran to me.

'By God, it's yourself,' he declared as he stood before me, staring into my tear-filled eyes.

'Clara, Clara,' he bellowed, as he drew me to his chest, 'Clara, she's home. Our girl is home.'

Clara raced out the door and flew towards me.

'I'm sorry,' I cried as she held me to her chest, 'I'm sorry …'

She shushed me and declared, staring into my eyes, 'You've nothing to be sorry about, do you hear me now. Are you well? Are you alright?'

I nodded lost for words.

'Good, that's good. That's all that matters, my darling' and she smiled, her eyes filled with the love of a mother.

'Mahala,' she whispered, tears now welling in her eyes. 'I sang this to the moon and stars every night you were gone, just as you chanted it for me in The Burren all those years before. And now you are here. You came home and, my darling, all is forgiven.'

Oh, the celebration that ensued that night and for the following week, when Aunt Maeve and Dòmhnall visited, along with Madame Rosaline, Sacnite and Nate. It was the reunion of all reunions and Gabriel, as always, took it all in his stride, despite it being an Irish madhouse, with passionate storytelling, bellowing laughter, endless meals and cups of tea and whiskey by the fireplace.

*Home … my heart was full.* Somehow, without me even sharing, Caellach knew the depths of my journey and his heart ached for all I had been through. He often held me in silence, our embrace the remedy for the pain in his heart. I assured him all was well, that I was grand, that I had healed and learnt and grown. He could not deny that I was older and wiser, more grounded yet more connected, more open yet more discerning. I was far from the wounded young woman who had run from the city. I was a woman with the battle scars to prove it. And I was damn proud of those scars, for I had unwittingly entered the battlefield and in there, I had discovered my wild, wise warrior and risen from the darkest of dark to become the Queen of my story. Caellach challenged Gabriel, testing his worth, but, within a day, he could see he was the man to meet my woman and our dance was one not choreographed in the heavens, but mastered with our feet on the ground from the beautiful complexity of the human experience.

Of course, in quieter times, I shared my experiences with Clara and Aunt Maeve, and they wept with me, laughed with me and celebrated with me.

'Quite the journey, my girl,' Aunt Maeve declared, 'Your Ma's would be proud, though I've no doubt they were keeping a close eye on you even when you didn't know if you were coming or going.'

We laughed, yet we all knew that it was only through a miracle that I hadn't found myself dead in a gutter. I shuddered at the thought because life was proving to be more than I could have possibly imagined.

Sitting by the fire, sipping tea and sharing stories late into the night on the eve of our parting, Aunt Maeve handed me an envelope. I looked between her and Clara seeking answers, but all Aunt Maeve said was, 'Athena made it very clear that I was only to give this to you when you spoke of your birth mother. Perhaps I should have given it to you after Caellach told you the true story of your birth, but he did not feel you were ready then. We agreed to give it to you after you went missing in the underground and returned with the red shawl wrapped about you, but then you disappeared with the fire. I trust you needed to experience all that you have over these past couple of years, especially losing your own baby boy. From all you have told us about the dreams and visions of the woman who birthed you, now is the time.'

It was true, I had felt a deep calling to return to the place of my birth since the rosary beads had mysteriously appeared in my hand. Their presence intimately connected me to the mysterious woman who was my mother, and for the first time in my life, I longed to find her. Aunt Maeve and Clara were completely silent, the crackling of the fire the only sound as I tentatively opened the envelope. I drew my fingers across the familiar handwriting and brought the notepaper to my nose, eager to recapture the smell of my beloved Ma Ma. As I closed my eyes, I could sense her presence surrounding me, assuring me it was time.

My Precious Marigold,

When you left for your new life with Clara and Caellach, I missed you terribly, more than I could have ever imagined. My heart ached with a raw gaping wound that stayed with me for many months as I grieved for you.

I had always been aware of the pain your birth mother must have felt being separated from you, but until I felt it myself, gnawing at every cell of my body, I really had no idea of its magnitude. Rightly or wrongly, I sought her out, the young woman who birthed you. Guided by my heart, I simply needed to hold her in my arms and silently honour her pain. We shared a unique bond, the love and loss of you, my sweet girl, and she welcomed me into her life, becoming my dearest companion in my latter years.

From the outset, she requested that I never reveal our connection to you or our family unless you specifically asked after her. She is adamant that she will never seek to find you because she does not want to disrupt your life. She is a woman of deep faith, despite the challenges that life has brought her, and believes if it is God's will, you will be reunited. She often says, 'Everything is the will of God, but men and women can make mistakes.' And so, she has chosen to let go and leave this one to God.

The Goddess I know is love and as my time to leave this realm nears, I offer you this as my final act of love for you, my daughter. I have trusted this message with Maeve, instructing her only to give it to you when you speak of your birth mother. I know within my heart and soul, my darling Marigold, that if you are reading this, then the Divine Mother has touched your heart, and you are ready to receive this message.

Brigid Malone, Kinvarra, The Burren.

Never a day passed when she did not pray for you, and it is my honour to be the bridge that reconnects you.
My Love Remains Forever,
Your Ma Ma

Arriving in Dublin the following evening, I was exhausted on all levels of my being. Farewelling my family once again was heartbreaking, though this time I assured them of my return. Who I would be on my return, I did not know. I understood that my return to Ireland and the ancient lands of the West Coast, as well as the possibility of reuniting with my birth mother, was to change me in ways I would never be able to define. I wondered, as I collapsed onto the bed in our little room in the bed-and-breakfast just outside Dublin, whether my soul would ever seek to rest in this life.

*We vowed not to waste it and nor shall we!* I giggled as my soul voice chimed in with such clarity that she could have been standing in the room beside me. Of course, she was closer even, within me. Gabriel dived onto the bed beside me and mused.

'What's so funny, my little one?'

'Everything and nothing! You, me, us, life, all of it!'

'Are you feeling overwhelmed being back here?' he queried, stroking my hair.

'I don't know. When the plane landed, I knew I was home. It was the strangest feeling, like my soul breathed with relief. I was flooded with a million images from the past, life when I was a child, but also beyond that, before that time. In the mountains and in the forest, with dragons and faeries, I knew I was one of them, I was part of them. And, oh, Gabriel, it sounds like insanity, even for me, but I feel like I carry their blood within me. While I'm excited to head west tomorrow, I'm also terrified. Not just about maybe finding my mother, but also discovering a lost part of me. I have this feeling, something or someone is waiting there for me and it's … oh, it's just a lot.'

'It is a lot, but I feel it, too. There's a reason we are here that is well beyond what we can comprehend. Let it remain a mystery until it is not.'

And he kissed me, gently at first, before more passionately.

'Does this help?' he smirked, knowing my desire.

We headed west the following morning, Gabriel remaining in Galway while I continued further into The Burren, a journey I had to do alone. I resisted the temptation to go straight to the village of Kinvarra and ask after Brigid Malone. Instead, I was called to the cemetery where Athena had been laid to rest beside Cynthia, my Ma's. I longed to be close to them again in the physical, even though they were with me so often in the imaginal realms. When I found their plot in the cemetery, I dropped to my knees and placed my hands on the ground.

*Home. I was home with my beloved Ma's.*

As the tears stained my face, I took the garnet beads from around my neck and, closing my eyes, I began to pray the Rosary, honouring the Divine Mother and my Ma's.

'Excuse me, lass. Where were you after getting ye rosary there?'

I did not see or hear her approach, my awareness only with my prayer, and I jumped, shocked by her presence.

'Oh, hello, sorry, I missed you,' I stuttered, 'These beads? Um … they were a gift. A gift from my mother.'

'Ah, they are beautiful, sure they are. I had a pair just like them myself, but I lost them a few months back now.'

She smiled, sadness in her eyes. I stared at the beads in my hands, my heart thumping through my chest, dizziness threatening to overwhelm me. I almost escaped into the realms where it was safe from the intensity of the emotions charging through my body, screaming at my mind, piercing my heart. Yet my soul was ever calm, holding me in the present, in the exquisite magic of *this* moment.

'You visiting your loved ones here?' she asked.

I nodded, unable to find words.

'How, like …,' she stumbled to ask the question she knew the answer to. 'How do ye know them, Athena and Cynthia?'

I sobbed, and she reached out to take my hand in hers and I knew her fully, never had I forgotten her touch.

'They were my Ma's.'

'Ah, I see, you were blessed to have them, sure you were.'

'Did you know them?'

'Aye, I did indeed. Athena there, a grand woman she was, a dear friend, confidant and guide. I miss her terribly, so I do.'

I nodded, for I knew her pain. With a breath, I threw caution to the wind and in the presence of my Ma's, I asked, 'Are you Brigid Malone?'

She nodded, her eyes glistening. She took my other hand in hers.

'I am Marigold,' I replied.

She drew me to her chest.

'My baby, oh, my baby.'

We remained holding the other for hours, finally reunited, and intent on writing the next chapters of our story as mother and daughter.

*In darkness the seed of love is planted,*
*in light the seed of love blossoms.*

# CHAPTER 50

# The Mystery

I returned to Galway when the night fell with plans to meet with my mother again the following morning. As stillness settled, I surrendered into the arms of my beloved. Cradled in the cocoon of his arms, the overwhelming surges of magical transformative energy flowed through me as orgasmic waves and he held me as I shared the beauty of my reunion.

'You were with me today. I could feel you. I always feel you with me,' I whispered, as I traced the line of his heart across his chest, its beat as one with my own.

'I'll always be with you, Marigold. Wherever you are, wherever I may be, I will be there with you, to hold you, to love you, to guide you home. I promise you.'

'And I will always be with you, Gabriel. Wherever you are, wherever I may be, I will be there with you, to hold you, to love you, to guide you home. I promise you.'

I placed my left hand on his heart, and he placed his right hand on mine. Bowing our heads together, we prayed with gratitude for our love and asked for our union to be blessed. From my bag, I gathered a bottle of oil, a blend of frankincense, myrrh and rose.

'I was guided to create this blend for us, to seal our love. I didn't know when I would be called to share it with you, yet I *knew*.'

I anointed his heart, lips and third eye.

'I receive you into my heart and I offer my soul to you, trusting in the sacredness of our union, now and for all eternity.'

Receiving my love, he reciprocated the ritual before drawing a sachet from beneath his pillow. Opening it, he smiled gently.

'I, too, was called to honour our union and I had these made for us as a sign of our love. I did not know when I would be guided to share them with you, yet I *knew*.'

Reverently, he placed two rings on a silk cloth before taking a white gold band embedded with a garnet and, gently kissing my forehead, he placed it on my finger beside the band he had given me in the hospital, the day of my Xavier.

'As one we were. As one we are. As one we will always be. No beginning, no end, an eternal tapestry woven through the mysteries.'

In turn, I guided a black titanium band onto his finger and tenderly echoed his covenant.

'As one we were. As one we are. As one we will always be. No beginning, no end, an eternal tapestry woven through the mysteries.'

Brushing the tears from my eyes, he drew my lips to his and zealously kissed me, my overwhelming joy bursting into laughter and tears as I met his passion fully and we bathed in our infinite love. We relished the ecstasy of our union and marvelled at the mystery and magic of creation, the transformation of consciousness to matter. Entwined in our bliss, Gabriel drew a small gold bangle from the sachet and, meeting the light in my eyes, he whispered, 'I didn't know when.'

*But we knew.*

# The Story After the Story

My name is Brigid Malone. I'm not much of a writer, so please forgive me. Truth be told, I'm not much of a storyteller, unlike my daughter Marigold, who is forever sharing her stories. My Ma told me to keep my mouth shut and not to air the dirty laundry. My Pa beat it into me. I guess I learnt to keep my business to myself, so I've never had a lot to say. My Marigold, she's always at me telling me I do have a story to tell, we all do and that I have to use my voice. Ah, she's full of advice, that one. Wise beyond her years. Always has been, but I'm after telling her only last night that I'm too old and stubborn to be changing now at the age of eighty-eight. She tells me, 'You're always changing, Mammy, from one moment to the next. It's never too late to tell your story.' I couldn't sleep last night, thinking about it. So, this morning, I went for a walk as the sun was coming up. I looked beyond the trees to the mountains, the Pyrenees that surround us. This morning, they were different. They remained solid, strong and ever present but I realised they are always changing from morning to night, summer to winter. I contemplated how I, too, have changed from season to season, and perhaps there was still time for me to grow some more. For a long time in my life, there was darkness. I suppose I was stuck in the night, unable to rise like the sun, but once Marigold came back into my life some fifty years ago, it was like the sun rose on a new day and I did change—there and then.

I'll never forget the shock on the faces of Mary O'Toole and Deidre Mulhern when I walked into the teahouse in the main street of Kinvarra the morning after Marigold and I stumbled across each other in the cemetery. Right auld gossips, they were. Those two couldn't believe it when I declared, 'Good morning, Mary, Deidre. This is my daughter, Marigold, and my son-in-law, Gabriel. They're after visiting me from the USA.'

Never in my days would I have even spoken to them. Sure, hadn't they always turned away from me thinking I was beneath them. Even though I'd sat beside them when we were little ones in the schoolhouse and made my Communion and the like with them. Yet that morning, something came over me and I just remember my heart being that full, like I'd never felt it before. I couldn't stop myself saying what perhaps I'd been longing to say for twenty-odd years, 'This is my daughter.'

Back then, word travelled fast and before I knew it, my Ma and Pa were on my doorstep. My Ma filled with shame and my Pa with rage. He pulled the belt from his pants, so he did, to whip me as he so often had done. I was a grown married woman and here, my own father thought he could whip me in my own home. Something came over me. I roared. It came from way down in my woman's parts. I told him never again would he lay a hand on me and that their nephew, my cousin, was the one responsible for impregnating me over twenty years before. I declared with a force I only wish I had known twenty years before that it was not my shame, it was *his* shame. My daughter was not shameful. She was a gift from God. They left and never came back. Not a word was ever spoken to me from either of them, or any of the family, from then until this day.

I didn't regret it because I was now free from them and their judgements. I had my own family, my husband Tom, a good man, a simple man, who was overfond of the drink but never a raised voice or hand to me. We never could have our own children. God's will, I suppose, but we had Marigold and Gabriel, and they were our family. Perhaps that girl of mine is right. Life is full of seasons and something within me seemed to take me from one to the next.

Now, I surely shouldn't admit this, given the fierce love I have for my Marigold, but never have I felt a love like the one I did when I held her daughter, my grandbaby, in my arms only nine months after we were reunited. Thea Rose birthed into my hands by the fire in my sitting room, her Mammy bringing her into the world with a grace I had never seen before. And Gabriel, he was something else, sure he was, holding us in that room all night. He brought us cups of tea, clean towels, he played music in the background and, sure, didn't he even rub our feet with some special oil. He made it very special, 'sacred' as my girl is so fond of saying, for both of us. 'It's your birth, too, Mammy,' my Marigold whispered as I held her daughter in my arms. I didn't understand what she meant. I often don't, but as time passes, I ponder all these things she says and eventually they make sense.

I was born again, the day of Thea Rose's birth. She was the light of my life and brought me joy beyond what I had ever experienced. They came often to Ireland, spending months at a time with me in Thea Rose's first seven years. Ever the gypsy, they travelled about Ireland, the US and South America, stopping a few weeks or months here and there. Homeless, I dared to say once, only for Marigold to look at me and say, 'Mammy, home is not where you live. Home is in here.'

She tapped on her chest and I rolled my eyes, telling her, 'That child needs a proper home.'

She laughed and pointed to Thea Rose, who was maybe four at the time and covered in flour with a mouth full of sultanas having helped me make a fruit cake.

'I think she's home, Mammy, don't you?'

It was awfully hard every time they left me. My home and my heart were empty, but I got on with getting on until their next visit. Eventually, they settled in Boston when Thea Rose was about seven years of age. She was after getting terribly sick and one of Marigold's witchy friends, Sacnite, I think, told her that the child needed structure and stability. It was a big change. Marigold and Gabriel had been travelling the world doing their special teaching, healing and what not, for a long time. I never really understood what they did, but since moving here to live with them on their farm in the south-west of France in early 2020, when the world went into the lockdowns and all, I've begun to see what it is they do.

Pilgrims travelling the Camino Trail come and stay with us, some for a night, others for two. Some stay longer and help out on the farm. The orchard needs a lot of work and all the fruit and vegetables we use are grown here. Gabriel and I are the cooks. He has a glass of Spanish red wine and I have an Irish whiskey, as we spend the afternoon together in the kitchen, singing, dancing and laughing as we prepare a feast for our guests. Marigold greets the travellers as they come in and settles them into the sleeping quarters, immediately making them feel both safe and at home. Of a night, we all sit around the long table in the barn and eat and drink and share stories. I like to sip on my whiskey and listen to the pilgrim's stories and the wisdom that Marigold and Gabriel share with them. They all have a story, much more than you first see, and between them, Marigold and Gabriel seem able to draw out what's beneath the surface. Often, there is laughter. Often, there are tears. Always, there is love. Not in a sappy way, with hugs and kisses and the like. No, it's a feeling. I feel it in my chest, the place where Marigold calls home. Sometimes, as I look about the table at our guests who feel like family, Marigold, Gabriel and, especially when Thea Rose, her wild Irish husband Niall and my gorgeous great-granddaughters Magdalena and Camille (Maggie and Cami) are staying, tears spring to my eyes because my heart is so full. Full of love and contentment.

I'm after getting awful soft in my old age. I never cried when I was younger. I was taught not to. My Ma told me it was weak, so I just never let those tears come, not even when I left my newborn baby alone on that bed of marigolds, nor when I held her again in my arms, or even when I held my Thea Rose. The first time tears came from my eyes was when I watched her dance on stage in Paris.

When they settled in Boston she insisted, because she was fierce like her mother, that she go to a fancy private school because she wanted to tie her hair back with ribbons, wear stockings, a skirt below her knees and a blazer. Marigold was horrified that her wild child longed to be prim and proper, but she always allowed Thea Rose to be true to her calling. This went on to include ballet classes with the tutus and buns and fancy point shoes. One class each week soon became two, then every afternoon for hours at a time. She was a natural and loved the structure and discipline required to perfect each step. She would come and visit me in the summer and spend hours with those shoes on moving through these seven steps, the beginner steps she called them. I didn't understand why she had to keep practicing because, in my eyes, she was no beginner and she had already perfected them.

'Oh no, Granny, even when you think you've mastered it, you have to keep practicing because sometimes you will just forget and then it affects the flow of the whole dance.'

I was not a dancer, never had I moved my body, not like my Marigold who would pick up any auld instrument and start playing and throwing her body around like a wild banshee, yet somehow still in flow with the rhythm. So different to the grace of Thea Rose's dance, yet somehow it was so alike. To watch them dance to their own rhythm was quite something. Something quite beautiful.

And so it was, I took an airplane and left my homeland for the first time when my Thea Rose was eighteen and danced for the French Ballet in Paris. My Tom had passed by then, so I had no reason to say no when Marigold and Gabriel insisted I come. I had refused them many a time to visit Boston, but something came over me this time and before I knew it, there I was having a cup of tea in some fancy café staring at the Eiffel Tower! An hour later, the tears rolled down my cheeks the moment Thea Rose took to the stage. I took my Marigold's hand, and I was taken to some magical place watching that child dance. She was … she is a pure gift from God.

The next time I went to Paris, I didn't wait for an invitation from Marigold. I went by myself and every time there after. I'd stay with my Thea Rose in her little apartment overlooking the Basilica of Sacre Coeur and I'd cook and clean for her, watch her performances and make sure she was behaving herself for she was a beautiful young woman and drew the eye of many a French man. We had all sorts of delightful adventures in Paris, and these were indeed happy days. With Thea Rose settled in Paris, Marigold and Gabriel continued their work in Boston, Gabriel as a psychologist working with inmates in some of the toughest prisons in the country, and Marigold as a doctor, working with the dying. When she told me she was working in palliative care, I didn't understand.

'Sure, after all the years you've been studying, why would you waste yourself on the dying? Aren't you meant to be keeping people alive?'

My Marigold, looked at me with eyes of deep wisdom and professed, 'Mammy, one of the most exquisite experiences in our life will be our death. It is my honour to support people to find the beauty in the darkness of death so their soul may transition with peace.'

As I near the end of my days, in this my last season, I am beginning to understand what she meant. I no longer fear the darkness in dying because I am finally truly living every day and I am at peace. And I'm sure to take that peace into my death. I have watched closely over these last few years, and I see the gift my Marigold offers to those who are often struggling to live. She and Gabriel alike show the pilgrims how to move through the hard moments, the dark times and find the light again.

As I sit here writing these words beneath a peach tree on the edge of the orchard, I think I may have found something I never knew I owned—my light. It's an awful New Age thing to say, and it goes against all I was taught. The Catholic Church teaches that God is the light and Jesus, his son, is the light of the world. But maybe God is the light in me, the thing Marigold calls my soul and, like Jesus, I can be a light in the world.

Sure, I'm old and my dance in this life is nearly done, but maybe my last little jig on the dancefloor of life might be sharing my light with those people who visit us on their pilgrimage. Perhaps I do have something special to share after all. Maybe within my story, there is wisdom that might help those young ones on their way. I shushed that daughter of mine the other night at dinner when she said to some Australian woman, 'Every village has their elder and ours is my Mammy, sitting right here beside me.'

I didn't think I was wise enough or interesting enough or vibrant enough to be the elder. I was just an old lady. But as I write this to you, something within me that I now know as my soul, is telling me I am enough. I am an elder and I pray my wisdom helps guide you on your journey through life.

> *Life is a dance choreographed by the soul.*
> *Every challenge has a lesson.*
> *Every season has a reason.*
> *Every moment is a gift.*
> *May your dance be blessed.*

## ACKNOWLEDGEMENTS

I wish to thank my publisher, The Kind Press, especially Natasha Gilmour who has held this book with such love and respect. You met Marigold's story with an open mind and heart and have honoured her story by never trying to change it, only ever meeting it with the intent of refinement to ensure the potency of her impact. Natasha, as an editor and publisher, you have helped me craft Marigold's story into what it now is and guided me in how to bring her to the world. As a friend, you have met me in my quirks, understanding me fully where others simply cannot, and you have walked beside me as a true soul companion in bringing this story from a vision into reality. The ladies and I thank you for again saying yes to journeying with us.

It is said it takes a village to raise a child, and over the last five years, it has taken a village of wise women to support me through the huge transformations required within me to channel Marigold's story. I am honoured to call these women my friends and have been able to call on them to assist me physically, mentally, emotionally and spiritually when I have needed that helping hand. In deepest gratitude to Patrice, Emily, Sara, Karen, Mary S, Julie M, Jess, Mary B, Julie C, Loreto, Renee, Allison, Michelle, Jo, Kerrie.

To my clients over the past five years, who reflected  so much of Marigold's story—her patterns, her shadow, her struggles, her lessons. As I worked with so many of you, I solidified the story of Marigold within me, which enabled me to bring it through, knowing her story was an important guide for others embarking on their own healing and growth journey.

I remain in deepest gratitude to Karen and Christina whom I trusted with the beautifully clunky, raw messiness of Marigold's story before an editing brush had come close to the manuscript. Thank you for receiving her, understanding her, seeing the beauty of her truth, in the light and dark. Your acceptance, reflections and insights were the medicine I needed to take the next steps to bring Marigold's story to the world.

Thank you to my friends and family, Mary, Brigid, Kevin, Peter, Lodewijk, Louise and our babes. When I step beyond my comfort and dive into the unknowns, I know that if I fly, you will celebrate with me, and if I fall, you will be there for me. That is love. I am so grateful for your love.

Mum, thank you for being you and keeping life so simple, the balance to my complexity. In our family, you are the Elder and we are so blessed to have you, your wisdom and your endless loving support.

To the long line of storytellers in my family, those I have known and those I never had the chance to meet, I feel you with me as I write, and I hear your voices woven throughout my books.

To my babes, Kokoda, Lucia and Xavier, I love and adore you three more than you will ever know. You make my world fuller, and I don't know who I would have become without you. Thank you for choosing me to be your Mumma. I love you.

Kokoda, thank you for being my toughest teacher, a barometer of truth and demanding I be *Nothing But Love.*

Lucia, thank you for the side eyes and always making me laugh, the reminder that it's not all that serious.

Xavier, thank you for adoring me in a way no other does, for encouraging me to keep writing and for your goodnight kisses.

To Luke, my beloved, you stand by me, ever patient, with endless unconditional love and support as I share my gifts with the world. Our love is pure and simple despite the complexities of life, and your presence by my side invites me to breathe and remember that all is well. Thank you for loving me, in my light and dark, my gentle and fierce, my calm and storm—the fullness of me.

Finally, Marigold, thank you for choosing and trusting me to share your story. And to the ladies, Clara, Aunt Maeve, Athena, Cynthia, Madame Rosaline, Sacnite and Brigid Malone, thank you for holding us as we danced over the last five years. With your support, Marigold could never give up on me and ensured I could never let her story go until I honoured it fully.

And here we are.

# ABOUT THE AUTHOR

*The Mysteries of Marigold* is Bernadette O'Connor's third book. *Let's Go Home, Finding There While Staying Here* (2018) and *Beneath the Veil* (2019) were received with international acclaim and inspired profound healing, growth and transformation in readers around the world.

Bernadette believes in the power of story as a creator of change, and, in addition to her writing, she has worked with thousands of people throughout the world as a healer, guide and mentor. She is honoured to support them to remember who they are and to live from love guided by their soul.

Bernadette lives on the East Coast of Australia with her husband, Luke, and three teenage children, Kokoda, Lucia and Xavier, the pulse of her heart and greatest inspiration for being a creator of change in the world.

Visit www.bernadetteoconnor.com